# THE FOREVER BRIDGE

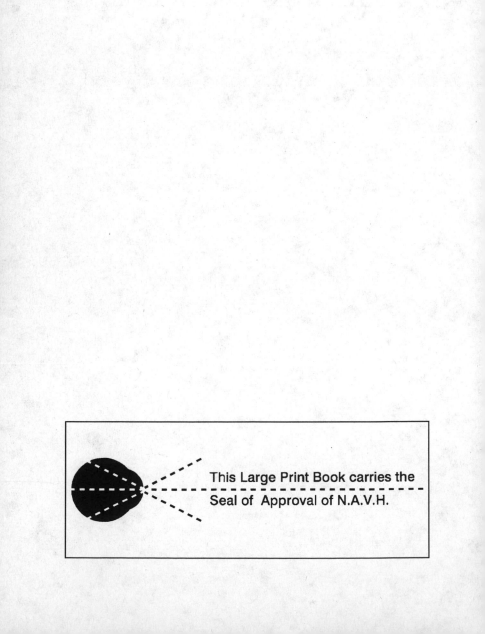

# THE FOREVER BRIDGE

## T. GREENWOOD

**THORNDIKE PRESS**
*A part of Gale, Cengage Learning*

Farmington Hills, Mich • San Francisco • New York • Waterville, Maine
Meriden, Conn • Mason, Ohio • Chicago

LIBRARY OF CONGRESS CATALOGING-IN-PUBLICATION DATA

Greenwood, T. (Tammy)
    The forever bridge / by T. Greenwood. — Large print edition.
        pages cm. — (Thorndike Press large print clean reads)
    ISBN 978-1-4104-7977-8 (hardcover) — ISBN 1-4104-7977-3 (hardcover)
    1. Life change events—Fiction. I. Title.
PS3557.R3978F67 2015
813'.54—dc23                                    2015005207

Published in 2015 by arrangement with Kensington Books, an imprint of Kensington Publishing Corp.

Printed in Mexico
1 2 3 4 5 6 7 19 18 17 16 15

*For Mikaela*

# ACKNOWLEDGMENTS

With gratitude to Peter Senftleben, Vida Engstrand, Henry Dunow, and the rest of my team for their hard work. To my writing friends for their ears and shoulders (especially Miranda Beverly-Whittemore, Jillian Cantor, and Amy Hatvany). To my family for believing in me. And, as always, to Patrick and the girls, who give me a zillion reasons to be grateful.

There is a land of the living and a land of the dead and the bridge is love, the only survival, the only meaning.
— Thornton Wilder,
*The Bridge of San Luis Rey*

Love is the voice under all silences, the hope which has no opposite in fear; the strength so strong mere force is feebleness: the truth more first than sun, more last than star . . .
— E. E. Cummings

Here is the night the world changes, your world changes. The night when certainties are shattered, and you are left with shards of your old truth, hunched over and picking up the broken pieces, wondering that they ever made anything whole. And the pieces are sharp, and the pieces will hurt you again and again and again.

Here is a bridge. Here is a river. Here is rain and a family and a car: a brown sedan that has seen better days. The leather seats that were a luxury to the original owner are now cracked, tears duct-taped and cold. It is late autumn in Vermont. It is too dark to see this, but you know that the corridor of trees that make a tunnel as you travel down the bumpy dirt road have turned from green to blazing crimson and yellow. That this is the beautiful burst of flames that occurs before everything dies.

Here, inside the car, the mother, Sylvie,

11

does her lipstick in the greasy mirror in the passenger-side visor. Here is the father, Robert, fiddling with the dial on the radio, attempting to get the game to come in and stay in. The first Celtics game of the season is on and Boston is down by seven against the Cavs after the first quarter. Here are two kids in the backseat. Ruby is nine and Jess is seven. They both have thick mops of brown hair. They both have a pair of startlingly green eyes. They are beautiful children. This is what Sylvie thinks. Robert is more concerned with the boy's ability to throw balls, with their heights, which he records on the Sheetrock in the unfinished room he is building for Ruby now that she is getting older. They can't afford the addition, but he also knows that part of his job is to not ask questions. It is to build this room and not complain. His job is to mark the kids' heights on the wall, to worry about the strength of the boy's arm. Let their mother be the one to worry about puberty and privacy. Let him just be the father.

He is preoccupied tonight as he is most nights. When the rain comes, he thinks not about the bald tires, about the bad brakes, but about something his brother said to him while they were snaking a backed-up toilet earlier in the day. *You're your own worst*

12

*enemy,* Bunk said as the electric snake rattled and whirred. *What the hell's that supposed to mean?* he'd asked. *Nothing. Sorry I said anything. Looks like we got it.* Robert's whole chest was hot with shame and rage, but he just said, *Got what? Paper towels,* Bunk said. *Goddamn people and their goddamn paper towels. It's like putting cement in the pipes.*

He still feels the anger in his shoulders. He rolls his neck to try to loosen them up.

Sylvie is thinking about the parent-teacher conference they are going to. She knows what to expect for Ruby. She is her brilliant shining star. (This girl, here in the backseat, so absorbed in her book she has forgotten where she is. *Who* she is even.) She is *gifted,* the teacher will say: a word which conjures up holidays. Makes Sylvie imagine pretty wrapped packages. Ruby is *special,* the teacher in her sensible shoes and cardigan sweater will say with a nod. And this will make Sylvie blush with pride. And then feel terrible, because Ruby is not her only child. Because Jess, the little one, is sweet and gentle, but he struggles, and it seems there is little she can do to help him. She has watched him cry in frustration over the words on the page, the numbers, the problems. She tells herself that all that matters is that he is good and kind. Still, it breaks her heart a little, the way the whole world seems, already, to be disappointed in him. She tilts the mirror to look at him, this sweet boy, face pressed to the glass, looking at the rain that is starting to come down now in patterned sheets. He is mesmerized by the world. Captivated. It is enough for him, she has to remind herself, and there is something so good about that.

Sharp, sharp slivers.

What if you were simply able to rearrange them, to build something from these remains, reassemble the broken pieces into something new? Something stronger? Something both similar to what was and yet entirely different? What if you were able to make something indestructible? Something permanent?

But here is the new truth: the pieces are chipped and broken, some of them lost. A shattered glass on a tile floor. Some of them working their way already under your skin. Shards that will burrow there, that sometimes will not bother you at all, but other times will make you wince with recollection. With the undeniable and unbearable pain of it all.

Here: the look on Sylvie's face when she turns to ask if she looks okay. And none of them know whom she is asking, whose opinion matters the most. She is asking each of them and all of them. Because they are not only *father, son, daughter,* they are a *family,* and so they nod a collective nod of approval. They all love her more than she can know.

Here: Robert's sigh when he resigns himself to nothing but static on the radio and clicks it off, filling the car with a peaceful silence.

Here: Ruby lost inside her book and Jess, hot cheek pressed to the glass, the rain making patterns on the window, and he watches, transfixed.

Here: the bridge, the covered bridge you've traveled a million times. The one on which you have closed your eyes and held your breath as you crossed over, the superstitions of childhood as powerful as God.

Here is the moment before it slips and shatters. Here is the river. Here is the bridge.

# SUNDAY

In the morning Sylvie is startled awake, as she is always startled awake. But usually it is the banging clanging of her own brain, the electric shock of her own fear, that acts as an alarm. It takes her several moments of heart-banging, neck-sweating delirium to realize that the sound she hears is not coming from her own imagination but rather from outside her window.

She is afraid to move. Afraid to breathe even. And so she holds her breath, worried that her own inhalations and exhalations will confuse her ears. Her head aches from the effort of separating the sounds she knows (birdsong, the wind, the river) from this new and unfamiliar one. It is like separating two intertwined necklaces from each other; she knows there are two distinct silver strands, but the chains are tangled together.

She thinks of the grocery boy, but it's only

Sunday; he won't be here until tomorrow. Once, on a Sunday a long time ago, a pair of women in ill-fitting dresses (*girls* really, with glasses and heavy shoes, clutching their *Watchtower*s) arrived and stood on her screened porch for nearly ten minutes. She watched them through the cracked vinyl shade in the living room. They giggled and whispered and knocked again and again, until finally they shrugged and left.

But this voice is low. A man's. Slowly, she rises out of bed, noting the stitch in her side. It's a new pain on her list of pains, and it is sharp. She clutches at her rib cage as if she can quell the cramp by containing it, and she stands. Her robe is waiting for her on the hook at the back of the door, and she slips into it as she slips into it every morning, grateful for both its comfort and familiarity. It is like the Superman cape Jess used to wear when he was three, a talisman.

She shuffles across the worn floorboards to the living room, to the window, which, if it were not battened down, would look out over the front yard. She recalls walking through the unfinished house, the timber skeleton, with Robert and Bunk more than ten years ago. The smell of sawdust was thick, as Robert pointed out the views they would have from all these unfinished win-

20

dows, promising her rooms filled with light. They'd bought this land enticed by the expansive front yard and, behind the house, the river and woods. She didn't know, when she stood there nodding and smiling, that the view wouldn't matter one day. That all that lovely green, those deep verdant woods, would instead become the stuff of nightmares. That most days she would leave the blackout shades closed, curtains on a stage of an old life drawn shut. Show over.

She carefully tugs at the bottom of the roller shade, feels its weight and magnetic resistance. It is fragile. She worries the whole thing might just crumble in her hands if she's not careful, that it will expose her. She gently pulls, just until it begins to show a will of its own, as though it *wants* to rise up and let in the light. Finally, she is able to reveal just an inch or two of the outside world, of that view that once was enough to make her think she could live here. That they could make a home.

She sits down in the straight-backed chair by the window, the place where she usually sits to put on her socks and shoes, and she peers through that sliver. The morning glories she planted so many years ago have been left to proliferate, covering the whole front of the house and filling this window.

She spies through the violet flowers, squinting as though this effort will make the thick leaves and indigo blossoms transparent. She needs to lift the shade higher in order to see. Her fingers tremble as she allows it to release just a couple inches more. Finally, there is a gap in the foliage that is strangling her house, and she looks through the peephole it makes.

Through the vines, she sees someone walking up the overgrown front walkway. He's got a phone, but he is talking *at* it, not into it; there's no cell reception out here. "Goddamnit," he mutters, looking at the useless phone, and then shoves it in his pocket. In the driveway, she can see the white van, and suddenly she is overcome by a flush of hot relief. *Bunk.* It's just Bunk, her brother-in-law. But why on earth is he coming to the house? Usually he drives by to check on her once a week, but he never comes *in:* never even comes up the drive. But now here he is, in his filthy work coveralls, walking toward her house. He's got a cigarette in the corner of his mouth which he finishes, crushes under his boot, and then picks up and deposits in one of his shirt pockets. He looks up, as if just remembering where he is.

By the time he makes his way up the steps

and opens the screen door to the porch, her entire body is trembling again. She feels like she might faint, the edges of her vision vignetting like an old photograph. His knock feels like fists against her chest.

She considers ignoring him, just as she ignored the Jehovah's Witnesses, the lost tourists, the salesmen and the Girl Scouts. But he knows she's inside. And if she doesn't answer, he will worry. She tries not to think of the bad news he could be delivering, of all of the terrible things he could tell her, of all the possible futures that she might be forced to face by simply answering the door. She is paralyzed, every muscle in her body momentarily atrophied.

*It's only Bunk,* she tells herself. *It's okay,* as she beckons every bit of courage she has, mustering the will from some primitive place, and makes her way to the kitchen where she unlocks the door.

Bunk stands on the porch, and she knows he is trying not to look around at the mess. The inside of the house is immaculate, but she has given up on anything beyond the front door. She knows he is silently assessing the disaster, and so she beckons him in.

"Morning, Syl," he says, stepping into the dim kitchen.

She nods and motions for him to sit at

the table.

"You got any coffee going yet?" he asks, and she shakes her head.

"Is something . . ." she begins, and is startled by the crackling sound of her own voice. When was the last time she spoke? "Did something happen?"

"No," he says, shaking his head. Smiling. Bunk's easy smile has always calmed her. Her body remembers this, and she sighs, her fear dissipating.

"You sure?" she manages. "Ruby?"

"Everything's good. Ruby's doing great."

Still, she is trembling as she goes to the counter to make a pot of coffee. She runs the cold water into the carafe and pours it into the machine. Her hands recollect this ritual. *Coffee, filter, mugs.* It steadies her.

"And Robert?" she asks. She can't look at him when she asks this, and so she simply watches the coffee drip into the pot. But she can feel his eyes on her back, and she knows he is reading the pain of Robert's name in the defeated curve of her spine, regret revealed in her slumped shoulders.

"He misses you," Bunk says, and she feels her throat close.

She turns to him, realizing, after it's too late, that her face is wide open, her hope exposed like an open wound.

"We all miss you," Bunk says, looking down at his hands. He's said too much.

As the coffee brews, she sits across from Bunk at the table. The stitch in her side persists, and she winces slightly as she sits.

"Listen, Syl," Bunk says. "I am actually here about Ruby. Rob and I were hoping she might be able to come stay with you for a week or so. Just still school starts up again."

She is confused. Ruby hasn't stayed with her for months. The last time had been a disaster. The last time, Ruby had to call 911. The memory of it is excruciating, embarrassing.

"I know you're still having a rough time," Bunk says, his eyes filled with concern. "But she's eleven now. Spends most of her time with her nose in a book or out riding her bike. She's an easy kid, Syl, mature. And she misses you too."

"Why now?" she asks in that strange, rusty voice.

Bunk smiles again. She notices that his teeth are worse than the last time they spoke. That whatever issue he's had with that canine tooth has gotten bad. She wishes he had the money to see a dentist. That he could take care of it.

"It's Larry," he says.

Larry is his and Robert's little brother. He lives on some tiny island off the coast of North Carolina. The last time she saw him, that anyone saw him, was at Jess's funeral almost two years ago.

"He's in a bad way," he says. "Which I'm sure ain't no surprise."

And Sylvie recalls Larry's glassy stare and trembling hands at the funeral. And she'd known it wasn't grief, wasn't sorrow that made him that pale and thin, that had turned him into a shadow of himself.

"It's kind of funny actually," Bunk continues. "We been talking about getting down there. Try to get him some help. 'Course the issue's been money. Ain't it always? But then Rob goes and wins five hundred dollars in one of those scratch-off lottery things. Up at Hudson's? So we thought, maybe it's a sign."

None of this makes any sense to her. For one thing, Robert hasn't won a thing in his life. He used to joke about his bad luck, back when misfortune meant silly things like locking himself out of the car or losing his house key in the snow. Before bad luck meant *accident,* meant *disaster.*

"Ruby can't come with us, for obvious reasons. We asked Gloria already, but she's got her hands full next week. And Rob and

I both think it would be good for her to stay here with you. Good for *both* of you."

She is shaking her head, despite herself.

Bunk reaches across the table for her hand. His knuckles are big, knobby things. His nails bitten to the quick. "Please, Syl. It's just a week. It'll be fine. She needs her mother. You know that, right?"

She nods, despite the fact that she knows that she is exactly what an eleven-year-old girl does *not* need.

Everyone thinks it began that night at the river. That the paralysis was instantaneous instead of a slow crippling that actually began years and years before. It's easier to explain this way, to blame the accident; this is something even the most callous people can understand. Believing that her life is what it is now, that she is who *she* is now, as a direct result of what happened to Jess elicits pity rather than disgust: sympathetic bemusement rather than horror.

Here is her life: a cave of leaves, a house strangled by morning glory vines, perched at the edge of a river. (That same river as the one under the bridge, only here it narrows and slows. Here it is a quiet, benevolent thing.) Inside the house, there are five rooms strung together like beads, though she only uses four of them anymore: bed-

27

room, kitchen, living room, bath. There is a screened porch as well, the only place of commerce, of contact: three plastic boxes left outside her front door on the warped wooden floor. One for groceries. One for books. One in which she puts her recyclables. All other debris is composted or burned. Every Monday the grocery delivery boy brings food and leaves it, like someone leaving scraps out for a feral cat. He can't seem to run fast enough back to his car afterwards and once safely inside, he revs the engine, blasts his stereo, and peels out of the long driveway backwards, as if afraid to turn his back. The books come every other Friday, selected from the lists she makes. The book-mobile driver, Effie, leaves the books and takes away her recycling and sometimes brings in the mail which accumulates in the mailbox at the end of the drive, shoving it through the rusty slot in the door. In the fall, a man drops off a cord of wood, already split, which keeps her warm until the following spring. Bunk comes by every week or so. When she sees his van idling at the end of the drive, she flicks the porch light on so he knows she's okay. There are no other visitors. She hasn't seen a doctor since the accident. Her teeth, unlike Bunk's, are good. She doesn't leave the property anymore. Except for the visit to the hospital last spring, she hasn't left in well over a year.

It's quiet here with only her and the other strange creatures that have sought refuge in these dark woods. And in this almost silence, she can, finally, hear the world speaking. It hums to her its dangers. Sings to her its risks, reminds her of her vulnerability. Without anyone to interrupt, it is possible to hear its premonitory song. It is her reveille. Her alarm.

She does not sleep well, despite the physical exhaustion of it all; the million raw nerves, the electric currents that inform every muscle and vein, refuse to desist. She depends on the pills the doctor prescribed to shut her body down each night. But despite this drug-induced respite, each morning just before the sun rises she is shaken awake like someone in a burning house, the whispered promise of all the potential disasters hissing hot in her ear.

Each day begins with a scalding shower, a sulfurous baptism. She washes her hair and body, enduring the nearly blistering assault until the water grows cold. As the sun rises, she eats alone: dry toast and black coffee. After breakfast, she scours the sink and counters and floors. She vacuums and sweeps and dusts. She boils her sheets and strings them out to dry on her back porch. She feeds the birds. She buries her coffee grounds and eggshells in the compost. By then it is time for lunch and this makes the kitchen dirty again and, on hot summer days, the sheets will have dried and she makes her bed. She irons clothes she no longer wears. She polishes Robert's old shoes, which makes her heart ache like something bruised. In the summer she tends to her garden, in the winter she shovels snow. These are her rituals, and this is her church. She relies on this domestic liturgy, on these quotidian sacraments, though she knows they are ultimately futile. Because hers is the religion of the damned.

But she can't blame the accident for this life, no more than she can blame the river, the rain, the bridge. No more than she can blame the other set of headlights that disappeared into that terrible night. No more than she can blame Robert even. Because all of this started so long ago, she isn't even sure anymore what the first vague rumblings felt like.

The cracks, the fault lines, may have been there even when she was child, but were too small to register: the seismic rumblings so deep under the surface that she didn't even notice them. Not until she became a mother. Not until that one morning, just three days home from the hospital when she lay with Ruby in the bed (this bed), studying her miniature features, her tiny hands and feet, as her fingers stroked her feathery hair, and then stumbled at the boney ridge. Locating the soft spot, the abyss between the two boney plates of Ruby's skull, she was overwhelmed by a crushing realization. For the first time, those quiet quivers, that tremulous feeling she sometimes felt, now shook and quaked with a violence she could barely comprehend, and she felt herself splitting in two, her *life* splitting in two. Because in this moment, as her fingers skipped across the fontanel, that fleshy undefined place bridged by the certainty of bone, of skull, she realized that she had not only the obligation to protect this child, this life, but also the power to destroy it.

It shook her to her core, the epicenter of this convulsion located deep in her chest. But instead of relief, the stillness that followed brought only further unease. And every single day afterwards, until the accident, provided a series of startling and painful aftershocks. She had spent her entire life waiting for that cataclysm which would render her powerless. In this way, the accident seemed not accidental at all, but rather *inevitable,* simply confirming what she'd been dreading all along.

She knows what people think, what people say about her. That she's lost her mind. That she's gone off the deep end. But they forgive her her eccentricities, because what else can they do? They try to empathize, to imagine how they might respond to this same loss. *A little boy. God, he was just a little boy.* But it is an impossible kind of imagining. There is no way to understand, and patience and tolerance go only so far. People expect you to eventually pick yourself up and move on. Grief has a shelf life, and hers expired long ago. And so she has exiled herself, alone and trembling in this chasm between *before* and *after.*

Ruby does not belong here.

Why can't Bunk understand this? But here he is, waiting for her to answer, as though this is not her life. As though there is any sort of normalcy to any of this. It's not as though he can't see with his own eyes what she has become. How the terror of every single moment has laid claim to her. Perhaps he still believes she might pull through this. But she is a rope trying to fit in the eye of a needle. There *is* no pulling through.

She's always liked Bunk, always respected

him as a man. He works hard. He is loyal to his brothers. A good uncle to Ruby and Jess. He was the first one, the only one after the accident who thought to say, *I believe you,* when she tried to explain that there was another car, that the headlights were blinding as they entered the covered bridge. Why else would Robert have steered them over the edge? Robert, who could remember nothing afterwards except for the score of the Celtics game, blamed himself for being distracted by the radio. By the rain. Ruby recollected nothing either; she'd been so lost inside her book. Bunk was the only one who would listen when Sylvie insisted that someone else was there. That someone else had caused the accident and then backed away into the night. *I believe you,* he'd said, sitting across from her at this same kitchen table nearly two years ago. *We'll find them, Syl.* He was the only one who knew exactly what she needed to hear, even if it was an impossible promise, a futile one.

And now he sits across from her with his imploring eyes and this proposition, and she tries to imagine having Ruby home again. She thinks of how it would feel to tuck her into bed. She thinks about the sound of her voice. Of the softness of her skin. God, how she misses her, nearly as much as she misses

Jess. She misses every single thing about her, the missing like a living thing. It breathes. But this is no place for a child, and she is no mother. Not anymore.

And here again is the fissure, the breaking. It starts in her center, as it always does. And that stitch, that cramp in her side spreads, splitting her. Bifurcating her. And her heart, banging hard in her chest, does not know which way to go. One part of her resists, protests. And the other, the one that controls that corroded voice box in her throat, relents.

"Isn't there some sort of storm coming that way?" she asks. She doesn't have a television anymore, but she does have a radio, and they've been talking about a hurricane that's supposed to hit the East Coast. *Irene.* That's what they're calling this one.

Bunk shrugs. "We'll be fine. Storm's way out in the Caribbean right now. Probably blow over by the time we're driving back home. It's just a week."

"One week," she says. Neither agreement nor refusal, but Bunk hears what he needs to hear.

"It'll be okay, Syl. I promise."

But after Bunk disappears down the road and she is alone again, she wonders at what she has done.

Things haven't been right with her mom in a while. Not since the accident. Ruby knows that. Still, it doesn't change the way her stomach bottoms out when Uncle Bunk, Daddy, and she pull into the driveway today and she sees the house.

She lives with her dad and her Uncle Bunk in town at Bunk's now. She used to come sleep at her mom's on the weekends, but since last time, the time the ambulance had to come and her mom had to go to the hospital, her mom's stopped asking her to stay with her. It's too hard, she thinks. Ruby reminds her of too many things that hurt her heart. The last time she even saw her mom it was spring, Easter, but here in the woods there was still snow up to her waist. They could barely see anything but the top bit of the house: the faded blue metal siding, the tar paper roof. But now that the snow is gone, now that they're nearing the end of summer, she can see what all that snow was hiding.

The first thing Ruby notices is the mailbox, which is lying on its side in the driveway. She bends down and tries to right it, but the post is wedged into the ground and won't budge. She opens the metal lid and a bunch of pincher bugs scramble in the sunlight. The envelopes and flyers inside are wet. She grabs them, and they disintegrate in her hands. She sees there's a card from her stuck against the back, one she sent almost two months ago with her spring class picture inside. She lifts the flap and realizes the whole thing is glued together, and so she tries to tear the envelope away, to salvage the picture, but it just peels her whole face off the paper. It was a good picture; she wasn't making that stupid face she usually makes in her class pictures, the one where she smiles with her mouth closed tight and her eyes bugged wide open. She was wearing the dress her mom likes, even though she never wears dresses anymore, the one her mom says brings out the green in her eyes.

Bunk is helping Daddy get out of the van. He's got Daddy's wheelchair out, and now he's leaning into the car to scoop him up. Ruby turns away. Daddy doesn't like her to watch this part. She doesn't blame him. There's no dignity in your little brother having to carry you like a baby. Once Ruby can hear the familiar grunt that means he's settled into the chair, she turns and motions for them to follow her to the house.

That's when she notices that all that waist-high snow has been replaced with hip-high weeds and grass. There is a path worn through the middle of it, probably from the guy who delivers groceries and the lady from the library who brings her mom books, but it still feels like the jungle. It is August, and the mosquitoes and horseflies are thick. She slaps them away from her ankles as she makes her way toward the house. She can hear Bunk struggle to push Daddy's chair through the weeds; the path is barely wide enough for a single person, never mind a wheelchair.

"Jesus Christ," Daddy mumbles, but Ruby doesn't turn around to look at him. She already knows what his expression looks like.

The driveway is longer than she remembers. It feels like a mile of twists and turns before they finally see the house.

"I warned you," Bunk says. Bunk came up last Sunday to talk to her mom about Ruby staying with her. Ruby heard him and

Daddy talking about it when they thought she was asleep, their voices as soft and low as music in the kitchen over the shuffling of cards. They don't know she listens.

Ruby feels her mouth twitching in the way it does just before she's going to cry, so she sucks in a breath to stop it.

Bunk and Daddy built this house before she was even born. They put up these walls with their own hands. They plumbed and wired it. They dug the well, put in the septic tank. They raised the roof and installed the windows. They insulated and painted. They put in the light fixtures, the toilet, the cabinets, the sink. And before the accident, Daddy started to build the addition that was supposed to be her new room, which now sticks out from the side of the house like an abandoned husk. It's framed up of course, with warped and faded Tyvek paper wrapped around it like a gift. But there's no roof over the top, and the woods beyond the house seem to want to reclaim this little piece of land. A sapling has worked its way up through the unfinished floor. There is a *tree* in the middle of this room, *her* room, its branches reaching out through the windows. The new green leaves climbing the unfinished walls.

The front porch is the same as it's been

since Ruby and her dad left, bamboo shades rolled down, their pull strings rotten. The three steps leading up to the door are missing one of the treads now. She suspects it's probably buried somewhere in the overgrown grass. The screen door hangs from one hinge, and there's a blanket tacked to the back of the door, so you can't see in.

"How the hell am I supposed to get into the house?" Daddy asks.

"I can carry you," Bunk says and then realizes that won't happen in a million years. "Here," he says, quickly realizing he needs to come up with another solution, and goes to the side of the house where there is a stack of plywood sheets leaning against the wall.

Bunk fashions a sort of ramp for Daddy's chair over the broken steps, though as soon as he puts the chair on, they all know it's probably going to just snap in half like a cracker. Still, he somehow manages to get Daddy up the ramp and through the broken door onto the porch.

Ruby can't help it now. Her mouth is twitching something fierce as she looks at the wicker loveseat where her mother used to sit with her and Jess on summer nights to read them stories and watch the fireflies. The wicker is ragged, as though something's been chewing on it, and the rose-covered cushions are torn, the stuffing pulled out. She moves closer and sees that the stuffing is mixed in with a pile of straw. It's some sort of *nest,* and wriggling inside are three baby raccoons. She closes her eyes and concentrates on pushing the lump that's in her throat back down. Neither Bunk nor Daddy says a word, but it doesn't matter, because Ruby knows exactly what they're thinking. They're thinking there's no way on earth they can leave her here for a whole week. They're thinking about how they're going to tell her mom that this is no place for an eleven-year-old kid to be. They're trying to figure out if a heart that's already broken can be broken all over again, wondering what would be left.

Daddy wheels himself up to the door and bangs his fist against the glass three times. Ruby hears scurrying and think it's the raccoons, but they're still sleeping. Maybe it's the mama raccoon. Or maybe it's something else altogether.

Her mom doesn't answer the door right away. And every second they wait makes Ruby nervous. She tries to imagine what she's doing inside the house. The last time they were here, it took her mom almost five whole minutes before she answered the door. But then when she finally did, she laughed and apologized and said she'd just been in the bathroom. That day Ruby gave her one of the cream-filled chocolate Russell Stover eggs she always used to like, and everything was okay. But this feels different. This feels scary. The twitchiness of Ruby's face moves down into her chest. She feels shaky all over, like there's a nest of baby raccoons stirring inside her ribs.

She can see the cracked vinyl shade in the door's window move a little, and this is enough to settle her down a little bit. And then when her mom opens the door, she feels most of that awful trembling feeling go away.

It's just her mom. The same mom she's known for eleven years, with her pretty twinkling dark eyes and soft hands which reach for her, and then she is hugging her, smelling the same familiar smell that makes her feel both happy and so sad she can't keep the tears inside anymore. And so Ruby lets them come, hot and certain, but her mom has her pressed so tightly against her chest it's like she's a sponge just sucking them all away.

When her mom pulls away, she holds on to Ruby's shoulders and pushes her back to look at her. She's almost as tall as she is

41

now, and her mom notices that first. She frowns and shakes her head. "You look like you've grown a foot," she says, smiling sadly. "I'm not ready for you to grow up yet. Can you please just stay little for a while longer?"

Then it's like she's noticing for the first time that Ruby didn't come alone. "Hi, Bunk," her mom says, smiling at Bunk, who leans in and gives her a little hug.

"Robert," her mother says, nodding at her dad, and then she reaches out awkwardly and takes his hand. They hold hands like this for a minute before Daddy spoils everything.

"Syl, you got raccoons living out here." He motions to the loveseat.

Her mom looks at the loveseat, and her face turns red. She brushes her hand as if she could just make it go away. "I know, I know. The mama came in through the broken screen this winter, I think. To get warm. And now we've got this."

Bunk says softly, "Syl, you can't have wild animals living in the house. You know that, right?"

She nods up and down, too many times. "I know. I'll get somebody to take care of it."

Daddy snorts.

"I *will,* Robert," she says, and now she's

the one with tears in her eyes. "I'll call him tomorrow."

Her mom is a terrible liar, though, and they all know she can't call anybody. Her phone went out during the last big storm this summer, and she never got it fixed. Every time Ruby's tried to call her, she's just gotten a busy signal. There's no cell reception up here either, so even if she had a cell phone she wouldn't be able to use it.

"I don't know about this," Daddy says suddenly to Bunk. "Maybe this isn't the best idea."

Ruby sees her mom's hands clench into fists at her sides. She's like a little girl, she thinks. She's seen her best friend, Izzy, do the same thing when she gets mad. She half expects her to stomp her foot. But she just keeps nodding.

"It's *fine,*" she says. "I'll call somebody. And I'll get the screen fixed."

She reaches for Ruby again with her tiny hands. And Ruby remembers all of a sudden the way she used to lie down next to her in her bed when she was little and stroke her hair until she fell asleep at night. How big her hands seemed then.

"You *want* to stay, don't you, Ruby?" she asks. Her voice sounds like two voices, one that is strong and deep. The voice she remembers singing in the shower. But it's like it's split into two now, like a thread that's been separated. And the other strand is high and fragile and scared.

Ruby nods, even though she's afraid to be here. She's afraid that she looks so much like her old mom but is so different at the same time. Still, Ruby misses her. She misses this house, or at least what it used to be. And she *does* want to be here. At least she thinks she does.

"We don't have a lot of other options, Rob," Bunk says. "And it's just a week."

Her dad nods. "I know."

Bunk is taking her dad down to visit Uncle Larry in North Carolina. They say it's because of the scratch-off ticket, that now they don't have any excuses not to go see him. They looked into flying, but it was too expensive, so they decided to just take the van down. Make a road trip of it. This is the official reason why they're dropping her off at her mom's. But there are other reasons, secret reasons they don't think Ruby knows about. The first is that Larry's got some problems. She doesn't really know what they are, but she's pretty sure it has something to do with drinking. Maybe even drugs. The second is about a little piece of land for sale down there. A house and a commercial fishing boat that Larry knows about. This is what Ruby has gathered from those nights when they thought she was sleeping. A few beers into the nights when they would forget to whisper, and their voices, her dad's dreams, found their way down the hall and under her closed door. About leaving behind all the bad memories. About taking the insurance money and selling the house. *This* house. About starting over. And helping Larry get himself back on track at the same time. But what Ruby hasn't been able to gather, the words that haven't found their way to her ears, are the ones that explain what will happen to her mom. Where *she* will go.

She looked up the town, Wanchese, on the Internet at the library, studied the little island off the coast of North Carolina. Tried to imagine their life there. But it was like trying to draw a picture of an animal you've never seen before. Like trying to imagine God.

She knows this is the real reason she isn't invited to come along, but her dad makes up excuses.

"You can't really afford to miss all those swimming lessons," her dad offered as if this were a bad thing. She *hates* swimming lessons.

"You wouldn't want to spend the last week of your summer with a couple of old dudes anyway," Bunk said, playfully punching her in the shoulder.

And while this didn't actually sound bad at all, it *was* the last week of summer. By the time they got back, it would be almost Labor Day. The leaves would be starting to turn, the mornings would be crisp, the air cold and quick instead of thick and slow. Summer would practically be gone.

"Besides, you'd miss the fair," her dad said, slapping his knee, as though he'd just solved a riddle.

And so Ruby nodded. They didn't want her to come along. And it had nothing to do with any of these excuses and everything to do with that little town she could barely find on the map. Ruby tried to convince herself she'd be better off staying behind. For one thing, she *would* miss the fair. She and Izzy had gone to the fair on opening day every single year since they could walk. It was a tradition. In ten years, she hadn't missed the fair even once.

There was also the model-bridge building contest, the one Mrs. McKnight told her about last spring. She's the Gifted and Talented teacher at school, and she's always finding cool projects for them to do. At first

Mrs. McKnight was worried that Ruby wouldn't want to do the bridge unit, that it wasn't a good idea, after the accident. Everyone at school knew what had happened that night at the river, at the bridge. "You don't have to do this, Ruby," she'd said after class when they were alone. But building bridges soothed her, made her feel like she had a purpose even. She couldn't explain how it felt like she was fixing something, like she was solving a problem with each drop of glue, each slender, bendable piece of balsa wood. And so after Mrs. McKnight saw how much Ruby enjoyed it, she encouraged her to enter the contest, which was sponsored by the college.

She and Izzy had been talking about it all summer, but they hadn't really gotten past the researching and planning. Izzy kept putting things off. She'd been acting weird all summer. Ruby couldn't put her finger on it, but every time she hung out with Izzy lately she felt *bad.* Like Izzy didn't really want her around but didn't know how to tell her. No matter, they were signed up and they had to have the model bridge designed and ready to be built by the middle of September. If Ruby took off to North Carolina, they'd never be ready in time.

The other thing that she kept coming back

to was her mom. If her dad and Bunk decided to take Ruby along with them, who would check in on her? She knew Bunk went by at least once a week just to make sure the house was still standing. Who would look after her if they were all gone? She tries not to think about moving away. About what would happen to her mom then.

"It'll be okay," she says to her dad. "It's just a week."

"I want your phone fixed," her dad says, and her mom nods. "And I want these goddamn rodents gone. I'm going to set some traps, and as soon as the mama is caught, you need to call Animal Control to come get them. If you can't take care of that, Ruby is coming with us."

"Of course," her mom says, nodding again. It's like her head is attached to a spring. "I promise."

They all go into the house, and she can see her father start to relax. Despite whatever it is he was expecting, the house is spic and span like it always is. Her mother could never stand the messes they all made. She was always chasing after them with a dish rag and a bottle of 409. She used to make her dad and Jess wipe down the toilet seat with a Clorox wipe every time they peed. She used to say that living with two men in the house was like living in a barn. To this, Jess would always push his nose up with his finger and snort like a pig and Daddy would make that great rumbly blowing sound through his nose like a horse.

Ruby's got her backpack, but Bunk has to go back to the car and get all her other stuff. It's not much really, just a duffle bag of clothes and books. It's only a week, and it's still summer; she doesn't need much besides her swimsuit and some T-shirts. Flip-flops and her Chucks. Her bike, which Bunk is wheeling up the tangled mess of a driveway. She's got a cell phone, but it won't work for anything but games out here.

Daddy tells Bunk where to find the traps, and Bunk disappears into the shed to look for them.

"They won't hurt her, will they?" Ruby asks.

"They're padded," he said. "Shouldn't hurt her at all."

Daddy is at the kitchen table thumbing through the phone book. "I want you to ride your bike up to Hudson's later today. See if you can use their phone. If not, there's a spot up there where you can get pretty good cell reception. Here's the number for Fairpoint. You need to tell them to come out and fix the line. Ruby, I'm not kidding. This

49

needs to get done today. I want you to call me to let me know as soon as it's taken care of. And Syl, you need to let her do this, you understand?"

Her mom nods.

Ruby leans down to give her father a hug and wishes she hadn't. Despite everything, she suddenly does *not* want to be left here. She wants nothing more than to leave with him and Bunk, to get in the van and go.

"You sure you're going to be okay?" her dad asks as Bunk wheels him back down the makeshift ramp.

Ruby nods even though she's *not* sure. Not sure at all. The lump in her throat is back and the words can't get past it.

When they pull away, she watches her father perched up in the front seat of the van, waving. But he's scowling too, like he's also having second thoughts. But Bunk keeps backing out anyway, and then the van is just a flash of white through all that thick green foliage.

It is morning, finally, and they are getting close. She can feel it. Nessa peers out the bus window at the blur of green, all of it shrouded in a hazy mist. A river coils like a snake below. It has been almost two years since she left Vermont, but she remembers this landscape. It is as familiar to her as her own skin.

*Home.*

When Nessa still spoke, this word in her mouth felt like a sigh. How strange, she thought, that it felt so similar to *whole,* to *hole.* A heavy exhalation followed by the meditative *om,* which was the very first sound. The sound of both beginning and end.

The baby kicks her gently in the ribs, and she presses her hand against her belly.

She is going home, though now the word itself — *home* — feels like a relic from childhood. A forgotten toy. A half-remembered story. It's been two years since she left, two years since she's uttered that word, that sigh. That incantation, that prayer.

She wonders if the pull that this place has is something else she inherited from her mother. For as many times as her mother left, this was the place her mother always sought when she was most lost. Like a flower seeks the sun. Like a junkie seeks a fix. She tries to imagine her own mother's journey home seventeen years ago, her own belly swollen with Nessa. Did she feel this same aching? Did she long for the same impossible thing? She squeezes her eyes shut and tries to dream her mother's face, her hands. But they are obscured by the same mist that obliterates the river.

This is definitely where it began. After she was born, she and her mother lived here, at the lake with her grandfather, until she was six years old. From those early years, Nessa remembers only yellow wallpaper, a drawer filled with pencils and tools and matches, a creaky staircase. These images themselves seen through the hazy lens of memory, distorted, lacking clarity. A voice (her mother's?), her feverish cheek resting against the cold porcelain sink and hand touching the space between her shoulders, a purple Tinkerbell nightgown riddled with holes. Her grandfather sitting in a chair by the fireplace, the steep corduroy climb onto his warm lap. Colorful books and his soft voice reading to her until her eyes were too heavy to hold open. This is the crumbling foundation of *Home:* soft sheets, the distant sound of a train.

She doesn't remember leaving back then. It's as though she fell asleep one night and woke up in a new life. A world where *Home* became nothing more than an idea. An abstract. A word signifying nothing. The memories of the apartments where she and her mother lived after this (*Hartford, Springfield, Worcester*) run together like ink in water: the smell of natural gas and mildew. Rust-ringed toilets and cigarette-singed counters. Men in and out of the house, in and out of her mother's bed. The rumble of a dryer, headlights racing across her ceiling at night, and the wailing of a neighbor's baby.

Then one afternoon, after school, she found her mother shoving her clothes into a suitcase again, her eyes wild. Desperate. Nessa swears she could smell the need coming off of her, like something chemical.

"Where are we going now?" Nessa had asked.

"We're going back," her mother said. "Home." And in that moment, the word sounded like a promise.

Nessa had stood watching her in the bedroom doorway, plucking a bit of peeling paint from the frame. And she'd allowed herself to believe. That Home, like God, was something other than a wish.

It was with this hope that they had come back here, taken a bus almost exactly like this one, her mother wringing her hands in her lap and smiling nervously the whole way. She hadn't had a drink in three days, and had made a terrific show of flushing her pills down the toilet. But when they got to the lake, none of it mattered. Nessa's grandfather had passed away while they were gone, and her mother hadn't even known.

Nessa imagines it's foolish of her as well to think that after two years her mother might still be living here in that cramped apartment above the hair salon. That she can just knock on the door, and that she will answer.

Since Nessa left, she's sent exactly two postcards to her mother: one when she arrived in LA, to let her know she was safe, and then another one a week ago from Portland, to say she was coming back. But she didn't offer a return address, because each time she'd written there hadn't been one to give.

She tries to remind herself that the important thing is that she has returned. That she has come back to take care of things. That she has stopped running away. Her grandfather taught her once that if she was ever lost in the woods, she should stay put, wait for someone to find her. She fears she might never find her mother if she's on the move again. But she tries not to think about what lies ahead if her mother has left, if she'll have to face this alone. Whenever she does, she feels her entire body tense, harden with fear.

*Home,* she prays silently, because she doesn't speak.

She tries to stretch. Her back hurts, and the baby is restless, tossing and turning inside her as though trying to get comfortable. Neither of them has been comfortable for weeks now. She continues to press her palm against her stomach which is so distended now she feels freakish, and the baby rolls again, listlessly.

*Home.*

But is this the beginning or end?

The bus exhales, stops.

"Quimby!" the bus driver says, and she

stands and makes her way down the long aisle to the doors.

Sylvie stands in the kitchen, her entire body trembling inside her robe. Ruby is standing on the porch still, watching Bunk's van pull away, until the rattling of the muffler is gone. It is only nine o'clock, but the sun is starting to burn through the misty morning.

"Why don't you come inside," Sylvie says, hoping the tremor does not reach her throat, doesn't expose how frayed she feels. She touches Ruby's shoulder tentatively, as if she might turn to dust with her touch. "I fixed up your room," she offers, and Ruby turns to her and nods.

Sylvie tries to see the house through Ruby's eyes. Her world from her daughter's perspective.

This is still Ruby's house. Even though it's been nearly six months since she's slept overnight here, Sylvie likes to think that her staying at Bunk's is just a temporary thing. Until she gets better. As if this is all just a passing malady rather than the chronic chaos it is. On good days, she imagines getting help. Getting past it. Getting over it. She is reminded of the game she used to play with Ruby and Jess when they were little. The one about the bear hunt. *We're going on a bear hunt! We're gonna catch a big one! I'm not afraid!* But then the whole journey is one obstacle after another. Things they have to go over, under, *through. We're coming to a wide river. And there's no bridge going over it. No tunnel going under it. It's just plain old water. And we're gonna have to swim . . .*

With Ruby beside her now, she realizes how dark she keeps the house. She clicks on one of the small lamps she uses for reading and the whole room is illuminated.

"Wow," Ruby says, her eyes widening.

Sylvie realizes this is the first time Ruby has seen the birds. She's only been collecting them since the spring, but the entire mantel over the fireplace is littered with glass jars. She has donated all of her old books to the library to make room in the built-in bookcases. And she's fashioned additional shelves out of some old two-by-fours and bricks she found in the shed.

"Are these real?" Ruby asks. She picks up the one with the barn swallow inside.

Sylvie nods. And she remembers the swallow, because it was the first.

It happened last spring, not long after she got out of the hospital. After Ruby's last visit. She had been washing the dishes, caught up in a strange reverie brought on by the medication and exhaustion, when she saw the flash of something against the window and heard what sounded like a gunshot. The sound tore through the haze enveloping her, and she dropped the dish she'd been washing, watching in disbelief as it shattered on the floor. Trembling, she pulled on her coat and opened the back door. It was the first time she'd walked outside in nearly a week. The cold air made every nerve ending feel raw. She found the swallow in the deep tangle of grass beneath the kitchen window. And as she knelt down, she'd felt overwhelmed with sadness. The violence of it, the suddenness too much.

Cradling the bird's warm body in her palm, she was transported back to her childhood, and she recalled her grandmother's collection of birds. After her mother left, her grandmother had tried to teach her, and Sylvie had watched her from a distance, because the process both fascinated and horrified her. Her grandmother had learned taxidermy from her *own* grandmother, this sanguinary art handed down from one generation to the next. This brutal craft was her inheritance, she supposed. Her birthright.

And the birds kept dying. A baby robin was next. A grouse. It was as though they were offering themselves to her, as though God were plucking them from the sky and presenting them to her, providing her hands with the distraction they craved. She requested books from the library on home taxidermy. And it really wasn't difficult. She had most of the tools she needed already at home: cotton balls, Borax, nail scissors, a needle and thread. And over time, she too became skilled in this particular art of preservation.

"This one is so small," Ruby says, peering in at the hummingbird.

The hummingbird had been difficult. She'd had to use tweezers and a magnifying glass. It was delicate work and had taken her nearly three full days. But the finished product was astonishing: the emerald throat, the eyes she'd replaced with tiny black glass beads, the illusion of flight achieved with invisible wires.

Ruby wanders around the living room looking at the birds, as though she's stumbled into a museum. And as she studies Sylvie's birds, Sylvie studies her. She's gotten taller, at least two or three inches since last Christmas when she and Robert moved out. Her hair has grown, her two braids traveling nearly to her waist. She is still a tomboy, wearing ratty cut-off jeans and a sweatshirt. Tall athletic socks and sneakers. Her long pale legs are riddled with bug bites and bruises. She is eleven now, but she is still such a child, her body still that of a little girl.

The sweatshirt is one Sylvie hasn't seen before, and this, more than almost anything, tears at her heart. A mother should be the one who shops for her daughter. When Ruby and Jess were little, she loved picking out clothes for them. The tiny T-shirts and jeans for Jess. The impossibly small high-top sneakers and baseball caps. And for Ruby, tiny dresses and rompers, the miniature tights and shoes. The fact that Ruby is wearing a sweatshirt Sylvie has never touched, never washed, never folded, makes her want to cry. And despite every effort not to, she feels her eyes well up.

Ruby looks up from the barred owl Sylvie finished last week. Ruby is smiling, but when she sees that Sylvie is crying, her face falls. And then she throws her shoulders back, hardens. "You don't have to do this,

Mom. I could just go stay at Bunk's house by myself. Or with Izzy. I'm sure Gloria wouldn't mind." Ruby looks at her blankly. "It's no big deal."

"No," Sylvie says, shaking her head, brushing her hand in front of her face. Ashamed that she is unable to control any of her emotions. "It's fine. I'll be fine." She stops before she makes any more promises she isn't able to keep. "I'm glad you're here. Really."

Ruby is holding the owl. "Can I maybe put this one in my room?" she asks.

"Of course," she says, nodding. "Any of them that you like. Here, follow me," she says, as though Ruby no longer remembers the layout of the small house. As though she needs a guide.

Behind her, Ruby carries the owl carefully down the hallway. When they get to her room, Sylvie pushes the door open gently, but doesn't go in. Her instinct is to turn away, as though there's something radioactive and glowing inside. But everything's exactly the same as it used to be. Ruby's bed and Jess's bed. The pictures of them stuck into the corners of the dresser mirror. Jess's Sox cap with the ketchup stain on the brim still hanging on the hook at the back of the door. There's the stuffed SpongeBob

62

Robert won for her at the fair. Empty hangers lined up in half of the closet. Ruby goes in and sets the owl on the nightstand. When Sylvie finally joins her inside, she shows her the room, like Ruby is only a tourist, and Sylvie is the guide, a docent to this sad museum.

"Thanks, Mom," Ruby says, and Sylvie takes it as her signal to leave.

"Okay. Let me know if you need anything. I'll make us some breakfast."

Sylvie returns to the kitchen and tries to imagine all the other mornings with Ruby. How many were there? Ten years of mornings. Thousands of breakfasts. As she pulls the dusty mixing bowl from her cupboard, she is transported back in time, when she used to make pancakes for the kids that looked like Mickey Mouse, chocolate-chip eyes, jelly mouths. The bowl, the ceramic bowl that Gloria made for her, conjures other mornings: the sound of bickering coming from the kids' room, the distant sound of the shower as Robert got ready for work. Some mornings she wouldn't even have gone to sleep yet, coming home after a delivery, bleary-eyed and exhausted, wanting nothing more than to slip under the covers and sleep. She remembers wishing she didn't have to make breakfast, check homework, pack lunches. She remembers wishing sometimes she were alone.

She clicks on the radio.

". . . now classified as Tropical Storm Irene, it's a slow-moving storm, expected to pass through Puerto Rico tomorrow and then head northwest through the Bahamas. It is difficult at this point to determine whether or not it will make landfall on the East Coast and what effects it will have . . ."

She thinks of rain. Of storms, and as she looks into the bowl, its depth is suddenly distorted. She grips the edge of the counter as if it can keep her from plummeting, keep her steady as the earth drops out from beneath her.

Ruby puts her clothes into the empty drawers, stacks her books next to the owl on her nightstand, and shoves the empty duffle bag under the bed. She looks around the room, remembers how excited she was to have her own room. How her dad promised a window seat that looked out over the river. She remembers how Jess talked and laughed in his sleep. How he would pounce on her bed to wake her up every morning, Superman cape flying behind him. How messy he was. How annoying. It makes her throat feel thick just thinking about how much he irritated her.

Since she and her dad left, she has been able to push him out of her mind, just as she used to push him away from her stuff, to the other side of the backseat, out of their room. He was easy like that. He never put up a fuss. When she started to annoy her, she just had to say, "Get out!" and he'd shrug his shoulders and go. She was not a very nice sister. She could be mean and selfish and unkind. There were times when she wished he'd vanish. When he broke her protractor, when he spilled grape juice on her Red Sox jersey. When he tried to explain his long and complicated dreams to her while she was still trying to sleep. These are the flashes that come to her, even as she tries to keep them at bay. Her own cruelty. Her failures. He is a reminder that she is not a good person. That, maybe, she was the one who wished him away.

But every now and then, there will be a bright memory that presents itself to her: just a flash that floods her entire body with that strange longing that is grief. Jess wrapped up in the towel that looked like an elephant, the one with the hood that had a trunk and ears and button eyes. He used to run through the house after a bath, making wet footprints on the floor. Of the way he always asked her to tie his shoes, and how he tickled the back of her neck with his tiny fingers as she bent over, again and again, to show him how to make two bunny ears. Or the way he said *pan-a-cakes* instead of pancakes, even after he knew better. Usually she tries not to think of Jess. Because thinking of Jess makes her entire heart hurt like something bruised in her chest. But now here she is, back in the room they shared. She grabs his baseball cap and puts it on her head.

She hasn't eaten since last night, but she's still not hungry. She knows her mother is cooking for her, though, and so she leaves the bedroom and goes to her in the kitchen.

Mickey Mouse pancakes. There is a stack of them on a plastic *Cat in the Hat* plate from when she was little. It embarrasses her, makes her feel sad. She's not hungry, but she mumbles, "Thanks," and sits down. As she eats, her mother hovers at the counter like she's waiting for her to do or say something. But Ruby doesn't know what to say that will make any of this okay. She's not hungry, but she nods when her mom offers her another one.

"So I've been thinking that maybe you could help me with the birds," her mom says, sitting down across from her at the table. Ruby notices for the first time that her robe is threadbare at the elbows, that her cheeks are hollow and her bones sharp. She reminds her of the swallow. Tiny, dark. "I mean, if you're interested at all. I could teach you."

Ruby nods.

"I know you're busy with swimming lessons. And with Izzy. Daddy says you still play with Izzy a lot?"

The word *play* crushes her. She is talking to a little girl. She is feeding a little girl. She thinks she's the same kid she was the last time she sat and had breakfast at this table with her. But she's not the same little girl. She's not a little girl at all. And the fact that her mom doesn't realize this suddenly makes her angry.

"Yeah, I'm going to be pretty busy," she says, pushing away the unfinished pancake. The ears are gone, the chocolate chip eyes smeared across the face.

Her mother nods hard and fast as she stands to take away the breakfast plates. Ruby looks down at the Cat in the Hat, the illustration worn, the plastic scratched.

"You know, I've been feeling a little under the weather. Didn't sleep well last night," her mother says with her back to Ruby. "I think I might need to go back to bed for just a little bit. Will you be okay if I take a little nap?"

"Yeah," she says. "I have stuff to do."

Nessa gathers her things and gets off the bus. She is the only passenger to disembark here. And she is keenly aware of the driver's eyes on her as she descends the steps. Keenly aware of the eyes that follow her as she makes her way down Quimby's main street. Keenly aware that invisibility might have been possible in Portland, but that here, she is as invisible as a blood stain on clean white sheets. And so she lowers her head and tries to walk with purpose, as though she belongs here.

It has only been a week since Nessa left Portland, but already the city and her time there feel like a dream. Three thousand miles away now, Portland is like this mist, hazy and dissipating. It is only rain against a window, gritty sheets, incense. It is the bare knob of Mica's shoulder. It is ancient bootleg cassette tapes playing in a boom box perched on a rotten windowsill. It is weed and stolen library books and strangers in and out of the house. Dirty dishes. Dirty feet. Dirty linoleum on the kitchen floor. It is the smell of curry, sickening and thick. No matter how hard she tried, Portland was never home.

She left on the Greyhound bus a week ago, with only this backpack on her back, a wad of stolen cash, and a name and a phone number scrawled on a piece of paper. In the warm glow of the reading light over her seat, she had spread it across her lap, smoothing it like a love letter, touching the script with her fingers, tracing the deep slants and shivery loops. By the time she got to Burlington, the paper was worn thin and soft like a baby blanket, rendered fragile with her constant worrying of it. It's the only thing she has, in case her mother is, indeed, gone.

She didn't sleep well on the bus. The smell of exhaust and gasoline and whatever it was they used to keep the bathrooms clean assaulted her. She was fortunate enough to have an open seat next to her for most of the trip, except for a stretch between Minneapolis and Chicago when a woman wearing a hijab sat next to her. They didn't speak for four hundred miles. At first she felt offended, that the woman didn't feel compelled to ask her when the baby was due, whether she was having a boy or a girl, or any other of the myriad questions she was asked a thousand times a day. That she wouldn't even get the opportunity to greet the woman's barrage, her curiosity, with the wall of silence she'd been building. But then, as the landscape outside the window changed from pine trees to corn to ramshackle houses, Nessa felt relieved by her companion's reticence. It was as though the woman also understood the power and beauty and *honesty* of silence. Perhaps she too enjoyed the freedom from chatty superficial niceties inevitably followed by painful, uncomfortable pauses. Instead they sat side by side, together but completely alone for four hundred miles. Respectful of each other's aloneness, not falling for the myth of fellowship, for the false intimacy created by such situations of proximity.

For years now, she's bought into that lie. Believed in the hollow promise of communion. Trusting that two bodies could forge an alliance. That it was as simple as flesh. As simple as whispers skipped across skin like a pebble across water. She's wanted so desperately to believe that attention (to lips, to hips) was the same as home.

But people lie. And people steal. And

people leave.

This is something else her mother taught her. People *always* leave. But she is not running away anymore. She will prove her mother wrong. She will make all of this right.

It's been two years, but it could be twenty. This place feels like a distant dream, both familiar and strange. If she's remembering correctly, the apartment she and her mother shared is not too far from the bus station, and so she walks, purposeful if uncertain, ready now for whatever awaits her. But still, tears sting her eyes.

She approaches the brick building, sees herself reflected in the salon window, and thinks about how she used to check her hair in this same glass each morning on her way to school. She barely recognizes the girl in the window now. Tattered, filthy clothes, dreadlocks. Swollen face and feet and a belly as large as a small moon. It stuns her. Who has she become? She peers closer, as if she can find an answer to this, but instead her reflection disappears, and she is not staring at herself anymore but at an old woman sitting under a hair dryer, her lips pursed in disdain at what she sees outside the window.

Startled, she steps away from the glass.

Her stomach rumbles with hunger.

Nessa studies the mailboxes along the wall by the door, searches for her mother's name, but the label on her mother's box has fallen off, leaving only its sticky ghost behind. And so she opens the door and climbs up the narrow stairs to the second floor. Her legs remember the depth of each tread, the steepness of each rise. The scent of cigarette smoke and the salon chemicals fill her with an odd nostalgia. Her heart beats hard in her chest, but the baby is motionless.

The hallway is longer than the one in her memory. Darker. She walks to the end.

And then she is at the door. Her mother's door. She presses her forehead against the wood and takes a deep breath. Her stomach contracts; it nearly takes her breath away. Her entire abdomen tightens like a fist.

She tries to imagine her mother's face when she opens the door, the look of relief and surprise. It's been two years since Nessa slipped away, two fugitive years. Of course, she's thought of her mother often. Dreamed herself inside these walls, tried to imagine her mother's worry, her fears. She used to think that her disappearance might actually help turn things around for her mother.

That maybe it would be the one thing that would, finally, make her get clean. On the darkest days in Portland, when she was hungry and alone, she even imagined that she was somehow doing this *for* her mother. As though her running away was some sort of sacrifice instead of the most selfish thing in the world.

But now, as she curls her fist to knock, she thinks about the day she and her mother returned to Quimby, when her mother told her to stay in the car when she walked up the long path to Nessa's grandfather's house. How she had watched her mother open the screen door, and how a stranger had stood in the doorway shaking his head. Her mother must have known that this was a fool's errand.

Nessa holds her breath, but hope is slipping away.

The door cracks open, and an elderly woman in a housedress peeks out at her.

"I got my own church," she says. "And I ain't buying nothing."

And Nessa is only surprised by how little this surprises her. She must have known all along that her mother was long gone.

It's Sunday so Ruby doesn't have swimming lessons. Thank God. She promised her dad she'd call the phone company, but she doubts she'll be able to get through to anyone on a Sunday. She figures she'd better call anyway so that when he checks in with her later she can at least say she tried.

She goes to her mother's bedroom door and knocks. "Mom?"

"Yeah, honey?" she says from inside the room. Her voice is too bright.

"I'm going to go into town to call the phone company. I might go to Izzy's house too. If that's okay. Do you need anything?"

Silence.

"Mom?" she says, feeling a flutter in her throat. Ruby hears her slippered feet, and then her mom opens the door. There are shadows under her eyes.

"There's a storm coming," she says.

Ruby is confused. The sky is bright blue.

It's already warming up outside. It looks like a beautiful day.

"I mean, when you talk to your dad. You should tell him to listen to the news. I worry about him and Bunk driving in bad weather."

"Okay," she says and shrugs. "Do you want anything from in town?"

Her mother shakes her head, and for one moment Ruby gets the strange sensation that *she* is the child. Ruby is nearly as tall as she is now. Her mom's hair is messy like a little girl's. Without makeup, she looks younger.

"Are you riding your bike?" she asks.

Ruby nods. How else would she get all the way into town?

"You have your helmet?"

She nods again, though she never wears her helmet.

"Are you sure it's not too far?"

"It's like four miles, Mom," she says, fearing suddenly that she's going to expect her to hang out here with her for the next week.

"You go the long way," she says, and her eyes grow wider. "Don't go over the bridge."

Ruby swallows. Nods.

At Bunk's house, she comes and goes as she pleases. She has her own key to the house, and she can get everywhere she needs to go on her bike. Her dad's only rules are that she be home by supper time, that she answers her phone if he calls, and that she doesn't cross the covered bridge. This last rule is the single thing he and her mother seem to agree on anymore.

She makes sure she's got her backpack, her helmet (her mom is watching from the window), and then she just puts her head down and goes. The dirt road her mom lives on is a little bit dangerous. Her bike is a ten-speed, so the tires are narrow; the smallest rock could throw her off into a ditch. But luckily, after a mile or so, the dirt turns to pavement, and then it's just big trucks she needs to worry about. Even going the long way, it only takes twenty minutes to ride into town, and it's downhill most of the way. She's barely even out of breath when she pulls up to Izzy's driveway and drops her bike on the gravel next to Grover's car.

Izzy lives in one of the big Victorian houses on the park in Quimby. She calls it "Miss Piggy" because it's big and pink and fussy. In her room there's a bell that used to be for the maid. There's also a dumbwaiter, which is like a tiny little elevator they use to bring up snacks from the kitchen. It's got three stories and a fake door in the library.

Her dad says that her great-grandpa was a bootlegger, and he used to hide liquor in there. Now it's just filled with boxes of stuff they can't seem to get rid of. It's easy to win at hide and seek in her house because there are so many good places to hide. Ruby hid in the old ice chest in the pantry once, and Izzy couldn't find her for forty-five minutes.

Izzy's great-grandpa used to own the sawmill, which meant he basically owned this town. He built the house back in the eighteen hundreds, so it's been passed down through her family for two hundred years: grandparents and aunts and uncles and cousins. But now it's just Izzy and her parents. And Grover. The mill closed down a long time ago. They're not rich, not anymore anyway.

Izzy's father, Neil, is a science teacher at the high school, and her mother, Gloria, is a potter. She makes bowls and plates and coffee mugs, which she sells at crafts fairs and at the artists' collective in town. Her pottery has sandy-looking bottoms and colors swirled like sunsets. A long time ago, Gloria made an entire set for Ruby's mother as a birthday gift. Her mom still eats and drinks out of these dishes every day. Ruby noticed she was using the mixing bowl this morning for the pancakes. To bring in a little extra money, they rent a room on the first floor out to an old man named Grover who, even though he's almost ninety years old, still drives a car. It's a big yellow station wagon, and it takes up the whole driveway, so Ruby's mom and dad have to park their cars on the street out front. Grover is a professor emeritus at the college. He almost won the Nobel Prize like fifty years ago, Izzy says.

Ruby has known Izzy since she was born. Literally. Ruby's mom was the one who drove through a snowstorm to bring Izzy into the world. Ruby was exactly one month old then, and her mom brought her with her because her dad was working that night too. Before the accident, he was a volunteer EMT. Her mom said Ruby slept through the whole thing, at least until Izzy was finally born, screaming bloody murder. Their moms liked each other right away, which is crazy because they probably wouldn't ever have met each other if not for Izzy's mom needing a midwife. But even though they didn't have anything but babies in common, that was enough. They became best friends. And it feels like she and Izzy have always been friends. Izzy is like family. Like a sister. And after the accident, it sometimes felt like Izzy's mom was her mom too.

Izzy answers the door wearing a tight pink T-shirt and a short denim skirt, wedge sandals. Ruby barely recognizes her.

"What are *you* all dressed up for?" Ruby asks her.

Izzy looks down at the skirt as if noticing it for the first time. She blushes a little and shrugs.

Usually Izzy lives in that stupid Yankees shirt she got a year ago, the only Yankees fan in the entire state of Vermont as far as Ruby knows. She just does it to be contrary. Izzy's always hated everything that most other kids like, especially other girls. She hates pepperoni and chocolate ice cream and jumping rope. She even hates Harry Potter. And she *hates* skirts. What Izzy does like are computers. But not video games and stuff like that. Someday she says she wants to be just like Steve Jobs. She wants to be a famous inventor. She's the smartest kid Ruby knows. Even smarter than Mark Blume in their class. That's why Ruby needs her help designing the bridge for the bridge building contest. Ruby's got a zillion ideas, but Izzy's the one who can turn those ideas into something real.

Mrs. McKnight told them about the

contest at the end of the school year. Signed them up for it and even paid the entry fee. She told them their only job was to design the best bridge they could design over the summer, and she'd make sure they had the supplies they needed to build it in the fall. The contest is in October, but Ruby can't seem to get Izzy as excited about it as she is.

"You stink," Izzy says, and Ruby lifts her arm and sniffs. She's right.

"Sorry," Ruby says, and Izzy pulls her into the house.

"There's a hurricane coming," Izzy says.

"Here?" She remembers her mother mentioning a storm.

"Well, not Vermont. But up the whole East Coast. It's going to hit the Carolinas first."

Ruby thinks about her dad and Bunk. About North Carolina. About her Uncle Larry, about the fishing boat.

"It's been all over the news," Izzy says.

Ruby's mother doesn't have a TV anymore.

"It's going to be bigger than Katrina," Izzy says.

"Who's Katrina?" Ruby asks.

Izzy's eyes get wide and she sighs. "*Katrina?* The hurricane in New Orleans?"

Izzy gets exasperated with Ruby a lot.

With the things she doesn't know. Izzy knows everything about everything, or at least it seems like it lately.

Ruby remembers now. Though it was so long ago, they were just little kids then. Kindergartners. "We were like five when that happened," she says.

"My parents went *down* there to help," Izzy says, still irritated beyond belief. "I stayed at your house for a week?"

"Oh yeah," Ruby says.

"You want some Wheat Thins?" Izzy asks then, and she notices that Izzy's socks match. Izzy's socks never match. And when Izzy turns around, she can see that her blond hair is brushed smooth. It's shiny, like the silky stuff inside a cornhusk. Normally, there's a big knot at the back, a permanent tangle that Gloria stopped fighting at the beginning of the summer. "A rat's nest," is what Ruby's mother would call it. And she gets a picture of her mother combing Izzy's tangles out, sitting outside their house back when they were just little kids. Maybe this was when Izzy came to stay with them. When her parents took off to Louisiana to volunteer to help all those people after Katrina. Ruby does remember, of course she does. It's just that sometimes she keeps memories in a locked box in her mind, pulling them out only when she needs them. This is one of them.

Izzy grabs a half-full box of Wheat Thins and a tub of whipped cream cheese and Ruby follows her down the hall. They both peek in at Grover, who is watching a movie in his room.

"Hi, Grover!" Ruby says.

"Hello, ladies!" he says, waving to them from his recliner.

He always leaves the door open in case they want to come in and visit. Sometimes they hang out and watch movies or play Gin Rummy with him. But today, Ruby is determined to make some progress with the bridge plans.

Izzy's mother is in the guest bathroom, crouched down looking at something on the floor. Her mother dyes her hair with streaks of hot pink now, ever since Izzy's aunt got breast cancer last year. "It's a gesture," she explains when people ask, and around here people always ask. "Solidarity."

"Hi, Gloria," Ruby says.

"Hi, Ruby," she says, standing up. She always looks just a bit startled, her eyes wide like Izzy's. "Wait a minute, will one of you guys get the door for me?" She's got her hands cupped together and she's peering into a gap where her thumbs come together.

"It's a daddy longlegs," she says.

Ruby rushes to the front door and opens it for her, and Gloria goes outside, releasing the insect into the grass by the front porch. For some reason this makes Ruby think about her mother's birds. Gloria's still wearing her pajamas, which have bright yellow ducks all over them.

"Did you hear about the hurricane coming up the coast?" Gloria asks when they go back in. "Probably going to be a rainy weekend ahead. You and your mom going to be okay?"

"Yeah. We'll be fine. Bunk patched the roof for her earlier this summer."

Gloria squeezes Ruby in a hug. She smells like clay. "How is she?" Gloria asks then, and her face looks sad. Ruby doesn't know the last time they even saw each other; she thinks she probably visited her at the hospital. But she doesn't know if she's been to see her at the house.

"She's good," Ruby lies.

"Well, you let her know we're here if she needs anything. Anything at all."

And she knows that while some people say things like this, they're just saying them to seem nice, but Gloria means it. After the accident she came to the house almost every single day for months. Until Ruby's dad got

84

out of the hospital, she even slept on the sofa some nights. But then her dad gave up, and after awhile, even Gloria could see that things weren't getting better. That maybe they might *never* get better.

"Come *on,*" Izzy says, exasperated again, and yanks her arm.

Izzy has her own computer, and so they've been doing most of the work at her house. Izzy's dad brought home a bridge-building software program from the high school. Ruby keeps a notebook with her ideas and sketches, but Izzy's the one who translates all her scribbles into something real, plugging them into the computer and watching as it generates the 3-D images. The competition is for the entire state. Which means there are going to be some pretty awesome bridges. They've looked at all the designs from last year online, and it's sort of intimidating. But Ruby has ideas. That's one thing she never runs out of.

Izzy's door has a TOXIC WASTE sign hanging on it, and she's not kidding. Her room is always a disaster. She's the messiest person Ruby knows. Ruby can't believe Gloria doesn't care; she just closes the door when it gets too bad. Ruby's mom would never let her room get like that.

But today when Izzy opens the door, it's

like they've slipped into an alternate universe. The bed is made, the carpet has been vacuumed, and all the crap that's usually all over the floor is neatly put away. There isn't a dirty dish or dirty T-shirt in sight. Her collection of snow globes is lined up on her bureau, and her desk is clear of debris.

Izzy pretends like everything's normal and goes to her desk to turn on her computer.

"You cleaned your room," Ruby says.

"Duh," Izzy says and all of a sudden Ruby gets that bad feeling she's been getting all summer.

"I just mean, it looks nice," Ruby says, trying to make everything better again. She just wants Izzy back. Normal, messy, tangled hair, mismatched-sock Izzy. She doesn't like this Izzy.

"So, listen," Izzy says, not looking at Ruby. "You can only stay a little while today."

"Huh?"

"Um, Marcy Davidson is coming over this afternoon."

*Marcy Davidson.* Ruby doesn't even know what to say. It feels like somebody knocked the wind out of her. Marcy Davidson lives down the street from Izzy in the big green house. The "Kermit" to Izzy's "Miss Piggy." Her parents own a realty company. Their faces are plastered on every FOR SALE sign in Quimby. She's one of the rich girls, one of the popular girls at school. And Izzy *hates* Marcy. Once, in the second grade, Izzy laughed while she was drinking milk and it came out of her nose. Marcy tortured her for the whole year, called her Snotface. Back then Marcy was mean, but now she is the meanest kind of mean: the kind where she's nice to your face and then says things behind your back. Ruby can't imagine any situation where Marcy would ever even be in the same room as Izzy, never mind coming over to her house to hang out.

*"What?"* Ruby asks.

"Her mom and dad are going to a conference in Boston, so she's staying here. I thought you knew. That's why you couldn't come this week. My mom told your dad."

Ruby feels as though someone is sitting on her chest. So this is why she's been sent to her mother's. Because her dad asked Gloria first and she said *no. "Marcy Davidson?"*

Izzy nods but she won't even look at Ruby. She's just staring at the computer screen as it boots up.

"Well, when are we supposed to finish the bridge designs then?" Ruby asks, trying hard not to cry.

Izzy shrugs. "We can work on them now.

Then maybe after her mom and dad come back next weekend. It's like no big deal, Ruby." There again, that awful condescending tone, making Ruby feel like she's an annoying little kid instead of her best friend. But it *is* a big deal. Ruby has been thinking about the bridge all summer. Even if Izzy doesn't think it matters. It does. To Ruby.

"What about the fair?" Ruby asks then, even though she already knows the answer.

"We're going on Wednesday," Izzy says. "You can come if you want."

But Ruby doesn't want. Ruby wants nothing to do with any of this. With Marcy, with this new Izzy. Ruby feels stupid. And still that crushing feeling in her chest. She wonders if she's too young to have a heart attack.

"I gotta get back to my mom's anyway," Ruby says. She wants to do something, say something that will make Izzy feel as bad as she feels right now. But instead she just says, "I guess I'll see you at swimming lessons tomorrow."

Ruby goes to her door then and realizes that Izzy's Einstein poster is gone. There's been a life-size poster of Einstein hanging there for as long as she can remember. But instead of Einstein and his crazy hair, there's a color poster of One Direction, pulled out of the middle of one of those teen magazines they sell at the drugstore. And as she looks at the guys' faces, bisected by the creases where it was folded in the magazine, she realizes that Izzy is changing. And this makes her chest ache more than any stupid bridge project. More than Marcy Davidson.

"Well, bye," Ruby says, hoping Izzy will say something, that it's not too late for her to come to her senses, but knowing that if she thinks she can be friends with Marcy Davidson, then sense left her a long time ago.

She takes the stairs two at a time and rushes past Grover's open door and then past Gloria, who is doing something in the kitchen. She leaves Izzy's house but she doesn't know where she should go. She doesn't want to go back to her mom's house. And so she pedals away from Izzy's house, past Marcy's house, and heads over to the library. But it's Sunday. Closed.

Outside she sits on the steps, dials the number for the phone company, and waits for almost fifteen minutes before somebody finally helps her. While she waits, she looks across the street. All of the shops are closed except for the salon and the drugstore. Suddenly, the door next to the salon swings open and a pregnant lady with long blond dreadlocks and a big backpack barrels out. Her face is red; it looks like she's been crying. She looks lost. She looks up and down the street before ducking down the alley between the used bookstore and the artist gallery. Ruby stands up, thinks about following her, but then a voice comes on the other line.

"Fairpoint, how can I help you?"

Ruby gives them her mom's address and tells them the phone's out. They say they'll send somebody tomorrow. They give her a confirmation number she writes in pen on her hand. She calls her dad then and tells him everything's taken care of. What she wants to tell him is to come home. That her mom is sad, that Izzy's being mean, and that she just wants him to come back. But instead she just says, "Where are you now?"

"Just crossed the border into Massachusetts. Listen, I'll call the house tomorrow. You said they're coming to fix the phone tomorrow morning, right?"

"Yeah. Tomorrow."

"How's your mom?" her dad asks then, and Ruby can picture his face. The way he draws a breath in whenever he talks about her. The way his eyebrows lower and his nostrils flare.

"She made Mickey Mouse pancakes," Ruby says.

As Nessa stumbles back down the stairs and outside, she feels sick. Dizzy.

Her mother is *gone.* And beyond the confirmation of this, the finality of this, there is the undeniable and inescapable fact that she is still hungry. Starving. Hunger doesn't care that her mother is gone. Baby animals in the wild, abandoned by their mother, still need food. Nourishment. Infants without their mothers' milk must find other ways to survive.

The last thing she ate was a bruised apple an old woman on the bus had offered her from her bag. It was mealy and sweet, but it had taken the edge off at least. Though now the edge has returned, dull and serrated.

In Portland, she had been able to scavenge. Foraging in Dumpsters and trash bins usually yielded enough to survive on. And even when it didn't, while it had pained her to do so, she'd also been able to count on the kindness (or pity) of strangers. She had only to sit on the sidewalk with her hand outstretched for a moment before someone would drop a dollar in her palm.

But here, the streets are not littered with the detritus of urban life. The sidewalk is clear of both trash and people. Leaving her mother's apartment building, she feels like a castaway, surfacing on a deserted island. Her mother is gone. But that does not change the simple truth: she needs food and she needs a place to sleep.

She has ten dollars in her pocket. It is the last of the money she stole from Mica. She had vowed to herself that she would not touch it. That it was her emergency fund. Though she wasn't sure how ten dollars might be able to save her in an emergency.

And so now, her stomach angry with hunger, the baby demanding, demanding, she ducks into a diner and takes a seat in a back booth.

Her heart stutters when she realizes that the waitress is a girl she remembers from high school, though she was older than Nessa, a couple of years ahead of her at school. Nessa always thought she had a friendly face: plump and inviting. Heart stammering, Nessa waits for recognition, for the waitress, *Marla,* to remember her.

But soon it is clear that she has no recollection of Nessa, or, perhaps, it's that Nessa is simply unrecognizable.

"Good morning," Marla chirps and hands her a menu.

Nessa wonders if she had stayed in Quimby if this would be her life now: a blue uniform, her name etched into a gold name tag. Sensible shoes.

"When are you due?" Marla asks brightly, setting down a carafe of ice water, lemons floating inside.

Nessa shakes her head, blushes.

A cloud passes over the waitress's face. "I'm sorry," she says. "None of my beeswax."

Nessa shakes her head, trying to relay, *No, no, it's okay.*

She points to the special, handwritten on a piece of paper paper-clipped to the menu.

"Okeydoke," the waitress says, her face nothing but sunshine again.

The special comes with eggs and bacon, hash browns, a biscuit heavy with creamy gravy. She eats and eats, and then uses the biscuit to wipe the plate clean. Afterwards, she drinks glass after glass of ice water, filling any empty spaces that remain. She leaves the ten-dollar bill on a $9.50 tab and starts to get up to leave, ashamed.

"Hey," the waitress says, reaching for her arm. Her fingers are so cold, it makes Nessa jump. Nessa looks down at the ten-dollar bill, feels her face redden.

"Listen, if you don't have nobody yet, there's a lady, a midwife. She delivered me and all my brothers."

Nessa looks up at her.

"Her name's Sylvie Dupont. Lives by the river, out near Hudson's, the general store? On the way to Lake Gormlaith."

Nessa nods, forces a smile. She hasn't thought that far ahead; she hasn't thought past her mother's door.

" 'Course since the accident, I'm not sure if she's still practicing."

She doesn't understand.

"She lost her little boy. Now she don't leave her house. But she might help you. If you went to her."

Nessa's stomach roils, the breakfast suddenly leaden in her stomach, bile rising in her throat. She feels like she might vomit. She needs to get out of here. She rushes to the ladies' room, feeling vertiginous. She locks the door and grips the edge of the sink. Once she has steadied herself, she runs cold water over a bunch of paper towels, and presses them against her forehead. When she puts them back under the faucet, the water runs brown into the sink.

Reeling, she rushes outside and back down the street. It is Sunday, and everything is closed. The streets are vacant; it is quiet. She stops when she gets to a pay phone. She pulls the slip of paper from her backpack and studies the name, the number. But even as she lifts the receiver to dial, she realizes she doesn't have a quarter. And never mind that even if she did, even if she dropped it into the slot and punched the numbers into the keypad, even if he answered, he would only be met with silence. It's been two years since she's uttered a single word.

In the darkness, Sylvie listens to the new sounds in the house. To the new *old* sounds. Her room and Ruby's room share a wall, and on the other side she hears Ruby as she jumps into her bed and clicks on her light. She hears a zipper, and when she closes her eyes, she can almost see Ruby's hand reaching into her backpack, finding whatever book she is reading. She wonders what world she will slip into tonight and knows this ability is something she has given her: a genetic inheritance like her dark hair and Robert's green eyes. Because the only time Sylvie leaves the house anymore is through the paper portals of her novels.

Sylvie wasn't a reader as a child like Ruby is. She didn't really start reading until after she became a midwife, after she realized that sleep would elude her on the nights when she was waiting for a baby to come. She never understood how Robert could sleep on the nights he was on call. At any moment he could receive word of an emergency, yet he still managed to close his eyes and fall into a deep slumber, his body claiming the rest it needed so that when the call did come (and it always came) he was alert and had the necessary strength to deal with whatever emergency was at hand. He has always been able to separate himself from the possibility of disaster and the actual disaster. She remembers hundreds of nights in this bed, as she lay reading (her eyes blurry with exhaustion) with Robert snoring next to her, waiting for the phone to ring. Expecting the shrill tremble of it, and wondering if it was life or death waiting on the other end of the line.

It was Gloria who gave her her first books, who brought her armloads of the novels she'd kept from college. They were mostly tattered paperbacks with yellow USED stickers along the spines. The pages were riddled with illegible notes in the margins, with yellow highlighter bleeding through to the other side. But she was grateful for the diversion, grew to rely on it. She wonders what she would do now without her books. What would distract her from all the new potential catastrophes, both real and imagined?

Tonight she tries to focus on the page, on one of the new books that Effie has delivered, but she is too tired to make sense of the words. The ink is blurry on the paper. Her days, as predictable and uneventful as they are, still manage to wear her down. Fear is a cumbersome thing. Regret even heavier. By the time she climbs into her bed at night, her limbs ache with the exhaustion of another day, though as she turns out the light and closes her eyes, her body rests but her mind races. Like a car long after the ignition has been turned off, the engine ticking, ticking. The hood still hot to the touch. Because while her days are predictable, as an ascetic's grim routine will be, her nights are capricious. Sleep is like the river. Changeable. Sometimes it is still, harmless, and sleep is nothing but a simple shutting down. But other times it is a violent thing, which pulls her into its current. On nights like these there is nothing to do but to surrender to its sway.

Nessa stands at the edge of the road and thrusts her thumb out into the night, her hand, her entire arm enclosed by the darkness. There is no moon. There are no streetlights. And there are no cars on the road to cast their beams on her. The night is swallowing her whole. Her backpack digs into her shoulders, and she wonders what she could sacrifice in order to lighten the load. What she could spare. She tries not to think about all the things she's given up or lost on this long journey.

After she left her mother's apartment in town, she walked all the way to Lake Gormlaith to her grandfather's old house. By the time she arrived, her ankles ached, and her feet and hands were tingling and swollen. His absence, unlike her mother's, was expected. Still, the unfamiliar car in the driveway, the toys in the yard, the child in a sagging diaper staring at her through the screen door made her throat grow thick. And so she'd kept walking, stopping only when she got to the boat access area, taking off her shoes and wading into the lake. The cold water had numbed her aching feet. And she considered just walking into the water, making her whole body insensate.

She is completely alone.

She's not sure where to go, now that she knows her mother is, indeed, gone. Or at least no longer living in that apartment. She hasn't really thought beyond this. Like most runaways, she has not considered much beyond the leaving. Her thoughts, her body, have been focused on *departure* rather than *destination.* Driven only by a vague, but urgent, need to return to the place where it began, or rather where it ended.

In her pocket, she touches the slip of paper. When she left Portland it had given her a sense of safety. But she wonders now if this too was foolish. What if it is like so many other broken promises? One made in haste, sincerity as ephemeral, as fleeting, as the night, as she herself seems to be. Still, it is all she has. She needs to find him.

If someone would just stop to offer her a ride, she would hand them the paper, ask them to help her. But she has been walking for hours now, and no one has stopped. Not one person has even slowed down. When she was in town she had felt as though all eyes were on her, but now, out here, she feels like a ghost: invisible. Haunting these desolate roads.

She continues to walk up the road, thumb jutted out into the darkness, walking backwards the way she has watched hitchhikers do on TV. She tries to be cavalier; she tries to be fearless. But the deeper she goes into the night, the more frightened she becomes.

When the pavement turns to dirt, her ankle twists and she falls to her knees. The backpack slings forward and knocks her in the head. She is down on all fours, like an animal, and scrambles to her feet as though she is being watched, even feels herself blushing a little with embarrassment. She is transported back to high school before she dropped out, anticipating the jeers, the catcalls, the hisses. But there is only the sound of the wind in the tops of the trees, the sound of crickets and bullfrogs. The sound of her own breath as she rises again to her feet.

She is not used to the wilderness anymore. The forest. She has slept on bus station benches and with her head resting on tables in coffee shops. Once, she dozed inside the cold fluorescent stall of a bathroom. But in the city there is always someone else awake, and there is always light. There is the semblance of life in a city. The illusion that you are not alone in the world.

For now, she just needs to find a place to sleep. To figure things out. She has not had a bed to sleep in in over a week; on the bus she slept sitting up, chin to her chest or cheek against the glass window. She forgets what it feels like to fully recline. And she is tired. So tired. So she keeps walking, determined now only to find a place where she can lie down. The baby begins its restless rolling again, and she feels the sting of tears in her eyes.

She walks and walks and walks, trusting that this road will take her somewhere. And finally, she sees a faint yellow glow in the distance. A house? It's far away, but it is like a beacon. Like a lighthouse welcoming, or warning. Nessa is smart enough to know there can be a fine line between *hazard* and *haven*.

Still, she walks toward the light, drawn, as she is always drawn, by the certainty of human kindness and sympathy. Trusting, as she always has, that people will want to take care of her. She knows this is what she inspires in people. No matter how filthy and ragged she may get, she knows that she has an innocent face, a harmlessness about her that people respond to. And now with the baby, she is almost always met with pity. She has fought it her entire life until now. Now she depends upon it.

And so she walks toward the light glowing in the house, and soon she is standing in the driveway. Or what might have once been a driveway. There is gravel, but the grass on either side is waist high. There are no cars. The mailbox post has fallen, and as she walks closer to the house she can see that all of the shades are drawn, furniture is pushed up against the windows of the porch. The one small light seems to be coming from the side of the house, and suddenly she is terrified. This is not the city. She doesn't know who might be living inside this ramshackle house, what sort of fairy-tale witch. She is Gretel without her Hansel, and the simple enticement of four walls and a roof is not enough. But she is also exhausted. She cannot walk another mile down this road that seems, right now, to lead to nowhere.

So, quietly, she walks around the side of the house where there seems to be an unfinished project underway, a skeleton of timber. She can hear the river in the distance, and it reminds her that she is thirsty.

She emptied her water bottle over an hour ago. As quietly as she can, she makes her way around to the back of the house, following the sound of the river. But just as she steps gingerly past what looks like a garden, a light fills the backyard, and she thinks, for a moment, that she has been struck by lightning. But there is no rain, no storm. She drops to the ground, again on all fours, and scurries across the grass until she is in the shadows again. She nearly tumbles into the river, which is actually more like a creek, and she peers back up at the house, waiting for someone to come out of the back door. To hunt her like the animal she has become. To kill her.

She crouches at the river's edge and waits until the light finally clicks off again before she cups her hands and dips them into the icy water to drink. It is dark again now, but she is left with the bright impression of the water, and she uses her memory of it to cross to the other side. And then she is running, running toward whatever shelter she can find.

Ruby is startled awake by the sound of something outside her window. At first she thinks it's just the wind, just rain. But it isn't raining. The moon is bright through the window; there are no clouds, and the sky is almost violet. She moves the pillow away from her ear and strains to hear. It sounds like rustling, like branches and leaves being crushed. An animal maybe. She thinks of the raccoons on the porch. She considers her mother's birds. When she opens her eyes, the owl peers at her intently. Twigs snap. And then the whole backyard is illuminated. She hates the motion sensor. It doesn't take much to set those lights off. Bats, birds, even chipmunks can fill the whole world with light with the slightest movement. And every time it goes on, it's like lightning just struck the house.

On the other side of her wall she hears her mother jolting out of bed. Ruby knows this sound. She also knows the sound her mother's nightstand drawer makes when it opens. She knows what she keeps in there, and the understanding makes her heart pound harder in her chest.

"Mom," she whispers, but her voice is too quiet for her to hear. "Mom?" she says again, louder. And whatever is outside the window stops moving. Stops making noise. She leans over and peers out the window, but there are only shadows: the dark outlines of trees against that indigo sky. Her mother's garden illuminated by the moon. There is only the river beyond this.

She lies back down and feels her heart slowing, returning to normal. And on the other side of her wall, she hears the drawer close. But her mother doesn't sleep. Ruby hears the light click on, and knows that she will stay like this: prone, alert, awake for the rest of the night, listening for trespassers and startling awake with each flash of imaginary lightning.

This is how it begins. It doesn't take much. Light. Sound. Something out of place. Simple discord is the trigger that detonates the explosion. That sets into motion the series of reactions that occur again and again, the dominos *click click clicking* in a beautiful, organized, and systematic destruction.

It is an illness, they tell Sylvie. *Generalized anxiety, panic disorder, PTSD, agoraphobia.* The labels meaningless, useless to her. And all of it, incurable. It is simply something she must learn to *manage.* To control. But what they don't realize, these doctors with their bald spots and diagnoses, is that she can no sooner control this than she can control a speeding bullet. Or *they* can control a mutating cancerous cell. It has a life of its own. Her fear is a breathing thing.

It may be a *mental* illness, but its manifests here: here in the hollow of her throat, in the sinews of her neck. In her gut. Sometimes even deep inside her breasts. It can feel like pain. It can also, sometimes, feel like desire. Like hunger. It's as though every yearning of the body, every extreme physical response is happening at once, hot and cold becoming one new sensation, a frigid incalescence that makes her sweat cold beads and shiver even as her limbs burn. When she tried to explain this feeling, one doctor suggested it was hormonal, only the early onset of menopause.

"I'm thirty-six years old," she had said.

And he'd smiled, condescended. "You'd be surprised."

She didn't bother to go on. To tell him about the way it feels like her heart is a train, a puffing, accelerating locomotive that is racing, but that there are no tracks beneath it. It has derailed inside her body, crashing inside her chest. She didn't talk about the vertigo that follows, the complete upending of her world. That once, one of the last times she went out in public, she had to lie down in the middle of the grocery store and even then the world would not stop turning. A broken carnival ride, the centripetal force not quite strong enough to keep her from being thrown off. There are not enough metaphors for what her body is doing to her. And despite what they say, it is her *body* that is defying her. It is not her mind; her mind is the only thing that seems to remain calm when her body is failing. It is her mind that saves her, that rights her. That is able to talk her body off the ledge. Her mind is the great hostage negotiator, convincing Madness into relinquishing her body. Into releasing her. She understands that this sounds insane. She is aware that this is not normal. But sadly, in this knowledge is no power.

When the floodlights click on outside, she is jolted from sleep, disoriented for only a moment before the first domino goes down. She knows what to expect. Even as her body begins its panic dance, her mind quietly waits. Stands at the edge of her body holding the megaphone, promising that it will all be over soon. Assuring everyone inside that if they remain calm and listen and do what it says, no one will be harmed.

*Harm.* Every inch of her body is informed by the possibility of harm.

She reaches into the drawer only when the locomotive Tilt-A-Whirl fever dream becomes too much, when she fears it has brought her, at last, to the end. When she believes, truly, that her heart will simply cease to beat. That it will retreat. That it will, at last, just shut down, systems overloaded, nuclear meltdown.

Here is the drawer. Here is the gun. Her grandmother's pistol passed down, like a recipe for strudel. Like brown eyes. Like mental illness. The gun.

The object has ceased to be what it is. It is no longer the symbol of safety it can be for some. It is not an instrument of destruction, a weapon. It is just cold comfort in her palm. The metallic shiver that cools her entire body down to a low simmer. It is just a symbol. An abstract. It is calm. It is calm. It is calm.

■ ■ ■ ■

# MONDAY

■ ■ ■ ■

In the morning, her mother offers her cereal, and Ruby is grateful that she has not made pancakes again. It is as though the absence of pancakes signifies a new understanding between them. Yet still, they sit across from each other at the table and she chews silently while her mother simply stares into her tea.

"Did you hear something outside last night?" her mother asks, softly, finally.

"Probably just the raccoons, Mom," Ruby says, and tries not to think about the drawer. About the way it made her feel. Sort of tender and vulnerable, like a new bruise.

Her mom nods, but Ruby can tell she doesn't believe her. Her eyes have that scared wild look they get sometimes. Like they got the last time.

"Really, Mom. It's nothing. Bunk set the traps. We'll catch the mama soon."

Her mom nods, agreeing with her, but

she's still wringing her hands. "You know, I read in the paper that people are going around stealing copper. Ripping pipes right out of people's houses," she said. "Wires."

Ruby tries to imagine someone coming to steal the house's innards. It's ridiculous. The last time she was here, the time when the ambulance came, started this way too. Her mom had convinced herself that somebody was trying to break in then as well. The whole time Ruby was there, she kept talking about vandals, about trespassers. When she misplaced her good scissors, she had made Bunk install motion lights on the back of the house. Never mind Ruby found the scissors under the bathroom sink a week later when she was looking for Q-tips; her mother still insisted that somebody had an eye on the house. That they had to be vigilant unless they wanted to lose everything. Ruby didn't remind her that everything was already lost.

"It might just be the wind," Ruby says. "Maybe from that storm everybody's been talking about." Ruby *has* noticed a shift in the air, and it's not just autumn coming on. She's sensitive to that sort of thing since the accident. They lost a lot of things that night: Jess, her daddy's legs. And even her mom too in a way, though not right away. But

Ruby was the only one who seemed to *gain* something. Because instead of getting numb to things the way people sometimes do, her senses seemed to get all fired up. Raw. In the fifth grade last year, Mrs. Lawson brought in a book written in braille. She made them close their eyes and run their fingers across the bumpy pages. The world is like that for her now. Textured. She can feel it, and, sometimes, if she pays close enough attention, she can even make out what it's trying to tell her. Last night it was telling her that something is coming, but it isn't burglars. It isn't as easy as thieves.

Her mom nods into her tea, but Ruby can still tell she's not convinced.

"I think maybe we need to build a fence."

"A fence?" Ruby says, and for some reason she thinks about the fence around Izzy's house in Quimby. It's a storybook fence, like *Tom Sawyer,* like *Dick and Jane,* protecting a storybook house. Going to Izzy's house is like heading right into the pages of a book. Even the sky in town is a fairytale sort of sky with cotton candy clouds, a bright yellow sun. Sometimes she half expects the grass itself to feel like paper under her feet. That somebody could turn the page, and Izzy and she would just disappear.

117

"Mom, I really don't know anything about building a fence."

"Oh, come on," she says, smiling. "Remember that time we helped Daddy build that fort for you and Jess?"

Jess. This is the first time she has heard her mother say his name in a long time. It stuns them both.

Ruby nods, thinks of Jess giving their dad instructions (*It needs a roof and a trap door and, and, and . . .*). She remembers her mother standing in the woods with them, watching, blowing warm air into her hands. It was fall, and the leaves were gone from the trees, lying in scattered heaps on the ground. Every step they took into the woods was so loud. Each crush and crumble amplified. And something about this memory, something about the recollection of that sound, and the memory of her mother making hot chocolate for all of them afterwards, the way their hands were chapped and pink from the cold, makes her nod.

"Okay."

"I think there are some sheets of plywood in the shed," her mom says, clearing the dirty dishes, carrying them to the sink. She turns her back to Ruby and says, "It can't be hard. We'll figure it out. Maybe after swimming lessons."

Swimming lessons. All summer long she's been spending five mornings a week at the town pool, but what her dad doesn't know, what her mother doesn't know, but what every other kid and all the teenaged lifeguards at the pool *do* know, is that Ruby has not once gotten into the water. For the entire summer, she has ridden her bike to the pool, gone to join her classmates, and then sat on the cold concrete edge, her feet dangling into the water, shivering, teeth chattering, boys jeering, teacher coaxing and then pleading and then finally retreating. Defeated. All of them. Whispers swirling in the chlorine-scented, cold-water mornings, *Her brother . . . I heard she almost drowned too . . .* For an hour every single weekday morning for the whole summer, she has watched the other kids, most of them at least four years younger than she, jumping and splashing and swimming. Blowing bubbles and floating on their backs and clinging to the edge of the pool while kicking their feet gleefully. And when the hour finally ended, she'd stand up, wrap her towel around her, meet Izzy, who is in the Junior Lifeguard class, and they'd go to the locker room where they would both stand under the weak spray. As long as she came home with wet hair, her dad didn't ask questions.

Today, she goes through the motions again, arriving at the pool just before the lesson is about to start. She leaves her bike with all the others on the grassy area outside the pool gate. She wraps her towel around her waist and goes to the entrance where some pimply teenage boy who smiles too much finds her name on the checklist and then says, "Have fun!"

She can see Izzy at the deep end of the pool. The Junior Lifeguard class all wear red Speedo bathing suits, but even from here she recognizes Izzy by her long blond hair. Today they are learning CPR; she can see the dummy lying at the edge of the pool, the line of students waiting to revive it.

Marcy Davidson is in the class too, though until today Ruby hasn't thought twice about her. The best policy, the *only* policy that works with Marcy, is to pretend she doesn't exist. To acknowledge her at all is to make yourself vulnerable. Both Ruby and Izzy have learned that the hard way. But today, instead of ignoring Marcy, Ruby watches her. She watches the way Izzy and she lean into each other, bare shoulders touching, heads touching, as they whisper.

Ruby walks as quickly as she can to her spot with the other Tadpoles and takes her usual seat at the edge. Her teacher, Nora, walks over to her and tickles her feet, as though she were seven (like the rest of the class) instead of eleven.

"Coming into the water today?" she asks Ruby (as she has asked Ruby every single day this summer). And Ruby shakes her head.

"Okay, you let me know if you change your mind," she says and moves on to the next kid. Ruby knows Nora has given up on her, which should be a relief, but her lack of effort today makes her feel even more like a lost cause.

From here Ruby watches Izzy and Marcy in their matching red suits, and feels her heart sink. The friendship bracelet that Ruby gave Izzy for her ninth birthday, the one she made (their favorite colors — purple and green — woven together with little wooden heart beads with their initials), the one that Izzy hasn't taken off once for the last two years, is gone. Her brown wrist is bare, leaving only the fluorescent white tan line where the bracelet used to be. She thinks for a minute that it must have finally broken, that the threads, eaten away by chlorine, finally snapped. But she knows how strong it was. Her dad let her use some of his fishing line to reinforce the delicate threads. She also knows that when it started to break before, Gloria helped her fix it. Izzy never takes it off. Not ever.

Ruby stares at Izzy as if she could communicate how mad and sad she is through telepathy (they used to practice reading each other's minds back in the fourth grade too). But Izzy is busy with Marcy. She doesn't even look Ruby's way. Ruby feels her eyes begin to sting and suddenly she realizes she can't sit through another swimming lesson. Not today. Not any day.

Besides, her dad is gone, and what can her mom do to stop her from just leaving? They might call her father, but he's in North Carolina. And the phone at her mom's is still out. She can leave. She can just go. And so that is exactly what she does.

She stands up, wraps the towel around her waist again, and walks to the kid at the gate. "I don't feel good. I'm going home," she says. It's as easy as that.

He looks at her, still grinning that stupid, pimply grin, but he doesn't stop her. And she wonders why she didn't think of this sooner.

She untangles her bike from the pile, kicking the pedal loose from somebody else's chain, and then takes off, wobbling until she gets momentum and then rights herself.

She pedals furiously, realizing she forgot to wet down her hair, but doesn't care. She's leaving. But to where? She can't go home, not yet. She cranks her head around to look back toward the pool, on the off chance that Izzy might have noticed and decided to come after her. But she can't see anything except for a blur of red bathing suits, all trying to bring that stupid dummy back to life.

She doesn't have any other friends she can go to, not really. There are plenty of girls she gets along with at school, but in the summertime it's just her and Izzy. Which was fine until now.

With her dad and Bunk gone, she really only has one other place she can go. And so she rides her bike to the library. It's not open yet, but she knows the children's librarian, Christine, sometimes comes early. And if she knocks, she'll let her in.

"Well, good morning, Ruby," Effie, the lady who drives the bookmobile, says, smiling at her. She can see she's got one of her daughters with her today. *Plum,* that's her name. She's in the first grade at Ruby's school. "Go ahead downstairs. Christine should be here any minute. I'll let her know you're down there. Do you know how to turn on the lights?"

Ruby nods and smiles, moving past them to the stairs. Downstairs in the quiet children's room, she immediately begins to feel calmer. More rational. She finds her favorite spot in the computer area and writes her name in careful cursive on the sign-in sheet even though there isn't anyone else here. The computers aren't on yet, so she turns each one on. She knows the password to get online and so she makes sure all of the computers are ready for when the library opens. Christine told her she's always welcome in the library, that she trusts her. This makes her feel grown-up, important. She doubts there's a single kid her age that has the same privilege.

It is here, in the musty children's room, all summer long, she's studied the world's most famous bridges, examined the photos, read about their designs. She's spent hours at the long counter of computers, exploring: traversing the great bodies of water via the most beautiful structures of all time. She's sat in the library for hours, clicking through the images of bridges, reading their specifications, their histories, their myths. Christine lets her print out some of the pictures, which she takes home and hangs in her room. The wall behind her desk is pocked with thumbtack holes from the photos. There must be a thousand bridges by now. She thinks about the One Direction poster on Izzy's door, and she feels that sinking awful feeling again. Maybe she should have seen this coming sooner. Maybe she should have realized that Izzy wasn't nearly as excited about bridges as she was. *Is.*

Ruby loves the great suspension bridges, of course. Everybody does. The Golden Gate Bridge. The Tsing Ma. The Ikuchi in Japan. She wonders at the cable-stayed bridges with their fans or harp designs: the Zhivopisny, the Machang, the Queen Elizabeth II. She is awed by the architecture of arches, the magical geometry of cantilevers and trusses. She has dreamed herself across rivers and lakes, bays and inlets, estuaries and straits. In that musty, dark basement she has stood in the pavilions of the most beautiful wind and river bridges of China. She has peered down from the deck of the Millau Viaduct in France to the River Tarn below. She has walked through the caterpillar-like Henderson Waves in Singapore, felt dizzy atop the Trift Bridge in the Swiss Alps and the Hussaini Hanging Bridge in Pakistan.

The language of bridges sounds like poetry to her. *Bascule, brace, caisson.*

*Camber, cantilever, catwalk.* She recites the terms like words on her vocabulary lists from school, as if there might be a test and that these are the answers: *diaphragm, gabion, lattice pylon.* This is her lullaby at night. It is her song. *Riprap, roller nest, strut, truss, vault.*

She hates Izzy for ditching her. There's no way they can get the bridge design done in time if Izzy is busy with Marcy Davidson. She's going to have to do this one alone. The bridge she wants to build is one that's never been made before. At least she doesn't think it has. Izzy says there's no way of knowing. With all the bodies of water and all the bridges in the world, there's bound to be one like the one in her dreams. But she doesn't think so. Because it feels like it belongs to her. Like it's hers alone. There aren't many things she can say that about, but this is one of them. She doesn't have a brother anymore. She doesn't really have her mother. Now she doesn't even have Izzy. But she does have this. This magical bridge, a bridge that will traverse any body of water. That combines the strength of the best suspension bridges with the beauty of the wind and rain bridges. That will seem to break the laws of physics, even as it depends on them. It will be a structural miracle.

By the time Christine comes down the stairs to the children's room, Ruby knows swimming lessons are over, and she has printed out three new bridges to consider as she finalizes her designs.

"You leaving already?" Christine asks as Ruby makes her way toward the stairs.

"Yeah," she says. "I'm staying at my mom's, and she needs me home."

"Oh," Christine says, and Ruby wonders how much she knows about her mom. It seems like the whole town knows about the accident. About what happened. But not everybody knows about all the stuff that happened afterwards. That's a secret that they've managed to keep.

"Well, have a nice day. Looks like that hurricane, Irene, is going to bring some rain. Hopefully it'll hold off until after the fair," Christine says. "Are you going this year?"

Ruby nods, but remembering Izzy and Marcy and thinking about going with them to the fair brings back all those bad feelings and so she just nods and says, "See ya."

Bridges, like ladders and cats and cemeteries, have their own set of superstitions. Hold your breath as you cross a bridge and make a wish. The only way to reverse the bad luck of a broken mirror is to throw the shards

127

into rushing water beneath a bridge. Never say good-bye to a friend on a bridge, or you will never see them again.

There are only two bridges in Quimby: the wide concrete bridge and the covered bridge out by the old mill. The quickest way back to her mom's house from town is across the covered bridge. And that was the route she used to take, they all used to take. She didn't used to think about it at all. She hardly even noticed it back then, other than remembering that she should always stop and listen to make sure there wasn't a car coming from the other direction. The bridge can only hold one car at a time, so you're supposed to honk to let pedestrians and bicyclists and other cars know you're coming. She would fly across that bridge coming and going without noticing the trusses or portals, the wing walls or decks. Without understanding the physics of a bridge, how a bridge's design depends on the laws of motion: on the irrefutable concepts of compression and tension and load. She didn't think. She didn't have to. She just crossed the bridge.

She is so angry with Izzy. She wishes she could rewind the last twenty-four hours. Rewind the entire last two years as a matter of fact. If she could do that then she'd just hit *pause* at the place before everything changed. She wants the feeling of the boards of the bridge deck beneath her tires again, feel the cool shade the roof makes. She wants to hear the river rushing beneath her. She wants to pause back at a time when her mom didn't live like this, back when everything was *normal*. Maybe she'd pause at a night when she was cooking something good for dinner in the kitchen. The homemade mac 'n' cheese she used to make with the buttery cracker top or the pot roast that would cook all day in the slow cooker, making the house smell like a holiday. Back when Jess would use her Legos without asking because she wasn't home and couldn't say no and they'd wind up wrestling on the living room floor until neither one of them could remember how it started. When their hearts pounded with the effort and despite the brawl, there was this untamed happiness. *Pause:* the grassy smell of his hair, the soft worn corduroys he wore torn at the knee, the smell of dinner and hungry stomachs. Back when her daddy was still a hero, instead of half a man, before the glossy stumps of his knees made her cheeks flush and her stomach turn, when he used to carry them, one under each strong arm, as though they were footballs instead of kids.

*Pause.* When their mother would shake her head, but smile, smile, smile. Back when she could ride her bike across that stupid bridge without thinking about anything but getting *home.* When home was a place she actually wanted to be. *Pause.* Just linger for a few minutes longer in this suspended place.

But there's no pause in real life. There's also no rewind. And there's definitely no delete. There's just *now* running on and on, and you can't ever stop it, no matter what you do.

Besides, she's not allowed to go that way anymore, by either her father or her mother. And so she takes the long way home, or what used to be home, and arrives at the house breathless, her legs trembling.

Nessa wakes up and for a few scattered, fractured moments, she has no idea where she is. She struggles to recollect all the places she has slept, all the beds she has shared, all of the floors and couches she has crashed on. Then she remembers Mica and rolls toward him, recalling the certain slant of his bed, the depth and breadth of it. But instead of a body, the hot hollow of his back or the soft skin of his stomach, she is greeted by something wet. Has he just taken a shower? Disoriented, now rising to the surface of consciousness like a diver ascending, she realizes the dampness is dew on grass.

When she opens her eyes, the first thing she sees is the silvery shimmery filament of a spider's web. She blinks and blinks, trying to focus, to make sense, and then her eyes adjust, bringing the images into sharp relief. The bright red of her sleeping bag, a large

131

willow tree making a canopy of branches and leaves around her, sun struggling through the green. She pulls her arm out of the sleeping bag and stares at the face of her grandfather's watch. It is enormous on her tiny wrist, like a cartoon watch. It is almost nine o'clock. She cannot believe she was able to sleep so late, especially outside. Especially curled up in a sleeping bag under a tree.

When she hears the sound of tires crushing gravel in the distance, she starts and struggles to get out of the sleeping bag. Her instinct is to run. Her instinct is always to run. But she is stuck, a fat caterpillar inside this bloodred cocoon, and so instead of trying to escape she burrows deeper, clutching the hard round pouch of her stomach, and feels the baby stir, just the small flutters she started to feel months ago. Like an insect's wings beating against her insides.

Inside the closed sleeping bag, she can smell herself, the impossible funk of her own flesh. She remembers the last shower she had at Mica's, the day before she left. She recalls the delicious heat of the water, the way it massaged her aching shoulders and back. She remembers the clean minty scent of the shampoo, working it into her dreads, and then rinsing them clean. She remembers the steam filling her chest, as though even her insides were getting clean. But she also remembers the dirty grout between the cracked tiles, the filthy washcloth draped over the faucet, the missing COLD handle. And she remembers the pubic hair, the black hair curled on the sliver of soap. That comma, causing her to pause for a moment, to hold her breath.

She is blonde. So is Mica. And yet.

The whole summer had been a series of *and yet*s. Speculations, silent accusations, explanations. Until this dark hair, this private punctuation mark causing her this one final, awful, lingering pause. It was the last straw, so to speak, this tiny little hair, this private thing shed from *who-knows-whose who-knows-what*. It really was as simple as that: a black, wiry anonymous hair on a bar of Ivory soap. It was enough to send her packing again. Onward.

But as she shoved her dirty T-shirts and crinkly long skirts into her backpack, she realized that her whole life she has been nothing but a ball stuck inside a pinball machine, racing intently toward nothing, meeting obstacle after obstacle along the way, walls she smashed into. Bouncing from one place to the next — never resting long before being thrust from whatever small com fort she has found. This comfort, that comfort, each no more permanent or reliable than the next.

But she had no money, none of her own anyway. And so in a fit of rage and desperation, she'd raided Mica's drawers, where she knew he kept his cash. He'd gotten the idea earlier that summer to grow weed in the attic of the rented house. There was a hidden crawlspace upstairs near the bathroom. And so he'd bought some seeds from some guy he knew, *magic beans* he called them, and spent every last cent he had on grow lights and timers, some primitive hydroponic equipment. Ten plants under hot lights hidden in the recesses of the house. And soon, the entire house smelled like Christmas. The pungent green scent seeped into the air, the misty air that filled the upstairs where they slept. All summer long he'd cared for them. At the worst moments, she was jealous of the plants, envied the way he nurtured them, the gentleness of his touch. At night he would check on them as though they were sleeping children. (She had even been foolish enough to think that this was evidence that he might make a good father.)

It took eight weeks before they were ready to harvest. And now, all that tenderness had offered its rewards. He'd harvested nearly three pounds of weed, which he'd hung to dry in their closet. Every item of clothing she owned was saturated with the scent of it. Earlier that week she knew he'd sold at least a pound of it, but he hadn't told her how much he got. "Enough to pay the rent," he'd said. "And the electricity bill." He'd laughed, the grow lights pulsing like something alive through the cracks in the attic crawl space door.

He was still sleeping, so she went quietly back into the bedroom, trailing water across the dusty floor, and she told herself that he owed her this. That she had somehow earned it. Stupid cheating motherfucker.

There should be at least a couple thousand dollars, she thought. But when she reached stealthily into the drawer, pushing aside the ragged pairs of boxer shorts and threadbare socks, just four hundred dollars remained. The rest of it was already gone. And this, almost more than anything, infuriated her. The first of the month when all the bills came due was weeks away, but he'd already spent it.

Only four hundred bucks, but it was enough to pay for a bus ticket. Enough to go home.

She'd been running away when she left

Vermont. But no one had followed. Though it killed her to think about it, her mother had probably been relieved. She was caught up in so much of her own shit back then, dealing with Nessa was just one more headache. But it had been two years; maybe things had changed with her mom, wherever she is. Nessa is practically an adult now. She'd be eighteen in just two more months. She wasn't a child anymore.

She'd walked out of Mica's, clutching the fistful of cash, not even glancing back up at that falling-down house as she made her way to the bus stop. She knew she didn't have long. As soon as Mica woke up and realized she'd stolen the money, he was certain to try to find her at all their haunts. She didn't have a single friend in Portland who wouldn't tell Mica exactly where she was. She had nowhere to go. No one to go to. The realization of this should have hit her in the gut like a fist, but instead she felt nothing. Her whole life, just bounced around like a pinball, aimless, pointless. *Ding, ding, ding.* She cupped the growing mound of her stomach and hung her head down to her chest. She felt nothing. No fear. No sadness. Not even any anger anymore.

She'd stood in the bus station at Pioneer Courthouse Square watching as each bus screeched to a halt, huffing in a strange exasperation, its doors opening, one impatient driver after the next waiting for her to make up her mind. And then she'd reached into her bag and pulled out the note. It was tattered now, worn from sitting in the bottom of her purse. The ink smudged. She touched her fingers to his name and tried not to think about the last time she'd been thrown out, hurled into the darkness by someone with such carelessness and thoughtlessness.

Maybe all of this, the pubic hair, the money, the baby, were all signs that it was time to go back home and deal with this. To go back to her mom. To find him. To make things right. She didn't believe in fate, but she did believe in being a decent human being.

Now, she peers out of the sleeping bag, which is too hot, the smell of her own body unbearable. The morning air smells clean, green; her nostrils flare with relief. She peers through the shaggy leaves of the tree, feeling like a child hiding under a table, peeking out from under the tablecloth. She can see a man in a uniform climbing a telephone pole. It's just a telephone man. An ordinary man. A man in a gray-green uniform with a job to do. A man who fixes things. The simplicity of this vision hits her hard. Like a whack on the back to someone with something lodged in his throat. The simple image of this man dislodges a blockage, and she can suddenly breathe again.

None of the men she knows are like this. None of them honest, purposeful, hardworking men. It's no wonder she's been so directionless. She has been surrounded by aimlessness, by purposelessness, her whole life. Her grandfather was the only decent man she ever knew, but he's long gone. Even Mica, who she wanted to believe could one day be this kind of man, an ordinary man, turned out to be as substantial and trustworthy as dust. The things she found attractive about him at first became the things she most despised. His tenderness became weakness. His affection toward others became betrayal. His easiness was really just apathy. Because while he seemed to care about everything (everyone), he really didn't care about anything at all. And this, more than that black hair, that dirty black coil on that clean white soap, was why she left.

She is afraid to move, to make a sound. She wishes her sleeping bag were green instead of red. She is hardly camouflaged here in the woods. She is like a crimson blood spot among all this green. But the man on the pole is so intent on his job, he does not notice her. She imagines herself an apple fallen to the ground. She is only a maple leaf, a wild strawberry, a poppy. She dreams herself a chameleon, blending into her surroundings, becoming one with her environment. Blending in.

It's been a long time since she's been this intimate with nature. When she left Vermont, she went as far away as she could, arriving in LA where she met a couple of girls who were driving to Portland. And on the way north from California, they slept inside coves and under piers, awakening each morning to the sound of the surf and the squealing squawk of gulls. She camped among the redwoods, slept in the back of pickup trucks, in backseats, in vans. When she first arrived in Portland, she lived with another girl in Woodstock Park for three weeks before she met Mica. Though in Portland, even in the park, it seemed like there were always others like her around. A community of wanderers. But now that she is back here where she started, there is no longer the illusion of friendship, or companionship. Even her mother is gone, and she is alone. Well, almost alone.

The baby kicks her hard just under her breastbone and she gasps at the pain. The man on the pole turns his head, as though looking for the source of the sound. She holds still, presses her hand against her stomach to still the baby. To still her own heart as it clangs and bangs inside her chest. She remains motionless, a statue, a tree, afraid to move even an inch. And soon he goes back to work, but she knows she needs to keep moving. She can't stay here, not in the naked light of morning. She needs to keep moving or to find proper shelter. A good place to hide until she can figure out where, exactly, to find him. How to go about this.

And so as soon as his truck pulls away, she scurries out of her sleeping bag, rolls everything back into her pack, and then takes off up the river's edge, thinking she will bathe here later. Tonight when the sun goes down again. She imagines the water taking the debris of the last week, the detritus of a lifetime disappearing downstream.

She has blisters on her feet from her sneakers, and so she slips them off and shoves them in the side pockets of her backpack. She doesn't have any socks, so her feet are bare. Tanned and dirty. The silver toe ring she lifted from a bikini shop in Venice Beach sparkles in the sun. Her heels are callused, conditioned to the elements: hot sand, burning pavement. She feels primitive without her shoes on, *free*. Her flesh barely registers the pine needles and branches, the twigs and stones and pinecones underneath her. She could belong to a different time, she thinks as she claws her way through the thick foliage. To a time before shoes, a time before clothes.

She only walks for about ten minutes before she sees the structure, and she can barely believe her luck. It looks like some sort of shack, a hunting cabin, she thinks. It is falling down, nobody's house. Abandoned. There is one window, but it is broken: a hole at the center of the glass from which an intricate pattern of spidery cracks emanates. The roof is caved in on one side, and the foliage has grown around it, camouflaging it. It is perfect. But it's on the other side of the river, which has, somehow, gotten wider here. It doesn't look deep, but the water is moving fast. One wrong step and she could get swept away, or at least dragged across the rocks. Her center of balance has shifted with the baby. She used to be agile, strong. Now she feels clumsy, uncertain in her own skin. But what choice does she have? And so she tentatively tests the first flat stone she can find. The water is freezing cold, and the rock is slippery, but her toes are strong and she has to trust her calluses. She grabs a low-hanging branch to steady herself and she holds on tightly as she makes her way to the next stone and the next. The shock of the water is somehow both violent and assuring. She is alive. She is awake. She is making progress across this body of water. By the time she reaches the opposite bank, she is trembling with adrenaline, and her chest swells with a sense of accomplishment. She looks around, as though waiting for approval from the trees. As though someone should applaud her efforts. But she is met only with the silent stare of a thousand invisible eyes. All creatures besides herself hiding in the dark green shadows.

She runs, the backpack slamming against her back. The tendons beneath the swell of her stomach stretching, aching. She knows this baby isn't going to wait much longer; she can only hope she'll wait long enough. She wonders for a moment about that midwife the waitress mentioned, and her throat swells. She hasn't seen a doctor since she slunk into the Planned Parenthood this winter and had her fears confirmed. And she has refused to do the math, to count backwards to figure out how close she is. But the baby reminds her, whispers and nudges. *Soon,* it says. *Soon.* The door to the shack is hanging from one hinge, but it is unlocked. It is open. It is hers. And it is home. For now.

The very first bridges in history were the ones made by nature: something as simple as a fallen tree across a ravine making it possible to cross from one place to another. And the earliest man-made bridges were simple: just limbs lashed together, stones. They served a basic purpose: to get from a familiar place to the unknown.

But while the earliest bridges were built simply out of necessity — to get safely from one place to the next — function was not enough. The Romans wanted not only utility but endurance. The oldest bridge that is still in existence, and still in use, is the Arkadiko Bridge in Greece. It was built in 1300 BC, an arch bridge built to traverse a stream, made using limestones, Cyclopean masonry. This bridge was made for chariots. Ruby dreams of going there someday, of traveling along the same stone steps as the Ancient Grecian people. As the gods even.

The Alcántara Bridge, built over the Tagus River in Spain, an arch bridge also made of stone, was inscribed: *Pontem perpetui mansurum in saecula* (I have built a bridge which will last forever). She has studied this bridge that has survived not only the elements but war. This everlasting bridge. She has sketched the arches in her notebook.

This is the kind of bridge Ruby wants to make. Not necessarily one made of stone or even of this design, but the kind of bridge that *survives,* that is immune to natural disasters and to destruction by people. She wants a bridge that won't crumble. That will last.

She doesn't need Izzy. She can do this on her own. But there are just a couple of weeks left until school starts. She needs to get the designs from Izzy. She needs to finish them and finalize her plans. The bridge they'll make at school will be miniature, just a model. But what if she could actually build a *real* bridge? To really test the design before the contest? The mere thought of it, the possibility of it, makes her not feel so bad about Izzy. About Marcy Davidson. And so, after the phone company guy comes and fixes the phone, she decides to take a walk down by the river. That's one thing she hasn't thought about, something they don't really take into account in the contest either. A bridge relies upon what it bridges. Upon the land that will support it.

"I'm going for a walk," Ruby says. Her mother is sitting at the table with a dead bird laid on newspaper in front of her. The smell of alcohol is strong. It turns Ruby's stomach.

"What about the fence?" her mother says.

"I'm doing research for a school project. It's *required.*"

"But school hasn't even started yet."

Ruby rolls her eyes even though there is no way in the world her mother would know about the bridge project or about Izzy or about anything that has her stomach in knots.

"It's a contest," Ruby says. "We had the whole summer to work on it. But Izzy was supposed to help, and now I'm doing it by myself."

"Oh," her mother says, and Ruby waits. For something. She doesn't even know what it is she wants. She doesn't really want to talk about Izzy, but she's mad at her mom for not knowing something is wrong. For not asking. She doesn't want to tell her about the way it made her feel to see Izzy and Marcy leaning into each other at the pool, the way her heart ached when she

146

noticed that the friendship bracelet was gone. Her mother doesn't know there was a friendship bracelet to begin with. She doesn't know the secret language that she and Izzy made up (the one like pig latin but with "izzyuby" instead of "ay" at the ends of words). She doesn't know that when she spends the night at Izzy's house, they like to sleep head to toe in Izzy's big bed. She doesn't know how much she loves the smell of the detergent that Gloria uses, that she falls asleep with Izzy's ankles pressed against her cheeks, smelling that smell in Izzy's extra pillow. She doesn't know about the times she and Izzy have dreamed themselves grown up, living next door to each other with their families. That they've got a name for the company they'll start together. That they have shared dreams the way other girls share hairbrushes and candy. And so she doesn't know how it feels like somebody tore her heart out. That she feels like she's missing something so big it left a sinkhole where it once was. She doesn't know that she feels, suddenly, like half a girl.

"Okay, then," her mom says, looking up from the dead bird.

Ruby could say something now. She could go to her, to sit in her mother's lap, let her stroke her hair. She can see in her mother's eyes that this is what she wants of her, but she has forgotten how to give it.

And so she does nothing.

And her mother looks down at the bird again. "Don't be gone long."

Ruby glances up at the clock on the wall. But the battery died a long time ago, and so it is always 7:21 in the kitchen. Always either dawn or dusk.

"And lock the door behind you?"

Ruby checks to make sure she has her key, and then she locks her mom inside. As she walks across the backyard, she wonders when the last time was that anybody mowed the grass. Something about this makes her angry. She thinks about Izzy's lawn again, about the tulips and irises that pop up in the spring, the yard littered not with trash and debris but daisies and black-eyed Susans. She starts to kick a beer can that has washed up onto the yard from the river like seashells on a beach and then instead, she stops, mid-kick, and picks it up. She tries to crush the can in her fist the way she's seen both her dad and Bunk do, but she's not strong enough. It just dents in on one side a little bit. And so she chucks it back onto the ground and takes off.

The river isn't wide enough here to make a bridge necessary. With a good run, she can leap across it. The water's pretty shallow here too, though if she's not running fast enough she might land in the marshy edge and get her feet wet. There's not much on the other side: just woods. Beyond that there's a farm and a cemetery. Sometimes Izzy and she used to go there and play. It's the old cemetery where everyone's been dead for a hundred years or more. The gravestones are crumbly. You can't even read the names on some of the stones because they're covered with moss. Jess is buried in the town cemetery by the high school in the new part where the stones are so shiny you can see your reflection in them. She's only been there once, for the burial. She spent the whole time staring at her shoes so she wouldn't have to look at that tiny white casket.

The river divides the people who live out here in the boonies from the rest of the town. They're almost like an island, she thinks, which is actually kind of nice. A bridge would change that though. The kind of bridge she plans to make anyway.

The idea behind a bridge is getting somebody safely from one place to another. But she wants her bridge to be more than that. The best bridges aren't just about function but about beauty too. Over forty million people either visit or cross the Golden Gate Bridge every single year. Of course, most of them are the people who are driving to and from work; those are the people who drive across without even thinking twice about it. But then there are those who go all the way to San Francisco just to see the Golden Gate Bridge, just to drive or walk across the 4,200 feet of the San Francisco Bay.

She walks along the river's other bank, studying the land at the edge, taking notes in her notebook. She worries a little that Izzy still has all of her designs on her computer. She can't imagine she would steal them, but you just never know. That's one thing she's certain of. People do surprising things. The people you trust the most are sometimes the ones who betray you the worst. And the people you love more than anything are the ones who will break your heart.

It's another windy day today, which is a good thing. It reminds her that building bridges is not just about designing something that will keep your feet dry. It's also about creating a structure that will withstand the elements. Rain, wind, snow, and ice. Vermont gets all of that and more. That's why covered bridges are so popular here. That's why every calendar of Vermont you ever see has one on the cover.

Finally, she gets to a place upstream where the river is wide, where its current is strong. The wind blows hard here, whipping through her open notebook, nearly yanking the pages out. She nods, feeling something scary and wonderful. She starts taking notes, continuing to walk up the river when all of a sudden she feels a cold shock as her foot dips into the water. She steps on a flat rock that's about an inch under water, but it's slippery and she is starting to go down. She clings to her notebook; the last thing she needs is to drop that in the river, and her whole body tries to stay upright. Finally she lurches forward and catches a tree branch, which extends itself like a hand to hold on to, and she is able to brace herself. Her heart is pounding hard in her chest. *That was close,* she thinks.

Instinctively she looks up then, as though somebody were watching her. And when she peers across the river toward the dense forest, she sees something move in the distance. She peers harder, shielding her eyes from the sun, which is blinding now. And beyond the trees, through the green of leaves, she can make out the outline of something. A cabin? An old sugarhouse maybe? It could simply be her imagination, but it looks as

151

though there are shadows moving behind the broken window. She wishes she could cross the river here, go check it out. But she's afraid it's too wide, and dangerous. Her mother would be furious if she knew that she was even this close to the water's edge.

She closes up her notebook and starts to walk back down toward her mother's house, looking behind her a few times to make sure nobody's come after her with a shotgun to shoo her off their property. She thinks of her mother, the drawer.

Even by the time she gets back to the house, she can't shake the feeling that somebody saw her slip in the water. She gets that feeling other times too though. Like somebody's keeping an eye on her. If she believed in God, she would say it was Jess, that maybe he was her guardian angel now. But she doesn't believe, not anymore anyway. God was something else she lost that night.

The birds occupy Sylvie's hands, but they cannot cease the buzzing of her mind. Not for long anyway. Despite being focused, fixated on the task (on the parting of feathers and splitting of flesh, the separation of sinews and the extrication of the innards). Despite the combined beauty and gore, her own fascination with the incredible complexity of the avian anatomy, the delicate bones serve as little more than reminders of fragility, of preciousness, of vulnerability.

She tries not to think about Ruby out there, doing whatever it is that she is doing. If she allows her mind to wander down that forest path, she may get lost in the terrifying woods of her own imagination. It seems Sylvie is constantly building fences between reality and possibility. It is her life's work now.

She thinks again about a fence for the backyard. She is vulnerable out here, the backyard accessible to anyone: the unfinished room providing opportunity for anyone at all to come into the house, only a hollow-core door and a flimsy locking doorknob keeping intruders out. Before Ruby came she was able to put this out of her mind, somewhat. To erect that wall between herself and the dangers lurking beyond the trees. What would anyone want with her anyway? But somehow Ruby's presence has made her aware of how very susceptible they are, how exposed.

On the table, the spotted sandpiper lies splayed, its freckled chest carefully dissected. Everything that once made it alive, all those exquisite diminutive organs (heart, lung, brain) are now gathered in a ziplock baggie on the table. She will toss these entrails outside later, let the mother raccoon find them. Maybe she should throw them near one of the traps. She picks up the tweezers and goes about the painstaking venture of removing its eyes.

The banging on her door startles her, yanks her sharply from her project. She feels her knees grow weak and she looks around the room, but for what she doesn't know. (A weapon? An escape route? Help?)

When the knock comes again, the sound is like gunshots, not the tentative knocks of the lady selling Avon or even Robert and Bunk. This knock is aggressive, threatening. *Bang, bang, bang.* Her hand flies to her chest as though it can keep that cage door shut, keep that wild creature inside. Under her fingertips, it beats and beats and beats. She stares at the door as the person knocks again.

She can see him, his silhouette behind the curtain, shifting his weight from one foot to another. And then he leans forward, his face pressed to the glass, and she feels as though she might vomit. He shields his eyes to block out his own reflection, and his features come into focus behind the sheer curtain.

She stares back at him, because she doesn't know what else to do.

"Ma'am?" His voice is muffled behind the glass.

She doesn't answer. Can't. Moments pass. A minute? Slowly. Time is so cruel, she thinks. So very cruel.

She watches him move away from the door, the dark outline of his body moving up and then down. The screen door on the porch opens and closes, opens and closes. She wonders if maybe Ruby called Animal Control and he's come to get the babies. But then she hears the sound of something tearing, and her heart starts to pace again, back and forth, like a tiger. Like a terrified and dangerous beast. And then he presses something against the glass. But it's just a piece of paper. He is writing something, using the window as a hard surface, the way one might use a book or someone's back. When he is finished, the screen door from the porch outside slams shut again, and she can hear his tires on the gravel of her drive, feel the bass of his stereo, and then there is nothing but the rhythmic aftermath of her own body.

She realizes as she stands that her muscles have been clenched this entire time, that she has not been breathing. She nearly collapses, her limbs like rubber bands that have been stretched too tight. Cautiously, she walks to the door. Even though she knows it is safe, that he is gone now, she distrusts his absence.

She tries the knob, fearful, even while knowing that it is locked. (She remembers the deadbolt sliding into place. She checked it. She always does: at least ten times every evening before she goes to bed. Sometimes she wakes up in the middle of the night to ensure that the deadbolt is turned, that the chain is latched tight. Throughout the day, it is one of her many, many rituals.) And it *is* locked; of course it is. There was never any real danger. She knows this, but that doesn't change the way her body feels as though it has just suffered a great trauma.

He has left the groceries in the bin on the porch, just as he has for the last couple of months. She has had at least a half dozen grocery boys, but this one with the fast car is new this summer. She has never seen any of their faces, except for this one's, pressed against the glass of her window.

She lifts one of the bags out of the bin and realizes he's left a note on top of the groceries.

*Storm's coming. Brought extra water, candles, and batteries. Need anything else just call the store.*

In addition to the usual three paper bags of groceries, there are four gallons of water on the porch floor and a small plastic bag with candles and batteries and an inexpensive flashlight. She plucks the receipt, which is stapled to one of the brown bags, and stares at the predictable list of items: milk, orange juice, oatmeal, ground beef, bananas. She scans the list, searching, but there are no extra charges. It is, to the penny, the same as it is (and has been) every single week. Suddenly the creature in her chest begins to swell, rising upward to her throat, nearly choking her. She swallows hard to push it back down into the place where it belongs. And it resists.

She brings the bag of items into the kitchen first and dumps its contents onto the part of the table that is not occupied by the sandpiper. She studies these ordinary objects as though they are arcane artifacts. And she supposes they are. Proof that someone somewhere still cares that she is here. That she is safe. That she is alive. It makes her feel something between comfort and unbearable shame.

Nessa unpacks her bag as though she is in a hotel instead of an abandoned shack in the woods. She has always done this. For all the years that she's been wandering, she has always needed to feel settled in, if only for the night. Her mother could live endlessly out of open suitcases, battered boxes, but Nessa at least liked to pretend that she might stay. That her life wasn't just a series of pit stops, that there was at least the semblance of permanence.

She takes her filthy clothes and folds them, making piles on the floor. She arranges her toiletries (trial sizes pilfered from the drugstore: deodorant, toothpaste, shampoo) on a broken table. When her backpack is empty, she pushes it into a corner and studies her new home.

In the center of the room is an enormous piece of metal equipment, which connects to some sort of chimney. Because the roof is caved in, the chimney stands alone, a freestanding spire made of crumbling brick held up by the benevolent branches of a tree. There is also a wood box whose empty bottom is littered with yellowed newspapers. A stove. She quickly realizes that this must have been a maple sugarhouse at one time; her grandfather had one as well in the woods behind his house at the lake, though it doesn't look like anyone has used this one in years.

There are some soggy-looking cardboard boxes under the broken window, and she wonders what's inside. She hopes there is maybe some canned food, something edible, because she is starving. She hasn't eaten since the diner yesterday. And even then she'd felt bile rising to her throat for hours afterwards. The baby makes it impossible to eat anything without it haunting her later.

She drags the box across the floor; it is so heavy she feels the muscles in her back strain with the effort. She peels back the damp flaps to open it, hoping for sustenance but instead finding magazines. *Hustler* magazines. There must be a hundred of them. She scans the date on the cover of one of them: 1981. The girl is totally nude save for a yellow plastic visor and a pair of yellow sweatbands around her wrists. She is holding a tennis racket between her legs. Nessa feels her face grow hot and she tries not to think about some guy out here alone in the woods with this collection of magazines and little else. She reaches for the next box and pulls it over. Inside is a lone mason jar filled with amber colored liquid. At first she assumes it must be some sort of backwoods moonshine, but then quickly understands that it is *syrup.* Of course.

She tries to pry the lid off, which is sealed tightly, almost too tightly. But it finally comes loose in her hand, and she dips her finger into the thick liquid. She sucks the sweet syrup from her fingers, but instead of quelling her hunger it seems to incite it. Her stomach rumbles, the baby kicks. And she sits down on the floor, her fingers sticky, and wonders where she will find her next meal. She doesn't have any money left. Not a dime.

And so for now, she needs to go out into the woods, see if maybe she can find something to eat. She had noticed some apple trees along the road last night as she was trying to hitch a ride. She wishes she had picked some and put them in her backpack. She tries not to think of Mica's house, the smell of it. The taste of the syrup pulls her back to that tiny kitchen, to that little oven and the turquoise and black tiles of that counter. Most mornings she would make pancakes. The ingredients were cheap, and the pancakes filled them up. They'd eat until their bellies were bursting. Until even the baby felt fat inside her. She would give anything for a pancake right now. She wouldn't even need butter.

She opens up the front door of the sugar shack again, just a crack, and peers out. There is nothing but pine and maple and birch trees as far as the eye can see. No apple trees. And certainly no ingredients for pancakes just sitting out there in the forest. She knows she can't stay here long if there is nothing to eat.

Seeing that it is safe to go outside, she tentatively steps out of the shelter of the shack and peers across the river, retracing her steps from last night. In the distance she can see the back of the house she saw before and is pretty sure she sees wooden stakes and chicken wire. This means there is a garden. *Vegetables.* God. Her mouth fills with saliva as she recollects the simple wonderful acidity of a tomato. The crisp green snap of peas. She'll go tonight. She'll wash herself in the river, and then she'll go eat. But for now, she needs to save her energy. To think of things besides food.

She goes back inside the shack, which is darker and cooler even than the forest around her, and spreads her sleeping bag out on the floor. It is still damp from the wet ground last night and so she brings it outside and lays it in a spot of sun to dry. Then instinctually she reaches into her pocket for the note, holds the soft worn paper in her hands and reads it for the thousandth time.

She hadn't thought she'd need to use it, but now here she is. Her mother is gone. She has no money. The baby is coming whether she likes it or not. It is all she has. *He* is all she has now. But there is no address, nothing but the phone number. She wonders what he will do when he sees her again. If he will even remember. And she wonders if he can give her back what she lost that night. If he's been keeping it safe for her.

After the daylight has disappeared, Nessa slips into the river to bathe. It is quiet here with only the rushing water and the sounds of the crickets and frogs. It is like a soft lullaby. She thinks of the words, what the lyrics might be. Rolls them around in her mouth like berries. Like stones. But she doesn't sing.

Silence is remarkably easy.

Nessa, for whom words are like gems, like beautiful stones, has not spoken a single one in so long she no longer remembers what they taste like on her tongue.

She has always loved words. From the moment she could understand the connection between the letters on the page and the sounds they made, she was enraptured by them. In her room, one of her rooms (she recollects green shag carpeting, a painted bureau the color of sky, Barbie dolls) she practiced the words, watching her mouth in the mirror.

At school Mrs. Marvel, the speech therapist, had her do the same, staring at her lips and tongue in a red plastic framed mirror, learning to imitate the therapist's own mouth. She tried, struggled to make those sounds. But the sounds never ever matched what she heard in her head, when she studied the letters on the page. When the words slipped out of her lips, they sounded wrong. Garbled. Throaty and swollen. Over time, she learned how to say only what needed to be said. To pretend that she was only shy instead of inept. They moved the first time, and somehow, at the new school no one cared whether or not she could pronounce those elusive words. They didn't care that entire syllables were inaccessible to her. That certain letters of the alphabet remained out of reach. And that every word she spoke was a tentative creature, coming out only when absolutely necessary.

And then, suddenly, when she was about twelve, it was as though *none* of it mattered any more. She still could not speak well, but *nobody* cared. She learned a new language then. Red lipstick on those plump, stubborn lips. She learned the language of hands and hips. Her body able to communicate in ways her mouth never could. Most of the words stayed trapped inside, while the world read her body instead.

She became the book that everyone wanted to read. The forbidden one that was both coveted and hidden, the one to be ashamed of. Still, hands, so many hands, thumbed through her pages, bending her spine until it grew weak. Until the pages were stained and tattered. Entire passages disappearing, ink blurred like the black mascara she wore that smudged under her eyes. It didn't take long before hers was the story everyone knew, the ending spoiled.

And then they moved again and again, and with each subsequent move she lost more and more words. Spoke less and less.

Relied on the cover to tell her story. Let people believe they knew her, just because they were able to hold her. To touch all those worn pages.

But you can only keep poetry imprisoned for so long. And while her throat often failed, her hands were still perfectly capable. She collected the words she couldn't speak in spiral notebooks. No special journals with locks and keys. No silly leather-bound diaries that called attention to themselves. They were safer this way, camouflaged inside the accoutrements of any student. And inside the notebooks, she wrote the things she wasn't able to speak. Those stubborn, evasive words. And she shared them with no one until him. And even then, she was reluctant. Words are precious things. She knows this. And she has come to get them back. She will do whatever it is she needs to do.

But tonight there is only one word that matters. Only one word that informs everything she does. *Hunger.* She is feeling sick and weak. As she bathes in the cold river, carefully rubbing the shampoo between her legs and under her arms, under her breasts which hang like low fruit, she knows that she must eat and soon. That she is in real danger.

166

She has known hunger before, but never like this. In the city, there was always a slice of pizza left on a table, some delicacy wrapped in wax paper left near the top of the trash. She could always find a loaf of bread, a stick of butter. There was almost always someone willing to exchange food for her attention.

She washes her clothes with the same shampoo, wrings the fabric out with her hands and then lays the wet clothes in a pile on the grass. She will hang them out to dry behind the shack. She gets out of the water and realizes she doesn't have a towel to dry herself, no clean dry clothes to put on. And so she slips back into a dirty skirt and the cleanest tank top she can find. All four pairs of underwear she has are soaking wet.

She looks at the back of the house across the river. Later, after the lights go out, she will go to the garden. She will scavenge on all fours, pillaging and ravaging. Harvesting, gaining sustenance.

Sylvie is so very tired tonight. Her body is angry, exhausted from the exertion of another day spent hanging by her fingertips from this horrendous cliff. She wonders, sometimes, how much longer she can hold on. There are times when she wishes she could just let go, stop clinging. Stop fighting the inevitable and irresistible pull. But while her body demands rest, her mind resists. Always vigilant, the night watchman standing guard over imaginary evils. She fluffs her pillow, arranges her blankets, pulls the crisp cold sheets up tight to her chin. Tucking herself in, as though she is her own grandmother, making sure she is safe and snug inside. But still, her mind races, her palms sweat. Her heart pounds and there is an electric sort of buzzing as though her brain might short out.

She reaches into her drawer, runs her fingers across the cold metal of the gun, and then rests them on the vial. She touches the corrugated plastic rim of the cap, holds the smooth orange canister in her hand. It immediately brings comfort; even the *promise* of sleep calms her. She tries not to rely on these, but there are times when she knows that without them the night will be endless. Unbearable. She is careful to take them only at night; she knows that it would be easy to start using them to help her get through her days as well.

She already checked in on Ruby to make sure she was asleep, wondered at the peacefulness of her body, her face. And standing there reminded her of a thousand other nights when she and Robert stood together in that doorway, his chest pressed against her back, their bodies making one shadow on the wooden floor. She remembers he was always the one to pull away first, "Come to bed," he'd say and reach for her hand, pulling her away, turning off the light. She could have watched them sleep for hours.

She has also already checked the locks on all the doors, something Robert used to do. She has paced the house, looking for vulnerabilities, for cracks or fissures, breaches in the fragile security. Without Robert here, she worries that she has missed something. And so she is vigilant.

Now she pops one, then two pills, under her tongue and swallows them dry, without water. Taking them this way makes her more aware, and, she thinks, somehow more accountable. If she can just get some sleep, she thinks, as the pills lodge in her throat and then make the slow achy descent down her throat, she will have the energy to be a normal mother tomorrow. Maybe a good night's sleep will give her exactly what she needs. As the time-release capsule begins to dissolve, as her mind's stubborn resistance to rest also begins to disintegrate she imagines the impossible: a call to Gloria, maybe she could bring Izzy over. They could sit on the back porch and drink tea, talk, while the girls play. If it's hot, she could hook up the sprinkler, the one that spins. The one that Ruby and Jess used to play in. As the medicine makes its way into her bloodstream, quieting the cacophony of her brain, she dreams other summers. She dreams of prismatic rainbows made from sunlight and a sprinkler. She dreams dirty little boy feet and grass-stained knees. She dreams a wet child wrapped in a towel on her lap. The thrumming of his heart under her fingers, dreams the way she used to press her palm against the soft bone of his chest just to feel that steady, certain rhythm.

How that was assurance. *Insurance.*

As the wild synapses of her brain shut down, as the live wires of her imagination fizzle out, there is only this: *Twilight. Mosquitoes.* Robert's warm hand on her shoulder as they both studied the long black eyelashes of his closed eyes. And Ruby, her little girl, playing in the sprinkler, breathless and blissful in the half light.

The narcotic paralysis is so powerful, the depth of this slumber so deep, the crash of glass, the flash of light, and the rustling sounds outside do not frighten her but rather integrate into the landscape of an analgesic dream. Sunlight, laughter, bare feet running across wet grass.

■ ■ ■ ■

# TUESDAY

■ ■ ■ ■

At the swimming pool on Tuesday morning, it's not the same boy with the clipboard at the gate. Instead it's one of the few adults who seem to run the pool and the park. He's Ruby's dad's age, and there's no way on earth he's going to let her leave in the middle of swimming lessons. When she tells him she's not feeling well, that she needs to go home, he shrugs and says, "Sorry, kid. Why don't you just sit and watch? I can't make you go in the water, but I can't let you leave."

And so she walks back to the Tadpoles and sits down on the edge of the water, drawing her knees up to her chest.

"Coming in?" Nora asks brightly, her optimism never wavering. But Ruby just shakes her head and stares at the water.

The air is loud with the sounds of children squealing, water splashing, and whistles blowing. It's all the sounds of summer at once. The ice cream truck that comes by and waits for the kids to be released pulls up, blares "Pop Goes the Weasel," and all of it is almost more than she can bear. She almost wishes she could just get in the water and let her ears fill, let the cool blue water of the pool drown out all those sounds.

She also can't stand to look over where the Junior Lifeguards are swimming. Watching Izzy pretending to be cool (flipping her hair, putting her hands on her hips, throwing her head back in laughter) makes her feel even more like a little kid than taking lessons with the Tadpoles. And so she stares at her feet, callused and brown from the summer. She studies the way her second toe seems to have an extra joint, making it longer than her big toe. Her mother told her once that this meant that she was descended from royalty. She thinks it just makes her look like a freak and none of her shoes fit right.

She looks up when she feels cold water dripping on her. Izzy is standing there, her arms crossed across her chest.

"Hi," Izzy says, and it sounds like an accusation. Like Ruby has done something wrong.

Ruby shields her eyes from the sun and peers up at Izzy's face. She's wearing

176

mascara. And lip gloss. At the pool.

"Hi," Ruby says.

Marcy is standing a couple of feet behind her, as though she is her bodyguard.

"My mom says we'll be by to pick you up for the fair tomorrow at ten. If you're still coming," Izzy says.

Ruby doesn't know what to say. She knows she should shake her head, say *No thanks, I'm going with somebody else.* But there *is* nobody else. Izzy is her best friend. *Was* her best friend until two days ago. These are uncharted waters, and she can't swim. She is doing everything in her power just to keep her head up. To keep from crying.

"Okay," she says, and Marcy sighs.

"And make sure you bring your own money," Izzy says then, and Ruby feels her throat grow thick. Of course she'll bring her own money. She always brings her own money. But the way Izzy says it made it sound like she is some sort of mooch. Like she is poor. The old Izzy never talked about money. Marcy nods, as though it's her job to make sure Ruby plays by these new rules.

"Well, bye!" Izzy says and walks away, Marcy following behind her.

As soon as the whistle blows and all of the kids scramble out of the water and the lifeguards jump in, she gathers her things and runs toward the gate. She has a dollar in her pocket, and on any other day she would go straight to the ice cream truck and order a rocket pop. She and Izzy would get them together and eat them as they sat on the swings in the playground. But the money in her pocket makes her think about the fair. About Marcy. And so she just gets on her bike and pedals away, her towel waving out behind her like a cape. She flies past the library, past Marcy's house and past Miss Piggy. Gloria is outside on the porch painting a chair. Ruby doesn't stop; she doesn't even wave when Gloria calls after her. Instead she rides her bike the short way, the wrong way.

It is out of habit that she finds herself here. But the moment the bridge comes into view, it's as though she has fallen into the pool. Her vision gets wavy, her ears fill, and her lungs collapse. She can't breathe.

Crying, she turns the bike around and rides the other way, back through town, back past the park and the library and the school. She goes the long way, the *safe* way, like she's supposed to, until she's back at her mom's house again.

She walks her bike up the overgrown drive and tries not to think about what Marcy will say when Gloria pulls up to pick her up tomorrow. She tries not to think of the disdain in Izzy's face.

She hears rustling by the shed and is startled to see her mother outside. She is dressed in an old pair of blue jeans and one of her dad's T-shirts. She looks smaller inside the old shirt. She's dragging a piece of plywood from the shed.

"What are you doing?" Ruby asks.

"Somebody came into the garden last night," she says. "I don't know why I didn't hear anything."

"How do you know?" Ruby asks.

"Well, half of the tomatoes are gone. The green beans are all picked over, and the watermelon is gone too."

"It could have been animals," Ruby offers. Though she can't imagine what animal would walk off with a watermelon.

"The bulb in the floodlight is smashed. There's glass everywhere."

"Wow," Ruby says. The idea that somebody was in the garden is strange. Everyone around here has a garden. What on earth would somebody want with her mom's tomatoes?

"Help me build this fence?" her mom says, and Ruby nods. But she doesn't know how to make a fence. She doesn't know the

179

first thing about fences. What she knows are bridges. When they did the unit on bridges last spring in fifth grade, Mrs. McKnight taught them how to make a bridge out of balsa wood. She worked on hers every single day for three weeks until it was finished. It was a thing of beauty, Mrs. McKnight said. She leaned over and whispered just that in her ear. "That," she said, "is a beautiful bridge. Ruby, I hope you realize that you have a very special talent. I think you may have found your calling."

She likes to think of the future this way: like a voice calling out to her. Like something speaking to you from far, far away. And the closer you get to it, the clearer the voice is. She imagines herself on one island, and that voice calling to her from another island she can't even make out yet it's so far away. And she knows, somehow, that her job is to build a bridge between the two.

The last time she was in the shed was not long after the accident, before her dad came home from the hospital and she tried to build a ramp up into the house for his chair. But the ramp split in half, and Bunk had to help her. She didn't know then what she knows now. About suspension, about load.

She helps her mom drag the sheets of plywood out of the shed and they stand together, staring at them. She thinks about the delicate pieces of balsa wood, the graph paper they used to map their bridge plans out. She recalls the precise task of gluing the pieces together, the pliability of the wood, the way it bent at her will. She thinks about how all those fragile pieces wound up making something so strong.

Her mom hands her her dad's old drill, but the battery's dead, so she searches everywhere for the long orange extension cord. It's like a spider den in the shed. She's not afraid of spiders, but she *is* afraid of snakes. She knows there aren't any poisonous ones living in Vermont, but her throat still gets thick every time one of them slithers out of the grass or out from under the porch.

She plugs the cord in the kitchen and runs it out under the door. It barely reaches the backyard where she tries to envision how this is all going to work. That is one thing she learned from building the bridge: you can't just start building. You need to think ahead, to plan.

The backyard is overgrown as well, the grass and weeds thick. The lawn mower is broken or else she'd get back here and take care of it herself. Jess and she used to have a swing set back here, but it rusted out and their dad took it to the dump. Now there are just the cement blocks he poured into the ground to hold the swing set steady, the rusty severed pipes from where he sawed the frame off. They also used to have a dog, a mutt named Foster, and the run he was chained up to still crisscrosses the backyard. The sight of that run makes her feel bad. She didn't love that dog the way she should have. Nobody did. He was a mean dog, but it was probably just because he hated being stuck outside, hated that nobody paid any attention to him unless he was barking. Ruby fed him every night but that was about it. Her dad wouldn't let him in the house; he said animals weren't meant to live inside. Maybe if he hadn't been tied up in the backyard he could have made a good pet. That's just one of those things she'll never know though. It seems to Ruby that life is made up of stuff like that. A billion questions with endless multiple choice answers. Sometimes you get them wrong, even when the right answer is sitting there in front of you.

"What do you think?" her mom asks.

"I don't know," Ruby says. "I guess we need to fasten the first one to the house somehow." She finds some hinges in the shed and drills them to the plywood, then she drills the other side of the hinge to the side of the house. It makes an awful sound and a few sparks when she drills into the metal siding. She tries to use what she remembers from building the model bridges to build the fence, but it's not the same.

A bridge is meant to connect people, but a fence is meant to keep people out. Or in.

One by one, they drag the big sheets of plywood from the shed to the backyard. One by one, they lean one up against the next, fastening them together with whatever hardware they can find in the shed. By the time they're done, they're both sweaty, their hands blistered, and the wind is blowing so hard Ruby's worried this house of wooden cards they just made is going to blow right over. It looks terrible. Like an eleven-year-old made it. The pieces don't stand up straight at all; they lean in on each other like football players in a huddle in a losing game. Defeated.

But her mom seems happy. "That'll do the trick," she says. And she reaches for Ruby's arm. Her skin feels electric; Ruby almost expects sparks to come flying off her. "Thank you."

She leans into her mother then, closing her eyes as she presses through that wild force field that encloses her mother. And for a single moment, she feels connected.

But then the phone rings, and her mom's eyes grow wide and scared again. They separate and Ruby's runs through the back door into the kitchen, picking up the phone. "Hello?"

"Hi, Ruby," her dad says.

"Hi, Daddy," she says, smiling, missing him suddenly more than she ever has.

"How's it going?" he asks.

She thinks about that pathetic fence. About whoever it was who knocked out the bulb and stole the watermelon. She thinks about Izzy and Marcy and the bridge. "It's okay," she says. "I'm going to the fair tomorrow."

"Oh good, baby. Gloria taking you?"

She nods, the lump in her throat swollen and thick. "Yep."

"Listen, remember there's that storm coming up the coast?" he says.

"Yeah. Irene."

"Well, they're saying now it could hit North Carolina sometime in the next few days. I'm not too worried about it, but just wanted to give you and your mom a heads up. We're going to help Uncle Larry shore up the house. Sandbags and all that. Hopefully, it'll pass real quick and then we'll be on our way home this weekend."

She nods again. She can't believe he's only been gone a couple of days. It feels like the whole world has turned upside down since he and Bunk left.

"Hey, thanks for getting your mom's phone back up. You caught that mama raccoon yet?"

"Nope."

"Well, keep checking," he says. "And as soon as you've got it, call Animal Control."

"Okay, Daddy," she says.

"Okay, baby girl. Listen, I love you. And I miss you."

"Miss you too, Daddy. Say hi to Bunk."

"Can I talk to your mom?"

Ruby looks up, but her mom isn't in the room. She can hear the shower running and she knows that she's doing this so she won't have to talk to her dad.

"I think she's taking a shower," Ruby says.

"Okeydoke. I'll call again tonight."

Ruby sits down at the table and sees that her mother has been working on another bird, one with a spotted chest. It's almost done; the invisible threads sewing shut the place where its heart used to be just need to be clipped. She's got some birch branches scattered across the table to give the bird a habitat inside its glass jar. When she's done, you won't even be able to tell that it's dead.

That its chest is empty, its heart replaced with puffs of cotton.

Nessa knows she needs to ration the food, but she is still so hungry. Deliriously hungry. She eats the tomatoes as though they are apples. She chews on the green beans, not even bothering to spit out the sharp ends. The watermelon she will save, though she salivates at the mere thought of that sweet pink flesh. She will eat the seeds. The rind.

She knows she can't stay here for long. Someone is bound to spot her here. Whoever owns the house with the garden she pillaged last night must know she's out here, even if they don't know exactly where.

She hung her wet clothes on the backside of the shack, but now they are damp with dew. The wind is incredible. Warm but almost violent. The clothes should dry quickly, and when the sun goes down again tonight, she'll leave. She needs to find her way back into town.

Inside the shack, she lies down on the

hard floor and stares up at the rotten ceiling. The baby squirms under her fingers, and she presses back. A way of communicating. She tries not to think about what will happen when the baby is ready to come out. She knows she needs to find him before that happens. This is something she cannot do on her own.

A fat housefly buzzes over her and smacks into the window again and again. She resists the urge to swat it. What a stupid creature, she thinks. There's a door right there. There are a thousand ways to get out. She feels tears coming to her eyes as she watches the fly hurl itself again and again and again against the unyielding glass.

Later, when the sun goes down, she gathers her clothes, which are finally dry. She rolls them and stuffs them into her backpack along with her sleeping bag, which still smells of a deep earthy funk, as though her body and the ground have merged together. For dinner, she smashes the watermelon open on a rock and eats the sweet insides with her hands. But there is little sustenance to be found. It is an illusion of nourishment: her mouth flooded with flavor, but her stomach still aching and angry even after it is gone.

She knows she needs to go back to the

garden again. She won't make it to morning without something else to eat. She needs to gather her strength. She may be walking for a while. It clearly looks as though she's gotten off track. None of this looks familiar. None of this looks like the place she used to know.

When the sun goes down, she slips off her shoes and makes her way across the river, the cold shock of it just as startling as it was before. It's amazing how the body forgets, the amnesia of the flesh. She is wet and trembling with cold and with fear as she makes her way to the house with the garden. She stops, confused.

There wasn't a fence here last night; she's sure of it. She looks around, perplexed. Disoriented. This is the same place. Then her heart pounds with the realization that this fence has been erected to keep her out. Though, it's not much of a fence. More like a ramshackle barricade. It's haphazard, pathetic, and something about it makes her feel almost sad. She considers just turning back, getting her stuff and then moving on. But she is hungry. So hungry. And so she walks the perimeter of the fence, looking for a way in, for a weakness in this ridiculous fortress.

She's forgotten her shoes on the other side

of the river, and the grass could be snow it is so cold. She pushes each board tentatively, waiting for something to give. But, despite its appearance, the fence is quite strong. She thinks about the garden on the other side. There were still some tomatoes left, lettuce, spinach. She thinks that if she is able to dig, she might find potatoes, rutabagas. She imagines those root vegetables filling her stomach, weighing her down. She thinks about the cold crisp snap of peas and bell peppers. Her stomach roils and rumbles, she imagines the baby, like a lion growling inside her. She pats her stomach as if to soothe, but it is as futile as trying to calm a wild animal.

The lights inside the house are all out, and it is so dark she can barely see her own hands. She uses the fence as a guide as she circles the garden. She is so quiet. She is invisible.

And then there is the loud crack of a gunshot, a firecracker? No matter its source, the bang is followed by excruciating pain, though it's nearly impossible to locate. It seems to begin in her toes, but it radiates up her calf and into her right hip. She drops to the ground, still soundlessly, her mouth failing, even now, to let go of the fury and anguish.

It is her foot. Has someone shot her foot? Bitten it? In the darkness, she gropes for her ankle and feels instead the coldness of metal. The pain is overwhelming, nauseating. She leans over and vomits onto the grass. Her mouth is filled with the now bitter recollection of melon.

It's a trap. At least she thinks it is. She's never seen one before. It seems like something medieval, a torture device, and her toes are trapped inside. She feels all around the mechanism, her fingers searching for release. But it is futile in this darkness. She wonders if she is going to faint.

When she hears the back door open, sees the light (the one she smashed last night) go on, she presses her body flat against the ground. She tries not to breathe.

"Who's there? What do you want?" The woman's voice is trembling. She sounds scared, and for a moment, Nessa feels like she should explain herself. That if she could, she would say, *I was only hungry.* But the words are trapped inside, just as her toes are captured. And so she holds her breath. It is agonizing. The baby kicks and kicks; her ribs ache.

An owl hoots and the woman says, "I have a gun. This is private property!"

Nessa doesn't move. Even the baby seems

to know the importance of stillness, of silence. It could be hours she stays here, body pressed to the cold ground. It could be years. Finally, she hears the door shut, and eventually the light clicks off, enclosing her in darkness again. But the pain has not lessened. If anything, it has gotten worse.

She has to get back to the sugarhouse. She'll have to drag the trap with her. She feels along the ground with her fingers, and finds that the trap is connected by a chain to a spike in the ground. She digs into the earth, releasing the spike, and then tries to stand. The trap cannot be that heavy, but it feels like an anchor as she attempts to walk. Finally, she decides that the best way might be to crawl on her hands and knees. The pain in her foot is a throbbing, living thing now. Each movement creates new sparks of sensation. It is as though the metal trap is somehow electrified. Her face is damp, her cheeks hot and streaked with tears and sweat when she reaches the river. She will have to stand to get across. It's too dangerous to crawl. She could drown. She could die here. And she worries that even if she can cross the river, she's not sure she can make it all the way back through the woods to the shack. She worries that the woman in the house will come out again, with her gun this time, and shoot her before she has reached the other side.

And so she uses every bit of willpower and strength she has to stand. Her center of balance is completely thrown now between the baby and the current of pain that is radiating up and down the whole right side of her body. But still, she has to choose: survive or die here? Nine months pregnant in what is, for all intents and purposes, a shallow creek. Is this her destiny?

She isn't sure how she manages to get through that icy water and back onto land. She is barely cognizant of anything but the pain as she negotiates the dark and impossible path leading back to the shack. She is elsewhere as she makes her way inside and lies down on top of her sleeping bag. She has separated from herself. From this body. From the baby even.

This is her true talent. This ability to stay and leave at the same time. She has done it since she was a little girl. There are two Nessas. There always have been. One who hangs around looking normal, while the other one hovers and then flees. Tonight that Nessa, the one made of *pain* and *hunger* and *baby,* lingers on the floor of this cold cabin. And the other Nessa, the one made of *light* and *poetry* and *air,* observes and then flutters away through the cracked glass in the window. She is elsewhere. She is nowhere at all.

■ ■ ■ ■

# WEDNESDAY

■ ■ ■ ■

In the morning, Ruby gets dressed and wonders if she just hides out in the house with her mom, if she doesn't answer the door when Izzy and Gloria come to get her, they'll just go away. She wonders if she pretends she no longer exists, if she ignores the phone calls and the knocks on the door, she can just disappear. That's what her mother has done.

It wasn't right away, of course. But slowly. So gradually you could barely see that it was happening. Her mom was like the moon, waning, just a little bit every single night, so slowly you barely realized that she had become only a sliver. That all the light had gone out save for a thumbnail. And over time, people just gave up. They stopped coming to check on her. Stopped knocking on the door. Even Gloria, who loved her mom like a sister, didn't know what to do anymore. She tried so hard, but was met with nothing but her mother's obstinacy. And so they gave her what they thought she wanted. They gave her her privacy, her seclusion. They left her alone.

At the time, it made Ruby angry. The day after Christmas last year when her dad made her pack her things, made her say good-bye, she'd been sobbing. She hadn't wanted to give up on her mother. She hadn't wanted to leave her out here alone to fend for herself. Ruby had thrown a tantrum as though she were still a baby. She'd pounded her fists and cried and refused to go. She remembers her throat felt raw, as though she were sick instead of desperately sad. But her mother had just hugged her, and then pushed her gently toward the door. And *this,* her mother's hands pushing her away, hurt more than the cracked ribs, the broken arm, the cuts that crisscrossed her face after the accident. Her father didn't understand that them being there was the one thing keeping her mother from disappearing entirely. That if they stayed, she would have to linger. Like a ghost, stuck in the purgatory between life and death, between two worlds. Her mother was haunted with them there.

But Ruby understands now, this inclination. This desire to slip away. To seclude herself. She understands how it feels to be an island, separate from everyone else, surrounded by nothing but water. Even when she is with people (at school, at Izzy's house, at the pool), she is aware of how alone she is. Nobody can reach her, not really. She and her mother are more similar than different, but she doesn't know how to tell her mom this. What words might explain that she understands.

Her mother looks as though she hasn't slept at all. Her hair is pulled back away from her face, which calls attention to her pale skin and dark eyes, with dark half circles like gray thumbprints beneath them. Her hands are shaking as she hands Ruby a glass of orange juice.

Ruby knows she was up all night, pacing. She heard her open the back door and yell into the night. The fence was supposed to make her feel safe, but now, instead, it seems to have convinced her even further that someone is trying to get in.

"What time are you leaving for the fair?" her mother asks, glancing furtively out the kitchen window.

Ruby doesn't want to go. She wants to stay here. She is overwhelmed by a memory of one day a few years ago when she felt this same incredible desire to stay home with her mother after everyone else was gone. She'd pretended she was sick, feigned a stomachache, a headache. She'd watched Jess climb into her dad's truck and then disappear through the trees. Her mother stayed home all day with her, playing Monopoly. They made brownies and ate the whole pan. They watched soap operas on TV and read out loud to each other until it was time to pick Jess up. It was one of the best days of her whole life.

"Gloria is coming at nine. The gates open at ten, but it's Children's Day, so she wants to get there early."

Her mother nods, but she doesn't seem to be listening. She is pacing back and forth, one arm wrapped around her waist, the other clinging to her mug of tea.

"I could stay here, Mom," she offers, hoping that maybe her mother will agree. Say, *Oh, that would be so nice.*

But instead her mother shakes her head, forces a smile. "Don't be silly. You can't miss the fair."

"It's okay," Ruby tries again. "It's not that big a deal."

But her mother is looking at her the same way she looked at her the day that Bunk came and loaded her dad's things, *her* things into the van. The day Ruby cried so hard her eyes ached and she lost her voice. She is pushing her away without even touching her. But this time, Ruby feels angry instead of hurt.

"I need money," she says, blinking hard so as not to cry. And she thinks of Izzy telling her to bring her own money. It feels like a wound being torn open.

"Oh," her mother says, looking around the kitchen as though a twenty-dollar bill might simply materialize. "I have some cash in my wallet." She finds her wallet on the counter and pulls out two crisp twenty-dollar bills.

Ruby wishes she hadn't asked. Something about all of this makes her feel bad. She finds herself doing this all the time lately: saying something or doing something in anger and only moments later feeling guilty and awful. But she can't stop herself. "That's too much, Mom," she says softly. Sorry.

But her mom shakes her head and presses the money into Ruby's palm. "You'll need a ticket to get in and for the rides. And lunch." And then she kisses the top of Ruby's head softly. "Maybe you can get a caramel apple."

Ruby remembers her first caramel apple then. When Jess was still in a stroller. They went to the fair, and she'd been mesmer-

201

ized by the rows and rows of apples in the window of the colorful truck. It had taken her nearly ten minutes to decide which kind she wanted. She didn't want to make a mistake. When she finally picked out the apple (a caramel apple with colored jimmies scattered across its golden surface), she was so excited. But three bites in, she realized the apple was bruised and mealy inside. The caramel was delicious and sweet and decadent, but inside the fruit was rotten. She didn't know how to tell her mother, who had been so eager to please her. And so she ate the whole thing, brown fleshy bruises and all.

"Thanks," she says. "We probably won't be back until after dark. Is that okay?" She is hoping, wishing futilely that her mother will change her mind. Ask her to stay home. *Need* her.

"Of course," her mom says, and she looks like she wants to say something else, like she has a secret she is about to share. But instead she just says, "I hope you have fun."

Ruby can't stand the idea of Izzy and Marcy seeing her mother's house, what has become of it. The baby raccoons are still living in the loveseat on the front porch. She can only imagine what Marcy would have to say about that. She already calls anybody who doesn't live in town a redneck. A hillbilly. A woodchuck. She teases the kids who live on this side of the river. She is merciless. Snobby and cruel. Ruby has no idea how she's going to endure an entire day at the fair with her, especially now that Izzy has fallen under her spell. What on earth was she thinking when she agreed to go?

She stuffs the money in her pocket and heads out the door to the front porch. There's a bad smell out here. The raccoons must be going to the bathroom somewhere. She thinks that maybe tomorrow she'll try to clean up the porch for her mom. The baby raccoons are asleep in the loveseat, curled into each other, making one furry pile. She wonders where the mother goes. If the babies worry about her not coming back.

She figures if she waits by the road, Gloria won't even have to pull into the driveway. If she can keep them from pulling in, the worst thing they'll see is the tipped-over mailbox. And she can just say a snowplow ran over it if they ask. She tries once again to right it, but it is too heavy. There is trash spilled on the ground. She picks up the debris and chucks it into the woods. Then just as she's making her way to the road, she realizes she left Jess's baseball cap in the backyard yesterday when they were building the fence, and so she decides to go grab it. It's supposed to be sunny today, and it'll be nice to keep the sun out of her eyes. She glances down the road to make sure they aren't coming and then runs back to the house.

When she gets to the shed, she sees that the trap her dad set is gone. She's been checking it every day for the mama raccoon, careful not to trip it. He said that the trap wouldn't hurt her; raccoons have thick feet, and the trap is padded. She'd made him promise that it wouldn't hurt her. That it wouldn't kill her. But now the trap is missing. *Gone.* She tries to imagine what sort of creature could drag an entire trap away with it. Certainly not a raccoon. Not unless she's a big one. That must have been what her mom heard last night. Maybe it's a bear, she thinks. Maybe that's who's been eating up all the vegetables in the garden.

She finds the baseball cap hanging on a nail sticking out of the shed's wall. It's a little too small, and so she lets the strap all the way out and pulls her ponytail tighter so that it fits down snug. Then she makes her way back down the overgrown driveway, past that broken mailbox, and sits down on a stump. She picks up a blade of grass and puts it between her fingers, presses her lips against it and blows. The whistle is shrill and piercing. Maybe it will scare away whatever got away with the trap.

She worries again about leaving her mom alone, especially if there's a bear out there. Especially if the bear is hurt now, dragging around a trap attached to its paw. She'll need to call her dad later and tell him what happened. Thinking about her dad also makes her think about the storm they say is coming up the coast. He said not to worry, but she does. She worries about everything. About her mom, about the storm. And about what she's gotten herself into by agreeing to this.

Gloria pulls up in Grover's big yellow car. Ruby can see Izzy and Marcy sitting in the backseat, one on each side of the enormously long bench seat. They are both wearing hot pink T-shirts with Hello Kitty on them. They both have sparkly nail polish and matching ponytails. Ruby barely recognizes Izzy with her hair pulled back. Her eyes wide, her face naked.

The window is rolled down; Gloria leans over. "Hey, Ruby! Hop on in."

Ruby thinks about squeezing in next to Izzy and Marcy in the backseat but neither of them seems to be moving an inch to make room. And so she opens the passenger door instead and sits down next to Gloria.

"How are you, sweetie?" Gloria asks. "Sorry about the Banana. My car's in the shop."

Ruby nods.

"Iz, aren't you going to say hi?" Gloria says, turning around to the backseat.

"Hi," both of the girls say in unison, as if they've practiced it. As if they are in a play. Ruby can't bring herself to turn around and look at them and so she mumbles, "Hi."

Gloria scowls a little and then smiles brightly. "I heard they have a new ride at the fair this year. What's it called, girls?" she says to the backseat.

"It's the Zipper," Marcy says. "You have to be five feet to go on it."

Ruby isn't anywhere near five feet, but she knows both Izzy and Marcy are. Marcy is the tallest girl in the whole class. She tells everyone she's going to be a model as soon as she hits five seven, which, by Ruby's estimation, will be by the time they're in the eighth grade.

In the backseat the girls giggle and talk. Ruby stares straight ahead at the road in front of them. It is still foggy out, the mist like ghosts in the trees. For a mile or so, it is nearly impossible to see through the thick haze. She is aware suddenly of how deep in the woods her mom lives. She never thinks about it, but with Marcy in the car, looking out the window at the thick trees surrounding them, she feels self-conscious.

"What do *do* all the way out here?" Marcy asks suddenly, and Ruby realizes she's talking to her. "I mean, do you like even get cable?"

Ruby thinks of the antenna on the roof, the snowy pictures on the screen of the small black-and-white TV they used to have so her dad could watch his basketball games. She thinks about her cell phone that doesn't work.

"My mom thinks that TV rots your brain," Ruby says, and Gloria turns to her, smiling.

"That is totally stupid," Marcy says. "No offense, Gloria."

Ruby feels her face get hot. Everyone their age calls her Mrs. Sinclair. She's the only kid she knows who is allowed to call her Gloria.

As Izzy and Marcy retreat back into their whispery little world in the backseat, Gloria asks softly, "Are you having a nice time at your mom's?"

Ruby nods, but her throat feels thick.

"I miss her, you know," Gloria says, and it

feels like she wants something from Ruby. Like she wants an explanation.

Ruby nods again.

The girls giggle in the backseat, and it makes her heart ache.

"I think we're moving to North Carolina," Ruby says, startling herself.

"What?" Gloria says. And the car goes silent in the back seat.

"You're *moving*?" Izzy says.

Ruby turns around then, and looks at Izzy in that stupid pink shirt with that stupid ponytail. "Yeah. Near my uncle. We're going to buy a house on a little island off the coast. It's like right on the beach." She can't stop herself now.

"No way," Marcy says.

Ruby shrugs. "It's called Wanchese. You can look it up if you want."

"When?" Izzy asks, and Ruby can hear just the faintest bit of something in her voice: sadness? Fear?

"I don't know. They're checking it out. If it works out, probably soon. My dad is going to buy a fishing boat there. And my mom will come with us too, of course." Now she is just lying. But strangely, she doesn't feel the way she has felt in the past when she stretches the truth. This feels good. Izzy's wide-eyed disbelief feels wonderful. Even Marcy's scowl feels good.

"I thought your parents were divorced," Marcy says.

"No, they're just separated. But they're getting back together." Ruby's chest hurts. Like she swallowed a rubber ball.

"Oh, Ruby," Gloria says then, and when Ruby turns to look at her, she sees that her eyes are wet. "I don't want you to move."

And suddenly it dawns on Ruby that she's just told the biggest fib in her life. For one thing, she's not even supposed to know that her dad is looking at a house, at a boat. She also has no idea, really, what his plans are. And the business about her mom is just wishful thinking. The enormity of the lie hits her like a punch in her gut. She blinks hard and looks out the window.

"I mean, we'll just have to see. It might not happen."

Marcy snorts, and it takes everything Ruby has not to turn around and glare at her.

At the fair, Izzy and Marcy cling to each other like the baby raccoons, and Ruby hangs back with Gloria. She goes on a couple of rides with them, though each time winds up sitting behind them in the cars, staring at the backs of their perfect ponytails: the Himalaya, the Chinese Dragon roller coaster, the haunted house. After they leave her wandering through the hall of mirrors in the Rock 'N' Roll Funhouse, she gives up and just sits with Gloria and watches as Marcy and Izzy go around and around and upside down. Gloria buys a bag of cotton candy and they share it as Marcy and Izzy run from one ride to the next. Ruby feels sick to her stomach and worn out by the time the sun starts to go down and the lights come on.

Izzy and Marcy seem to have forgotten she's even there. They hold hands, locking pinkies, and Ruby just wants to go home.

"Hey, let's go up in the Ferris wheel," Gloria says quietly as Izzy and Marcy get in line for the Zipper for the hundredth time. "Just you and me."

Ruby nods, and Gloria reaches for her hand, taking her to the metal ramp, which leads up to the Ferris wheel. There's a long line, and as they wait to get on, Ruby studies the architecture of the ride. She examines the physics of it, marvels at the beauty of the steel and lights. It's miraculous to her that just two days ago, all of this wasn't here. It was disassembled, packed away in trucks or on trains. It is amazing that something that looks so permanent can be so ephemeral.

"Ready?" Gloria asks, as the carnie motions for them to come up and get in the bucket.

Ruby nods and they climb in, let the man lower the thick metal bar across their laps. The whole mechanism lurches and they begin their ascent.

Gloria doesn't look like anybody's mom. She's what her dad calls a *throwback*. A hippie. Today, she's wearing a T-shirt that says *In Science We Trust* with one of those Darwin fishes on it. The pink streaks in her hair have faded; now it's just back to regular sandy blond. She wears it in two low pigtails like a little girl. Earlier she was wearing big black sunglasses that made her look like a bug, but now that the sun has gone down, she's put them away in her giant purse.

When Ruby was little, she used to think that Gloria was like Mary Poppins. That same exact purse has always held exactly whatever it was that she and Izzy needed: Goldfish crackers or Fruit Roll-Ups, drawing pads and Magic Markers, beads to make necklaces, baby aspirin for headaches or Dramamine when one of them got carsick. An extra pair of tights if it got cold, and once a metal spoon that Izzy used to eat yogurt on a class field trip. She looks at the bag sitting next to Gloria in the Ferris wheel cart and wonders what she keeps in there now, if she could pull out something and make everything all right.

As they rise up, Ruby peers down at the midway below. It is twilight, and the sky is a strange, electric blue. Franklin Mountain is just a silhouette against that incredible sky. And below, below, becoming farther and farther away, are all the lights and rides and noises and smells of the fair.

"I'm sorry about Izzy," Gloria says as the Ferris wheel stops to let on some more people.

Ruby looks down at her hands, at her nails that she has bitten down to the quick.

"I don't know why she's being so terrible. But she *is* being terrible and it's not your fault."

Ruby nods.

"Are you really moving?" Gloria asks quietly.

Ruby feels her mouth twitch. "Actually, my mom doesn't know about North Carolina," she says. "I just overheard my dad and Bunk talking. It might not even happen. I'm not even supposed to know."

Gloria smiles and reaches across the seat and touches her hand. Ruby can see her skin is freckled with dried clay. She can

212

almost smell it, and she remembers loving that smell when she was younger. When she and Izzy curled up together and Gloria read them books or they watched movies projected on a sheet Gloria hung on the back of their house, she would breathe that earthy scent, and it made her feel calm.

Ruby looks down at the sparkling midway below them, life bustling and humming without her. She is far away from everything, alone up here, suspended by nothing but physics, by some engineer's dream. In a week, all of this that holds her up will be gone. Just a recollection.

"You must miss Jess," Gloria says. "*I* miss him."

Ruby nods but she can't look at her. She squeezes her eyes shut and sees Jess's face, his bright eyes and red cheeks. She pulls Jess's baseball cap down over her eyes so Gloria won't see that she's crying. And she knows there isn't a single thing in Gloria's bag that can help her now.

At eight o'clock, they make their way back to the parking lot to Grover's car. Izzy and Marcy spent all of their money playing a dart game until they won matching plastic sunglasses. They are neon green. It is dark out, but they wear them anyway. They look like a weird set of twins in their matching outfits.

The ride home is quiet. Gloria tunes into the public radio station and they are talking about the storm. It's expected to hit the coast of North Carolina tonight. They interview residents in the Outer Banks who have evacuated.

"Isn't that where you said your uncle lives?" Izzy asks. It's the first time she's spoken directly to Ruby for hours.

"Yeah," Ruby says. "I'm sure they're fine though. My dad would have called."

When they get to the turn for Ruby's mom's driveway, she says, "You can just drop me off here."

"Don't be silly, Ruby. It's dark. I don't want you walking in the dark." Gloria maneuvers the big yellow car between the two giant oaks that serve as a gateway.

Ruby feels her heart start to thump in her chest. Izzy and Marcy are quiet now in the backseat, sharing a pair of headphones, listening to Marcy's iPod. She hopes they won't notice. She hopes they will ignore the house just like they've managed to ignore her all day. But when Gloria pulls up in front of the house, the floodlights come on, almost blinding them. Gloria's hand flies to her mouth, and Ruby feels like her heart might explode.

"Jesus," Gloria says, but Ruby is already out of the car, running toward the house.

Illuminated in the headlights, the flood-light, lit up like something at the midway, are two giant sheets of plywood. Both of them are spray painted in neon orange paint: KEEP OUT! NO TRESPASSING! STAY AWAY!

Nessa's toes throb. They are swollen, filled with blood and turning a deep bluish purple. They look deformed, monstrous. And the pain pulses like a drum with every heartbeat.

When the sun came up earlier that morning, she was able to release the trap. It was a lot simpler than it seemed last night as she was dragging the damn thing with her across the river. If she'd had more than the sliver of moon to see by, she could have done it sooner and she probably wouldn't be in this predicament right now. She's pretty sure at least three of her toes are broken. The pain is incredible. She can't even walk. It is incessant, insistent.

And the baby seems to know that her body's efforts and energies have now all shifted to her right foot. She is not the rolling, jabbing entity she was just yesterday. She is still. Demanding nothing. Nessa feels like a failure. That she is distracted from the work of carrying this baby. Even her own body has neglected it. She wonders if this is her true legacy from her mother.

The sun has gone down again, but now she cannot leave. She can barely even walk. But she needs to eat. The *baby* needs her to eat. She found an old PowerBar in a forgotten pocket of her backpack, and it felt like a miracle. But that was three hours ago, and she is starving again. She crawled around outside the shack earlier and found some more crab apples, a couple of blackberries that were still green. They did nothing to assuage her hunger. She worries she will die out here.

She knows that soon she will have no choice but to take her chances and go knock on someone's door, to depend, once again, on the benevolence of strangers. She will have to scratch out her pleas on a piece of paper, look at their alarmed faces when they realize she doesn't speak. She will have to endure the sidelong glances as they offer her food or water or a place to sleep. She knows, though, that her silence makes her suspect. It always has. It is nearly impossible for people to believe that someone is unwilling or incapable of voicing their concerns, their wants, their needs. What they don't know is that her voice has failed her. Words, she can trust, but her own assertions, requests, denials, and pleas have almost always gone unheard. And so when she refuses to speak, when she proves incapable of explaining herself, they will not trust her. They might even call the police. And if they call the police, she could get in trouble. Her mother could get in trouble. She's seventeen years old, not allowed to be on her own in the world yet. Never mind the stolen money. Never mind the baby. Never mind all that she knows but has not spoken.

*Words.* She rifles through her bag, looking for the notebook where she stores them. These tiny little gems, hidden away from the world. Her words, the ones captured in her unwilling throat. The words are tiny, scribbled in her nearly illegible writing. Page after page of this. If you look at it from far away, it looks like the scribbles of a child. Near the back of the notebook, she finds a blank sheet of paper and tears it out.

The ink in her pen has dried up, and her pencil is just a stub. But it is enough. She writes carefully. *I AM HUNGRY. PLEASE HELP.*

Sylvie heard Gloria's car pull up, saw the headlights through the window, but still, Ruby's violent entrance startles her. Ruby unlocks the door and storms into the kitchen, her face red. Sylvie nearly drops the hermit thrush she's working on at the table.

"Why did you do that?" Ruby cries, and Sylvie feels her en tire body clenching like a fist.

She knows she's talking about the signs. And she was going to wait until after Ruby got home. But it started getting dark, and she was terrified that whoever was out there last night would be back. She couldn't wait any longer. It's not her fault. She's just trying to keep them safe.

"I'm sorry," she says. "You heard them last night though, didn't you?"

"It was an animal!" Ruby screams. "It got caught in the trap Daddy set for the raccoon. It was just an *animal*!"

Sylvie feels her face grow hot. How can she explain to Ruby the way every nerve of her body feels danger coming? How can she articulate this terror to a child? How can she make sense of the illogical, the nonsensical? The insane?

"They think you're crazy!" Ruby hisses.

Sylvie shakes her head, feels tears coming to her eyes.

"Normal people don't live like this!" Ruby's hair has come loose from her ponytail, and tears are running down her face.

"I'm just trying to keep you safe. Can't you understand that? After everything that happened, Ruby. You were there when your brother . . ." She stops. She can't say the words or else she will be there again. She will be inside the car as it slips into the water, watching from inside as the river presses against the glass, as she sinks and the others are thrown. As those lights fade away in the distance and she is swallowed by the darkness.

"It's too late!" Ruby says. "Don't you get it? Jess is dead. And Daddy is going to take me away too. You're going to have *nobody*, Mom. And it's your fault!"

Sylvie covers her ears with her hands, shakes her head. She can't listen. The words sting, striking her somewhere in the heart and then shattering like buckshot, piercing every bit of her. And then Ruby is running out the back door, kicking at the fence they built, kicking and kicking as Sylvie stands, powerless, and watches. One of the boards yields and then Ruby is scrambling over it, running toward the river, disappearing into the dark, dark woods.

Sylvie knows she should go after her, but when she gets to the broken fence, she can't move. She is paralyzed, a dog with an electric collar. This fence is fallible, but the invisible one she has erected is strong.

"Ruby!" she cries out, but her voice is powerless as well.

Ruby runs and runs, even though she knows her mother won't come after her. This is something she can be certain of. She leaps across the river, her ankle twisting as she lands, but she recovers quickly, shaking the pain away. She doesn't look back. She doesn't know where she's going, but she knows she can't go home. She wishes she'd gone out the front door and gotten her bike instead. Then she could have ridden back into town, gone to Izzy's house. But she imagines knocking on Miss Piggy's door, Izzy and Marcy answering the door in matching pajamas, and she knows she has nowhere to go anymore. The realization of this is almost more than she can stand.

She feels herself starting to cry, but it's not just the leaky eyes she gets sometimes when she feels sad, but rather the kind of crying that starts in your stomach, that rises up into your shoulders and shakes you. The kind of crying you can't control. She runs, even as her whole body is trembling, as though she could run away from the crying itself. As though it's something she can escape.

It is so dark out here in the woods, the moon completely covered in clouds now, she could be running into another night. She could be slipping backwards through time. As though this darkness is a portal. A giant black hole into which she has fallen. Alice's rabbit hole. She runs headlong into the past. Fearless, but not aimless. And then it begins to sprinkle and she is rewinding, she is doing the impossible. She is pulled, somehow, back through the last two years, through the dark abyss into this night. Into these woods. By the edge of this river.

Here is the sound of the river, of wood creaking, moaning. The sounds of water filling her ears. Here is the scent of pine, the smell of rain, the crush and crumble of leaves. The crack and hiss of an engine. Here are the colors red and blue, like carnival lights reflecting off everything. Here is the taste of mud in her mouth, blood in her mouth. The sound of her father keening, her mother moaning, and Jess's silence.

Silence. She has stopped crying. It feels as though she has hit a wall, the bottom of the rabbit hole? Regardless, it is as though her body is simply incapable of feeling even another ounce of sorrow. Her tears spent. Her eyes impoverished.

It is quiet, but she doesn't feel like she is alone.

She has traveled upstream so far she can't see her mother's house anymore. Her legs are shaking with the effort. She can feel the scratches on her bare legs from the branches and brush. She can feel blood trickling down one calf. The rain is light, cooling her skin, which feels feverish. Hot to the touch. She climbs up the embankment and looks around, suddenly scared of all the creatures that live in these woods. *She* is the trespasser here. The vandal.

As the rain starts to come down a little harder, she moves toward a dark, thick grove of trees, hoping to find shelter. Her ankle reminds her of the earlier stumble, and she turns it again as though working out a kink. She pushes through the thick foliage, the overgrowth of trees, and suddenly, her eyes, accustomed to the darkness now, make out a crumbling hunting cabin, or a sugar shack? How has she never found this building before? She has walked through these woods a thousand times. She feels disoriented. How far has she gone?

She moves toward the door of the shack, when suddenly there is the sound of rustling inside the cabin. She backs up, afraid.

"Hello?" she says softly.

Nothing. The rain starts to come down a little harder.

"Hello?" she says again, louder this time, feeling her voice rising up from her stomach. Like the choir teacher at school always says, *from the diaphragm.* And Ruby is overwhelmed by fear. "Is anybody in there?" she asks again.

Again, there is the sound of floors creaking, of someone moving around.

She pushes tentatively against the broken door. She knows she should just turn around, run back to her mother's house. She shouldn't be here. She thinks about the gun in her mother's drawer, wonders if whoever is inside here has a drawer as well. A gun inside. But her common sense, her logic, also seems to be lagging behind, still trying to catch up with her, and so she pushes the door open and steps inside.

At first she doesn't see anything except for the weak glow of a candle in the middle of the floor. But then she sees the girl. And she recognizes her instantly. It's the girl she saw in town on Sunday, the one who disappeared down the alley.

The girl is backed into the corner now, like a frightened animal. Her blond hair is knotted, dreadlocks braided around her head like a crown; she looks like an illustrated girl. Like a fairytale girl. But she is pregnant, her belly enormous. She sits like a child though, her legs splayed out in front of her. When Ruby's eyes adjust to this new light, she can see the piece of paper she is holding up. It says, *I AM HUNGRY. PLEASE HELP.* And scratched at the bottom, it says, *PLEASE DON'T HURT ME.*

Nessa presses her back hard into the corner of the shack, as though she can disappear into the walls. She holds the sign she has made out in front of her like a shield. When the voice outside ceases, the only thing she hears is her own pulse beating in her ears. She cranks her jaw to try to open her mouth, but it does nothing.

When the door to the shack opens, she is ready for whatever the following moments hold for her. She has learned to accept her fate. To acknowledge her powerlessness. To embrace it even. She knows suddenly that living like this, on the run, has prepared her for this moment. Its inevitability has finally come to fruition.

She holds the sign out in front of her, and looks up at the figure in the doorway.

But even in the weak glow of the candle, she can see it is only a child. Just a girl. She looks as though she's only about ten or eleven years old. She has long dark hair pulled into a messy ponytail. Big eyes and tiny features. Nessa suddenly feels the fear, the wild thumping rattling fear, begin to melt. It is candle wax, dripping hot down her throat and into her stomach.

"Who are you?" the little girl asks, not moving any closer. "What are you doing here?"

And here is the question, the one with all the words. (All those unspoken words, like beads collected in a jar. A million glass beads, each one a moment from her life until now, but jumbled inside her. She lost the ability a long time ago to string the words together. The last time she tried, the string that held them together snapped, and the beads, the words, slipped off the string, tumbled back into chaos. And she was left with this.)

Nessa shakes her head.

"Here," the girl says, slowly coming closer and then sitting down on the floor across from Nessa. Indian style, as though they are only sitting by a campfire. As though they are Girl Scouts. "I have some candy."

She reaches into her pocket and pulls out three Tootsie Rolls, which she holds out to Nessa as though she is some sort of wild animal. Nessa reaches for them tentatively and then squeezes them in her hand. They are warm. She unwraps one of the candies and puts it in her mouth. She doesn't chew but rather lets the sweetness fill her mouth, which floods with saliva. It is somehow both satisfying and completely unfulfilling. Her body responds to this small bit of nourishment by reasserting its hunger. The baby kicks hard as the burst of sugar reaches it. And then her stomach growls, hungrily, angrily. Demanding more. She wonders about starvation, if because of the baby the length of time before she begins to starve is half. Or is it exponential? She imagines it like a math problem. She considers cells multiplying, while strangely her body divides.

"You can't talk?" the girl asks.

Nessa shakes her head.

"Can you hear?" the girl asks.

Nessa nods.

"There's a girl at my school who can't talk, but it's because she's deaf."

Nessa unwraps the second candy and puts it into her mouth, the baby kicks again, this time hitting her bladder. She needs to pee. She puts her finger out as though to say, "Wait here," and the little girl nods. She rises to her feet, and the pain in her foot is blinding. She starts to see stars and reaches for the wall to steady herself.

The girl scrambles to her feet and offers her her arm. "Are you hurt?" she asks.

Nessa nods again and leans against her, tears starting to fill her eyes.

"My dad can't walk. He's in a wheelchair. I help him all the time. I know what to do," she says, though Nessa hasn't offered her a single word.

The girl guides her as she hobbles out the door. Nessa motions with her chin that she's okay and that the girl should go back into the cabin. The girl releases her and Nessa makes her way along the side of the cabin and pulls up her skirt to pee. The sound of her urine echoes the sound of the river. The grass is wet from her pee, wet from the rain. She has nothing to wipe with but damp leaves. She struggles to get herself situated again and then hops back to the door where the girl is waiting for her and helps her back into the cabin.

"I can go get help," the girl says.

Nessa shakes her head.

The girl shrugs, but doesn't persist.

"Here," she says, handing her a pencil. "Make a list of what you need. I'll come back in the morning. Will you be okay until the morning?"

Nessa nods and takes the pencil from her.

She flips the paper over and thinks about what she needs. It is overwhelming. The words come like a hailstorm, and she scribbles and scribbles until her wrist aches with the effort. She hands the list, this odd poem, to the girl and the girl says, "Okay, okay. We have all that."

She has written *Bread, milk, cheese, apples, meat* on this list. *Tylenol, ice, bandages.* She doesn't show her the other list, the one with his name, with his phone number, with all the other things she yearns for. Not yet.

"Are you sure you'll be okay? You could come with me, you know, to my house," the girl says, but even as she offers this kindness, Nessa senses a hesitancy. A pause and uncertainty. And so she shakes her head, no. She has learned the nuances of generosity. The limits.

The girl stands to leave, and studies the list again.

"You're having a baby," she says, as though simply to acknowledge this obvious truth.

Nessa nods and the baby reaffirms this fact by kicking her in the ribs. She winces with the sharp pain of it.

"Okay," the girl says, and then she is gone.

The candle has burned down, the flame is out. Nessa is alone again with only her hunger to keep her company. She tries to get comfortable in the nest she's made with her sleeping bag on the floor. But as she drifts into that strange place between wakefulness and sleep, she worries that she is delirious, hallucinating, that she has only dreamed this little girl. That she is simply a figment of her imagination.

Sylvie stands at the edge of the yard listening to her own voice as it echoes Ruby's name. And then she listens as the sound of Ruby's footsteps recedes in the distance. She thinks about running after her, but her legs refuse. Her whole body refuses. Her will is no match for her body's stubborn refusal.

Her only comfort is that Ruby knows these woods. She and Jess were practically born in them. From the time they were little, they claimed them as their own. Sylvie used to joke that they were feral children, more animal than human. For the first few years here, they didn't even wear clothes, attired instead in mud and grass, twigs in their hair and leaves on their bodies. They disappeared into the woods and came out again only when she called them for dinner. It was their playground. Their world. But even as she finds a small solace in the fact that Ruby is no stranger to the woods, she cannot forget that there is someone else out there. There is someone close who wants something from her. No matter how hard she tries to explain it away: the broken bulb, the trampled garden, the loud crash and the scurrying away, the fact remains that they are not alone. And now Ruby is running right into the darkness. Headlong into danger. It feels as though she's doing this on purpose. To test Sylvie. To see what it will take to get her to finally leave the house.

It kills her. This cruelty. Ruby knows that she is powerless, that she cannot go. That this house has a magnetic pull, an invisible tether. It makes her think of Foster, and that awful run that Robert installed. The dog running up and down the same path all day every day. And the horrible way it would snap him back if he tried to test it, to go farther. She used to hate that, watching him get excited about a rabbit or a squirrel — the way he'd forget he was chained up and would shoot out toward the animal only to be choked back in, nearly strangled to death if he persisted. She remembers the wincing sound, the whimpering that would follow. The anguish of both the frustration and the pain.

She stands in the backyard waiting for

something, anything, for nearly ten minutes. In the floodlight, she feels as though she is standing on a stage, unable to see a single face in the audience, as they wait for her to deliver her first line, to do something. Anything.

When the phone rings, it sends shock waves through her whole body, but it also confuses her. It is such a foreign sound, like something from a half-forgotten dream. She looks toward her house, as though trying to decipher the sound coming from inside. *The phone.* Maybe it's Ruby. Maybe she's gone far enough away from the house that she has reception in her phone. She tries to imagine she's just gone to Hudson's up the road, that she's on the phone, sipping on a Coke she's gotten from one of their coolers. That she's eating penny candy by the handful.

She rushes to the counter and picks up the receiver. It feels heavy in her hands as she presses it against her ear.

"Syl?" *Robert.*

"Hi," she says. She sits down, her legs shaky underneath her.

"How is everything?" he asks. "Ruby?"

She nods. She can't lie to him. "She's angry," she says. She tries to picture him on the other end of the line. His callused hands

235

holding the phone, his kind face changed in the last year, laugh lines becoming worry lines.

"At me?" he asks softly, and her throat grows thick at his assumption that he has somehow done something wrong.

"No," she says, feeling terrible that she has allowed him to feel even one moment of guilt. "At me."

"Listen, Syl," he says then, and he sounds the way he sounds when he is about to deliver bad news. She knows this tone of voice better than she should. It was the same voice she heard the day he said he was taking Ruby to move in with Bunk. It was the same voice he used when he told her he'd forgotten how to love her.

"The storm is expected to hit here by the weekend. I don't know how soon we're going to be able to get back. They're talking about closing the bridge to the mainland down. We could be delayed. And there's a good chance we won't have power, which means my cell phone might go out. But we're safe. I don't want you to worry."

She almost laughs. Telling her not to worry is like telling the sky not to be blue. Like telling the rain not to fall.

"Can I talk to Ruby?" he asks.

She pauses. Should she tell him? What

would be the point? What can he do? He's
stuck on an island in North Carolina.
Stranded. It's not as thought the truth is
going to help him. It's not as though he can
do anything. But she has never been able to
lie to him. Not even when the lies were less
painful than the truth.

"She's run off to the woods. But I'm sure
she'll be back. She's just angry with me."

There is nothing but an awful silence at
the end of the line.

"Jesus, Sylvie. Why didn't you say something? How long has she been gone? Have
you gone to look for her?"

His words are like a barrage, like gunfire.
She ducks her head as though she can
escape. But every single one feels like an accusation. And worse, deserved.

"I . . ." she starts, but what can she
promise? What can she offer him anymore?

Just then, the back door opens, and Ruby
walks in. Her face is red, and her eyes are
swollen.

"She's back," she says into the phone.
"I'm sorry. Everything's fine. She's here."

She drops the phone and goes to Ruby.
She grabs her shoulders first, as though she
wants to shake her, but then she just pulls
her in close and ignores the way Ruby's
body stiffens. The way it refuses to yield.

She doesn't care; because she is back. She is home. She is safe.

■ ■ ■ ■

# THURSDAY

■ ■ ■ ■

In the morning Ruby packs her bag with all the items from the girl's list. She has not spoken to her mother since last night. She is already learning from the girl, the one who is waiting for her in the woods, the power of silence.

Last night after she got home, her mother tucked her into bed, stroked her hair, whispered her apologies until Ruby's eyes were heavy with sleep. But Ruby didn't say a word. She didn't have to. Her running away had provided everything she needed to say. Now she offers her mom only a few words, and she has no choice but to accept them.

"I'm not going to swimming lessons today. I have to work on my school project. I'll be home later." Her mother looks at her with those sorrowful eyes, and so Ruby offers, "I'll be safe. I promise."

Ruby makes sandwiches, slathering slices

of bread with mustard and mayonnaise. Heaping piles of deli meat and thick slabs of sharp cheddar cheese. She wraps the sandwiches and fills baggies with crackers and cookies and dried fruit. She empties the box of granola she finds in one cupboard into a Tupperware container and pours milk into a Thermos. She closes the bathroom door and raids the medicine cabinet for something that might help the girl. Tylenol, an Ace bandage. She fills a baggie with ice.

Her mother is consumed with the evisceration of a plover she found in the bushes this morning. Its black belly is splayed open, its guts bleeding into a blanket of newspaper on the table. It makes Ruby's stomach turn.

"I think maybe we should call Animal Control about the babies. In case the mother isn't coming back," Ruby says.

"I don't know if today is a good day," her mom says, shaking her head, and this makes Ruby bristle. Why does it matter? Why can't she just be ready for visitors? Why can't she just take care of things like a normal mother? "I just mean, maybe tomorrow would be a better day."

And Ruby wonders what her logic is. Each day here is the same as the last. Each day is equal. Each day is identical to the one before it and the one that will come after.

Her mother depends on this monotony, this safety in similarity.

"The trap is gone, which means the mother might be hurt. The babies will die without her," Ruby says. Why can't her mother understand this? "They need to come get the babies. Somebody needs to take care of them."

Her mother sighs and looks out the window at the porch where the baby raccoons are stirring. "They seem okay," she says.

"God, Mom, we can't have animals living on the porch. Don't you get it?" Ruby is angry again. It feels like she is always angry now, as if the bitter sadness she usually feels around her mother has turned into pure rage. She clenches her fists and then resumes packing her bag.

"Is it something I can help you with?" her mother tries again. "This project? Is it something we could work on together?"

Ruby almost laughs. And this makes her sad. When did the idea of her mother helping her with anything become ludicrous? When did the idea of her being a regular mom go out the window? Did it happen that night when Jess died? Or did it happen before? She can't remember anymore. It doesn't matter.

"No," she says. And she doesn't even

bother with the nicety of an explanation.

"Really, if you just tell me what it is . . ." her mother starts.

But she just heaves her pack onto her back and walks out the back door, letting it slam shut. It echoes like a gunshot, like something more violent than it is.

She can feel her mother's eyes on her through the window as she walks away.

Her body still buzzing with anger, she kicks at the loose fence wall again, the wood relenting and splintering.

Her mother opens the back door and says, "Ruby?"

Ruby turns to her. Her mother's arms are wrapped around her waist, and her face looks sad. Ruby's throat feels thick. If she doesn't go now, she never will.

"I'll be home in a little bit," she says.

"Okay," her mother says, nodding. "Be safe."

It is windy today, the wind is howling through the tops of the trees. It sounds like a woman moaning, like an animal. Ruby looks up as though she might be able to locate the origin of that keening. But there is only blue sky, green leaves, and pressing sunlight. There is no sign of rain, of a storm. She makes her way to the river's edge.

■ ■ ■ ■

In her research, Ruby has learned about all
the world's great bridges, those made of
wood and steel and stone. But she has also
learned about the imaginary ones, the ones
made of dreams and fear. In many religions,
there is a bridge that exists between the
world of the living and the world of the
dead. In Zoroastrianism, this is the Chinvat
Bridge. When a soul dies, it must cross this
bridge. And depending on the person's life,
it will appear differently to each person who
crosses it. For someone who has been
wicked, the bridge is narrow, and fraught
with demons who will drag them from the
bridge. If the person has led a good life, the
bridge will be wide and offer safe passage
from one realm to the next. There is a
similar bridge in the Muslim religion as
well. It is called the As-Sirāt, and it is thin
and razor sharp. For those who have not led
righteous lives, the fires of Hell below the
bridge make their passage impossible. But
for those who have been good, their passage
is expedited, and they are able to cross the
bridge quickly to reach Hauzu'l-Kausar, the
lake of abundance or paradise. Ruby thinks
about bridges between this world and

245

whatever exists beyond this one. She likes to imagine that when you pass from this life to the next, that there is a structure, a place that will keep you safe as you pass. She thinks about kindness and evil.

She runs and leaps, not needing a bridge here at this narrow place between worlds. It is easy, this passing from the island her mother has made to the rest of the world. And she wonders if it's because this is the opposite of these stories, of these myths. Because here she crosses from the land of the dead to the land of the living.

Right after the accident, nobody worried about Sylvie wanting to stay at home. People could understand her fear of driving, of getting in a car even. They gave her her space. Room to grieve and to breathe. But months went by, winter came, and still she wouldn't go anywhere unless she absolutely had to.

She couldn't work, couldn't listen to the urgency in the women's voices as they waited for their babies to come, the excitement and the fear. She used to pride herself on being able to measure how dilated a woman was simply by talking to her on the phone, but now their voices only reminded her of what could be lost. She could no longer make that long trek toward uncertainty in the middle of the night; she realized how many times she had tempted fate and felt both fortunate and foolish. And so the women who had counted on her to bring their babies safely into the world stopped calling. Rumors circulated, she was sure, that she'd had a breakdown. That she'd lost her marbles. But what they couldn't understand was that it wasn't *grief* that confined her. It wasn't her sadness or sorrow that made her shun the rest of the world. They didn't know that seclusion began long before Jess and Ruby were even born.

People wonder if she is lonely. This is what Gloria would ask when she still came by. "Aren't you lonely?" she would say, fear and tenderness and frustration in her eyes. But the answer wasn't simple. Perhaps the question should be, rather, are you *lonelier*?

Yes, she lives a secluded life here. Indeed, she has opted to cloister herself in this small house by the river, but is she any more isolated than she once was? Probably from an outsider's perspective. The prevailing assumption is that if one is surrounded by people that one is not alone. But even then, even all those years when she was never physically by herself, she was beginning to feel the chasm growing between her and the rest of the world. It was like a small tear in the seam of a dress, a certain pulling away. A ripping. And once it started, there was no stopping it. Of course, she tried so hard to keep it together, to tether herself to the world. She filled her life with people. With friends and family. But even then she knew that the mere presence of people in one's life cannot eliminate the terrifying sense of one's aloneness in the world. Being surrounded by people is not the same as connection. As friendship. As love. When Robert came along, she believed for a little while that she had found the answer, the bridge that crossed the deep canyon. And the children too became links between herself and normalcy. The accident didn't start it, it just proved the faultiness, the tenuousness of these connections.

But that bridge is gone now. Robert and Ruby are gone. Jess is gone.

And so *yes,* she is lonely. She feels that ragged tear where she once ripped herself away from the rest of the world every day, though its violence has faded into a dull aching reminder. But she is not any lonelier than she was before she sequestered herself.

There is no verb form for the word *recluse.* There is only the noun. And it is she. A woman who is tired of being terrified and finds little solace, even in the confines of her own home. *Reclude.* That is a verb, but it is the exact opposite of what it sounds like. To reclude means to open. To *un*close.

*Recluse. Reclude.* A door that swings two ways. One way opens to the world. And the other shuts it away.

The girl listens to Nessa.

For the first time in so long (months, years, lifetimes?) someone seems to hear her. To *want* to hear her anyway. Because the words remain trapped inside. But this little girl sits patiently, her face as wide open as a flower, and Nessa wonders if she might wait forever to hear what it is that she has to say.

The girl came to her with a backpack filled with food. She offered Nessa sandwiches, grapes sweet and plump on their branches. She held the Thermos to her lips and helped her drink, as though she were a child herself. The milk ran down her chin as she gulped and gulped. It was cold and thick and delicious.

She is still ravenous, each bite inspiring her hunger rather than appeasing it. She feels like she could eat forever. Her mouth fills with a flood of tastes: salty turkey, sharp cheese, sweet tomatoes. The bread is thick and soft and good. She eats cookies and a dark ripe plum. Drinks more milk, wipes her face with the back of her sleeve.

"My name is Ruby," the girl says finally, when Nessa takes a break from gorging herself. Breathless from the wild chewing and swallowing. She offers Nessa her hand and Nessa looks at it in wonderment.

Her whole life has been made up of hands. People have always wanted to touch her. "The way you want to touch a painting in a museum," her mother used to say. At first she said this with pride, but later she said it with a hint of something else. Something bitter. By the time she was a teenager, her mother seemed disgusted by it, by this need Nessa inspired in people.

Even as a child, she remembers people touching her. Her hair, mostly. Gripping her chin. Touching her back and tickling her feet. As she grew older, people were more able to control this impulse, knowing that it was less acceptable to reach out and stroke the hair of a young woman than it was a little girl. But she could see it in their eyes, this desire, this urge to hold on. Because beauty is an elusive thing. It comes and goes. She has always understood that it is fleeting, and she doesn't blame those who

252

wanted to capture it. She pities them instead for believing that the ephemeral can somehow be contained. She, of all people, knows this is a foolish endeavor. But here is this girl reaching out for her, though oddly she seems to want nothing in return.

"My mother lives in that house, the one across the river," she says.

Nessa nods. The house where she hurt her foot, where she stole vegetables.

The girl pops a grape into her own mouth and chews solemnly. She reaches into the backpack again and pulls out a bottle. She unscrews the top and shakes two pills into her tiny palm. "Here, take these," she says, handing her the pills and the Thermos of milk. "It's just Tylenol. It will make your foot feel better."

Nessa accepts the pills, remembers vaguely the list of things she is not supposed to eat, drink, or swallow because of the baby. No sushi, no alcohol, no aspirin. She pops the two dry pills in her mouth and swallows them with another cold rush of milk.

"Do you want me to help you with your foot?" the girl asks.

Nessa nods. Because of the baby, she can barely even see her feet anymore. She tried to examine the damage the trap had done, but felt light-headed when she bent over.

She knows that it is cut, swollen. Damaged, maybe even broken.

"I took a first aid class at school," Ruby says. "It was just for PE, so I don't really remember much. I mean, I can do this. But I probably couldn't do CPR or anything."

Nessa sits with her feet out in front of her, and the little girl slips off her thick sock. The entire top of her foot is swollen, and her toes look like sausages too. Her toenails are long. She can't remember the last time she clipped them. Her ankles are filthy and there is thick sludge between her toes. She is embarrassed, but the girl does not even flinch. Instead, she pulls a bag of ice from the magical backpack. Most of it has melted, but it still feels wonderfully cold on Nessa's foot, which seems to be radiating heat now, even without the thick wool sock on.

"Your big toe is cut a little bit," Ruby says. "I brought some first aid cream and a Band-Aid. But I think they might be broken. I don't know how to fix that."

Nessa looks at the little girl tending to her feet and is overwhelmed with gratitude. With bewilderment. Where did this child come from? Who sent her here? She wants to ask her questions. She is curious about so many things. If she could, she would ask her why she looks so sad. Because despite the fact that she is still just a child, her face and eyes look older. Wiser and more wounded and wearied than they should. She would like to ask her what happened that changed her. But as she wraps the Band-Aid around her toe and then a soft Ace bandage around her foot, it's as though she is swaddling her, and the words are also wrapped somewhere inside.

It is quiet inside the shack, though outside there is a bird calling over and over again, its overture ignored. Still, it shrieks out again and again, as though mere repetition will demand a response.

The girl hands Nessa a handful of dried apricots, and she puts them in her mouth. The fruit is thick and sweet.

"My brother died," the little girl says suddenly, as though Nessa has actually spoken the words she's been thinking. "He was only seven."

Nessa's eyes widen.

"My mom is really sick, she won't leave the house, but my dad wants us to move away. And my best friend is mean now. *Really* mean."

Nessa battles the tears that are welling up in her eyes. She remembers the waitress at the diner. It couldn't be, she thinks. This couldn't *possibly* be the midwife's daughter?

"But I'm going to build a bridge," the girl says suddenly. And her face brightens. All that sadness seems, for a moment, to slip away. She reaches into her backpack and digs through one of the pockets. "Do you want to see?" she asks, and Nessa leans forward. This, this movement toward instead of away, her *Yes.*

"Look," she says, and suddenly her face and voice belong to that of a little girl again. An excited little girl. This is the sound of hope, Nessa thinks.

"This is the Ponte di Rialto in Venice. That's in Italy. Isn't it beautiful?"

Nessa leans forward again. *Yes.* Her fingers touch the photograph. The white stone bridge with the portico in the center. The impossible architecture of it. The beauty is astonishing.

"It burned once. And then it collapsed while people were watching a parade on it. But they rebuilt it again and again. Nobody expected it to last, but it's been used the last four hundred years. It's a miracle."

No, she thinks. *This is the miracle.* Right here.

She is Ruby's secret. This new friend. Her name is Nessa. She wrote that down for her. She doesn't know how she wound up in the woods behind their house, she only knows that she can't tell anyone she's there. That it's her job to protect her.

Ruby hates to leave her there alone and hurt, but she has to go into town before Izzy and Marcy get out of swimming lessons. She needs to get the plans she and Izzy made for the bridge. She can't do anything until she has the designs that Izzy started on the computer. Not if she wants to win the contest. She hopes that if she gets to her house early enough, that Gloria can help her.

She doesn't even bother going inside her mother's house again. She just goes around to the front yard, gets her bike, and rides away. She imagines her mother watching her as she pedals into the misty morning.

She squeezes her eyes shut for a second and thinks about the bird, its entrails bleeding through the morning paper.

The wind is furious today. It seems to be trying to knock her off of her bike. She thinks about her father, about the storm. She doesn't let herself imagine what will happen if their trip home is delayed, if she has to stay here once school starts. And then she realizes how selfish she is being. That her Uncle Larry's house could be in danger. They studied hurricanes in fifth grade. She remembers the pictures of all the destruction. She tries to recollect the science behind the devastation, the simple combinations that create a storm that wreaks such havoc.

When she gets into town, she rides past the entrance to the pool but doesn't even bother to look through the gates for Izzy. It's only ten, she and Marcy will be there for another half hour. She knows that they are probably giggling and sharing a towel in the chilly morning air. She imagines they are wearing their matching sunglasses from the fair yesterday. She needs to get to Gloria first.

She drops her bike in the driveway in front of Miss Piggy and then thinks that maybe she should pull it around to the back so Izzy doesn't know she's there. She walks it around Grover's car and leans it against the back fence railing. She can hear somebody in the kitchen, and so instead of going to the front of the house, she knocks tentatively on the back door.

"Ruby Tuesday!" Izzy's Dad, Neil, says, opening the door wide. He's still wearing his pajamas. Since school let out he's let his beard grow too, and he looks like Sasquatch. He's six and a half feet tall. He used to give her and Izzy rides on his shoulders, and they had to duck so they wouldn't hit their heads on the ceiling.

"Come in, come in," he says. "I just made some babies." He gestures to the giant Dutch pancakes that are his specialty. They look like cartoon pancakes, giant puffy things cooked in cast iron skillets. They are Ruby's favorite.

"Where's Izzy?" he asks. "You guys done with swim lessons already?"

She shakes her head and sits down on one of the stools at the counter, which is covered with junk mail and dirty dishes. "I quit swimming lessons."

"Oh," he says and slips a Dutch baby onto a plate. "I see." He pushes the plate in front of her. "Raspberries? I just picked them this morning."

She nods, and he drops a handful of berries onto the pancake and dusts it with powdered sugar. He hands her a jar filled with warm syrup, and she drizzles it over the pancake. She knows she should ask about the bridge plans and leave before Izzy gets back, but she is drawn to the familiarity and warmth of this kitchen.

"Are you meeting Izzy and Marcy?"

She shakes her head, and he scowls. He sits down next to her with his own pancake and smothers it in berries and sugar and syrup. He looks toward the doorway and then leans in conspiratorially. "If it's any consolation, I'm not much of a fan of Marcy Davidson's either."

She feels a smile creeping across her face despite herself, and she sighs.

"Ruby!" Gloria says, swinging the back door open. She's been in the shed throwing pots. She's wearing her overalls that are covered with clay and glaze. "They hardly even need me to stand up," she always joked.

"I know you don't have a TV up at your mom's, but have you listened to the news about the storm at all?"

"My dad called," she says. "They're getting ready for it."

Gloria grabs the newspaper off the counter

and flips through, searching for something. She gets to the weather and points at a map of the U.S., a comma-shaped orange-and-red-and-blue blob moving along the East Coast.

"They're expecting landfall this weekend. In the Carolinas and then moving up the coast. I hope they're not planning to drive through this mess," she says, shaking her head.

Ruby nods. And then she thinks about the girl in the shack. The shack whose roof is caved in. There's no way she can stay dry in there. For a moment she feels like she should say something to Gloria about her. To tell her about the girl. But then she stops herself. Nessa doesn't want anyone to know that she was there. She made that clear.

"I'm sure your uncle has been through this before. They'll be fine. But we're going to get some wet weather up here. Maybe even some flooding. Do you guys have any sandbags?"

Ruby takes a mental inventory of the shed. Plywood, tools, the broken lawnmower. "I don't think so."

"Well, I can get some extras and bring them up to your mom." She pauses. "Would that be okay? If I brought some by?"

Ruby is quiet. She thinks about the signs

261

her mom made, and the look on Gloria's face when she pulled up to the house last night.

"I'd like to see her," Gloria says.

Ruby nods and takes another bite of her pancake so she doesn't have to speak.

"I've got to turn the heat up on the kiln in about a half hour. But if you hang out, I can give you a ride back home and drop the sandbags at the same time. Sound good?"

It doesn't sound good, not at all, because in a half hour Izzy and Marcy will be back. But she doesn't have much of a choice. She stays in the kitchen with Gloria and Neil until she hears Izzy and Marcy coming through the front of the house. They are laughing as they enter the kitchen doorway, but when Marcy sees Ruby, she crosses her arms and frowns.

Izzy says, "Hi," and then stands there like she's found an alien at the counter eating her dad's Dutch babies instead of her oldest friend in the world.

"Hi," Ruby says, and then, because she knows that with Izzy's parents there she'll be safe, she says, "I just came by to get the bridge designs from your computer. I was hoping you could print them out."

Izzy's face goes white the way it always does when she's starting to panic.

Marcy says, "What bridge designs?"

"Um, Ruby and I were partners for the contest. Before, um . . ."

"Oh," Marcy says dismissively and rolls her eyes.

"Marcy and I have actually decided to be a team," Izzy starts, her face going from white to red, and she stutters. "You know, since she's staying here and everything. It's just easier, you know, like because she's already here and because it's coming up so soon."

"We were working on it all summer!" Ruby says, feeling anger welling up inside of her. "For two whole months. Those are *my* ideas."

Gloria says, "Maybe the three of you could be a team?"

Ruby shakes her head and looks to Neil for help, and he nods. "Izzy, you can't just take the plans you and Ruby worked on together. If you and Marcy are a team, then you have to start from scratch. But I don't really see why this is necessary, if you and Ruby have already done so much work . . ."

"Forget it!" Ruby says, and she feels like if she doesn't get out of the house, she's going to cry. "I'll just do it on my own. Take the stupid plans." She realizes that in eleven years, she's never ever yelled at Izzy. Not even once. It feels awful. It makes her whole body ache.

"No," Neil says, shaking his head. "Izzy, go print out what you've got right now."

But Ruby is already grabbing her backpack and walking out the back door, wondering how this all backfired and where she should go from here. She hears their muffled voices inside and then Gloria is coming out the back and putting her arm around her. She resists but then leans into her, unable to refuse this small comfort.

"She's being terrible," Gloria says. "I'm so sorry. I'll talk to her."

Ruby shakes her head. "Why? It's not going to change her mind. You can't change people's minds." And suddenly she is overwhelmed by a sense of powerlessness. She thinks about her dad wanting to move them away, about her mom refusing to leave the house, about Izzy and Marcy. People will do what they want to do. There's nothing you can do to stop it. And now, here is Gloria wanting to go see her mom.

Gloria picks up Ruby's bike and puts it in the back of her truck. "We'll stop by the hardware store and get some sandbags on the way. Okay?" And because Ruby knows that nothing she says matters at all anymore, she just nods. And as they drive out of town toward the hardware store, she tries to imagine the sort of bridge Marcy Davidson would come up with. She'd probably want to bedazzle it. Ruby thinks of her sparkly cell phone cover, and snorts. Marcy Davidson is about the worst partner Izzy could possibly choose. She cheats off her neighbor's papers and even copies during art. She's got about as many original ideas as that mama raccoon.

The raccoon. Shoot! She still hasn't spoken to the people at Animal Control. But if the girl is the one who tripped the trap, then that means the mama raccoon is still out there somewhere. While she still has reception, she dials the number for Animal Control and explains about the trap, about the mother, the babies on the porch. They say they can't come out until tomorrow. When she hangs up, she leans against the window of the truck and watches the trees grow thick around them.

"I'll get you those plans, Ruby," Gloria says as they finish loading sandbags into the back of the truck. "I'm so sorry she's being such a pill."

"Whatever," Ruby says. "It was a stupid idea anyway."

Sylvie hears the truck pull up and peers through the shade. It's Gloria. The passenger door of the truck swings open, and Ruby gets out. And for a moment, she fears that something has happened. Why else would Gloria be bringing Ruby home? But there is Ruby, and she is fine. She is safe. Gloria goes to the back of the truck, lowers the tailgate, and unloads Ruby's bicycle. Then she starts unloading bags of something, carrying them to the side of the house.

Ruby opens the front door without knocking. She simply slips her key into the lock and turns the knob. It always stuns Sylvie how simple entry can be.

"What is she doing?" Sylvie asks. "What's in the bags?"

"It's sand."

"Oh," Sylvie says, remembering the supplies sent by the grocery store, and peers out the window at the bright blue sky.

Gloria comes to the doorway again and stands at the threshold, as though uncertain if she should go any farther. "Hi Syl," she says.

Sylvie pauses and then reaches for her hand. "Come in," she says and forces herself to smile. "I'll make some tea."

She is aware of how ridiculous this is: her best friend, walking across the kitchen floor as though it is littered with glass. Gloria, who used to come into this kitchen and help herself. Who used to throw open the cupboards and refrigerator doors, who used to pluck cartons of ice cream from the freezer and eat straight from the container. Gloria who helped paint these very walls one Sunday afternoon. Who molded and shaped and fired the dishes that live inside the cupboards. Who has listened to every complaint, every bit of joy that Sylvie had to share at this table. Gloria, who has drunk gallons and gallons of tea in this very spot. And still, she doesn't belong here anymore.

Sylvie is trying so hard, but it feels like swimming upstream. She is so out of practice. She has forgotten the lovely rhythms and cadences of women's conversation. Of the pleasant silences. She has forgotten how to share a space, a story, a moment with another person. She feels clumsy and awkward and foolish.

"Ruby says Robert's down south visiting Larry?" Gloria asks, sitting down tentatively in one of the kitchen chairs, as though she doesn't trust its legs to hold her. "Is he worried about the hurricane?"

Sylvie nods. "He says they've evacuated a lot of houses on the island, but that he and Bunk are going to stick it out. Larry's dealt with this before. *Isabel,* I think. That was the last one."

Gloria fiddles with the sugar bowl that sits in the center of the table. "We're not supposed to get much here except some wind and a lot of rain. I'm worried though about you being so close to the river."

Sylvie thinks about the quiet stream that flows behind her house. It's hardly a river here. It's barely more than a creek. It is harmless.

"You could come stay with us for the weekend, you know," Gloria says hopefully. "It might be fun. We've got hurricane lamps if we lose power. It'd be nice to have all of us girls together."

And for a moment, Sylvie tries to imagine it. She dreams herself getting into the passenger seat of Gloria's truck, Ruby squeezed between them. She tries to imagine the bumps beneath her as they roll down the road. She tries to dream herself through the rickety front gate of their house, into the foyer where boots and sneakers all lie in a smelly heap. She tries to remember the feeling of the air inside, the scent of it. Clay and cinnamon and candle wax. And for a few strange moments, she thinks she could actually do it. She could just nod her head *yes,* pack a suitcase, and follow Gloria out the door. She could leap back into her old life, without more thought than she would stepping into the tub after a long day.

Gloria reaches across the table and takes Sylvie's hand. Sylvie looks at their hands together at the center of the table and for one moment is unable to differentiate between the two. They both have long fingers, slender wrists, though Gloria's hands are dark from a summer spent in the garden and her own are the color of milk. Gloria wears clunky silver and turquoise rings on nearly every finger, including her long, boney thumbs. Her hands are splattered with clay, and her watch battery is dead.

She dreams herself inside that kerosene lantern house, onto the front porch where they might sit together and watch the rain as it falls around them. And she tries to

269

remember how this feeling (of friendship, of sitting with another woman, another mother) used to be almost enough to make her feel safe. But then as Gloria squeezes Sylvie's hand, wanting, demanding, waiting and urging, her mind clicks, as it always clicks, into that strange overdrive. The engine in her chest restless and revving.

Here is what would actually happen if she were to walk out her front door to the truck. Once inside the cab of the truck, she would feel trapped. Watching the world buzz past her in the window would make her nauseated, turn her stomach, make her feel as though she can't breathe. But she would have to pretend that everything was okay, because why wouldn't everything be okay? Is she insane? And she'd feel like a fool asking to turn around and go home. And even once she was able to free herself from the confines of that truck, she'd suddenly be on display. She would belong, in a single moment, to the world, and the world would want from her. Grover wanting to hug her, Neil wanting to kiss both her cheeks. She already knows that her bones are not sturdy. She can't trust her legs to hold her up. (This is how it happened last year — that wild slow collapsing. It started at the ankles. It spread to the hips.) And Gloria would watch her and wonder what terrible mistake she'd made. And when the power went out, it wouldn't be coziness and comfort she would feel as Gloria flicked the key to the lamps and turned up the flames, but *fear*. Fear of fire. Of the crackle and hiss of the tiny flames. Fear of darkness. Of powerlessness. She wouldn't be able to sit with Gloria on the porch, on that beautiful broad porch where they used to share their secrets, their shames. Instead, she would start to tremble, the storm entering her body. She would be electrified, a rod collecting all the storm's energy, and she would become dangerous.

She can't bear the frustration, the humiliation, the terror. She can't bear that she has failed in every conceivable way: as a wife, as a mother, as a friend. She is pathetic and she knows that at some point Gloria will understand this, and then there will never be a moment like this again, a moment when Gloria looks her in the eyes and really believes that she can be saved. That she is even worth saving.

As if sensing the danger lurking underneath her skin, running through her veins like something toxic, Gloria releases her hand. She has given Sylvie all the time she has, with only so much patience for her reticence, for her resistance.

"I guess I can't make you leave," Gloria says, shrugging her shoulders, and Sylvie senses a hint of anger in Gloria's voice. Of frustration. Of resignation. Perhaps Sylvie was wrong; Gloria has *already* given up on her. What was she thinking? She is a lost cause.

"Would you at least like me to bring Ruby to my house for the weekend?"

Sylvie's eyes sting, and all of a sudden it feels not like Gloria is making a generous offer but rather challenging her. Saying, *I am better than you at this. Ruby deserves better. Than you. Than this.* It makes Sylvie's shoulders stiffen, her chin jut forward in defiance.

"We're fine," a voice says. But it's not her own. It's Ruby, standing in the doorway now.

"Are you sure, honey?" Gloria asks, as though she's the mother. As though she's the only one capable of taking care.

"We're fine," Sylvie echoes, sensing this is what Ruby needs right now. That this is what she's asking for, and Sylvie wants to give it to her. And somehow, for this sliver of a moment they are allies. They are in this together: a team, soldiers in the same war. But then just as quickly, Ruby slips away, slinks from the doorway and down the hall.

Sylvie and Gloria listen as her door closes shut.

"Let me know if you change your mind," Gloria says, rising from the table. "I put the sandbags out in the driveway. I can help you put them up against the back of the house . . ."

"That's okay. Ruby can help me," Sylvie says. "Thank you."

Sylvie stands up and moves toward Gloria. She opens her arms, tentatively, and Gloria's eyes fill. Sylvie leans into her, squeezing her own eyes shut at the familiar smell of clay and Gloria's shampoo. The hug briefly, awkwardly, and then Gloria pulls away, wiping at her eyes with the back of her wrist.

"You call me if you need anything. I can come get you. It's not a problem," she says.

And Sylvie nods.

As Gloria walks out the front door, Sylvie feels an impossible urge, the improbable urge, to change her mind. To just follow her. To go. To *let* Gloria take care of her. To ride out the storm together in that big safe house. But it is too late. It is always, always just a few strokes of time too late. And so instead she reaches for Gloria and squeezes her hand. "I'm sorry," she says. It's all she has left. Apologies for what she has become.

Now that she has been discovered, Nessa worries that it is only a matter of time until Ruby tells someone that she's here. Nessa trusts her, yes, but she is still only a child. Nessa tries not to think about what will happen to her if she is caught. To the baby. She's been on the run for almost two years now; she knows she can't run forever. And she still has two months until she is eighteen. Before she can stop feeling as though she is being hunted. She should be running *away* from here, she knows this, but the pull of this place is almost too strong to resist. Even though there was safety in distance, safety in the miles she put between herself and her past, between herself and the night she left here, she knows that nothing could be forgotten or forgiven until she came home.

*Home.* Again, that silly word. What does that mean now with both her grandfather and her mother gone? It's simply the last place where she had a bed she didn't share with anyone else. The last place where she had a schedule, a routine, places to be, where she had a semblance of a life.

Her mother had brought her back here, to get her out of the city, as though things might be different. She seemed to think they could become different people here, as though they could both change. Even with her grandfather gone, it seemed like maybe her mother had been right. That this was exactly what they had needed. But it only took one night spent out at the bar instead of in front of the TV before her mother brought someone home with her. Before *two* became *three* again. Before everything was exactly the same as it used to be. It didn't matter that they were here, that they were home.

It wasn't so long ago, but the memories are hazy. All of it like some sort of underwater dream, filtered through a watery lens. Her bedroom in that apartment above the salon was a tiny room off the kitchen; this she remembers. Her mother's new boyfriend, Rusty, liked to eat bacon sandwiches for breakfast. And so she awoke to the crackle and hiss and strong scent of bacon frying every morning. That and the smell of weed. Her mother worked second shift at the Cumberland Farms, and so she slept in most days. Those mornings Nessa and Rusty moved side by side, soundlessly in the kitchen as she got ready for school, and he got ready for whatever it was that he did. She never really knew. He worked off and on, but mostly he was a fixture in their apartment, joint in hand, Xbox on the TV, a bobbing head. A scruffy beard. The funk of a dirty towel in the bathroom. And it was only a matter of time before her mother started using again as well. She tried to hide it at first, but, as always, gave up these efforts to conceal the obvious.

And so Nessa stayed away. She slipped away before her mother woke up each morning and came home late at night when she was at work. She tried to ignore the mounting evidence on the coffee table, in the trashcans, in her mother's rheumy eyes.

She might never have found him if she hadn't been looking for somewhere else to go. She knows now she was drawn to him not out of desire, but out of necessity.

Nessa met Declan at school.

He came to talk to her English class about poetry; he was a real-life poet. He had an accent, though it was faint. It just played

276

with the edges of his words. It was the accent of someone whose parents were immigrants. Just an inherited slant to the words. Almost imperceptible. But Nessa, who barely spoke herself even then, was keenly aware of the patterns of other people's speech. It became more pronounced as he read his poetry from the paperback chapbook he brought, the one he kept shoved in his back pocket. She remembered thinking that was an odd way to treat your own words, as though they were printed on a takeout menu or a Xeroxed program for a school play. A lot of things about him made her think he was careless. She should have known.

She recalls tree bark, the scrape of it against her back. When he found her after school that day, sitting under the tree where she liked to read, he'd come so close, she'd pressed her back against the bark. He'd been eager like that from the beginning. She was unaccustomed to this forwardness; it frightened her. But even as she began to walk away from him, mumbling something about going home (*home,* that meaningless word), instead of letting her go, instead of watching her walk away like all the other hungry boys would have done, he'd moved to walk with her. This had startled her, but made her wonder if he might be different somehow. If she didn't have the same sort of power over him that she seemed to have over the others.

He might have sensed that she was lying, because as they walked, he didn't ask her where they were going (she didn't know). And he didn't look confused, bemused, when she walked him in circles, stopping right in front of that same tree an hour later. He only shook her hand, and said, "If you'd like to give me some of your writing to look at, I'd be happy to take a peek."

And this, this more than that wild longing in all the other boys' eyes, was what made her nod. He wanted her *words*. He had asked for her voice. He cared about what she had to say, not just the way her lips moved around the words.

He didn't come back to the school again. But she met him every single day that fall. She watched the seasons change through the windows of his beat-up Honda, the one whose headlights sometimes failed, and through the windows in the drafty converted barn where he lived.

Because she didn't get home from work until nearly midnight and slept until ten or eleven every morning, her mother also didn't notice that Nessa wasn't sleeping in her own bed anymore. Her mother didn't notice the marks on her neck, the plum-colored bruises from where he sucked at her throat, as though he could heal her voice, a leech bleeding out the poison. Her unfocused eyes weren't trained on Nessa anymore, only on Rusty and whatever Rusty brought home for her. Whatever vials and baggies littered the secondhand coffee table.

Most mornings, Declan would drop her off a block away from the school, and she could still smell him on her as she walked through the fallen autumn leaves to school. She didn't have any friends. Not a single girlfriend to tell about the way they slept curled around each other like slugs in the barn loft, like runaways, in the drafty building.

Perhaps she was practicing even then.

She also had no one to tell about the way he refused to kiss her or even look at her as he fucked her. She had no one to tell, no words to explain the way he sometimes wanted her to do things that made her feel ashamed. That sometimes those things hurt her.

And so she got out of his car each morning, a block away from school, as though he were just her dad (though he wasn't quite old enough to be her dad) and walked alone, in the cold silent autumn mornings, to school.

He was careless. Careless with her, careless with his words. He never thought beyond the next sentence. Perhaps this is a poet's way, she thought. To worry about life one moment at a time, one line. Never seeing the stanza until it forms. The shape of the poem creating itself, *accidental.*

He treated her like a child, a little girl. But then again, she *was* a little girl, wasn't she? She couldn't remember anyone ever telling her that she'd grown up. She still wore her hair in two pigtails. She still slept with a teddy bear on the nights when she did go home. She still liked to drink chocolate milk and watch cartoons and she preferred to sleep with a light on. It was as though only her body had transformed, and even then, she didn't really look like a woman, but just some sort of approximation of a woman. And she certainly didn't feel grown.

He was careless, because, in the end he didn't care. Not really. He was made up of words, but behind the words was nothing. He was nothing but a bunch of pretty syllables and sounds. He was assonance and consonance, a meticulously metered line, reliant only on rhythms designed to please the ear. But the words themselves, all those pretty words, were meaningless.

She might have left anyway. She might have fled into the darkness, directionless save for the vague notion of getting *away*. She can't say now whether everything that happened that night precipitated her departure or simply expedited it. It doesn't matter really. What matters is what happened.

It sits in a quiet corner of her mind like a naughty child, sequestered to an endless sentence of time out. This memory, like so many of the others. The room where she keeps them made not of walls, but only of corners. Of angles, of shadows providing dark places where the punishing thoughts reside. She has never spoken of that night, because after that night she stopped speaking altogether, her voice lost. Or stolen. Does it matter? It seems the most precious lost things are beyond retrieval now.

She ran away from him, but it didn't matter; there were so many others. They blur together now. The boy she sat next to on the bus on her way out of town (the college boy with the soft sweatshirt and cold hands) the one who shared her overhead light because his was broken, the one whose thick tongue probed inside her mouth as though searching for something he'd lost. The guy she met in the motel swimming pool, the one whose father owned the motel. The one who took her to the rooftop and set off firecrackers that made her ears ache and her eyes sting with their beautiful explosions. The man who gave her the job doing dishes in exchange for a room to stay in a stucco building behind his house. She was cold that night; the space heater was on the fritz. And so she'd gone to him, and he'd let her into his warm bed. The others are just a collection of vague details: grass-stained jeans, tanned feet, a canvas tent, music at an outdoor concert. The taste of greasy Carmex, of peppermint, of coffee and clove cigarettes. Naked skin and sinewy muscles. Short flat fingernails and cheeks as rough as sand. When she remembers the journey across the country to LA and then up to Portland, it is the men she remembers, but they are a blur of hands and hips. Lips and throats. All of it twisted into dirty sheets riddled with cigarette burns like bullet holes. And then there was Mica.

He found her in the park, like a feral kitten, and brought her to the big falling-down house with the slanted floors and tall, cracked windows. The house with the living room that was so cavernous and empty you could roller-skate there. The place where people came and went, where the attic was filled with pot plants growing under humming buzzing lights. The hydroponic lullaby bringing the deepest sleep she'd had in years. Since she was a little girl. *Home?*

But then later as her belly began to grow, as she swelled (with happiness, with love, with this life inside of her), she could feel Mica slipping away. Rolling away from her hands as they tried to hold on. Sitting too close to the new girl who joined them for dinner that one night when Ryan made mutton stew. Dancing too closely with Francesca (Jessica, Monica) at the concert in the park, while she sat, her belly like a giant anthill, like a dormant volcano, like an impassable mountain. He became every other man, just a fading recollection, an impression leaving only the vague scent of patchouli and grass and sex on her hands.

The thing about silence is that instead of explanations, instead of questions, instead of pleading or complaining or yelling, your only option is *doing.* Saying is one thing, but without words to fall back on you are required to act. Silence necessitates action to get your point across. And so instead of demanding to know who had left that black hair on her white soap in their shower, instead of begging him to love her and his baby, instead of yelling at him, chastising him, unleashing her fury in a meaningless string of syllables, she said nothing. She simply got out of the shower, wrung the water from her hair, put on a clean sundress, put the rest of her clothes in her backpack and stole his pitiful stash of cash. And then soundlessly left. Her departure the quiet period at the end of this particular sentence. He would have to read her absence in the empty drawer.

She'd reached the end of the world, or so it seemed, and good pinball that she was, her instinct was then to just go back. It was simple physics really, this rebounding. But she knew that heading back the way she had come also meant returning to the same merciless bumper that has sent her flying in the first place. This time she would ready herself. This time she would aim; she would move with purpose. With direction.

That night as her mother disappears into
the recesses of the house (Ruby hears the
water running into the tub, knows that she
will be there for at least an hour), Ruby
closes her bedroom door, fills her backpack
with food, water. A bar of soap, a flashlight
she found in the kitchen, a pillow. She stuffs
everything into her backpack and carefully
slips out the back door, like a thief, only
backwards. She is giving rather than stealing, breaking out rather than breaking in.

The air is strange, almost electrified. She
thinks about the storm that is coming and
about the bags of sand that Gloria has left
to keep them safe. She knows she should
move them against the back of the house,
that she and her mom should prepare. But
hurricane preparations seem silly on this
star-filled night. The sky is the color of a
ripe plum, it is warm, and the air hums with
possibility.

Ruby knows the girl wants to leave. She hasn't said a word, but Ruby can sense a restlessness in her eyes. As soon as her foot is better, she will go, make her way to wherever it is that she's headed. All of this she has communicated with nothing more than gestures. And her impending departure hits Ruby like a dull fist in the chest. There is something so comforting about her being out there. Taking care of her has given Ruby a sense of purpose. Without the bridge to build, without Izzy, without her father and Bunk, she has felt so alone. She wonders if this is what her mother feels like. This odd absence from the world. It is different than feeling out of place. It is more like feeling like you have become a shadow. Dimension-less. Inconsequential.

She walks through the brush, crushing twigs and leaves and other brush under her feet. She wonders if the girl can hear her. She calls out softly. "It's only me," she says.

The girl pushes open the door, and ushers her into the tiny dark room.

Ruby sits with her and silently watches as she eats. She uses both hands, stuffing her mouth and chewing loudly. She even growls a little, her body's response to the cheese and fruit. To the leftover chicken, the skin crisp and freckled with pepper. When she finishes, Ruby can see the slick grease on her lips. Crumbs across her big belly.

Ruby gestures toward the girl's foot, and she nods as though to say, "It's okay."

"I brought you some books," she says then, reaching into her backpack and pulling out the books she pilfered from her mother's shelf. When she selected them, she thought she was being helpful, but now as the girl scowls, she worries that she's made a mistake. *Mayo Clinic Guide to a Healthy Pregnancy. What to Expect When You're Expecting.* Nessa pushes them aside, shaking her head, and instead reaches for a worn paperback copy of *Bridge to Terabithia* that Ruby always keeps in her backpack. This is Ruby's favorite book, and from the look in the girl's eyes, it is hers as well. This makes Ruby smile. And as her smile widens, her face hurts. How long has it been since she's smiled? But despite the discomfort of her happiness, she continues to grin as the girl thumbs through the pages, nodding, touching her belly absently as she reads. She notices the girls lips move as she reads, like the kindergartners at school. And suddenly she realizes that this girl is not much older than she is. Despite the fact that she's going to have a baby, that she's all alone in the world. She needs to know how many years are between them.

"How old are you?" Ruby asks.

The girl looks up from the book, absently, as though she is being pulled from another world. She sets the book down and holds up both hands. Ten fingers. She closes them and reopens them, showing seven fingers this time. Seventeen. She's just six years older than Ruby. This is somehow both thrilling and terrifying to her.

"Do you want to see something?" Ruby asks, and Nessa nods.

She has brought the sketches of the bridge and now she shows the girl, who runs her fingertips, which are callused with filthy nails, across the drawings. She flips through the pages quickly, as though she is reading a catalogue and trying to pick out a dress or a new pair of shoes. She stops at the last page and presses the binding open so she can study it. She holds it close to her face, scrunches her nose and looks. Really looks.

This is the one that she hasn't shown to Izzy. The one that she has only dreamed of and hasn't shared. Izzy would say it was impossible: the one that, at first glance, defies all rules of physics. Only Ruby knows that it only *looks* impossible. And the illusion of unachievable construction, of architecture that relies somehow on magic rather than geometry, is exactly what she's been trying to achieve. Izzy, who is practical at best and annoyingly pragmatic at worst, would scoff at it. Would roll her eyes. And for the first time, looking at the bridge with this girl whose face is alight with wonder at what she's created, she feels a plunk of sadness. About Izzy. About what if their friendship is just *over*?

When the girl presses her hand against her belly, looking uncomfortable, shifting her weight, Ruby hands her the pillow she's brought and the girl puts it behind her back. The girl tilts her head, as though trying to figure something out. Her eyes are glossy. Ruby wonders what questions she is keeping inside. She reaches then into her bag, which lies next to her, and pulls out a slip of paper. It is folded into a tiny square, like the paper fortunetellers that she and Izzy used to make. She hands it to Ruby, presses it into her palm. And she knows with this gesture that she is asking for her help. That this piece of paper may be the most important thing in the world. And so Ruby looks at it. It's just a name, a man's name, and a phone number. A phone number she knows as well as her own. Ruby cocks her head, confused. She doesn't understand.

"Where did you get this?" Ruby asks,

wondering now if it's truly an accident that she's wound up here. That they've found each other.

But Nessa doesn't speak, and Ruby gingerly puts it in her own pocket.

Nessa leans against the broken wall of the shack, and Ruby turns off the flashlight. After a while the girl starts to drift off to sleep, and Ruby peers down at her. It strikes her that this is like some odd fairytale. She wonders, for just a quick second, whether the girl even exists or not. What moral there might be to this story. And how it will end.

She leaves reluctantly to go home. She knows that the girl won't stay here forever, that she has a reason for being here, and that reason is folded up inside that note in her pocket. That her job is to help her. And so, she feels strangely serene as she walks back toward her mother's house. Despite everything that's happened with Izzy, despite being worried about her dad, despite her mother, she feels like she has a mission now. A purpose.

The wind is really howling. It sounds like wolves. Like something wounded in the woods. She runs downstream until the river narrows and she is able to pass. It seems to be moving more quickly than usual, and when her foot dips into the water it rushes fast and cold over her foot, as if it has somewhere to go. She runs across the lawn toward the broken fence. The house is completely dark. She feels herself awash with relief. Her mother isn't awake, waiting to reprimand her, to demand to know where she was. She can slip back into the house, into her bed, unnoticed.

The hot bath makes Sylvie drowsy, and it is all she can do to dry herself off and put on her nightgown before crawling into the warm softness of her bed. She walks down the hall, sees the light under Ruby's door has gone out. She must have gone to sleep already. She said at dinner that she just wanted to go to bed early. She considers opening the door and checking on her, but she knows that sleep is a gift and doesn't want to steal that from her.

She agonizes over whether or not to take a pill tonight. The pills work well, *too* well. Sometimes, when she takes them, it feels as though she has fallen into a pit of quicksand. A well filled with sludge and mud and leaves. It is not sleep, but a sort of *death* she experiences when she takes the medication. But sometimes she has no choice. Sometimes, it is the only way to quiet her mind.

She senses that tonight might be one of those nights. Gloria's visit has reopened a wound. Once, several years ago, she cut her finger on an aluminum lid. The cut was thin but very deep. The slice healed quickly, surprisingly so. But even though it looked fine on the outside, it still ached inside. It was as though the tissues beneath the skin's surface were still damaged. Every time she bumped it on something, the pain nearly brought her to her knees.

She is worried about Robert as well. He is another wound that goes deeper than simple flesh. He is an ache that runs deeper inside her than almost any. Yet, they pretend for each other, for Ruby, that being apart is for the best. That the pain isn't bottomless. The wound festering under the fragile pink flesh that conceals it.

But her worry now is as vivid and real as it has ever been. She has tried to call his cell number, but it goes straight to voice mail. She has not been able to get much information from the radio, only that the storm should make landfall in the Carolinas tonight or tomorrow. She and Robert went there years ago when they were first married. Larry's house is just a few blocks from the ocean. When she closes her eyes she thinks of the footage of the tsunami in Asia, she worries about the hurricane carrying Robert and Bunk away. And she knows that this loss would be one she wouldn't survive. Because as long as Robert still breathes, there is hope. There is possibility of healing. Of *true* healing. Despite every bit of better judgment, she clings to this.

As she pulls back the sheets and climbs into the bed, she remembers the way he always made sure to face her when they fell asleep at night. She remembers his arm, pulling her close into his body, the strong clean smell of his skin, his callused hands running down her back. He never turned away until after she'd fallen asleep.

She tries and fails to turn off the flickering, skipping machine that is her mind. It makes her think of the old microfiche machines they used to have before the Internet. Every single night she scrolls backwards through the sepia recollections, moments blurring past and then coming suddenly into focus again. She tries not to linger too long on any of the images, just long enough to orient herself, but still, each of them causes deep pangs of regret and shame. The entire process just another exercise in self-loathing.

And so she reaches into the drawer and opens the bottle, tossing the pill down her throat like you might feed a pill to a dog. So that before she can second guess the decision, it is already gone.

There are strings pulling at her limbs; she is a marionette, a wooden doll. She can't seem to lift her eyelids though, those strings somehow unattached, or severed. Still, there is the sound of something against the far wall of her bedroom, and she knows that she must climb out of the well, must rise up from these impossible depths to acknowledge it. Her heart is pounding wildly inside her chest, but her legs and arms and neck will not comply.

Finally, through sheer will, she is able to sit up. The effort exhausts her further, though, and she can feel cold sweat running down her sides. And even as she is upright, her entire body feels weighed down, as though someone has poured cement down her throat, into her belly, filling her legs and arms. She is leaden. She has been rendered into stone.

The sound is under her window, the one

that faces the backyard. It is loud. Insistent. But also careful. Whoever is making the sound is trying to be quiet. They've come back. She wishes she had left the signs up. As if her words of warning were enough to keep someone away. She is even, for a moment, angry at Ruby for shaming her into taking them down.

She opens the drawer, and the bottle, now nearly empty, rolls toward the front. She reaches past it and pulls out the gun.

She drags her body, her burden, from the warm bed and shuffles across the cold floor like an old woman, clutching the gun as though it can somehow ground her. As though it is enough. And she makes her way to the kitchen. She peers out the kitchen window at the backyard, but it is dark. Despite the movement, the motion in the backyard, whoever is out there has managed to not set off the sensors. The floodlight is out. She wonders if they have smashed the bulb again the way they did before. If she somehow slept through another bit of careful destruction.

She flicks on the wall switch for the kitchen light to act as a warning, but the light does not come on. Confused, she looks toward the stove where the time is usually illuminated in blue block numbers, but it is also out. She opens the refrigerator door to warm darkness. The power has failed, and she wonders if the pill made her sleep through a storm. If the hurricane has come and gone already. She wonders how many hours she has lost. How many days, how many years.

But the air is quiet, no rain. Only the deep low hum of wind. She runs her hand across the counter, looking for the flashlight the grocery delivery boy dropped off, but she can't find it. She fumbles like a blind person through the kitchen, terrified of whatever the darkness is hiding outside. But when she hears that sound again, crushing leaves and scratching, she throws open the back-door. And when she sees the dark form moving through her backyard, she raises the gun and aims.

Nessa is startled awake by the explosion. It punctuates whatever strange dream she was having. And for only a second, she is unable to determine which world it came from: the world of her dreams or this one. This one of howling wind and hard floors, and an aching back. This one made of hunger and discomfort and longing.

She sits up, rubbing the sleep from her eyes, and looks first for the little girl, Ruby. She must have left while she was still sleeping. She peers around the small room, but it is too dark to see, and her eyes are still struggling to focus on this landscape, rather than her dreamscape. She has gone from a world of color to a world not of black and white but only black. She has awakened not to sunlight but to incredible darkness.

It was a gunshot, she realizes. This becomes immediately clear and she surfaces back into this world. The loud reverberating pop is not a sound of nature but of man. And she struggles to remember what season it is. She remembers when she lived here that some of the boys, the ones in her classes, were excused from school to go hunt with their fathers. These were the same ones who started school late in the fall because they were busy haying their families' fields. They were also the ones who came late to school because before school they had to milk the cows and feed and water the horses. These were the boys who wore soft plaid shirts and whose Wranglers' pockets had faded round circles from their packs of Skoal. These were the boys who tasted like winter. Like tobacco and pine. She loved the wood smoke smell of them. As if they were part of the woods themselves, these boys. A whole new species of man.

But it is summer now. Deer season is during the school year, after the leaves have fallen from the trees. She remembers the trucks driving like the Fourth of July parade through town with wide-eyed deer tethered down in the back. She remembers the smell of horse shit on their work boots and the way their skin smelled like sweet grass.

There is a strange silence that follows the explosion, and then Nessa becomes oriented, her eyes adjusting, and the silence is followed by a low, deep wailing. A keening. She squeezes her eyes shut. The sound is soft but certain, and difficult to separate from the prevailing rush of wind through the trees. But she is overwhelmed suddenly by a sense of urgency. A connection that makes no logical sense (besides proximity) between the little girl and that violent sound. She just knows that something terrible has happened, and she rises as though she can do something about it. But as she stands, hobbled by three broken toes and her enormous belly, she knows that it is ludicrous. She is worthless. Who can she help like this? She has been rendered a child by motherhood. It is ludicrous but true. She is helpless, dependent, afraid.

And so she sits in the doorway of the shack, her ears pricked for whatever comes next. An ineffectual bystander. Once again, an impotent witness.

She has killed her. For one blinding, horrific moment, Sylvie stares at her daughter who has collapsed to the ground and thinks, *she's dead.* She drops the gun on the porch and feels herself turning inside out. Her heart rises up through her throat, exits from her mouth in a deafening lament that peels her skin back. That cracks her ribs at the sternum, flaying her. She feels her insides exposed (lungs, liver, large and small intestines). Her heart beats outside herself now, the inner workings of her body revealed to be just that — an imperfect and unoriginal anatomy. A machine of blood and breath both similar and entirely different from every other woman in the entire world. In a fractured second, she is eviscerated, just one of her broken birds.

But then, Ruby looks up at her, her eyes wet, and Sylvie sees that she is not dead, not at all. There is a moment of confusion and then the stunning revelation that she has made an error. She has not shot Ruby, but whatever it is that she holds in her arms. Ruby is okay. Unharmed. But whatever she is holding, the *animal,* is large, gray, and bleeding. Her heart that beats beyond her begins to sink. To collapse in on itself.

It's the mama raccoon.

Sylvie should be overwhelmed by relief. She should feel that same heart-pounding adrenaline rush she felt the one time they lost Jess at the JC Penney and found him inside one of the round racks of clothing, hiding among a colorful sea of women's blouses. The way she has felt a hundred times when she braked just in time, her car stopping just short of another's bumper, the slow graceful skid across an icy road. The stammering relief each time she unwound a baby, blue and breathless, from its umbilical cord. She should feel the fear and terror abating like a tidal wave receding from a ravaged and unsteady shore. She should feel reprieve.

But instead, the grief continues, a tsunami of sorrow.

Ruby is on her knees and crying, sobbing, her whole body is shaking as she cradles the raccoon in her tiny arms. Sylvie has to keep herself from reprimanding her about germs, rabies, about the danger of wild things.

Tears run down Ruby's pale cheeks, leaving red scars in their wake. Her eyes are frantic and angry.

"You killed her!" Ruby screams, her voice raw and scathing. "You killed the mama."

Sylvie blinks hard, trying to refocus, as though she can change the scene before her by simply adjusting her vision. Here is her daughter, bug bites and scab-covered arms. A dirty T-shirt and jeans. It is cold, but she doesn't have a sweater. Why is she outside? Where did she come from? Was she running away again? Will she ever come back?

The animal twitches in Ruby's arms, which startles both of them, and Sylvie feels the raw edges of her own nerves, no longer protected by that layer of skin. The failure of epidermis. She is vulnerable now, excoriated. The raccoon releases itself all over Ruby's arms, urine soaking her cut-off jeans, but still Ruby clings to her. She buries her face in the animal's fur.

At the same time, Sylvie thinks she has begun to cry, the tears coming not only from her eyes but from her whole body. It's as though without flesh, the tears from all the years are now unleashed, the dam broken. That without her body to hold them captive, they are convicts, fleeing imprisonment. The tears soak her, a fever breaking into a cold sweat. She is drenched in her own sorrow.

The power clicks back on, filling the backyard with light. And in this new bright light, she can see it is *not* sorrow but rain beading up on the cool white of her neck and shoulders. Rain coming down in sharp drops, each a sort of painful reprimand. Even the sky is chastising her. She looks up then at the starless night for some sort of explanation, to face her punishment, to acknowledge her culpability perhaps. She focuses on the rain that is coming down like bullets, and accepts the assault. Welcomes it even. And as the rain soaks her hair, streams down her face, penetrates her nightgown, she wonders if this is what it feels like to be at war. Constant terror. Paranoia confirmed by violence. Unnecessary death, moments of respite that feel like admonishments instead.

"You killed her," Ruby cries again, trembling in the cold rain, but the anger is gone, and now her voice is filled only with the sounds of disappointment. And Sylvie can't decide which is worse: to have enraged her or to have failed her in yet another indescribable and unforgivable way.

Her mother finally leaves, finally retreats back into the house, but Ruby stays outside in the rain, holding on to the raccoon. Her throat is raw from crying, and her chest aches. She is soaked and cold, the rain still coming, unrelenting, as she clings to the lifeless animal. She knows she needs to do something for the babies. She needs to make sure that they get fed, but she has no idea how to take care of them. She wouldn't even know where to start. Milk? Water? What do raccoons even eat? The fact that she doesn't know what to do to help them further infuriates her. She cannot believe how angry she is at her mother. The rage feels like an infection, like an illness. She is feverish and sick with it.

Finally, when she is beginning to feel numb with the cold, she lays the raccoon down, covers it with an old blue tarp. And she goes into the house, expecting to be alone, expecting that she will need to go find a clean towel to dry off, that she will need to heat up water to make tea to begin to thaw her insides out. That she will need to take care of herself as her mother, once again, disappears. But surprisingly, she finds her mother sitting at the kitchen table. There is a stack of clean dry towels sitting next to a teapot. Steam rises from the spout like ghosts. She can hear water running in the tub in the bathroom. Her mother's face is calm, pale. She looks at Ruby through the haze of steam and says, "I'm sorry."

Ruby waits for something else. An excuse. And explanation. Her mind plays tricks on her, and she is transported back to a different night. Another midnight kitchen. Another pot of tea and dry towels and running bathwater. Another apology. But this is no déjà vu, this is only history repeating itself. Again and again, an endless loop.

"You killed her," Ruby says. "And she has babies to take care of. What will happen to them now? Who will take care of them now?"

Her mother squeezes her eyes shut and shakes her head, and Ruby waits. She won't back down this time. She doesn't want apologies. She doesn't want promises. Promises are as empty as the clothes hanging on Jess's side of the closet. She wants answers.

But her mother had nothing to give her then, that other night when the river soaked her clothes and hair. When she and her mother sat alone in this kitchen. Jess gone, Daddy at the hospital. Red and blue lights spinning like a carnival ride across the front yard. And her mother gives her nothing now. And so she stands to leave her, to go to her room. Ignore the hot bath, the warm towels, the tea. She will sleep in these wet clothes, the wild smell of the raccoon still on her hands, the metallic scent of blood still on her clothes. But just as she stands to leave, her mother says, "Wait."

And so she does. She waits. She allows herself to hope that her mother will do something. That she will make things better. That is her job. That is what a mother is supposed to do.

"Come here," her mother says, but her voice is fragile. Uncertain.

Ruby goes to her, and her mother takes one of the towels and wraps it around her. Ruby squeezes her eyes shut and lets her mother enclose her. Swaddle her.

He mother pulls her onto her lap, as though she is still just a little girl, and Ruby feels her throat swelling with something indescribable. Want. Sorrow.

She studies her mother's face, wills her to look at her. To see her. If she could just *see* her.

But the moment passes. She was there, *here* with Ruby. But she is gone again. She rubs the towel absently against Ruby's arms. But she is elsewhere.

"Do you remember that story? The one about the bear hunt?" her mother asks.

Ruby nods. Of course she does. It was Jess's favorite. He used to act out the whole story, *We're going on a bear hunt. We're gonna catch a big one! I'm not afraid! Are you?* Her senses are flooded, a deluge. The pounding of Jess's feet on the wooden floors, his laughter something raw and deep and good. His voice filling the quiet room. *I'm not afraid!*

She shakes her head. She does not want to slip into this place her mother has gone. She cannot let her lungs fill with the cool wet recollections of Jess (of applesauce and strawberry milk). Ruby shakes her head, trying hard not to dip below the surface: his freckled cheeks, the bright green rims around his pupils, the earthy scent of his hair. But her mother is gone, sinking to the cold dark bottom.

■ ■ ■ ■

# Friday

■ ■ ■ ■

Sometimes bridges fail.

Ruby knows this, yet still searches for evidence of their fallibility. She needs to understand that this is a common occurrence, that she is not the only one to watch as something that is supposed to be indestructible is destroyed. As something that is supposed to create safe passage becomes a death trap.

The Rialto Bridge collapsed under the weight of too many spectators at a wedding parade. In 1845, seventy-nine people died when people gathered on the Yarmouth Bridge to watch a circus clown go down the river in a barrel pulled by geese. Most of the people who died were children. A one-hundred-and-fifty-year-old pedestrian bridge in Bhagalpur, India, collapsed onto a railway train that was passing beneath it, killing more than thirty people.

Poor design. Structural weakness. Inability

to sustain load. Earthquakes, fires, and floods have caused the collapse of dozens of bridges. But accidents, *accidents* seem to be the primary cause behind the failure of bridges. Trains, and barges, and trucks. Collisions. Human error.

Inverythan, Bussey, Duplessis.

She is not allowed to go over the covered bridge anymore. But what are they afraid of? That it will happen again? That there is anything left to lose?

And so on Friday morning, she takes the short way from her mother's house into town, and within ten minutes she can see the bridge in the distance. It looks innocuous. As though the worst thing in the world didn't happen right there. There is no evidence that the accident was anything but a dream. She doesn't know what she expected. But it is not this. It is fully repaired. Clean slate tiles on the roof, brand new boards on the deck. The sunlight glistens in the river below.

She rides her bike slowly, cautiously to the bridge, noticing then that it is *not* the same. They have built pedestrian walkways on either side of the main passage. You can walk or ride your bike through here now without the danger of a car not seeing you. This should give her comfort as she rolls her bike over the bridge, but it doesn't take away the truth that the bridge is still only built to hold one car. Whoever is passing through by vehicle is no safer than before. You have to trust that another car coming will alert you. Three quick honks to say, "I'm here. Wait for me to pass."

And she knows that sometimes bridges fail. Sometimes people fail. No matter how safe you are, there is always, always the possibility of someone else's carelessness.

Today is the last day of swimming lessons. The pool will close, summer will end. School will start again. Her father will come back. She will return to that tiny room that used to be the laundry room at Bunk's house. Everything will be normal. She keeps telling herself this, though she knows it is a lie. The piece of paper in her hand, the note from Nessa, is evidence of this. She doesn't know what it means yet, but she does know that it may just change everything. If Nessa finds what she is looking for, she will leave her. She won't need her anymore.

She stands at the entrance to the bridge and peers down at the river below. She considers letting it drop into the rushing water. She imagines it bobbing on the surface at first, and then slowly being caught up in the churning tumult of the current. She thinks of the ink blurring, the clues smudging. She understands that with one simple flick of the wrist she could bring about a certain erasure. She thinks how easy it would be to change the course of history that way. How, for once, destiny is in her hands. But if ink on a page creates a truth, then isn't that truth impervious to destruction? She thinks of the sketch in her notebook, the bridge that Nessa had marveled at. Does erasing it, destroying it, make it any less real?

And so she takes the note and carefully folds it back up according to its remembered creases and gets on her bicycle. She rides along the narrow walkway of the bridge, holding her breath the entire way, and when she arrives on the other side, unscathed, unharmed, she knows that she has just managed the impossible. That if her mother could see her now, maybe this would be enough to convince her. This might change the way she sees the world. This: the fact that she has crossed this bridge, and nothing has happened to her, that she is still the same girl with a stinging scab on one knee, dirty hair, and a strong beating heart that she was before she crossed it. That one can tempt fate without fate giving in to that temptation. That sometimes life is as simple as that.

She is going to the pool. It is the last day of lessons, and she knows it is probably the only way she will get a chance to talk to Izzy. And regardless of what has happened between them, what inky truths have started to blur, she needs her right now. Izzy is the only one left that can help her. She rides her bike, aware of her trembling knees and the hot rush of relief that spreads from her shoulders down into her hands that grip the handlebars until she gets to the pool and then she takes a deep breath and goes through the gate.

The sky is strange. It seems like a nice day, but there is a humming thrumming feeling to the air. And she wonders if this is the storm's warning. Like a moaning fog-horn, a gentle reminder of danger ahead.

She has no choice but to pretend that nothing has changed. That she belongs here. And so she undresses, leaving her clothes in a colorful heap near Izzy's beach bag, which is sitting at one of the picnic tables.

She goes to her lesson, and she sits on the edge of the pool. She is attentive as Nora comes by with her big white teeth and shrill whistle. She tickles each of the little kids' feet as she passes, but stops when she gets to Ruby. Instead she winks and says, "So you've decided to join us again. Good to see you."

Ruby stares into the sterile water, into that chlorinated dream. She wonders who thought of making a pool, who dreamed of creating a new kind of body of water, one made of blue water and concrete and so much sunlight.

Around her the other students kick their feet, disrupting the cold quiet surface of the water with their joy and enthusiasm. Nora encourages this. As though she is telling them that they are the ones in charge. That the water must yield to them rather than the other way around. And so Ruby kicks her feet as well, enjoying the resistance the water gives and the sharp cold certainty of the splash.

"Okay, everybody, are we ready?" Nora asks. She is standing armpit deep in the water in front of them. She is wearing a red suit like Izzy's, and her hair is tucked up underneath a red rubber cap.

Nora lifts her whistle, looks down the row of expectant faces, stopping at Ruby and nodding. It's as though she knows. It's as though she is somehow able to see the sudden loss of fear in Ruby's face. It's as though she is saying, "You can do it. Don't

318

be afraid." And so when Nora puts the whistle to her lips and lets loose that wild trebly signal, Ruby pushes herself off the edge of the pool and dips into the water.

She slips into its cold blue recesses inch by inch until she is up to her neck in it, and then when the whistle blows again, she does as she is expected to do. She no longer resists. She bends her knees and allows the water to creep up her neck, feels as her hair gets wet, the water flowing over her closed mouth and then a sudden whoosh as it enters her ears, the quick blindness as she closes her eyes and then nothing but silence and darkness as she disappears completely under the water's surface.

When she emerges — seconds? hours? — later, the teacher is smiling and clapping. "That was awesome," she says. "That was great!"

Ruby blinks the water out of her eyes, feels the chlorinated sting of it. She brushes her hair away from her face and breathes again. Amazed that she has surfaced. That she was able to plumb those depths and arrive again, alive, unharmed. It is like the way she felt after crossing the bridge earlier. It's as though she is testing everything today, every risk, and she's finding that her mother is *wrong,* that there is nothing to fear. This realization would normally feed the anger she feels at her mother who has given into her dread, who has surrendered to it. But Ruby knows she is guilty of this as well. That she has also believed the world to be an unkind place, a series of traps and land-mines. She is no different than her mother, but because she's a kid, it's okay. Children are supposed to be afraid. Children are sup-posed to need the grown-ups in their lives to assure them: that the boogeyman isn't real, that they will never be hungry, that they will wake up in the morning.

And so it is with this new fearlessness, this terrific intrepidity that she searches for Izzy after the last whistle blows. The Junior Lifeguards are taking their certificate test today. This is what they have been working toward all summer. And because she knows Izzy (or at least used to know Izzy), she knows that Izzy is nervous about this. Izzy gets nervous about every test at school, even the weekly spelling and vocabulary tests in English. She hates to be wrong, and so whenever presented with the possibility of making an error, failing in any way, she stiffens. Freezes. Once, in the third grade spelling bee, she misspelled *clamor* in the final round, losing to Hughie Bartell, and she refused to leave the stage. She couldn't believe she'd misspelled the word, and with tears in her eyes, she kept shaking her head and asking Mrs. Vanderbilt, the PTA president, to repeat the correct spelling. After that, she refused to participate in anything that might put her on that stage again; Gloria even had to send a special note saying she was excused from the school's production of *A Charlie Brown Christmas* they did every year.

It's for this reason that Ruby watches from the safety of the picnic tables where she can't be blamed for any errors Izzy might make during her certification testing. She watches as the students perform timed laps, an endurance test, as they leap into the water and save a struggling swimmer. As they each dive into the deepest end of the pool and pull up a ten-pound weight. They finish the pool tests and then, wrapped in towels, sit down to take the written test from the Red Cross. Ruby knows this is what Izzy is most worried about. Written tests always give Izzy grief. She gets herself so worked up that she makes silly mistakes. On math tests, she'll do the problems perfectly on the scratch paper and then transpose numbers when she's writing the answer down. Or, sometimes, she just gets so stuck on one test question that she can't move on to the next one. Izzy is a genius when it comes to just about everything except taking tests.

But Ruby watches her, hunched over the little test booklet, clutching her pencil in her fist like she has since they were little, and she wishes she could root her on. Because despite the last week, Izzy is still her best friend in the world and she knows how much this means to her. She wants her to pass. She wants her not to make any mistakes.

The whistle blows again, and the lifeguard instructor gathers the booklets.

Ruby watches as Izzy finds Marcy, and they cling to each other as the instructor disappears into the locker room to grade the tests.

Figuring it's probably a good time to distract Izzy, Ruby walks the long walk from the shallow end to the deep end and takes a breath before walking over to them.

"Hi," Ruby says, mustering up every bit of courage she has. "I just wanted to wish you good luck."

Izzy and Marcy look up at the same time. Marcy scowls, "We already took the test."

"I know. I just mean, I hope you pass."

Izzy smiles and nods. "Thanks."

"And I was also thinking I could maybe talk to you after lessons," Ruby says, feeling an awful sinking in her chest. She thinks of that weight sinking to the bottom of the pool. She knows she needs to dive down and retrieve it. She needs to rise to the surface, not drown in this moment.

Izzy looks at Marcy as if for permission, and Marcy shrugs.

"Okay," Izzy says, offering an identical shrug of the shoulders. "Maybe we could all go back to my house?"

"I was kind of hoping I could talk to you alone," Ruby says. The weight is heavy, and still plummeting. "It's sort of important."

Izzy cocks her head, and opens her eyes wider. It's like she knows that Ruby is serious. "Okay," she says, this time without waiting for a go-ahead from Marcy.

"Marcy, I can meet you back at my house in just a little bit," she says apologetically.

Marcy rolls her eyes. "Whatever."

"You know," Ruby starts. She is holding the weight, she can see the light above the surface. She feels buoyed, buoyant, light. "You're not a very nice person."

"*Excuse* me?" Marcy says, her face turning red.

"Just saying," Ruby shrugs in her best approximation of Marcy's own dismissal.

The whistle blows again, and the girls stand up. They both run to the far end of the pool where the lifeguard is standing with a stack of certificates.

"Izzy Sinclair," she says without ceremony. Marcy gives her a stupid girly hug, and Izzy goes to get her certificate. She stands with Marcy as they wait for Marcy's name to be called. But when she gets to the last certificate, it's for Madison Young. Marcy didn't pass.

"For the rest of you, we'll see you next year."

Marcy stands with her hands on her hips, her face red. Izzy tries to give her a hug, but Marcy pushes her off. Izzy looks at her with disbelief (as if Marcy is doing anything different than she's done for the last thousand years). And Ruby finds herself both feeling terrible for Izzy and starting to smile.

Izzy leaves Marcy, who is now demanding the teacher tell her exactly what she did wrong, and finds Ruby waiting for her.

"Congratulations," Ruby says. "Can I see?" She gestures to the certificate.

She studies the calligraphy, and Izzy's name hastily written in the blank in Sharpie. They've misspelled her last name, which she knows will drive Izzy crazy later, but for now, she is beaming. "That is awesome," Ruby says.

"Thanks."

"Well thank you for talking to me," Ruby says. "We haven't talked for, like, a long time."

Izzy nods. "Did you bring your bike?"

"Yeah," she says.

"Maybe we could ride over to Carmine's and get ice cream," Izzy says, and suddenly it feels like everything is back to normal, like this whole past week has been nothing but a bad dream.

They get their bikes and climb on, Izzy riding out to the front like she always does, and Ruby following behind. She notices that Izzy has a 1D sticker on the back of her helmet that is new. But other than that, she's the same old Izzy. Skinny legs pumping furiously, wet hair flying out behind her.

They get ice cream from the window of Carmine's and then walk over to the park by the train tracks. There's a statue of Arthur Quimby, who founded the town, there. He was from the Revolutionary War; he had something to do with the Green Mountain boys, but Ruby can never remember what. But the statue is big, and it has cool granite steps, shaded by his hulking figure. They settle onto the steps and lick their ice cream silently for a few minutes.

"So what's up?" Izzy says finally. She has a small sliver of peppermint stuck to her cheek. Ruby motions to it, and she flicks it away.

Ruby hates to spoil this moment, but she did come for a reason. She didn't just tell Marcy off for the fun of it (even though it *was* pretty fun). She needs to tell Izzy about Nessa. It feels like so much has happened in the last five days. It used to be that she and Izzy were together every minute of every day. There's no way a secret, even a small one, could survive. But here she was, with this giant one. She isn't even sure how to start.

"Listen, I need your help. But you *cannot* tell your parents. Do you promise?"

Izzy's eyes widen, but she nods. She offers Ruby her pinky, bent and ready to lock with her own. Something about this gesture makes Ruby miss her even more than she has all week. She lifts her own pinky finger and hooks it against hers.

And then she tells her: about how she found the girl hurt in the sugar shack, about how even though she doesn't talk, Ruby worries that she's in danger and that's why she's hiding. Then she pulls the piece of paper out of her back pocket, unfolds it.

"She's looking for somebody named George Downs," Ruby says, reading from the slip of paper.

Izzy has her ice cream cone in one hand and a napkin in the other, so she crumples up the napkin and sets it down on the cool granite. "Who's *George Downs*?" she asks.

"I have no idea."

"And she's pregnant? Like a little pregnant or *really* pregnant?" Izzy asks.

"I don't know," Ruby says. "She's pretty big." She stands up and holds her arms out in front of her, making a round belly with her bent elbows. "Like this."

"Couldn't your mom help her?" Izzy asks, but then her face reddens, probably remembering that her mother can't help anyone anymore. "So she's living in the *woods*?"

"Yes, I told you all this," Ruby says.

"Why didn't she just call him? You said she has his number?" she motions to the note.

Ruby looks down at the slip of paper again.

"She doesn't talk," Ruby says.

"Is she deaf?" Izzy asks.

"No."

"Are you sure?"

"Yes, Iz."

"Maybe she like robbed a bank or something," Izzy says, her eyes growing wide. "Maybe she's some sort of fugitive."

"I don't think so," Ruby says, shaking her head.

"Then why is she hiding?"

"She hurt her foot," Ruby says. And while this explains her immobility, it doesn't explain why she hasn't just asked Ruby if she knows anybody who can give her a ride into town. Ruby is more confused than she was before. "I think she's afraid of whatever it is she's looking for. Like maybe she's afraid of this George Downs guy."

"She gave this to you?" Izzy asks, reaching for the note in Ruby's hand. As she reads it, her forehead crinkles the way it does when she's trying to work out a difficult math problem.

"Yeah," Ruby says, feeling her heart pounding hard in her chest.

"But Ruby," Izzy says, her eyes wide, "that's *my* phone number."

Sylvie brings the raccoon inside, leaving a dark, slick puddle of blood in the backyard. She had thought about just putting it in a bag or box and burying it. But she can't forget that look on Ruby's face, the tremble in her voice when she accused her. When she called her a *killer,* the word more destructive and painful than a bullet.

She sets it next to the robin she's been working on at the kitchen table, which is covered with a bleach-stained towel. Compared to the birds, the raccoon seems like some sort of monster. It is enormous; she'd been surprised by how heavy it was when she lifted it up. She'd had to struggle to hold on to it with one arm as she opened the back door. She is accustomed to the delicacy of birds, to their tiny bones and hearts and feathers. She doesn't know the first thing about the taxidermy of mammals, and so she searches for instructions in her grandmother's book and then sets about skinning the raccoon. She stumbles when she gets to the bone in the tail, overwhelmed by the smell of it. She finds a bandana in the junk drawer and draws it across her face. It smells of Robert. Of sawdust and his aftershave. She swoons for a moment, overwhelmed by something so old and primitive, it's hard to even identify anymore.

But she cannot be distracted. She needs to get this project done as quickly as possible. She splits the tail, and removes the bone, runs it under the sprayer in the sink until all the fat slips down the drain. She scrapes the rest of the fat from the hide until there is nothing left but the fur. She splits the eyes, the lips, and turns the ears. She salts the hide, but she needs a board to tack it onto to dry for the next twenty-four hours.

Outside, the wind is howling, but the sky is a bright, bright blue. She knows the storm is coming, that the rain last night was just a prelude, and the wind seems to echo its portentous call. She finds one of the signs, NO TRESPASSING scrawled in neon spray paint, and she tries to recall her state of mind when she painted them. The only thing she recollects, however, is Ruby's fury.

Ruby had been right. It was just the raccoon making noises in the night. *This* raccoon. Only an animal, just as Ruby had said. She is crazy, she thinks. Paranoid. Certifiable. And, though there is no logic behind it, she feels angry at the raccoon for fooling her, for triggering that place in her brain that causes her to panic, to go into survival-mode. As she carries the hide outside, she even thinks that justice has somehow been served. This is the kind of thinking that got her sent to the hospital, though. She knows. She knows that this is the sort of reasoning that caused the spiral last time, that day like a tunneling tornado in her brain.

She tacks the hide carefully to one of the boards. In twenty-four hours she'll be able to reassemble it, to bend its flesh back over a frame, to sew up the incisions she has made, to replace the eyes. She will give it life again, or the semblance of life. It's the best she can do.

She leans the board against the side of the house where the sun is shining the brightest; it will help quicken the drying process. Then she goes through the screen door to the porch. The baby raccoons are sleeping now, and the sight of them tears at her heart a little. She will need to have someone come get them now. With their mother gone, they probably won't survive for long. She wonders what she should feed them, if they will drink from a bowl of milk like kittens. She reaches to open the front door, but it's locked. Of course it is. She always locks herself in. She goes outside again and around to the back of the house, pushing her way through the gap in the fence and up the back steps. The door is closed, though she is sure she left it open. This crazy wind must have blown it shut. She reaches for the handle, but as she tugs, nothing happens. The handle is stuck. She tries again, this time with more force. Certainly, it's just stuck. But as she grows more and more anxious, tugging harder and harder at the handle, she realizes that it is also locked. Somehow, the wind must have blown it with such force that the little safety latch clicked into place. She is locked outside of her house.

She stares at the backyard, the tangle of weeds, the pathetic fence. Her garden is overgrown and bountiful despite the pillaging raccoon. She doesn't know when Ruby will be home with the key. She doesn't know how long she'll be out here. She tries hard to focus on her breath, conscious of each inhalation and exhalation, taking care not to hyperventilate. This was a trick they taught her at the hospital. Counting each breath, concentrating on the air coming in through her mouth and going out through her nose. She sits down on the back steps and bends over, her chest resting on her knees.

The wind whips through the backyard, creating a cyclone in the fenced-in area. She feels it striking her, lifting her hair. Whispering across the exposed skin of her neck and shoulders.

*One, two, three.* She breathes in and starts to tick off a checklist. Did she leave the oven on, the dryer on, the iron on? Is there anything inside that might ignite a fire? She thinks about Ruby's room. Is there anything in there that could suddenly combust? The uncertainty of it makes her forget to count.

Inside the house, the phone rings, and so she goes around to the front of the house, stepping onto the front porch, where she stands helpless before the locked front door. The phone rings again inside. It seems to be shriller this time, insistent. And on the loveseat the baby raccoons are making a horrible sound as well. It sounds like a rattle, a chattering, rattling screech, as they search and search for their mother. She sits down on the front steps with her back to the screen door and covers her ears. But still, despite the press of flesh against her ears, the phone screams and the babies cry and it's all so loud, you can barely hear the sound of her own slow and quiet sobbing.

She is stuck outside. She can't get into her house. She feels exposed, her entire body a raw nerve. And because of all the noise, this cacophony of misery, she doesn't hear the truck as it pulls up the driveway.

Nessa knows this sky. She has seen it before. Like one magician understanding another magician's trick. She has seen this illusory sky, this sleight of hand. It is a deception, a good one, but a lie no less. This ominous blue and sunlight. In Cleveland, in Salinas, in Denver, and in Portland; she has been audience to this particular chimera a hundred times. She understands the machinations behind it. There is a storm coming. A big storm.

She knows she needs to leave these woods, that the baby will not wait much longer.

The baby, like the sky, makes false promises of peace. Of safety. She hasn't been counting the days, the weeks. She has relied only on her body to tell her how close she is to its arrival. She is vaguely aware of seasons passing; this is her pregnancy's third season. It's going to happen soon.

Her foot still aches, but the pain no longer

has the same immediacy and urgency as before. It has softened into a dull ache, like the memory of pain. The swelling has subsided, and the colors have gone from deep plum to a less disturbing greenish-yellow. And so she tests it, tries to put weight on it, but there again is the sharp reminder of her injury. And she knows that her healing is fallacious. Broken bones take time to heal, more time than she has been here. Though time strikes her as a construct as well. Deceitful, even whimsical in its deception. Because the months that it has taken for this baby to grow, for her body to be transformed by it, suddenly seem but only a moment in her entire lifetime. A whisper. Each long day on the road and all those nights spent trying to find a safe warm place to stay were agonizing in the moment, time dragging like a wounded leg behind her. But now, in this long and excruciating moment, she can gather her memories in one handful. Like a palm full of colored beads. She stares at them, mystified that they had each once seemed so enormous.

Not only is the sky a liar and time deceptive, but these woods too (while they have provided a good hiding place) are not as benevolent as they seem. Her broken bones are evidence of this. She tries not to think of all the other dangers that are lurking out there.

She is hungry again, though there is plenty to eat. Ruby has brought enough food to practically last her through the winter. She has cans of peaches and green beans. Hard-boiled eggs and granola bars. She has cereal and little tubes of yogurt. But every time she tries to eat, the food will not go down beyond the burning place in her chest. The first time she felt it, she thought she was having a heart attack. That the fiery flume meant that she was dying.

The baby has dropped in the last couple of days. She can even see it in the way it distorts her shape. For a long time, her belly started to round just under her breasts, as though someone had shoved a basketball under there. But now, she can feel the baby in her hips, her lower back in a new kind of constant pain. There is not a single position in which she is comfortable. She can feel her tendons stretching, complaining each time she tries to move. And still, her foot.

She will wait for Ruby to come back. She needs to stay just one more night, and then she can go. If Ruby's mother, the midwife, cannot help her, then Ruby will help her find him. She gave her the note and after looking confused, Ruby had nodded. But

337

that was so long ago. She is rattled still by the gunshot she heard last night. She worries that Ruby might never come back. That she is stranded here in the woods. That she will have to find her own way.

She doesn't know exactly what she will do when she finally finds him. It's not as though she has words she can offer anymore. Her silence is so absolute, she has to rely on other ways of communicating. Besides, there are no words for what she needs to tell him. They haven't invented that language yet. The vocabulary of loss and regret.

She peers out through the door, and listens as the wind howls. Watches as it bends the trees. They resist, but she can see how some of them acquiesce, how some of them bow down, surrendering, to its unrelenting assault. Dead leaves and loose pine needles blow across the ground, giving the illusion that the earth is somehow moving. Even the river seems to be hustled along by the wind's insistence.

She needs a distraction as she waits. She needs something to do until Ruby comes again with the answers she needs. With the solution to the puzzle she's been trying so hard to solve. She tries not to think about what will happen if Ruby never returns. If there are no answers to this question (the only question anymore), no solution to this problem.

In school, she had a teacher who loved conundrums. Each week, she sent the children home with one to solve. *How much dirt is there in a hole that measures three feet wide and three feet deep?* She would puzzle over the questions, scribbling her mathematical musings along the margins of the paper. She would come up with an answer and then second-guess herself. And then, inevitably, the answer was not at all what she'd been shooting for. It was never as complicated as she made it. The answer always seemed obvious, and always made her feel a bit foolish. *How much dirt is there in a hole that measures three feet wide and three feet deep?* None. A hole doesn't have any dirt in it. A hole is empty.

She wonders if the puzzle she's been trying to solve is simply like one of these conundrums. If the answer is somehow there, *obvious,* in front of her. She tries to come at the question from all directions. To sneak up on it rather than tackling it head on. She tries to think of the least obvious answer. She thinks of it as something solvable, something with a solution. The idea that it might not have one is more than she can bear.

The baby slips farther down. She feels it this time. It plummets and lands heavily on her pelvis. It nearly takes her breath away with its sudden certainty. She doesn't know what this means, but she can only imagine that there isn't much time left. That it is readying itself. Like someone jumping from an airplane. She imagines the baby strapping on a tiny little parachute, miniature goggles, a harness. It is fearless, this little one. She thinks it might be a girl, a girl who is unafraid of anything. For whom the conundrums are obvious. Who never complicates the simple things, but simply dives headlong into life.

Sylvie considers hiding. But the man in the truck has already seen her sitting on the steps. It's too late. She thinks of running, of scurrying away like an animal, disappearing into the trees. But, as always, she is paralyzed.

"I got a call about some raccoons?" he says, leaning out the open window of the truck.

She crosses her arms over her chest, keenly aware how strange it must seem that she is wandering around outside in her nightgown.

"Ma'am?" he says.

"Yes," she nods. "They're here on the front porch."

He gets out of the truck and goes around the back to get a cage, and she stands up. He lumbers up the walkway, and she feels her skin grow hot with shame as he looks away from her, embarrassed that she is outside in only her ratty nightgown. She looks around frantically as though her robe will suddenly materialize.

She thinks for a minute about telling him that she's locked herself out. Any normal person would just explain the situation, ask for help. If he's anything like Bunk or Robert, he's got tools in his truck that could dismantle the lock on the back door. But as he averts his eyes and walks past her, she thinks maybe it would be better if she just lets him do what he has come to do. Ruby will be home soon with the key.

She follows him onto the porch and looks around furtively, registering what it is that he must see: the stacks of junk, the empty plastic bins. The drawn shades and the wild animals who have made a home there. They stir as his feet fall heavily on the sagging floor of the porch.

"You seen the mother?" he asks.

It feels like an accusation. She shakes her head. And she thinks about the mother's skin stretched across the plywood. About what it is that she is trying to do. Trying to preserve.

The baby raccoons chatter loudly. They wriggle and cry.

Within a couple of minutes he has gathered them into the cage. He still won't look at her, even as he shakes her hand and says, "All set. If you see the mother around, you give us a call."

And then he is in the truck, lighting a cigarette, and backing up. Soon he is gone, and the beating of her heart slowly settles back into its steady rhythm.

Inside the house, the phone rings again. Sylvie looks desperately at the locked door and wonders if she should break a window to let herself in. But that would mean she'd have a broken window to contend with, an easy way in for vandals, for animals, for thieves. And so she watches the closed door and wills the ringing to stop. She doesn't have an answering machine anymore. The last one broke, but because she never leaves, she hasn't had a need for one. She thinks of Robert, wonders if the storm has reached his brother's house. The radio had said that it was a slow-moving storm, and that the Carolinas and mid-Atlantic could expect sustained winds and a lot of rain.

She wonders if it is him. She wonders if he is okay. And then she thinks it might be Ruby. God, what if something has happened to Ruby? What if she is trying to reach her and can't?

She doesn't know what to do. She circles the house as though there is a secret door she has forgotten existed. When she gets to the backyard, she looks at the broken fence. If there hadn't been this hole, then the mother raccoon would never have found her way in. And she wouldn't have shot it. Ruby wouldn't be so furious with her, and she wouldn't have taken off again like this. And so she pulls the fallen board back up. It is cracked and splintered, but she is able to right it, to close the entrance. She searches for something to use to attach it to the other piece of plywood. She sees the pile of hardware that they had assembled from the mishmash in the shed. But the hammer is inside the house. She grabs a long nail and then searches for something to use to pound it in. She finds a rock and attempts to nail the plywood sheets together at the seams. But there is nothing to hold them together as she pounds, and the broken sheet falls down again, followed by the sheets on either side of it. She is sweating and breathless, and even as she understands how ludicrous all of this is, she cannot help but feel like her entire world is crashing down around her. That her life is no different than this miserably constructed fence. She has tried to do a job that she is not equipped to do. And this is the result: a faulty house of cards. A pathetic attempt at a fortress. An ineffectual citadel. She is a fool.

It is sprinkling now, just a little bit. She wonders how much of the storm they'll actually get up here. And when the real rain will start. What she does know is that she is still wearing her nightgown, and the wind is tearing through the worn nylon.

"What's going on?" Ruby asks.

It startles Sylvie, and she stumbles backward; she feels like she's knocked the wind out of herself.

"I locked myself out," she says. And she feels like a child.

"I have my key," Ruby says, fumbling in her pocket. A slip of paper falls out, and Ruby looks nervously at Sylvie as she scrambles to pick it up.

"What's that?" Sylvie asks.

"Nothing," Ruby says and then slips her key into the deadbolt, letting her back in. She practically falls into the house, as though into a warm bath. She is safe again. Safe.

But Ruby is still angry with her. She barely looks at Sylvie as she walks into the kitchen, opens the fridge, looking for something.

The phone rings again. And again.

"Aren't you going to get that?" Ruby asks, her eyes wide and angry.

And so Sylvie picks up the receiver. It is as heavy as a brick in her hand. An anvil. An anchor.

"Hello?" she says, her voice barely above a whisper, waiting.

But there is only the staccato buzz of the dial tone on the other end.

They are out of milk. Ruby sees the empty plastic jug on the table, next to her mother's coffee mug. The babies wouldn't drink it out of the bowl, but earlier that morning when she dipped her finger in the milk and dropped it into their open mouths, they sucked greedily at her. She thinks about them out there on the porch, completely unaware that their mother is dead. That she is never coming back.

She grabs her backpack again and throws it on her shoulders.

"Where are you going?" her mother asks.

"Up to Hudson's," she says. "We're out of milk."

Her mother dips the tea bag in and out of her mug, rhythmically, like a metronome. When she looks up, Ruby can see dark circles under her eyes. And for a strange moment, she imagines that she too is a mother raccoon. It's a ridiculous thought,

one of those odd things she thinks sometimes. That the world is upside down, and
that they are really walking on the sky. That
if she were to try hard enough she could
will herself to fly. She thinks of it as dream-
thinking, those thoughts that make no sense
when you're awake, but have a certain logic
when you are half asleep. And for this tiny
moment, she imagines her mother trans-
forming, growing a coat of prickly brown
and gray fur. The sad tired circles under her
eyes expanding until they make a mask. She
imagines her ears pricking up to the top of
her head, a tail pushing its way out of her
body. She imagines her dropping to all fours
and scurrying away into the forest.

"Do we need anything else?" Ruby asks.

Her mother shakes her head, and so she
heaves the heavy backpack up onto her
shoulders, and starts toward the door.

"Ruby?" her mother says, and she turns
to her again. She is remarkably grateful to
find that she has not transformed into an
animal but is still her mother. Still just a
woman with tired eyes.

"Yeah?"

"I'm sorry about the mama raccoon."

Ruby nods; she doesn't know what to say.
How to respond.

Her mother stares back down into the

steaming mug of tea. It's the one she and Jess gave her three Christmases ago. It says *World's Best Mom.*

"It's okay," Ruby says. "It was an accident." And that word, *accident,* is like a sliver under her skin, surfacing, stinging.

"I could have hurt you," her mother says, and her voice hitches, like fabric snagging on a barbed wire fence. "I thought I did hurt you."

"But you didn't," Ruby says. "I'm fine."

"I know." Her mother nods and smiles, but the smile is weak, a broken sort of smile.

"Okay, I really should go," Ruby says and shrugs the strap of her backpack that has slipped a bit.

"I'm going to make an appointment," her mother says as she heads toward the door. And for a minute Ruby thinks she means Animal Control. To have them come out and get the babies. To take them away. She has forgotten to tell her that she already did. But then her mother says, "For help. I know I need some help."

Ruby turns to look at her mother, at her earnest face full of promises. And Ruby is silenced again. It's as though she is reaching into a bag looking for the right item to pull out, the one that her mother is looking for. The one that she needs. But the bag is empty, and she gropes futilely in the abyss. She has nothing to say because she knows that this promise, as much as her mother believes she can keep it, is as hollow as a reed.

She walks out onto the front porch, and it is strangely quiet. Eerily quiet. She pushes the innards of the cushion aside, but the babies are gone. They're *gone.*

"What did you do?" she says to her mother. "Where did they go?" But strangely the rage that had filled her like something hot and liquid has cooled. It pools in her shoulders. And the sorrow and disappointment is worse than any sort of anger. Ruby can still smell the wild, gamey scent of the mama raccoon in her sweatshirt. There is a bit of the mother's blood on the cuff.

"The man came," her mother says. "You called him . . . he said he got a call."

The phone begins to ring again and they both look at it, hanging on the wall like some sort of foreign object. When it is obvious that her mother isn't going to answer it, Ruby lunges for it. "Hello?"

"Ruby, it's Daddy. Listen, I can't talk long. Can you put your mother on please?"

She doesn't want to pass the phone to her mother though. What she wants is for him to be back here. She clings to the phone, clutches it like a life preserver holding her afloat.

"Honey, I've only got a little bit of juice left. I really need to talk to your mom."

And so she reluctantly passes the receiver to her mom. "It's Daddy."

Her mother takes the phone and slips around the corner, the cord curling behind her like a tail. Ruby listens.

"You can't drive in a storm like this," she says. "That's crazy."

She watches as her mother starts to pace back and forth across the kitchen floor, and Ruby remembers the day after the accident. When the phone wouldn't stop ringing. All day long her mother walked back and forth across this same floor, muttering, *Thank you, I'm okay. We'll be okay. No, we don't need anything.* She remembers that her mother wore herself out, walking miles across the same ten feet of linoleum. How finally, she couldn't walk another inch and just left the phone sitting on the counter and went to bed. That she didn't get out of bed after that for almost a whole week.

"Robert?" she says, stopping. She looks at the phone again, as though it's a piece of technology she's never seen before. "Hello?"

"Where is he?" Ruby asks, forgetting about the raccoons, concerned only with her father now. With his safety.

Her mother looks at her as though she's forgotten she's here. "They're leaving early tomorrow, they want to get on the road before the storm hits. It could take a few days though, if they have to stop."

Ruby is overwhelmed with relief. Bunk and Daddy are coming. By Monday morning, this whole week will be like some sort of strange dream. But then she thinks about Nessa and realizes that she needs to get her out of the shack before her dad comes back. Once she's back at her dad's house, she won't be able to help her anymore. She heads to the front door. She can't help the raccoon babies, but she can still help Nessa. Whoever that guy, George Downs, is doesn't matter anymore. Izzy had never heard of him; he was nobody she knew. He is just a name on a piece of paper. But Ruby is here. She is real. And she can help her.

"Actually, I think you should stay here," her mother says. "Daddy says the storm is heading up the coast, and we're going to get a lot of rain. I want you to help me get those sandbags up against the back of the house. He says the wind might be bad too and that we should board up the windows."

Ruby looks at her mother in disbelief. Incredulous. "It's not even sprinkling outside. The storm isn't even supposed to get here until Sunday."

"I'm sorry. I need your help. I promised your father I would do this."

She tries not to think of Nessa out there in the woods by herself. She'll need to wait until tonight, she thinks. But then she remembers what happened the last time she snuck out at night. She tries to blink away the image of her mother standing in the yard with the gun. She'll have to go to her in the morning. She prays she won't try to leave, that she won't disappear. That she won't think that she's left her.

She helps her mother drag the sandbags up against the back of the house. The fence they made is broken now, the plywood sheets lying in heaps. When she sees the raccoon hide pinned to the board, she feels bile rising in her throat and tears coming to her eyes. At first she considers ignoring it, leaving it like that. Just forgetting whatever it is that her mother is trying to do. But instead, she gets a hammer and tears the nails out of the wood, ripping the pelt from the board. She carries it down to the river and hurls it with every ounce of her strength into the water. It bobs and dips, snagging for a moment on a rock, and then it is gone.

She takes the plywood boards that her

mother spray painted and drills them against the windows, turning them so that the lettering faces inward rather than outward. But she realizes when they are done and back inside that now the words are screaming at them through the windows. NO TRESPASSING! KEEP OUT! The house even darker now without the benefit of even the sunlight, normally filtered through dark curtains. Now there is nothing but darkness.

Nessa slips in and out of sleep inside the shack all afternoon. She feels feverish, almost ill. She wonders, vaguely, if somehow her toe has gotten infected and that the infection has spread to her blood. She wonders if it is possible to die from this. If she might just slip into sleep and stay there. Delirious, she waits for Ruby to arrive. But as the sun passes across the sky, changing the shadows inside the dark cool shack, she does not come. What if she never comes?

When the first pain arrives, like a shiver across her abdomen, she recalls the first time she bled: the wrecked feeling of her body, the way the pain gripped her. She remembers being alone in the apartment, the aching, empty feeling of it, her mother out again. Some nights her mom wouldn't get home until the sun was beginning to rise. Some nights she didn't come home at all. Nessa had squatted over the toilet with its cracked seat and rust-ringed bowl, touched the damp place between her legs, and thought that she was sick. That she was dying. She was eleven years old, and no one had ever taken the time to tell her that this would happen and not to be afraid. That this terrifying grip of her uterus was just her body's way of readying itself. She remembers a pilly pink bath mat and the dark, nearly black blood that dripped across it as she crawled to the bathtub where she ran the water so hot that steam filled the bathroom like ghosts. She remembers that she wanted her mother then, more than she had ever wanted her before, this longing the most pure thing she'd ever felt. The need as sharp and exacting as a sword. That when she sank into the tub, the water turning cloudy and pink, she had wished her mother home.

She wonders about her mother now, as her body recollects that first pain, that precursor, that prelude, to this. And then she tries to imagine her mother carrying her like this, about her mother's body being consumed by her. But it is impossible. Like imagining the future. Or like trying to remember the deep, deep past.

Her mother could be anywhere now. Or nowhere at all. By the time Nessa left

Quimby, her mother had lost her job again, and she and Rusty were talking about moving back to the city. But all these months later there could have been a dozen cities, a dozen jobs, a dozen other men. She had been a fool to think she'd find her here. That she would have waited for Nessa to come home.

She lies on her side on the cold floor, studies the green of leaves through the hole in the roof. She cups her hand underneath the swollen flesh of her belly, but the baby does not respond to her touch. And while her body tenses and contracts beneath her fingers, the baby does not stir. Not even a bit. And when the wave of pain washes over her, Nessa wonders if somehow, she has killed her.

Sometimes, unless Sylvie takes the pills, the only way to make herself sleep is to count. As a little girl, her grandmother, exasperated by Sylvie's insomnia, suggested that she count sheep. But there were no sheep to count, none outside her window in the pastures beyond their house. There were houses and lowing cows, but not a single sheep for miles and miles. And none inside her imagination. What lived inside her imagination were animals of a different sort. They were faceless, nameless, bleating creatures. She couldn't bring herself to count them; the numbers didn't go high enough. Far enough. And counting them, acknowledging them only seemed to make them multiply. There was no lullaby here.

Instead she counted her heartbeats. They were rhythmic and steady and certain, and while seemingly endless, she knew they had a limit. She could count them until she became an old woman, but one day they would cease, the ticking metronome would wind down, and there would be nothing left but silence. Peace. This was the only thing that gave her comfort back then, the only thing that kept the wild thoughts at bay.

And so this is her habit. She lies on her back so that her breasts fall to each side of her, as though parting to make way for her palms. She lifts her nightshirt up so that there is no confusion, no barrier between her heart and her hand. She presses her right palm flat against her flesh, searching for the cadence of her own body. And she wonders if this comfort hearkens back to a time before time, when she lived inside her mother's womb. When the sound of blood and heart and breath were the only sounds. She has always felt strangely about ushering infants from this dark peace into the violent world. When she was still delivering babies, she insisted that the mothers keep the lights dim, the rooms quiet, the fires in the hearth warm. And as soon as the babies emerged from their mothers' bodies, she would rush them back to their mothers' bare chests where they could be close to that sound again. Making the transition from womb to world as painless as possible. She tried not to think about what happened after she left.

When the bright light of morning came, the loud day with its smells and sounds. These poor new beings exposed, vulnerable to the everyday assaults. And it made her sad, that this is something they would eventually adapt to. That they might never, ever again in their lives find the safety they once had inside their mothers' bodies. That this is the only truth of life: you are vulnerable. You are defenseless.

When she tried to call Robert back earlier, her call went straight to voice mail. Not one ring, not even the possibility of connection. He'd said that he and Bunk were leaving in the morning, that they were going to try to beat the storm, to somehow outrun the wind and the rain. But she, of all people, knows that this is foolish. Futile. Because the storm will always catch up to you, no matter how fast you run.

After Ruby went to bed, she sat in the kitchen with the volume on the radio turned low, listening to the coverage of the storm. Late tonight, it was expected to reach the coast of North Carolina. A-hundred-mile-an-hour winds, storm surges from six to eleven feet. The president, who was vacationing on Martha's Vineyard, had cut his vacation short, gone home. In New York, residents of the lower-lying areas had been ordered to evacuate. The subways would close tomorrow. Airports would also be shut down.

She heard Ruby stir in the other room and turned the volume down even lower, until the voice on the radio was only like the patter of rain, the distant rumble of thunder.

*Robert.* If she could reach him what would she say? Stay where you are? Hunker down? Wait until the storm has passed? It wouldn't matter. Because this was always the fundamental difference between them. Her instinct was to seek shelter, but his was to flee.

She presses her hand harder into her chest, momentarily losing the beat of her heart, panicking with the thought that this is when it stops. That this is the night it fails. But her fear kick-starts her heart and it pounds reassuringly against her hand. *I'm here, I'm here.* And she begins to count, starting over where she left off. Thirty-one, thirty-two, thirty-three.

# ■ ■ ■ ■

# SATURDAY

# ■ ■ ■ ■

Ruby dreams of bridges.

In Europe there are at least a dozen bridges named The Devil's Bridge. Most of them are stone arch bridges built during the medieval times, and all of them have some sort of folklore about the Devil associated with them. They traverse mountains, impossible terrains, and the legends arise from the impossibility of their architecture — the suspicion that the Devil himself must have had a hand in building them, that no human could have accomplished such a feat. In Germany, in Romania, in France and Italy and Spain there are Devil's bridges: Die Teufelsbrücke, Moara Dracului, Ponte del Diavolo, Pont du Diable, Puente del Diablo. Each of them is a miracle of masonry and engineering, spanning great divides.

In these stories, in all of these stories, it is said that the townspeople, needing a bridge to reach from one impossible place to another, sought the Devil's assistance, and the Devil (having no use for payments of livestock or gold) agreed to assist, with the understanding that the first one to cross the bridge would be sacrificed, so that he might add them to his collection of souls. Not wanting to make such a sacrifice, the townspeople would then trick the Devil by sending across goats or other animals in their stead. In most of the stories, the townspeople prevail. In some, they are even able to trick the Devil himself into crossing first.

But Ruby knows that these are just stories. Just myths. Because the Devil, the real Devil, cannot be fooled.

Ruby sleeps deeply, her mother's owl standing watch over her. And as she sleeps, she dreams of bridges. Of all the bridges of the world. Her mind gathering the materials, rolling the stones and calculating the geometric patterns that will create the miracle she needs. A bridge impervious to storms, to destruction, to accidents. A bridge the Devil himself might build. And in the luminous depths of sleep she dreams of his collection of souls, and searches through the sea of faces, looking for the one she lost.

■ ■ ■ ■

In the morning, she tells her mother she is going into town. Says that if the storm really is coming tomorrow they will need more batteries, another flashlight, supplies. She brings her backpack.

"I'm going to stop by Izzy's house too." She hopes that this new peace she and Izzy forged over ice cream under the Arthur Quimby statue is real and not something else she dreamed. While Izzy is being nice again, *herself* again, she hopes she can talk to her about the bridge contest. Convince Izzy that she needs her; that none of this matters if they aren't able to work on it together. Plus, the storm is coming and once it does, who knows when she'll be able to talk to her.

Still, outside, the sky is clear and bright. The storm feels like a rumor. A lie. The only intimation of its impending arrival is this odd, hot wind. But she rides headlong into it all the way to Izzy's house, lets it sting her eyes and skin.

At Izzy's house, Ruby sits on her bed, and it feels almost like the last week hasn't happened. Ruby even notices that there is a pile of dirty clothes on the floor, a plate with the crusts of a peanut butter sandwich on the nightstand. A glass with a hard disc of milk in the bottom.

Marcy has gone across the street to her house to get something she's forgotten. Ruby knows she doesn't have long.

Marcy's suitcase sits open on the window seat, her clothes tidily folded inside. When Izzy gets up to go to the bathroom, Ruby has to resist the urge to rummage through them, as though she could find some sort of explanation in the skinny jeans and chiffon blouses. As though Marcy's socks and underwear and tiny padded bras could somehow explain how it is that Ruby almost lost her best friend this week.

Izzy comes back into the room, and Ruby feels proud of herself for not spying. For not being the snoop she wanted to be.

"Iz?" Ruby starts.

"Yeah?"

"I was hoping we could maybe still . . ."

Ruby can hear the front door opening, knows that it must be Marcy and wonders at what point she stopped ringing the Sinclairs' doorbell. She's only been staying here a week. Even Ruby, who has known Izzy and her parents her whole life, still rings the doorbell.

She hears Marcy and Gloria downstairs talking.

"I was thinking maybe . . ."

"I'm sorry about the fair," Izzy says suddenly, interrupting her.

Ruby feels her apology ping in her chest like a plucked string on a guitar. It reverberates.

"It's okay," she says. "I get it." And she *does* get it, sort of. And she wonders if she would have done the same thing if it had been her instead of Izzy who Marcy decided to make her new best friend.

Ruby notices that Izzy's hair is starting to tangle again. There is a sort of dreadlock starting to form behind her ear. Something about this makes Ruby feel better. The old Izzy is still here. She hasn't disappeared.

"When do Marcy's parents come back from Boston?" Ruby asks.

"Supposedly tomorrow, but Mom's worried about the storm messing up the flight."

"Oh," Ruby says, and tries to imagine what would happen if Marcy's parents' plane crashed. What if they died and she was an orphan? Would she have to stay with Izzy and Gloria and Neil forever? "I kind of can't wait," Ruby tries, testing these waters.

"I know, right?" Izzy says, breaking into a smile. She looks toward the door; they can both still hear Marcy and Gloria talking downstairs.

"She snores," Izzy whispers, like a gift. "Louder than Grover."

This makes Ruby giggle.

But before she can ask her about the bridge, Marcy stomps up the stairs and Ruby looks at Izzy to try to read what might happen next. She fears that this quiet truce, this return to normalcy, will slip away as quickly as it was returned to her. Once, her mother lost an earring from a pair her dad gave her down the kitchen drain. She reached her hand into the garbage disposal and was able to fish it out, but then she dropped it again. And this time she wasn't able to get it back. This time it had slipped past the carrot peels and lemon rinds, somehow disappearing into one of the holes in the mechanism. For a whole week her mother couldn't bring herself to turn the garbage disposal on, holding out hope that she'd be able to figure out a way to get the earring back. But finally, fruit flies started to gather in swarms at the lip of the drain and the house started to smell like garbage and she had no choice. It feels like this. Precarious. Like she'd better hold on tight or she might just lose Izzy for good.

"What are *you* guys talking about?" Marcy

asks, in a way that makes it sound as though whatever their answer is, she'll think it's childish. She flops on Izzy's bed like she owns the place, and picks up the pillow that Izzy's grandmother cross-stitched for her (*It's Not Easy Being a Princess*), clutching it to her chest. "Is it about that stupid bridge contest?"

Ruby studies Izzy, waiting to see what she does, how she responds.

Izzy fiddles with a Rubik's Cube that used to belong to her dad that she keeps on her bureau, and Ruby feels sick to her stomach. Marcy starts to pluck at a loose thread on the second *s* in *Princess* in the cross-stitch. It's been loose forever, but Gloria doesn't sew, and so Izzy has just been careful with it. Ruby watches as the thread starts to unravel from the fabric. As *Princess* becomes *Princes.*

Izzy lunges forward then and swipes the pillow out of Marcy's hands. "That's not yours," she says. "And the bridge contest isn't stupid. The winner gets to go to Seattle for the national competition. You said you wanted to do it with me."

Marcy relinquishes the pillow and rolls her eyes. "Sounds like a nerd festival to me," she says.

Ruby feels her face flushing red. She

371

wishes she could snap her fingers and disappear.

"Well, I'd rather be a nerd than a stuck-up b—" Izzy starts, Marcy's jaw falls open, and then there is a horrible sound from downstairs. It's actually two sounds, which seem to happen at almost the same time: first, there is an enormous crash, and then there is Gloria screaming.

Izzy and Ruby leave Marcy sitting dumbstruck and wordless on the bed and rush down the stairs, flying down the creaky boards, clinging to the rickety banister so as not to slip. Gloria is still screaming. "Neil! Neil! Come here quick!!"

They follow the sound of her voice to the kitchen where they see Grover spread out across the kitchen floor, all six feet four of him, like Gulliver. Izzy's dad comes into the kitchen from the back where he has been mowing the yard. He hasn't heard Gloria screaming and doesn't see Grover right away. "What's going on?" he asks and then says, "Oh shit."

He rushes to the phone and calls 911. Gloria drops down to her knees and presses her ear against Grover's broad chest. "He's not breathing. Tell them to come quick."

Ruby and Marcy stand in the doorway, afraid to move.

Izzy says, "I know CPR. I can use CPR."

Ruby thinks of the mannequin at the pool, and wonders how you ever go from that to this. This is a *real* man. A man with gray prickly whiskers and thick knuckles. He's a man who can beat anybody at Chinese Checkers and likes to drink his coffee mixed with vanilla ice cream. Grover has lived here since Izzy and Ruby were only three or four. He's been like a grandfather to Izzy. To them both.

As Izzy kneels down next to him and starts to go through the procedures she's learned at the pool, Marcy leans into Ruby and whispers, "Is he dead?"

"Oh, shut up," Ruby hisses, and Marcy pouts.

Luckily, the firehouse is right around the corner from Miss Piggy, and so it only takes about two minutes for the ambulance to arrive. The paramedics rush into the kitchen and Ruby and Marcy press themselves against the wall so as to not get in their way. He is breathing; his heart is beating. One of the paramedics pats Izzy on the back and says, "Good work. You may have saved his life."

Izzy still looks like a ghost of herself.

"Girls, why don't you go outside. Get some fresh air," Neil says, ushering them toward the front door. They obey, but once outside they aren't sure what to do. Marcy sits on the porch swing. Izzy and Ruby go sit by the giant oak tree, plucking whirlybirds off the ground.

"Do you think he'll be okay?" Ruby asks Izzy softly.

Izzy shrugs. "I hope so."

"I can't believe you know how to do that," Ruby says, but Izzy just nods.

Ruby recalls the night the ambulance came to get her mom last spring. She has tried to put this memory away, to push it to the back of her mind, but sometimes, it haunts her. She'd been in her room reading before bed, listening to her mother pacing in the other room. For hours her mom had been circling the house, checking the windows, the doors. Ruby knew something was wrong when the sound of her mother's feet shuffling across the wooden floors ceased. Still, she waited. She clutched her book, tried hard to focus on the words that were blurred and swimmy across the page. But the house just got quieter and quieter until the silence was nearly deafening. Terrified, she'd opened her door and gone to look for her mother.

The bathroom door was closed, and so she gently knocked, pressing her cheek against the cool wood.

"Mom?"

When there was no answer, she felt panic, like something liquid and hot, spreading from her chest out across her whole body. And so she turned the doorknob, which she was surprised to find unlocked. There was the sound of something falling to the floor; it startled her.

Her mother was crouched in the empty tub, clutching the sides, her eyes wild and terrified. But when Ruby reached out to her, she'd only cowered. Like an animal. Like something trapped. Ruby had been all alone.

"Should I call Daddy?" Ruby had asked, but her mother shook her head.

"I'm scared," Ruby said then, and her mother started to cry. Her entire body was trembling, quivering. "Mama?"

"I need . . ." her mother said, quaking. "I just need a doctor."

Ruby nodded and nodded. "Okay, okay." And then she ran to the kitchen and dialed 911.

She didn't tell anyone about the gun that had been sitting next to the bathtub. Before the paramedics arrived, she'd gingerly picked it up and returned it to the drawer where it belonged. And she wondered what would have happened if she hadn't found her in time. If she'd left her mother alone in the bathroom. Only she knows what her mother was thinking that night. It seems sometimes that her entire world is made of secrets, like swollen dangerous things she carries in her heart.

The paramedics are only inside Izzy's house for a few minutes before they push the stretcher outside, lifting it down the steps. Gloria follows behind, wringing her hands. As they load him into the back of the ambulance, Gloria answers the paramedic's questions.

"How old is he?" the guy asks, writing her answers down on a clipboard.

"Eighty-one," she says. "He'll be eighty-two next week."

"You his daughter?"

"Oh no, he just lives with us," she says. "He's our tenant. He rents a room."

"Any next of kin?" the paramedic asks, and it sounds like he's reading off a checklist.

Gloria shakes her head. "Just us. We're like his family. Is he going to be okay?"

"What's his name?" he asks.

"Grover," she says, but then pauses, shakes her head and laughs awkwardly. "But that's just a nickname, sorry."

The paramedic looks impatient.

"His real name is George. George Downs."

Sylvie still can't get ahold of Robert, and she worries. But strangely, she finds comfort in this new anxiety, grounded as it is in something *real* for a change. There is legitimacy to this fear. It has a cause. A purpose.

The radio said that here in Vermont they could expect three to seven inches of rain as well as sustained winds of thirty-five to forty miles per hour. The governor has already declared a state of emergency, anticipating downed trees and power lines. There will likely be some flooding of rivers and streams. Still, no one is being evacuated; perhaps the powers that be know that most Vermonters wouldn't heed an evacuation order anyway. People here are used to blizzards and arctic temperatures. To endless winters. A storm, even a big storm, is nothing to fear.

As she waits for Ruby to return home, she fills empty milk jugs with water. She show-

378

ers and then fills the bathtub with clean water. She locates every candle, every match. She makes ice and finds an old Styrofoam cooler on the front porch. She is a survivalist, she thinks. A survivor.

When Ruby comes into the house, breathless, Sylvie is digging through the junk drawer looking for the battery charger, trying to remember where the rechargeable batteries are.

"Mama," Ruby says, running toward her, clinging to her.

Ruby's arms feel strange around her. Sylvie cannot remember the last time she clung to her like this.

"What's the matter, honey?" she asks, feeling her insides melting like wax. Puddling, pooling.

"Grover's at the hospital," she says. Her shoulders shudder and she starts to cry.

"What happened?" Sylvie asks.

"Izzy gave him CPR and then the ambulance came. And now he's at the hospital. And did you know his real name isn't Grover? It's George? *George Downs?*" Ruby is sobbing, tears soaking into Sylvie's shirt.

Sylvie's body responds to this need in a way that surprises her. As Ruby clings to her, it's as though each nerve, each muscle, each sinew recollects. And she cradles her.

She holds her tightly and bends to breathe the scent of her hair. She can feel Ruby's ribs beneath her fingers, the hard boney cage that surrounds her chest.

"Okay, slow down," she says when Ruby pulls away.

"He might die."

Sylvie thinks about the kind old gentleman who has been like a grandfather to Izzy, to Ruby even. Ruby's only experience with death has been losing Jess.

"I'm scared," Ruby sobs, her face streaked with tears, and her nose running.

Sylvie shakes her head. *No, no, no,* she wants to say. *There's nothing to be afraid of.* But how can she tell her this? How can she, of all people, assure her that *anything* will be okay? And so she says, "He's very old, honey."

Ruby shakes her head hard. "He can't die. What if somebody needs him? What if somebody is looking for him and he doesn't know?"

"What are you talking about?" Sylvie says, confused. Ruby seems almost delirious. Her whole body is still wracked with sorrow, her tiny chest heaving.

"Nothing," she says. "It's nothing."

Ruby needs to get to Nessa to tell her about Grover. She needs to ask her how she knows him. What she wants with him. She needs to tell Nessa that he's sick. She tries not to think about what will happen if he doesn't get better, and she tries not to think about the look on Gloria's face, on Izzy's face, as they put him in the ambulance and took off down the street with the lights and sirens clearing their way. But when dusk falls that night, she knows that her mother is not going to let her go anywhere. It is not raining yet, but the sky has turned an ominous shade of gray, and the air feels thick. With the windows boarded up, it is dark inside the house.

Things feel strange with her mother. She is almost embarrassed now by how upset she got when she came home earlier. It's been such a long time since her mother held her like that. Since Ruby needed her to.

Afterwards, when she had finally stopped sobbing, she pulled away from her mother, excused herself and went to the bathroom, where she washed her face with cold water.

"Mama, where's our old TV?" she asks now.

"What old TV?"

"The TV we used to have, before?"

After the accident, her mother couldn't watch TV anymore. It didn't matter what channel they put it on. The news, the stories about all that suffering, of women murdering their husbands and children drowning in backyard pools, of accidents and storms and wars were too much. And the soap operas and sitcoms, all those make-believe people with their make-believe problems seemed to mock her. And so one afternoon, not long before Ruby and her dad moved out, her mother ripped the plug out of the wall, heaved the TV up, and carried it outside.

"In the shed maybe?" her mother says. "Why?"

Outside, Ruby examines the sky as if it has some sort of answers. It isn't raining, and the sky is a benevolent shade of indigo. But she also thinks about how quickly things can take a turn for the worse. How the world can flip upside down in just an instant. How everything that seemed certain is no longer true.

In the shed, she searches and searches until she locates the TV in the corner. It's so much smaller than she remembers. Bunk has a huge fifty-inch flat screen that takes up the entire living room wall. She lifts it up, following the cord, which has snagged on a pile of tools, and carries it back to the house.

Inside, her mother sits on the couch as she plugs it in and attaches it to the antenna wires. The antenna is still up on the roof. She finds the converter box they got a few years back in the junk drawer and hooks it up. Within minutes, there is a fairly sharp picture on the screen. She flips through the four channels they get (ABC, CBS, PBS, and a station that just broadcasts weather). This was the station she always used to flip past, but now she lingers there, looking for anything to confirm her mother's concerns. To prove that a storm is coming. That there is reason for her mother to worry. Reason for her mother to keep her prisoner here.

And she is right. The storm is headed north. There is a red banner flashing across the top of the screen saying SPECIAL WEATHER ALERT. They sit watching the forecast on the TV, waiting for the rain.

When it starts, they look at each other, eyes widening in something between disbelief and relief. It's as though they've been waiting for this their whole lives.

In her room, she listens as the rain taps and then pounds against the roof. She used to love this sound. She used to love storms. Jess was afraid of thunder, and so on nights like these, she would let him curl up in the bed with her. He always smelled so musty, dusty. Like such a boy. He liked to lie on his stomach, hands tucked between his legs. And every time the thunder rumbled and lightning flashed, she would rub his back. Just small quiet circles to calm him. She could feel his muscles tense underneath her fingers.

But this is not a normal storm. And she is alone in this bed, alone in this room.

She thinks of Nessa in the woods, and her heart aches with the idea that she might think that Ruby has forgotten her. She needs to get to her before the storm gets too bad. Before it's dangerous. The forecast said to expect rain all day tomorrow, winds, and later some flooding.

She can't leave now. Her mother is glued to the TV set, refusing to go to bed. And even if she could, after what happened with the raccoon, she's afraid to go out in the night. Of what could happen to her in the darkness.

She'll need to go to Nessa in the morning, to help her. To figure out where she should go.

When thunder growls like an animal, and she can feel its violent tremble rattle the windows, she wishes Jess back. Wishes his cold bare feet against her calves. The smell of grass and dirt, his musty breath. Because while she liked to think he needed her to protect him during the storms, she needed him to protect her too.

■ ■ ■ ■

# SUNDAY

■ ■ ■ ■

The agony is not inside her, but rather the other way around. Nessa is *inside* her pain. That is where she is. She has never felt anything like this in her entire life. It isn't the way they described it in the books she found on the library shelves and then pored over in the quiet shadows of the carrels. Every single one of those books described it as a gradual thing, a slow pain building, after hours (even days), to some sort of marvelous crescendo. But this does not feel like gentle, manageable waves of pain. It feels like a tidal wave, a tsunami. It feels as though her body is *made* of pain, as though she is no longer a *body* at all but rather one enormous ache. It is dull, persistent, a low hum and thrum that she can feel in her bones.

She wonders if she will die here in the woods.

She hasn't seen a doctor once since she

got pregnant, unless you count the trip to Planned Parenthood to confirm the pregnancy, the one after which she left clutching the brochures with colorful illustrations of girls her age, girls *in trouble,* girls with what the nurse practitioner had referred to as "options." She did go to the MinuteClinic once this winter when she had a cough that wouldn't quit. They'd asked her if she could be pregnant, and she'd nodded yes, and so they had prescribed her rest and tea and lozenges. She'd coughed so hard she'd thought she might just cough the baby out. But other than that, she has lived by the rules in the stolen library books. She has tried not to worry about all the things that can go wrong. She skipped the chapters that talked about preeclampsia, gestational diabetes, miscarriage. She didn't eat sushi (this was easy) or tuna (which was not so easy). She pilfered a bottle of prenatal vitamins from the drugstore, which she took religiously until she left Portland, remembering two hours into her bus ride that she'd left them in Mica's medicine cabinet.

She has tried to eat well, at least as well as she has been able, which has been difficult given her lack of money. There have been times that she's gone hungry, that the ache in her belly has made her afraid that the baby was going to come early. How foolish she had been to think that those hollow pangs were anything like labor. How silly she'd been. How stupidly naïve.

Because this is indescribable. Sometimes words fail.

She tries and tries to picture the pain as a poem, as something with a rhythm, a body, a form. She tries to study it line by line, the end-stopped lines when the pain recedes, the enjambment where respite is an illusion and the line runs on and on. She tries to imagine her pain on a page. The way the pen would feel in her hand. She tries to think only of the movement of ink, the continuous scribble and scrawl.

But this is an endless poem, one without stanza breaks, without line breaks even. If this pain were a poem, the words would rush to the margins, push *through* the margins, continue on the back of the paper. It would be the scrawling of a madman, filling page after page after page.

It has a sound, this pain. The ticktocking iambs, this clamorous scansion. The rhythm is deafening.

Ruby waits and waits. Morning passes. They eat lunch, and she thinks only of Nessa. Time crawls, the day stretches out, each hour swollen. She knows that eventually her mother will need a nap. Exhausted by another night spent wide awake, catching up on sleep during the day is not only necessary but inevitable. But she doesn't sleep; she can't pull herself away from the TV.

It is only when the reception on the TV goes out that her mother finally yawns and says, "I just need to lie down for a bit. You'll be okay?" And Ruby nods.

And while she is sleeping, Ruby slips out of the house and into the rain. She leaves a note on the kitchen counter, promises that she will be home soon. That she had something important that she has to do.

She is afraid to go behind the house in case her mother wakes up and hears her, and so she rides her bike up the muddy road and then cuts into the forest just past the old water shed. She leaves her bike there, hidden under some fallen fir branches. There is no path here, and so she has to forge her own. She can feel the branches scraping and scratching at her skin. By the time she gets to the river, she realizes she has gone too far upstream. Here the river is wider, the water deeper, the current stronger. It is pouring rain now, and the ground is slick. She considers walking back downstream to cross and then coming back up again on the other side of the river, but it will take too long. Nessa is waiting for her. And as soon as her mother wakes up, she will be waiting for her as well.

She sets her pack down on the ground and looks around to see if there is anything she can use to get across. At first she sees nothing and then spots a fallen birch about a hundred yards upstream. She drags it back to where she's left her backpack and stands it upright. She needs to drop it, just so, so that when it falls, it traverses the river. Then she simply needs to walk across it. She has good balance. Her gym teacher said so when they did their gymnastics unit in PE.

It doesn't fall straight the first time, but rather at an angle that leaves the top of the tree about three feet from the opposite bank. She considers trying to lift it again, but then figures she can just leap from the end to the embankment. She takes off her shoes and socks, stuffs them in her backpack, and starts across. The water laps at her ankles. It's not that deep, maybe two or three feet, but still she is nervous as she inches her way across. She grips the tree with her bare toes, curling them like a monkey to hold on. About halfway across, the tree rolls and she loses her balance. It feels as though it is happening slowly and not to her, as though she is watching it happen to someone else. An instant replay even as it occurs.

She tries to right herself, but it is too late. One leg is in the water, and the backpack on her back has slipped downward and is pulling her along with it. And then she is in the water. It is waist high and cold. Shocking.

She grabs for the tree and wills it not to budge again. Slowly, she walks through the rushing current, using the tree to keep her steady, until she reaches the other side. As she climbs up the muddy embankment on the opposite side, she finally realizes her fear. It's as if it's just now catching up with her. Her heart is thumping in her chest, her cheeks are flushed hot, and she is trembling all over. The current of the river like electricity. It's as though she has touched a live wire. She scrambles up the embankment and stares down at the river, at the tree, which has come loose from its tentative moorings and is rushing downstream now, like a twig. It hits a large rock and splits into two, each half taking its own separate course.

She thinks about how fearless she had been on Friday, about the new bravado that she'd felt at the bridge, at the pool, with Marcy. At the time it felt wonderful, a small miracle. As though some sort of weight had suddenly been lifted; she felt unbound, untied, *free.* But now as she watches the tree smash against the rocks, as the cold river water seeps into her jeans and sweatshirt and skin, she wonders if she'd simply been foolish. Maybe her mother is right. The world is a dangerous place: always conspiring to harm you. What more evidence does she need?

She is trembling, freezing, as she makes her way through the woods to the sugar shack. Her clothes are heavy. She peels off the wet sweatshirt and feels a little better, but still, her jeans and T-shirt are soaked through as well. Even her shoes, tucked in her backpack, are wet. And the food she'd packed for Nessa, the granola and breakfast bars anyway, are ruined. Only the canned food is okay. She hopes there is enough here. That they can salvage her next meal or two.

She makes her way to the sugar shack and knocks gently at the door, like she's just going to a friend's house to visit. Nessa doesn't answer.

Ruby knocks again and pushes the door gently open.

Nessa is sitting on the floor. Ruby can make out her shape in the dim light that is filtering in through the broken part of the roof. At the misty rain falling around her.

"Hey!" Ruby says brightly. "I brought more food! And I found him. George Downs? But . . ." She feels her throat start to swell up and she swallows before she speaks again so she won't cry. Nessa, of course, doesn't speak. And when Ruby's eyes adjust to the light, she sees that something isn't right. Nessa is sitting on the floor, surrounded by a strange pool of water, as though there has been a deluge, a flood. And then, when the girl's head rolls back on her neck, her throat exposed, she realizes what is happening. Her water's broken. The baby is coming.

"Oh my God," Ruby says. And this startles Nessa out of the words inside her head, off of the page behind her eyes, the ink dissolving into scattered pixelated fragments. "Is the baby coming?"

Nessa somehow remembers how to move her neck, how to nod up and down to communicate *yes, yes.*

"We need to get you across the river, to my house," she says. "My mother can help you."

But already Ruby's words are also scattering, fracturing, as the next surge comes. It is electric, thunder imbued with lightning. It starts in her spine, somewhere in the deep marrow. And it takes the form of a tail, the vestigial, primal remnants of another lifetime. She imagines it hitting the floor, sweeping in great arcs of pain, a warning. And when she is able to focus again, her eyes no longer rolling back in her head,

Ruby looks terrified.

"What do you need?" Ruby asks her. "What can I get for you? I have water. Do you want water?"

Nessa remembers the opposite of *yes*, though the word escapes her. She remembers only the back and forth shake of her head, and she tries to relinquish the memories of all the other times she has made this small and futile gesture, always failing to communicate. *He was careless. He didn't care.*

"Are you cold?" the girl asks, and it must be because her body is quaking. She doesn't know how to tell her that despite the trembling, it's as though her entire body is smoldering.

"Hot?" Ruby asks, and Nessa could kiss her.

And so she takes something from her pack and presses it against Nessa's forehead. Something cold. A water bottle? Whatever it is, it cools her, calms her. Gives her something to focus on. It's like a rock in the middle of a stream. The pain rushes around it, but there is stillness where it sits in the center.

"I'll stay here with you then," she says, "if you can't come with me." The girl looks as though she might cry. "I can help you." And then, blinking the tears away, and wiping them with the back of one filthy sleeve, she says, "I'm not afraid."

When Sylvie woke and found the note sitting on the counter, she felt her knees weaken beneath her. It took every reserve of strength she had to not collapse. She was a fool to think that what happened yesterday between them meant anything. That the tenderness and helplessness she felt in Ruby's little body had anything to do with her. That one embrace could make up for months and months of failures. For what happened that night last spring.

Now at dusk, she stands on the front porch, staring out at her empty driveway, listening to the rain and waiting for Ruby to come home. It is coming down hard now, and the wind is howling; the trees bending in abeyance to its assault.

She had picked up the phone to call Ruby's cell number, but then worried about what would happen if she didn't answer. She knows she needs to call Gloria. Her hope is that she is just at Izzy's house, doing whatever it is that she and Izzy do. She tries to imagine her inside that warm, safe house. She can practically see Ruby sitting at a stool at their cluttered kitchen counter, sipping at one of Gloria's mugs filled with cocoa. She can smell the fire in the fireplace. She can hear the bluesy music that Neil loves coming from their stereo. Ruby is safe. She knows this. Gloria probably just talked her into staying, to waiting out the storm. Sylvie wonders if maybe her own phone has just gone out again. Maybe Ruby has tried to call but hasn't been able to get through. She lifts the receiver and waits for the hollow confirmation. But the dial tone is strong and steady. Her hands begin to tremble.

She tries to remember the last time she used the phone to call Gloria, the last time she reached out to her. She is amazed when her fingers recollect the numbers, the pattern across the keypad. She clicks them rapidly before she has time to change her mind. And then she presses the cold receiver to her ear. Her entire body is trembling.

"Hello?" It's Gloria, and it sounds like she's eating something.

Sylvie pictures her sitting at the counter with the girls, maybe eating some homemade oatmeal cookies with them. Suddenly the kitchen smells not only of the wood fire but also of brown sugar, raisins.

"*Hello?*" Gloria repeats, a tinge of irritation in her voice this time.

"Gloria, it's me. Sylvie."

A pause. "Sylvie! Hi! Holy cow, do you hear the rain out there? Are you sure you guys don't want to come into town and stay with us? I can come get you. It's not too bad out yet, but it will be."

"Um, no, we're okay. I was actually calling because I was wondering if Ruby is with you. I was napping, and I think maybe she went into town?"

Another longer, deeper pause. An awful pause. And in this terrible moment, Sylvie anticipates exactly what Gloria will say and everything that will happen next. In a fraction of a second, she is able to envision the next thirty years of her life. Ruby has disappeared. She is lost; she is gone. Someone has taken her, or she has run away. The only certainty is this uncertainty. This is the beginning of a nightmare from which she will never wake up.

"Syl, Ruby hasn't been here. I've been home all morning. Izzy's been here too."

Sylvie begins to rock back and forth, her body remembering the strange primitive motion of motherhood, that instinctual

402

soothing of a body in motion. Only now her children are gone; her arms are empty. She is soothing a memory. She is pacifying a ghost.

"I'm coming over," Gloria says. "We'll find her, Syl. It's going to be okay."

"No," she starts. But what is she saying no to? No, don't help this nightmare to end? No, I am not standing alone in a dark kitchen rocking on my heels like a mental patient? No, I don't need you?

"The truck's dead, and Neil's run out for a minute in Grover's car. But as soon as he comes back, I'll come get you."

"Okay," Sylvie says. It is this easy. "Thank you."

Outside the wind moans, but she doesn't know anymore if it is a warning or a lament.

Ruby knows that she needs to go get help. That if she cannot get Nessa to her mother, perhaps she can get her mother to Nessa. But even though she knows that this is the logical, the *simple* answer, she also knows that it is illogical, impossible. Her mother has not left the house in a year and a half. Why would she leave now to help some girl she doesn't even know? For some figment of Ruby's imagination?

Ruby paces around the small wooden shack, listening as the rain pounds against the roof. Water now pours through the collapsed portion of the roof, spilling into an old sap bucket that she has placed here. Nessa is lying on her side, her knees curled up, as though she is only a child with a stomachache. Ruby remembers her mother instructing her to do the same on the nights when her belly roared and complained.

Outside the sky is strangely dark. It is only

twilight, but there are low, ominous clouds moving in from the east. They look like illustrated clouds in a child's picture book. The world looks like a painting. The rain is insistent but also strangely soothing. It is a storm without thunder or lightning. Only wind and this incessant rain. She wonders how much this shack can withstand, how much it would take for the entire roof to collapse.

The sounds that Nessa makes are not human sounds. There are no words, only guttural complaints. Glottal pleas.

Ruby is terrified. She tries to give Nessa water, and as she drips the water from the bottle onto Nessa's dry lips, she thinks of the baby raccoons. How this thirst, this impulse is the same. She can do this. She can help her. But then Nessa is rolling over onto her hands and knees, swaying, and vomits up all the water she has given her. There is a slick pool of water and bile on the rough-hewn floor. Ruby takes the rest of the water and splashes it on the puddle, trying to wash it away. Nessa rocks back and forth, her belly grazing the ground, and vomits again.

"I need to go get help," Ruby says, articulating exactly what she's been thinking. Waiting for Nessa to either affirm this or reject it. Should she stay here or should she go?

Nessa's eyes are rolling back in her head. Ruby and Izzy stayed up late one night and found a horror movie on one of the cable channels. It was about a girl who was possessed by the Devil. This is what she looked like. And she realizes that Nessa, the girl she found cowering in the woods a few days ago, is gone now. She has been consumed by pain, withdrawn into it. She has disappeared. All that remains is the body, this aching, rocking body. And Ruby knows that the choice is hers alone to make.

"I'll be back," she says, touching a tentative finger to Nessa's forehead. "I'm going to get help. I'll get my mother. She'll have to come."

Nessa's face relaxes a little, and in the second before she is overtaken by pain again, Ruby can see her answer. Her *Yes. Please. Help.*

Ruby has left her now, and Nessa doesn't know if she will ever come back. There is the definite possibility that she will have to deliver this baby alone. She wonders at the stories of teenage girls who have given birth in high school bathrooms, in fast-food restaurants. Closing themselves behind the clean white doors and delivering their own infants without anyone hearing them. Without anyone suspecting anything. Who are these girls and their painless labors? Who are these children who are able to somehow exist outside their pregnancies? She has always been baffled by the stories of girls who manage to hide their swollen bellies from their families. How sometimes, they don't even realize they are pregnant themselves until the baby is screaming in their arms. It seems like something made up. How could anyone be oblivious to such incredible transformation, to their body's own miraculous violence?

She doesn't really know anything about birth. These were the chapters she only skimmed in the library books. Because when she was reading them, this hour seemed impossibly far away. A speculation, a distant dream. She knows nothing of what to do. What had she been thinking?

Her logic has never transcended the moment. Not really. She has never been one to think beyond the immediate impulse. She wants something, she takes it. She feels something (hunger, lust, anger), she feeds it (with food, with sex, with fists). Even with the baby inside of her, she has still lived in this moment-by-moment way, hoping that when *this* moment finally came, she would simply react to it in the same way she has responded to any other problems.

But now here she is, and she is both gripped and paralyzed by the enormity of what is about to happen. Though the pain seems endless, limitless, boundless, she knows enough to know that it will not go on forever. This baby will come out eventually. And with its release, the pain will be released as well.

She needs to trust that Ruby will come back. That she will not have to do this alone. She is bringing her mother. The midwife.

Pain is a time machine. It transports her. She is reeling backward, removed from her body. Removed even from this rain, from this dark forest, from the storm that is gathering outside. She is at once inside and outside. She is body, and she is ethereal. She is the rain, beating against the roof. She is the aching moan of the wind.

She returns to the position on her side, with her knees drawn up as far as they can go, her belly pressing against the thick flesh of her thighs. And waits for the next wave of pain to come. And when it does, she slips away, out of this body into another body. Another time.

Ruby forgets the lies she has told. The fabrications come undone as she runs through the rain back downstream to the place where the river is usually narrower, but she is disoriented in the dark, in the storm. Has she gone the wrong way? She wonders as she stares at the wide expanse of rushing water. As she hears the roar of an angry river, rushing toward some unknown destination.

She stands, bewildered, on the bank and peers at the backside of her mother's house, at the broken fence and the sandbags lined up along its edge. She needs to get across the river and get to her mother. To convince her, somehow, to come with her to Nessa. She knows Nessa doesn't want her to call an ambulance, but she will if she has to. She will do whatever it takes to make sure she and the baby are okay.

Ruby knows she's just going to have to

leap. It's not that much deeper and wider than it was; it just looks that way in the rain. And so she backs up and runs headlong into the storm, eyes squinted against the rain, and holds her breath as she jumps.

She lands on the opposite side of the river, and it feels as though the river is inside her body now, as though her blood has been replaced by this angry, muddy current. She can barely feel her legs anymore as she runs toward the house. The entire fence has collapsed now, and the remaining boards are scattered about the backyard like playing cards, leaving the back of the house exposed.

She runs to the backdoor and reaches for the handle. It is locked. She bangs and bangs and bangs. The lights are on, and she can see her mother moving around inside, but then the lights go out and everything is dark. She is filled with rage. Is her mother hiding inside? Is it possible that she is simply pretending she isn't home so that she won't have to answer the door?

She runs around to the front of the house, up onto the porch, and smashes the door with her fists until they ache with pain. She wonders if she has broken her bones. If she might just bang until they are all broken and she is just a pile of dust.

A voice swims to her through the rushing water in the gutter. "Ruby?"

And then the door opens and her mother's shadowy face swims out of the darkness, a strange, ghostly white, disembodied face.

"Mom, you have to come with me," Ruby says, breathless.

"Where have you been?" her mother says, her voice changing from relieved to angry. "I called Gloria and she said you weren't there. I've been worried sick," she says, her voice trembling and furious. "God, Ruby. Why are you doing this to me?"

Ruby stands in the doorway, incredulous. "Why am I doing this to *you*?" she says, almost laughing. She thinks then of Nessa on the floor of the sugar shack, the sounds coming from her throat. All of the agony in the world concentrated in her body.

"I *need* you," she says, and she realizes that she is crying now. Because these three words are the ones she's been waiting to say for so long. The words she's been most afraid of. The ones she fears will go unheard. "I need you," she says again, only this time more firmly. She is giving her mother one last chance, an ultimatum. If she says *no,* if she shakes her head in the way that she always does, if she slips away from her, hiding in her cowardice, lost inside her fear, she will walk out into the storm alone. She will let her mother go. She will walk away and never, ever look back again.

"I need you," Ruby says.

And Sylvie feels her entire world starting to cave in. It's as though the weight of these words, the impact with which they strike, are the same as the car hitting the side of the bridge. Of the car with her family nestled inside as it smashes into the bridge and that other car backs away, leaving them to bear the impact alone. As she stands on the porch with only inches between her daughter and her impossible demands, she is once again hurtling inside the car, free-floating like an astronaut as they crush through the bridge and tumble down into the water. She is watching as the steering wheel comes down on Robert's lap, crushing his legs before the door swings open, releasing him into the night. She is sitting in the front seat, holding her mascara in one hand as she watches the glass shatter, as the current tugs her and Jess into its

414

arms, as she watches Ruby hurled like a ball toward the shore. She is pulled into the rush of dark water, blinded and deaf to anything but Jess's cries. She can see his one pale arm, his sweet small face illuminated by the headlights that are still, miraculously, shining like a spotlight on the scene in the river.

"Mommy!" he cries, and she tries, she tries so hard to reach him, but the closer she gets the harder the river pulls, and then, in only moments, his head dips under the water, and then, a moment later, that pale white arm is gone. A recollection. A memory.

After this moment, there was nothing left but this crippling fear.

She remembers almost nothing of the hospital that night, of the days and weeks after the accident. There were pills and sleep. Robert was in the hospital for nearly a month before he came home. They'd had to amputate both legs. There was no way to save them. There was a funeral, outside, a cold sunny day before Christmas, a casket that looked as though it were made for a doll. There was Ruby sitting on the couch watching cartoons and eating cereal. There was Bunk lumbering around the house fixing whatever he could fix. Gloria with her sad eyes sitting at her kitchen table like an odd guardian. And there was her fear. The fear she had lived with since she was a little girl, the fear she kept quiet in the back corner of her mind. But now the fear lived *inside* her. It controlled her hands. It maneuvered her eyes and mouth. It spoke through her. She was only a marionette, she realized, and Fear her puppeteer.

"I need you," Robert had said, with his worried face as he learned to navigate this strange new world. *I need you to help me, to love me.*

"I need you," Gloria had said as she waited and waited and waited for her to get better. *I need your friendship, your company.*

"I need you," said all the mothers. *To bring my baby into the world, to take care of me, to make us safe.*

"I need you," Ruby says. "I *need* you."

It takes everything she has to go to the closet. She is resisting every impulse, defying every instinct.

She hasn't worn this coat since the night of the accident. When the paramedics found her, she was a mile downstream, clinging to a rock, screaming Jess's name; her bright red coat ultimately saved her. She reaches into the pockets and feels something inside. It's an envelope. She pulls it out now; it has long since dried and hardened. It is stiff as she unfolds it. The kids' report cards. The reason they'd been headed toward the school during the storm. As Ruby waits in the other room, Sylvie unfolds the fragile paper, studies the assessment of her child. Her eyes scan the paper and go to where the teacher has handwritten her notes, which, despite the river, are miraculously preserved. *Jess is a hardworking and sweet boy, but he is easily discouraged. It is difficult to get him to participate in class, but only because he lacks confidence. He is shy and somewhat fearful of new things. And while he does not test well . . .* Here, the last words written about her son. This odd obituary. This strange eulogy. She remembers being frustrated when she first read this. She'd been a little angry, even, with Jess. *Why don't you raise your hand in class? What are you afraid of?* As though she herself had not been tentative like this. As though he wasn't exactly like she had been as a child.

She sets the report card on her bureau and unfolds Ruby's. *Ruby is such a bright child. She is eager to learn, kind to others, and a joy to teach. I feel lucky to have her as my student.* This, more than the note about Jess, feels like a blow: these observations by someone who had only known Ruby for a few months, who had not seen her take her first steps or listened to her sing or watched as she helped Jess put blocks in the shape sorter; someone who didn't know she liked plain donuts and meatball grinders and that her favorite color was orange; someone who didn't know she talked in her sleep or that she broke her arm when she was three. And still, this woman felt fortunate to know her. This *stranger* counted Ruby as one of her blessings. She feels oddly jealous and then just filled with remorse. How could she have let things go so wrong? How could she deny herself what she has left? How she could have deprived Ruby a mother all this time? What kind of mother was she? And what has she become?

Ruby leads the way through the house, grabbing things along the way and stuffing them into her backpack. She has heated up water and poured it into her Thermos. She has towels, scissors. She's talking rapidly about a girl in the woods, a runaway. Sylvie has no idea what she is talking about, but still she listens. She tries to understand.

"There's a girl in the woods, Mama. And she's having a baby."

Sylvie's eyes widen.

"Just come," she says. "Please. She needs us."

Nessa has become the pain now. She has ceased to exist as anything but this throe. Her entire body is burning up. She is fever. She is heat. She is not a body but an element. Volcanic. Molten. She feels as if a fire is starting; her flesh burns so badly. It recalls the first time, when the boy whose name she can't remember but whose hands and eyes she won't forget, kissed her until her face was sticky with his saliva, an ineffectual balm for the searing pain he'd caused. It is a memory of other times, when the men were too rough. When they cared for nothing but their own pleasure, even if it caused her pain. It is the memory of fire that lives between her legs now. A sort of primordial remembrance. She could be the first woman ever. She could be Eve.

She needs to get outside of her body, because it is about to destroy her. And so she crawls on hands and knees, lowing like an ancient beast, as she makes her way through the broken wall. The rain greets her with its cold hands, pulling her, even as it pushes. She lies in a pile of wet leaves, presses the cold wet mud against her skin, and opens her eyes until the rain fills them, until she is not only mute but blind as well. And, for a moment, there is respite. Cool rain on hot skin; the fire sizzles even as it smolders on. She feels as though someone is tearing her body apart, as though she is being ripped down her center, just threads holding together a seam. The girl is gone. When did she go? Was she ever there at all? Maybe Nessa dreamed her, conjured her. Maybe she is feverish, delirious, foolish, and deluded. She might die here, she thinks, and this thought is punctuated by a loud, wild creaking and the sudden and momentary certainty that something terrible is about to happen.

Ruby tries to open the back door, but the wind pushes back, resists like a child on the other side who doesn't want them to come out. She pushes harder, pressing her shoulder into it, leaning with all of her weight. The door swings open and she stumbles down the steps. When her eyes adjust to the darkness, she feels like she's stepped into a dream.

The first thing she notices is that the river is no longer the quiet creek it was yesterday. It is wide and high, and it roars like the engine of a car. She takes the flashlight and shines a weak spotlight into the distance. It doesn't seem possible, but the river has come closer to the house as well now.

She turns around to see if her mother is following her. But her mother stands in the doorway, her old red coat wrapped around her, her arms wrapped around her waist. She is looking at the river too. Suddenly,

Ruby is overwhelmed by a memory of her mother standing at the edge of the river after they finally found Jess. She had stood like this then too. She was soaking wet, and someone, one of her dad's friends, another paramedic, wrapped his arm around her shoulders. But she'd only stood there, shaking, staring out at the water in the same strange way. As though she were watching the world end and was powerless to do anything about it.

"Are you coming?" Ruby says to her mother, afraid of her answer. Afraid that she will only stand there just as she had that night, staring out into the darkness like a statue.

But instead her mother pulls the hood of her coat up over her head, pulls the drawstrings tight and nods at Ruby.

"Quick!" Ruby says to her. "We need to cross here. Upstream it's going to be too hard."

The rain pounds down on them, and Sylvie has to will her legs to move. She feels as though she is a tree that has grown roots in this spot. That she is tethered to this house by a strange underground network of nerves, intricate and complicated. Is this paralysis from her own stubborn unwillingness, she wonders, or *inability*? What if she was wrong? What if she is simply *incapable* of leaving this house, this little plot of land? What if this sentence, this exile is not self-imposed at all, but rather inflicted upon her? Mandated. What if there are greater powers than her own fear at work here?

The rain is loud as it hits the hood of her jacket; it pounds against her ears like a heartbeat.

Ruby is standing at the place where land

becomes water, waiting for her. Her face is blank, neither hopeless nor hopeful. Just *waiting.*

This moment is a gift, she knows. It is being offered to her — by Ruby, of course, but perhaps, even by the universe. If she refuses, if she turns away from this cosmic generosity, she is suddenly certain that something terrible will happen. And that terrible thing will be that she never sees her daughter again. And so when Ruby hollers into the storm, "Hurry, Mom!" Sylvie wills her legs to move, her body to respond. She can feel the network, the nervous system resisting. It is electric, magnetic even. But she wills herself forward, one step at a time. Her legs feel thick and heavy, as though she is tearing roots from the ground. As though she is ripping her own body from the earth. But then she is walking toward Ruby, and then she is running toward Ruby, and the house is behind her.

And nothing is happening.

She is not being sucked back into its clutch, there is nothing stronger than her own wish, her own desire, her own yearning. She wants desperately to be free of this, and then, suddenly, miraculously, she is. She just *is.*

"Take my hand," Ruby says. "We need to

cross here. It's too deep up ahead." Ruby extends her tiny hand out to her, and Sylvie grasps it. How many times has she held her daughter's hand as they crossed the street? There was always something so pacifying about the moment when palms touched and fingers locked in this way; as long as she was holding on to Ruby nothing could happen to her.

They move together like one strange multi-limbed body, first running and then leaping across the narrowest part of the river. It rushes against their ankles, tugs at their legs, but they are still able to cross and get to the other side. Sylvie can feel the cold water seeping into her pant legs, even her coat. It should weigh her down, but here, staring at the backside of her house from the opposite embankment, she feels lighter. So much weight lifted.

"Come," Ruby urges, and pulls her hand, a gentle reminder that this journey has only started.

They make their way through the dark woods, Ruby leading the way. The storm feels like something alive, a beast howling into the night. It is raining so hard now, the air feels like it too is alive. But rather than frightening her, it seems, rather, to urge them on.

Ruby carries the flashlight, and the weak beam bobs and dips as they run, illuminating nothing but rain and trees, spruce and fir and cedar, their evergreen scent heady and thick. Maple, birch, beech, elm, and ash with their tender leaves. But despite the darkness, Sylvie feels overwhelmed by all of her other senses: the heady scent of the trees, the snapping of twigs and crush of leaves under their feet as they run, the howling of the wind and the roar of the rain and the river behind them. She is disoriented, but Ruby seems certain; she is not forging a new path but following along one she already knows by heart.

Ruby rushes ahead and then stops, turning as if to make sure that Sylvie is still behind her. In the dim light of the flashlight, Sylvie can see the relief in Ruby's face. It tears at her heart. Ruby had expected her to disappear. That she would fail, again. Somehow, this makes Sylvie's resolve grow stronger. She will not abandon her again. She will never leave her.

"This way," Ruby says then, her words being sucked into the wind. "In the sugar shack."

You wouldn't know it was there if you weren't looking for it. It is a crumbling sugarhouse enveloped in foliage. One side has sunken into the ground, and the roof is caved in. It doesn't look as though it has been used for years. It's like something from a childhood fairy tale. Like something from a dream.

Ruby shines the flashlight toward the door, which has come off of its hinges. "She's in here," she says but hesitates at the doorway, as though afraid of entering, as if she is second guessing her decision to bring Sylvie here.

"It's okay," Sylvie says. "I'm right here."

And so Ruby pushes the door gently open and Sylvie follows close behind. They step through into the dark room, and for a moment all of the smells and sounds are silenced here. It is a quiet dark cave. But as Ruby scans the room with the flashlight, she becomes frantic. The room is empty.

Ruby scans the room with the flashlight, terrified that Nessa has tried to leave on her own, gone out into the storm to find help. She sweeps the room with the light, as if she has missed some dark corner where she might be cowering, hiding. But there is nothing in here. No girl. It's as though she never existed. As though she only dreamed her.

"She was just here," she says to her mother, who stands shivering in the doorway. "I swear. Her water broke right here," she says, gesturing to the floor. She drops to her knees and presses her hand against the floor. And it is wet. But it could just be rain that has come through the cracks in the roof overhead.

Ruby feels like she might vomit. She looks at her mother, afraid that she will think that she was trying to trick her. That she will be angry. But her mother just kneels down next to her.

"Where do you think she's gone?"

"I don't know," Ruby says. "I don't know why she would have left. I told her you were a midwife, that you could help her." Ruby feels her entire chest expanding, her heart swelling inside of it. She sits down on the floor and looks into the dark abyss of the shack.

Her mother sits down next to her, puts her arm across her shoulder, and says, "It's okay. We'll find her."

Ruby sets the flashlight down on the floor. It creates a narrow beam of light which points outside into the storm, into the night. "I'm sorry I brought you here," she says.

Her mother shakes her head. "No, no . . ."

"I know you didn't want to leave."

"It's okay," she says and pulls Ruby in tighter. "Listen, we'll find her. She'll be okay."

Ruby breathes the scent of her mother, and the scent of woods and rain and river transport her. She is sitting on the embankment as they pull Jess's body from the river. That night, her mother had stood at the edge of the river by the broken bridge, refusing to go home. Finally, Bunk came and pulled her away, and she fought and fought.

"You don't understand!" she kept screaming. "There was another car! There was another car! It was coming toward us, but then it just disappeared."

Ruby had not seen another car. She had been so lost inside her book, so lost inside the story, she hadn't realized they were falling until she saw the river outside her window, until she heard the horrific sound of her father screaming. But her mother insisted that there was another car, even as her father said, *No, no.* She must have been mistaken. It must have been the way the rain hit the streetlights. An illusion. Because there was not a single shred of evidence that there had been any other vehicle near the bridge that night. It was an accident. That is all. Robert had been distracted. There was a storm. The tires were bald, and the bridge was old. That is all. Sometimes the world is cruel. Sometimes it conspires against you, no matter what you do.

"What's her name?" Ruby's mother says softly.

She looks up at her mother's face, sees how this year has changed her. There are lines around her mouth and at the edges of her eyes. The deep circles beneath her eyes are like strange shadows.

"It's Nessa," she says.

She nods then and stands up. "Okay. Then let's find her. I'm sure she hasn't gone far."

They go back out through the front door of the shack, calling her name. They circle the shack, widening the perimeter like any good search team. But it feels as though they are looking for a ghost. The sky is furious, and the wind is nearly deafening now. The entire world seems to be made of water. Below them the river rushes with a new purpose, toward what, she isn't sure.

Even if they were to find her, Sylvie doesn't know what they can do for her. This was not part of her midwife training. Every single child she has brought into this world has been ushered into clean sheets and warm arms. Into soft light.

She tries not to think about the possibility that there is no girl. That this is all just a dream of Ruby's, a delusion. She tries not to think about the distinct possibility that she has passed on her own paranoia. That she has infected Ruby with her own irrational fears, her terribly vivid imagination. She needs to believe her, because the alternative is unbearable. But still, there is nothing here but woods and rain and river. The entire search seems ridiculous, futile. They are chasing a dream girl, a chimera, a ghost.

Ruby slips around to the back of the shack, taking the only light with her, and Sylvie is enveloped in a roaring blindness. She relies on sound alone to guide her back to her daughter. She runs and trips on a stump. She hears the fabric of her pant leg rip, and then feels the shocking cold of the rain against her exposed skin.

"Ruby!" she hollers, stumbling blindly toward the place where she disappeared. She uses the edge of the shack to guide her, and then she is on the other side, staring at the back of Ruby's head. She is squatting on the ground. She turns to Sylvie, and cries, "Mom. Come here."

Maybe it is just this overwhelming pain, but the only memory Nessa has now, the only one there is room for, is of the night she left. It was the reason for leaving, but now it is the reason for coming home. It has driven her back here. It has *pulled* her back like some sort of invisible thread. Each day since then like a bead, but the thread is too short, and she has to keep pulling and pulling to get more slack. And now, here she is, all those beads have slipped off the strand, and she is somehow back where she started, at the hard metal clasp that holds it all together. She is delirious, covered in wet leaves, but she knows that this is her only job now: to fasten this metal clasp. To bring things, everything, full circle.

When she opens her eyes again, they fill with rain, but she sees that Ruby has come back. She is overwhelmed with relief. Gratitude. This girl, with her ratty braids and

434

tiny hands and gentle eyes. She kneels down next to Nessa on the wet ground and puts her hand on her forehead, as though she is Nessa's mother. Her skin is so cool against the furnace that is Nessa's flesh. She smiles, even as the pain rips through her again.

"I brought my mom," the girl says. "She can help you."

Nessa focuses her eyes on the place behind the girl. Into the dark abyss of the storm. She can see the dark shape of a person, a woman. Ruby turns to her and shines the flashlight so that she is illuminated. She is wearing a jacket with a hood, and she can only see her face. But in the bright beam of light (*the headlights, flicking on suddenly, suddenly*) the recognition is absolutely certain.

She can taste the metal in her mouth. She can hear the *click, click* of her teeth. The pain is beginning to take the shape of a connection, and she is electrified as the two points of metal touch. She bites down, bites hard, her teeth grinding into each other, her mouth flooded with the tastes of gold, silver, platinum, and rust. She squeezes her eyes shut, bears down, concentrates on the clasp, holding it open just long enough to slip the loop in, and releasing it. And at once, everything is connected.

Here is the night the world changes, your world changes. A night of passages. From summer to fall. From childhood to adulthood. From careful whispers to total silence. You have left so much behind already, but tonight you will leave the rest behind for good. You will burn bridges tonight. You will barely stop to wonder at the flames.

Here is a man. Here are his hands. Here is his face you can barely recollect anymore. Here is the cold seat of his car, the cold wind through the crack in the window. Here is a song on the radio that sounds like the hollow insides of a tin can. Here is the joint he passes you that you put to your lips. It crackles and hisses, and the fire burns your throat before the calm descends.

Here is your body, though it doesn't feel like it belongs to you. He has claimed it somehow, made it his own. He has annexed your ribs, your skin. Here is your body sore and weeping. *Seeping.* You can smell him in your hair and on your hands.

Here is the book he has given you, his words pressed into the fleshy paper. A souvenir? A token. A reminder. Even before it is over, it has already begun to end. He thinks he will let you go quietly. That this letting go will be an easy thing. He doesn't know then that it will not be gentle, this severing, but violent. How could he?

Here is a river. Here is rain and a girl and a man in a car. Here you are, realizing that one day soon he will drop you off and never come back to get you again. And because you have been left before, this feels inevitable, though certainty and predictability doesn't make it hurt any less; it only makes it hurt more.

The rain taps its condolences, its reassurances against the glass. And as you lean into the cold window, it could be any window at all. It could be the window of that one apartment where you lived with your mother, with its black-and-white floors like a checkerboard, the brown cookie jar, the curtains with the pom-poms on the hem. It could be the place you stayed when you were seven: the room in the big yellow house next to the school, where you sat at the window and watched the children get dropped off by their parents. Longed for those kisses and the brightly colored lunch boxes and rain boots. It could be the window in the motel where you stayed one summer, the one that smelled of cigarettes and mold, but that also had a broken vending machine where you could get free Pepsi whenever you wanted one. It could be the window in your classroom, any classroom, in any of the towns and cities where you lived. It could be the window in the classroom where you first met him when he came to talk to your class. Where until the day he walked in, you'd spent most every day staring out the window, waiting for the scenery to change.

Here is a man who does not belong to you. You should be accustomed to this, to this borrowing. To the temporariness of all things. Everything you have known has been yours only on loan, on lien. Your mother has taught you that anything, everything, can be repossessed.

But the sting of your body echoes the sting of all those other departures. And for a moment, you wonder if you might still have a chance to change everything.

Here is the rain, here is the river, here is the man who does not love you. Here is a girl, a stupid girl, clinging to the words he

has offered as consolation.
    Here is the bridge.

In this body made of pain, Nessa is once again sitting next to him in the front seat of the car that night. She is not wearing her seat belt so that she can sit closer to him. He is bringing her to the barn where he lives; his hand is up her skirt, playing. She can feel his fingers parting her, as though he is trying to find something. It hurts and feels good at the same time. And as they approach the bridge, she can feel the cre-scendo that precedes the diminuendo, the thrumming ache across her abdomen.

She sees the headlights coming, but she is caught up in her own ecstasy. She is high too, they are both stoned on the weed they smoked in the ice-arena parking lot. And now, as his fingers continue to push and probe and he grabs her hand and presses it against the hard knob in his lap, she is too high to remind him that he needs to honk. To warn the car that's coming through.

The bridge is only wide enough for one vehicle. And as they round the corner, she can see that his headlights have dimmed again, because he hasn't bothered to get them fixed. He is careless, careless, and so it is a ghost car. Invisible in the night as they move toward the bridge, but then, just as they are about to enter the bridge, his lights come on, illuminating the faces of the people in the car. She can see the small *o*'s of their mouths as they materialize, as they realize what is happening. She sees the woman and watches the man yank the wheel as though he can still right things, as though he can change their trajectory, their destiny with one precise correction.

But it is too late. Declan hits the brakes, but the other car swerves to avoid them, and she hears the crush and scream of metal as it strikes the side of the bridge.

She watches through the rain-splattered windshield as the car teeters at the edge of the bridge and then as all of it collapses: as the walls break, as the roof caves in, as the car plummets into the river.

"Stop!" she screams at him. "Stop!"

She has *spoken,* she is sure of it, but for some reason he cannot hear her. It's as if she has not spoken at all, as if this one word — this demand, this plea — this desperate utterance is completely imperceptible to his ear. Because he does *not* stop.

Instead he backs up, as though he could just reverse everything that has happened, as though he can simply rewind. And then, he flips the car around and accelerates.

She scrambles into the backseat and stares through the odd viewfinder that is the rear window. When she turns back to him again, he meets her glance in the rearview mirror, looks her in the eye, sees the wreckage he has caused, and keeps on going.

Now, for a moment, she feels like she has returned. That instead of fleeing she is *inside* that covered bridge, enclosed in darkness, on the edge of disaster. The wind howls, the rain is beating down now, and she is worried the roof will collapse. That this is the world's way of punishing her, or exacting its perfect and precise revenge.

Sylvie peers into the girl's face. She is able to tell simply by her pallor, by the way her eyes have gone blank, unfocused, far away, that she is inside herself now. It won't be long. She is both absent and fully present. Her body is doing the work now, while her mind disappears.

They need to get her back inside the shack. It is wet and filthy out here. It is too dark to see. Somehow Sylvie is able to coax her onto her knees and the girl crawls, like an infant, like an animal, back into the shack. Inside she rocks and moans. Sylvie has seen women give birth in this position. She readies herself for what will come next.

"I need to check your cervix," she says to the girl, who nods, nods. She is compliant; she will do anything Sylvie says. And so she eases her onto her back on the floor, slipping the rolled up towel that Ruby brought under her head. She uses hand sanitizer that

Ruby has also brought to clean her hands, and she reaches inside the girl whose body convulses and resists. Despite the frigid air around them, the girl's body is furiously hot. Feverish. She tries not to think about infection. About what could go wrong.

She is fully dilated. The baby is coming.

Her hands remember. All of this. Sylvie is in a fugue state as she goes through all of the necessary motions. She layers the floor beneath the girl with clean towels. She takes the Thermos of hot water and pours it onto another fresh towel. She will use this to clean the baby. She takes a lighter from her pocket and sterilizes the scissors. And then she does what she has always done best. She calms the girl, she assures her that she can do this. That there is nothing, not a single thing, in the world that she should fear.

Ruby watches, mesmerized, from the corner of the room. She has propped the flashlight up so that it shines down on Nessa and her mother, providing just enough light for her to see. For them all to see. She watches in wonder and amazement, as her mother pushes and pulls, as she whispers, coddles and coaxes. "Yes, yes, this is it. Just one more push. The baby is coming."

Ruby is amazed by how calm her mother is, how that frantic unease that seems to have settled into her body has now disappeared. It's as though her focus is so intense, her purpose so certain, that any fear she might have has no room.

Nessa writhes beneath her hands, her hips pushing skyward, her head thrown back. She is bathed in rain and sweat and mud. Everything seems to go on forever. The baby presses and then retreats. Teasing. Nessa's entire body moans.

And then, it is so fast. There is the whooshing sound of something rushing into the world, the slip and squall. Her mother's hands move quickly, unwinding the baby from the cord, unwrapping it like a gift, and then using the baster to suction its mouth and nose, as though drawing its first breaths from it with these instruments. The entire shack is rocking and swaying in the storm, but for a brief moment, there is nothing but silence. And then the baby's cries fill the air. *Life.*

Her mother works quickly, cutting the cord and tying it off, easing the infant onto Nessa's chest, and covering them both with the warm, wet towel. Then she delivers the afterbirth, which Ruby knows about from her mother's books, and Nessa peers at the baby, her chest rising and falling, as her breathing slows. As the rapid panting quiets to the slow intake and outtake of breath.

Ruby kneels near Nessa's head and looks at the baby. Its face is red, its head elongated from the birth canal (another detail she learned from the books). Its eyes are unfocused but open, trying hard to find light, to find her mother.

"It's a girl," Ruby says, her throat swelling, her heart expanding in her chest.

Nessa looks at Ruby as though she has

forgotten that she is in the room. She smiles. There is a thick wet lock of hair across her forehead. Ruby brushes it away, and Nessa closes her eyes. When she opens them again, the baby's arm has come loose from the towel, and it flails out, pale and white in the darkness. Her hand is so small, each finger no bigger than a stem. As her fist uncurls, it is like a flower, a white moonflower opening. Nessa and Ruby are mesmerized. And then she opens her mouth and cries.

Outside, the wind beats against the side of the shack, and Ruby thinks of the three little pigs. The story used to terrify her and Jess when they were little. The wooden house was always the second to go, vulnerable to the Big Bad Wolf's rage. Only the brick house was safe from his wrath. She remembers her mother's promises, "But this house, this house is safe. Daddy built it, and it is stronger than any brick house. It's made of wood, but it's also made with love. And not a single thing in the world, not even a wolf, can destroy that."

She feels tears coming to her eyes as she watches her mother clean up, pulling fresh towels from the backpack, taking the baby from Nessa and cleaning the blood from her body, and then swaddling her tightly.

She wonders at the ease with which her

447

mother shows Nessa how to offer the baby her breast. She isn't even embarrassed to watch as the baby roots to find her nipple and then latches on. She watches her mother's hands remembering these tasks. And Ruby is suddenly filled with a tremendous sense of peace. For a moment, *this* moment, it feels like everything is going to be okay. That something stolen has been returned to her. That something lost has been found.

Even as the next gust of wind tears through the hole in the roof, sending rain and leaves down into the shack, even as the roof caves in a little more, she knows that everything is going to be all right. Even as the door is torn from its hinges, the inside merging with the outside world, she is certain that everything will, somehow, be fine.

"Ruby, I need to go get help," her mom says.

Ruby shakes her head. Feels the storm swelling inside her body, as though that open door brought the hurricane inside her. She is confused about where her body ends and the hurricane begins.

"I'll be back," her mother says. "I just need to get to a phone."

"Is everything okay with the baby?" Ruby asks softly, afraid of the answer.

"I think so, but her breathing is a little rapid. She needs to see a doctor."

"I'm coming with you," Ruby says. She doesn't want her mother to go.

"No, Ruby," her mother says. "I need you to stay here with Nessa and the baby."

And then she is leaning over Nessa, as though she is the child, saying gently, "I'm going to get help. I'll be right back. Just stay here, keep the baby dry and warm." She turns to Ruby and kisses her on the forehead. "I'll be right back."

But Ruby knows that promises, even those well-intended ones, can be broken.

In ten years, she never lost a baby. In the hundreds of births where she acted as midwife, not a single infant was lost. There were times when she was afraid, of course. Once, with the mother who lived way out in the woods in a trailer with her family of six. She'd given birth to all of her children at home, and despite having gestational diabetes, she'd insisted on another home birth. The baby was too large, her pelvis too small. And after twenty-four hours of labor, she finally relented and Sylvie called Robert and they took her to the hospital in an ambulance. She'd had mothers who hemorrhaged, and infants who'd aspirated on meconium. But she had always known exactly what to do to keep them safe. She'd never lost a child. Never lost a mother. When it comes to bringing babies into the world, there is no room for fear.

But now, as she rushes through the wind

and rain, she worries. She worries that this baby will not survive. The rattle in the tiny barrel of her chest was faint but certain. She worries about meconium, about RSV. Clearly there has been no prenatal care, and if this had been a normal home birth, she would have come ready with antibiotics for the mother. She needs to get to a phone. The infant, the girl, should both be taken to a hospital where they can be monitored.

When they left the house, her phone was still working. But she can't imagine that it is working anymore. Storms much smaller than this one have taken the phone line out.

She runs along the river's edge; she doesn't have the flashlight, and is relying exclusively on her memory and the sound of the river to guide her. She tries to remember the last time she ran like this. This movement of her body feels like a dream, though even in dreams she has not left the confines of her home. But now, her legs are flying, her feet are barely touching the ground beneath her. Her entire body is intent, purposeful, resolute. And she cannot fight this strange momentum.

She looks to her left at the river, waiting to find a place where it is narrow enough to cross. But the river is high and wide and rushing wildly downstream. She hears something else then, and it makes her stop. Her legs cease. Her heart even seems to stutter and stall. She holds her breath.

"Mom!"

The wind is calling her; it is only the tempest around her.

"Mama!"

And she knows it is not the sky, the voice of the leaves. It is Ruby, and she is running toward her. "Stop, Mama! Wait for me."

"What are you doing?" she asks.

"We need to build a bridge," Ruby answers.

They work in the dark, and Sylvie watches in wonder as her daughter builds the bridge. Branches and twigs, tethered and braided. Fallen limbs, lowered, and suspended. It is as though she is watching some sort of performance, as if Ruby is a magician, conjuring this wondrous construction out of the earth itself. She is building, blindly, in the rain. It seems she has been rehearsing for this moment, this illusion, her whole life.

Sylvie stands at the river's edge, assisting her daughter as she asks her to retrieve the fallen branches, the round barrels inside the shack.

The river is wide and angry and deep

here, though tamer than by the sugar shack. For now. They just need to get across the river. To the house. To the high ground of the road. Ruby works like someone possessed, her hands a blur of purpose and grass. This is madness, this is brilliance, this is miraculous.

Ruby is building what looks like some sort of raft, and for a moment Sylvie wonders if she plans to get on the raft and go, to flee, to allow the river to embrace her in its watery arms.

"Go get the towels and the scissors," Ruby says.

And Sylvie nods and runs back to the shack.

Inside, the girl is sitting up now, and some of the color has returned to her face. She is holding the baby against her chest. When she sees Sylvie, tears start to roll down her cheeks. She is trembling, and clutching the baby as though she is a child who doesn't want to give her doll away. Her bottom lip is trembling, and for the first time Sylvie realizes that she is still just a girl. A child.

"We're almost done," she says. "Ruby is amazing. She's building a bridge."

The girl is crying harder now, soundlessly but her eyes are awash with tears.

Sylvie squats down next to her and

touches her bare shoulder. Her skin is so hot.

"Help," the girl says, her voice like something broken. "Please help her."

Here the river is an untamed thing, and as Ruby labors, she knows suddenly that everything (all of her research, her plans) have been leading up to this moment. This is her chance. This is the *why*. This is the *how*.

Pontoon bridges, or floating bridges, have been used since ancient times when either the resources to build a permanent bridge were not available or when the bridge was meant to be temporary. These types of bridges were especially useful during battles when troops needed to cross a river but didn't want the enemy to follow. The bridge could easily be destroyed after a successful crossing or broken down and carried on the march. She dreams herself a warrior, not in flight, but instead in *pursuit*.

This is what Ruby thinks as she builds the bridge. She also tries to remember everything she has learned about the engineering: recalling the physics of a floating bridge. You need to take into consideration the weight of the load, and the displacement of water. She tries not to think about the river. She tries not to consider what will happen if her design fails.

When her mother returns with the towels, she sets about quickly cutting them into strips and together they braid them into ropes. Now she needs only to anchor the bridge. To moor it.

She and her mother roll the largest rocks they can find to the river's edge. They tie their homemade ropes around the rocks and then to the raft she has made. And then they lower the bridge into the water.

Her mother does not say a word; she simply follows Ruby's lead. Ruby can tell she is worried, but she also sees something she hasn't seen in her mother's face in so long. Trust. Belief. She believes that Ruby can do this. That the bridge will get them across.

"How is the baby?" Ruby asks, her words disappearing into the howling wind.

Her mother nods, but she seems uncertain. They need to hurry. And so she steps onto the bridge, feeling the river rushing beneath her. Her mother begins to follow, but Ruby shakes her head. The bridge is only strong enough to bear the load of one person, one *small* person.

"No," Ruby says. "You stay here until I get across. Then you can come."

Somehow, she makes it to the opposite bank, not far upstream from her mother's house, which stands shuddering in the wind. She leaps off the floating bridge and braces herself against the wind, which feels like something wicked now, like something with ill intent. Her mother stands on the opposite side; they are separated now by the river. By this angry channel.

"Now?" her mother hollers across to her.

But Ruby feels a rumbling, like thunder only deeper. She feels it in her knees. In the very pit of her stomach. She looks upstream, as if she can locate the origin of this ominous forewarning. But there is nothing but darkness.

"Wait!" she hollers to her mother, listening to her gut. To that cautionary whisper in her ear, the one passed down to her from her mother. She runs away from the river, her body reacting before her brain can even process what is happening.

And then, it is as though she is in a dream. There is a sound like an explosion, like a bomb has detonated. The river expands, and then there is a wall of water rushing downstream. It seems to be a living thing, a wild beast set loose from its cage.

"Run!" she hollers to her mother as she claws at the muddy embankment to get to higher ground, and she watches as her mother scrambles away from the river's edge to higher ground as well. Soon Ruby is high enough up that it is as if she is only watching a film. Looking down from above like some sort of god. As if this is only some kind of amphitheater.

She and her mother remain in their respective posts and watch in wonder and horror as the river rips through the earth below them, as it thunders and pillages, as it tears. They watch the bridge, which splinters and shatters and is carried downstream, the barrels and boards as they drift away, and it feels as though she is dreaming. As though she might open her eyes and find herself back in her bed, staring at the owl's piercing black eyes. But she is not dreaming, and the river rushes onward, intently, intensely, pulling trees from their roots and earth in its wake, toward the house.

They both watch as it approaches the trembling house, through the blur of night and water and tears. They watch as it grabs the unfinished room first, the timber snapping like pick-up sticks. They watch as it tugs and pulls at the foundation, loosening the house as though it is nothing but a child's baby tooth. A white bit of bone to pluck from the soft gums of the earth.

And then it is gone.

The house is *gone,* swallowed up by the giant tongue of the river, the lapping, thrusting mouth, disappearing into its dark throat. But strangely, the contents of the house linger, bobbing and dipping before disappearing. The birds, freed of their glass cages, seem to fly across the surface of the water. All those sad birds and their hollow chests. It is beautiful. It is terrifying.

"Oh my God," her mother might be saying, though her voice is lost in the steady thrum of the river. "Oh my God." But Ruby is rendered speechless. Words failing. Her own voice seemingly sucked away with the house into the surge before them.

And still the river keeps moving. It is merciless, unrepentant.

Here is the night the world changes, your world changes. This is the night when all those safe, soft places become terrifying and dangerous. This is the night when you need to decide whether to fight or to give in.

Here is your daughter. And here is a river. This river that stole your son, the river that stole your entire life as you knew it. What have you done to anger the river? What have you done to inspire such violence and rage? Because it *is* angry. This you can hear in its roaring admonishments, in its castigation and watery tirade.

Here is the river, swelling like a tsunami, deafening in its rebuke. The dam must have broken, somewhere miles upstream. Another broken bridge. Another failure. Because it is unbridled now, ardent and vehement. Fed by the constant rain, grown urgent in its vengeful quest. It is coming for you. What will you do?

460

Last time, you let the river take your child. Stunned by its audacity, you gave in. Like Moses's mother, you offered him up, your only son, watched as he was carried away, trusting (you fool) the river's promises to keep him safe. But here you are now, and the river has taken your house and now has come for your other child. It has come, even, for you.

Sylvie feels as though the storm has entered her body now. She stands at the edge of that violence, peering at the brutal water, at the wreckage of her house as it passes her. And so she moves toward the water. She will swim if she needs to. She will fight the current with her fists, with every bit of her strength. But as she gets closer, Ruby screams to her from the opposite shore.

"No, Mama. No. *Stay.*"

Sylvie shakes her head, resists.

"Please. Stay with Nessa. With the baby." Ruby stands on the other side of the river from her, across this vast expanse of violent water. But Sylvie feels closer to her than she has in years. Maybe ever. "I need you to stay."

Ruby runs to the spot where her house stood. It seems impossible that it is gone. That destruction can be so very simple and complete. The world is ravaged. It is as though a bomb has landed here. Only the cement foundation remains, a deep hole in the earth. She stands in the driveway, the one that leads to nothing, staring into its quiet depths which are now filling with water, a mud-and-rain-filled swimming pool. Oddly, the shed is still standing, though the door and part of the roof have been blown off. She reaches into the pocket of her jacket; thankfully, she still has her cell phone, but the battery is nearly dead. She turns it off to save any remaining juice she might have.

She prays that her bicycle is still where she left it upstream, buried under the brush, and is amazed to find it there, the kickstand somehow still propping it upright. She gets on her bicycle and heads up the road. She is pedaling furiously, and hardly making any progress at all. It feels like one of those terrible dreams where you run and run, but your legs won't move.

The wind is still so strong, it nearly knocks her off the bicycle, and she can barely see with the rain in her eyes. But she knows this road. Or at least she used to know this road. Now it too is like a river: water rushing down each side, a sea of mud. Soon it is clear that she is not going to be able to get her tires to move through this rushing sludge. She gets off her bicycle and begins to run. She is exhausted, her body resisting, but she is determined.

It feels like her legs are made of cement. And she thinks again about the foundation of the house. All that remains: the permanence of stone. She wishes the bridge she just made could have lasted. That it could have survived. That it might be here after the storm is gone, evidence of something, though she isn't sure of what.

When she gets to the top of the hill to Hudson's, the lights are out, of course. The parking lot is empty. What did she expect? The windows are boarded up, and there is a piece of paper with a Magic Marker missive, melting in the rain. *Closed for Hur-*

*ricane.* The Coke machine is toppled over, the bench where the old guys sit and smoke is tipped over too.

She stands under the awning by the front door and pulls her phone out of her pocket. She clicks it on, making a silent wish. The battery indicator is red, but there are three bars. She has reception. But she has almost no time left. She pushes the numbers 911 and waits for someone to answer.

Nessa drifts in and out of sleep. Her body is exhausted, but her mind is wide awake and wild with racing thoughts. She is both here and not here. She is floating, moored only by this second heartbeat against her chest.

She thinks about the woman's face, about that red jacket. *She lost her son.* Is it possible this is the same woman she saw that night? Or is she only seeing ghosts everywhere she turns? She's come back here to find her, to tell her what happened that night. To give her an explanation for the unexplainable. But now, somehow, this woman has found *her* instead.

Nessa has been watching her whole life in reverse since the accident, every glance at her past a look through that rearview mirror. She remembers memorizing the details of the vehicle, of the bridge. Looking out of the window from the backseat like a child watching the world pass by. She remembers screaming at Declan to stop the car, to go back. But he just kept driving, his headlights gone out again as they raced away from town, across the other bridge, and then into the woods. She remembers he lit the joint that he dug out of the ashtray. That he used one hand to steer and the other to smoke. She remembers the way the smell of weed, the sweet scent of smoke, filled the cab. But she could think only of the car in the river, filling slowly with water.

She crawled back into the front seat, pounded the dash with her fists as he went faster and faster, turning onto the long dirt road that led to his barn. She remembers that he was sweating. She could see the beads of perspiration glistening on his forehead every time he took a hit off the joint and his face was illuminated, briefly, by the bright orange glow of the hissing burning paper.

"How can you do this?" she asked as he wiped at the sweat with the back of his wrist. "There were people in that car. They're hurt. What if nobody finds them?" The words, the pleas come easily, steadily. They are like a string of hard beads making their way from her throat to her tongue. It is the most she has said to him in the last three months.

But somehow, he still couldn't hear her. None of it registered. Her words were like this dark car in the night. Their syllables rushed through the darkness, but they were somehow *not there.*

She looked at him, pushed her face as close to him as she could and screamed, "Why don't you stop! What kind of person are you?"

And she realized she had no *idea* what kind of person he was. She knew the feeling of his tongue on her body, the urging of his hands and hips. She knew the smell of his skin, the taste of his sweat. She knew the words he chose to put down on paper. She thought of those useless words, those carefully chosen words. The lies. Because this is who he was: a man who could cause an accident, and instead of staying to help, *leave.* He was careless, thoughtless, selfish, and he apparently had no conscience, because now he took his hand from the wheel and hit her hard across the face.

"Shut the fuck up!" he growled.

And she did. As his fist made contact with the soft bone of her jaw, and she felt it come loose, just a door on a hinge, she was silenced.

He slowed the car to a stop, and reached across her for the door handle, pushing the door open and then shoving her out. The world spun beneath her. The air was cold, the ground was hard. Rocks and gravel pierced her skin, she could feel her flesh tearing each time it came in contact with the road. But then she landed in grass and mud, and she was grateful for the coldness, the stillness. The silence.

And by the time she was able to stand up again, to focus her eyes, regain her equilibrium, his car was gone. He was gone.

She headed back the way they had come, walking, stumbling down the long dirt road. Her jaw throbbed with each step. Her entire body felt pummeled. She didn't know where she was going or what she would do when she get there. Should she go home? What was home anyway? Her mother sitting upright on a couch, eyes fixed on nothing. Drowsy and muttering in her Oxy haze. The crackle and hiss of bacon, of rolling papers, of Rusty's breath in her ear when he got too close, when he crossed that invisible, that impossible, line. *Home,* the word in her broken mouth, suddenly no different than *Hole.*

She barely remembers the walk back to the bridge. It must have taken her an hour or more. She had to keep stopping to sit down, to vomit. At one point she lost consciousness and then woke again, disoriented and weeping. She remembers one of her molars coming out, and she searched for it in the grass, desperate, for some reason, to keep it.

By the time she got back to the bridge, the ambulances had come. There was a lone police car parked cockeyed near the bridge, blockades with reflectors blocking the bridge. Three or four cars were parked at the edge of the road, a small huddled group of people stood at the edge of the river, staring at the bridge. She squeezed her eyes shut to block out the shadowy faces of the man and the woman in the car, the silent terror on the other side of the glass. She wondered if they were dead. She wondered if she and Declan had killed them.

Nessa saw the woman before she heard her, standing at the edge of the water in her red coat, like a vessel burst and bleeding. And then she heard the low, aching howl. Like a wounded animal. The anguished cry of sorrow itself. The wordless moan. And she knew as the woman's voice ruptured, the consonants abstracted, the vowels discarnate, that words were futile things. Deceptive and ineffectual.

And so instead of going to the officer like she should have, instead of trying to explain, to make sense of what happened, instead of falling to her knees, confessing, accusing, pleading, she ran. For miles, she ran until the pavement turned to dirt and then back again. Through the mud and tall grass, through the crush of fallen leaves until she arrived at the overpass, that concrete monolith. Then she climbed up and stuck out her thumb.

The station wagon was the first car to come. It looked like a hearse as it pulled up next to her, and she wondered if she had, somehow, died. If, perhaps, she was only a ghost. This is what she was thinking when the man reached across the seat and opened the door for her. That she was already dead.

But she realized then that the car was not a hearse. Instead, in the rain, it was a yellow submarine, just like in the song her mother used to sing when she gave her a bath at night. And she thought about her mother, about what leaving her would mean. This was the unbearable part. Because she knew that rather than terror, rather than anger even, there would be nothing but relief. That *Home* was the same as *Poem*. Just a word on a page of a book she once borrowed.

The man rolled down the passenger window and leaned toward her. "You okay, miss?" he asked. But she couldn't speak to answer.

He motioned for her to get into the car and she obeyed. He looked like somebody's grandfather. His eyes were kind.

He drove without asking another question, until he looked and saw that the side of her face was swollen. "Do you need to go to the hospital?"

She shook her head, *No, no.*

He reached into the dashboard and handed her a crumpled up piece of paper and a pen.

She was shaking as she wrote, "Bus station?"

He nodded. "What is your name?" he asked then, and she wrote, *Nessa.*

"My name is George Downs," he said, smiling, an even exchange. "But you can call me Grover."

The days she spent on the road are hazy now. George, the man in the car, had left her at the bus station, given her his phone number on a piece of paper, and she carefully tucked it into her pocket. He'd promised her that if she ever came back to Quimby, that if she ever needed anything, to find him. She couldn't understand his generosity, his kindness. It seemed unconditional, without strings when there were always, always strings. He gave her money for a bus ticket. He kissed her on the forehead, and she could feel the wet press of his lips for days. She imagined that it was like a seal, closing that night inside a clean white envelope. Protecting her.

She took the bus to LA, as far as the ticket would take her, but then she was on her own again. She ate what she found and slept where she could. She felt ethereal, invisible, now that she no longer spoke. It was as though her voice had given her a body, and now, in this new silence, there was no body either. She had, finally, attained invisibility. If not for her hunger, she might have had no body at all.

She felt both aimless and purposeful. Each day was a matter of survival; but there was no greater objective than this. She learned to exist at the periphery of things, to be every face, rather than no face. This gave her freedom she had never had before. She was unnoticed. She disappeared. And this invisibility empowered her. Fear slipped away. She became undaunted.

But now, as she tries to recollect those days, those months, those years, they too are fading. It's as though her memory is failing. She is seventeen years old, but it feels like she is seventy, and trying so hard to recollect the last two years of her life, a nearly impossible task.

It took her jaw nearly three months to heal. And by the time it was better, she was so accustomed to her own silence, she no longer felt compelled to speak. It was as though she'd left her voice, her words on the side of that road. As though she'd forgotten to pack it in her backpack.

The woman in the red coat sits with her now, stroking her hair as she slips in and out of time. In and out of places. Each time she wakes up, she believes for a few confused moments that she is in another bed. Another person's arms. But it only takes that warm, breathing, heart-beating baby on her chest to bring her back.

Had she spoken? Had she really spoken to this woman? *Help. Help,* she thinks. The word so simple, yet so rife with need.

She knows the baby is not well. She knows that this breathing is not the steady inhalation and exhalation it should be. But what does she expect? She has been living off of whatever scraps she can find to eat. She hasn't had a good night's sleep in months. She hasn't seen a doctor. She hasn't taken care of herself. She has been careless. And now, she will be punished.

She looks up at the woman's face, studies the fine angles of her nose and chin. She peers into her dark eyes. They're the kind of eyes that keep secrets.

"I know you," she says to the woman.

"What's that?" the woman asks, caught up in her own quiet reverie.

"I was there." It is too late now. The words have built up like water behind a dam. There is a flash flood coming. It is unstoppable.

The woman's hands stop in her hair, and she can feel her fingertips go as cold as ice on her fiery skin.

"What?"

"I came back. And I saw you, standing at the river."

"The flood?" the woman asks, her eyes wide. Terrified.

Nessa shakes her head. "His lights," she says, trying to select the words that could possibly explain what he did. How he fled. "They didn't work. You didn't see us."

The woman sits back on her heels as if she has, indeed, seen a ghost. That she is face-to-face with an apparition. She backs up, scurrying like a frightened animal toward the door. She scrambles to her feet.

Nessa searches for the words, but they swim before her, elusive like shiny fish

474

beneath the surface of water. If she can just catch the right one, she thinks, it will be okay. She can make all of this better.

"What do you want?" the woman asks. "What do you want from me?"

The baby sputters and coughs, the sound coming from her chest like a terrible whistle. Like the storm is inside her. She presses the baby to her chest, harder, as though she can offer her own lungs. Her own heart.

And then the word comes; it rises to the surface, a dead fish floating on still water. It is flaccid and sick. "I'm sorry," she offers and remembers that words are not enough. Words fail. Still, she tries. "I was so afraid."

The woman looks at her in horror and then she is gone, disappearing out into the darkness, and Nessa is alone again. Only now, she is *not* alone. The baby's chest whistles and it sounds like a scream for help.

Ruby gives the dispatcher the address of a house that no longer exists. "There's a lady who just had a baby on the other side of the river. I think the shack where she's staying is on the Monroes' property. Please send somebody. My mother is there too." And then the phone goes dead, and there is an odd silence. Her ears feel strange, achy in the absence of sound. Of course, there is still the steady sound of the rain on the ground. But here, she can no longer hear the river.

She has no idea how she's going to get back across to the other side where her mother and Nessa are. The bridge she made is gone. It's as though it resided only in her imagination, existed in the world for a single purposeful moment, and then disappeared back into her dreams again. There is not a single bit of evidence to prove that it ever existed at all except that she is here. Alive.

That she survived.

She starts back down the road, imagining that the ambulances will come to the house. Or to the place where the house used to be anyway. She will need to show them how to get to her mother. And to Nessa and the baby.

Her shoes are soaked, her feet freezing cold. She looks down at her hands, and they are covered in rain and mud and leaves. She must look like some sort of yeti walking along the edge of the road. She must look like a beast.

It is pitch-black now; it feels like when the battery in her phone died, everything else went dead as well. How could she not have noticed how dark it is? It feels as though she is walking inside a black hole, as though she has been swallowed. She remembers a story her mother used to read her about Jonah and the whale. When Jonah disappears into the whale's mouth, he has a candle, which illuminates the inside. It used to bother her. She always thought that if she were the one to write the book, she would have made those pages black. Just two dark pages so you would know what Jonah really felt like inside the whale. There are no streetlights out here, not a single flicker of light. She is inside those imagined pages. Inside the belly of the whale.

She thinks she must be close to the turn to her mother's. Despite the darkness, her body somehow remembers the curve of the road, the configuration of trees. And so she is confused when suddenly she is blinded by two bright lights. She shields her eyes, struggles to make sense of it. But then logic clicks in, like puzzle pieces snapping into place. The car pulls up next to her, and the window rolls down. It's Grover's station wagon, and Gloria is inside.

"Ruby! Jesus, I could barely see you out here," she says. "Get in!"

Inside, the car is warm and dry. There's a Joni Mitchell CD in the stereo. It's pretty much the only music Gloria ever listens to. It drives Izzy crazy, but Ruby likes it. There's something soft and peaceful about that kind of music. Like a lullaby.

She doesn't realize she's crying until Gloria reaches into her glove box and pulls out a tissue.

"The house is gone," Ruby says. And saying it out loud feels strange. Like it wasn't true until she said it.

"What?" Gloria asks, her eyes wide.

"The river. There was a flood. It's gone."

"Where's your mom?" Gloria asks gently, but Ruby can tell she is horrified. Terrified.

Ruby is crying so hard now, she can hardly get the story out. But somehow, Gloria is able to decipher enough from her blubbering, and she drives past the turn to her mother's house and heads back out onto the main road.

"Where are we going?" Ruby asks. "We can't leave them."

"I know," she says. "We'll go around, over the other bridge. I think it's the Monroes' farm across the river from your mom's place. It's probably their sugar shack. Don't worry. And here . . . take my phone. As soon as we get reception, call 911 again."

Ruby stares out the window at the rain. She feels like she is inside the whale now. Swallowed up.

"Ruby?" Gloria says, and she looks at her. She is gripping the steering wheel with both hands. "It's going to be okay. I promise."

The midwife is gone for only a few minutes, but in those moments alone with the baby, Nessa tries not to imagine what will happen if she doesn't come back. If she has left her here. She presses the baby against her, and tries only to focus on the heartbeat she feels underneath the barrel cage of bone. Like a bird inside, beating its small wings. But then, just as her own heart begins to pound with fear, the woman returns.

She stands in the doorway of the shack. "Tell me what happened," she says.

"His name is Declan O'Dell," Nessa says. "He was driving. His headlights didn't work right. It was an accident, but I couldn't make him stop. He wouldn't listen."

The woman stands there, but she doesn't say a word, and for a moment Nessa worries that somehow, she has stolen the woman's voice. Perhaps she has taken her ability to form words; maybe breaking her own silence has muted someone else. But then, as the woman lifts the baby from Nessa's chest, her words come to her as soft as rain.

"My son died that night."

Nessa's chest feels bare, exposed. Her heart feels hollow in the baby's absence.

"He was seven years old." This sounds like an accusation, like a plea.

Nessa struggles, searching for something to say that will make any of this okay. That might comfort or appease her. That might undo the damage she has done. She scours her vocabulary for the phrase or sentiment that might act as a balm to this old wound. But words are simply syllables, abstract constructions. Meaningless in their own right. Any words she might offer her on their own could not change history. They could not give her her son back. And so, for now, she says nothing.

And the woman studies her, though it doesn't seem like she is waiting for anything. It's as though she too realizes the inanity of words. The pointlessness.

"I think the baby may have an infection," the woman says. "We need to get her to a hospital. Ruby's gone to call an ambulance. But it may be awhile."

Nessa watches the woman who is holding the baby in her arms. But it isn't *fear* that she feels. This woman, whose life was shattered that night at the bridge. This woman who should despise her. Instead, Nessa trusts her. She trusts her in a way she has not trusted a single person in her life.

"We need to keep her hydrated. Let's try to get her to latch on again, okay?"

Nessa nods. She will do whatever this woman says.

She brings the baby back to her and positions her under Nessa's breast.

"Here, if you flatten your breast out like a pancake and tickle the roof of her mouth with your nipple, she'll latch on. Your milk hasn't come in yet, but the colostrum is good for her. And it will keep her hydrated."

The baby cries. And her chest rattles with each exhalation.

Nessa peers down into the small face of the baby, at the dark eyelashes and dark hair. She doesn't look like anyone she knows. Mica is her father, but what does this even mean anymore? Instead, she thinks, she is a child of the road. A gypsy child conjured from pavement and neon and cornfields. Conceived of stars rushing across the sky, of cold grass and endless rivers. She belongs to no man. She is Nessa's alone.

The baby wails again, and so Nessa does

exactly as Ruby's mother says, squeezing her breast and thrusting it gently into the baby's mouth. It feels both utterly strange and somehow exactly the right thing to do.

"Here," the woman says, and turns the baby so that she is facing Nessa, pressed directly into her chest. "Like this."

And then the baby is latching on. And for a moment, just one quiet moment, she feels like everything is going to be okay.

"Why did you come back here?" the woman asks. "What do you want?"

Nessa looks up into this woman's face, which is open as a flower. She thinks about George, about the soft kiss on her forehead. She thinks about Ruby offering her that warm Tootsie Roll from her pocket, about all the beautiful bridges.

"I just wanted to come home," she says.

Sylvie should feel rage. She should want revenge. She should want explanations. But strangely, she feels none of this. For the last two years, she has been trying to come up with some sort of logic for what happened that night. She has studied the trajectories. Analyzed every factor. She has lived her life backwards, trying to figure out every turn of events that must have transpired in order for those two cars to meet on the bridge at that precise moment. She has considered all of the little things she could have done, the simple delays that would have prevented this. But considering this, she has worked herself into a frenzy. If it truly is this simple, then maybe there have been countless other accidents that have somehow been avoided, disasters averted. And the possibility of this has overwhelmed her. How do you live your life when every single decision you make could precipitate such tragic consequences?

How do you live, when death is only waiting for you to slip up?

Closing herself inside that house seemed to be the only answer. If her world was confined to this small space, to those four walls, to those quiet rituals, then she would be safe. But now she knows that there is no such thing as safety. Here is the evidence. This storm that carried her house away. Her house, her home, is *gone.* It was swept away as casually as someone rubbing a smudge of chocolate from a child's face. And if she had been inside the house, she would be gone as well. This thought nearly overwhelms her.

Because somehow, this girl, this strange girl with the ratty hair and blue eyes, this odd Madonna is the one who saved her. She studies her, the way she would study a painting. Looking for meaning in the quiet brushstrokes of her hair, in the textured patterns of her flesh. She examines the angles of her shoulders, the quiet slope of her back and the swell of her breast as she feeds her baby. There are no answers here. Only more and more questions.

How do you not believe in fate? How do you ever think that you are the one in control? How could she have been so foolish as to think that she had any authority over her future? How could she have been so brazen as to think that this had anything at all to do with her?

And so instead of rage, she is suddenly filled with a sense of *thankfulness.* Her chest inflates with a sense of kinship she hasn't felt before. This girl is not to blame. No one really is to blame. Even the man, *Declan* she says, is culpable only of cowardice.

Because the world sometimes conspires against us even as we embrace it. And sometimes the world embraces us, even *as* we forsake it. Maybe this is God, she thinks. This quiet, easy truth. And religion, the acceptance of it.

Nessa hears something outside the shack, and for a moment she worries that the river has risen again, that it has somehow gone over the high banks and that it will sweep the sugar shack, and them inside of it, away. She tries to imagine that journey, the one she might take on this river. She wonders where it would carry her this time.

But then there is light filling the room. And there is Ruby and another woman.

Sylvie rushes to Ruby and embraces her. She looks like she might swallow her up in her arms. And Ruby clings to her, as though she is trying not to drown.

The other woman moves quickly. "Stay here. I'm going to go meet the ambulance. I'll bring them here. It will just be a few minutes. Is everybody okay?"

Nessa nods. And together, Ruby and her mother nod.

And then there are the men in uniforms.

It feels official. It feels like something on TV. They know what they are doing and move with certainty and purpose.

"We need to take the baby from you," one man says, and despite the width of his shoulders and the seriousness of his face, his voice is gentle. When she shakes her head and clings to the baby, he says softly, "We'll give her back. I promise."

And so they take the baby, who is screaming again, and it feels as though Nessa's heart is being torn from her as they carry her outside. They have brought a stretcher. They help her lie down on its hard white sheets, and then they fasten her. It feels strange to be tethered to a board like this. It makes her think of a papoose, as if *she* is the infant.

Outside, the rain is still coming down hard and sharp. It feels like splinters on her face. The journey from the shack to the dirt road feels endless. She can still hear the baby crying, and so she says, "It's okay. It's okay," hoping that her voice will somehow reach her.

The men walk like soldiers through the woods, and she stares up into that unforgiving sky. Nessa lets the rain fill her eyes, wet her face. It feels like a baptism. Like a blessing.

The lights are bright once they are out of the woods. There is a car parked cockeyed in the field, and the ambulance is parked next to it.

She feels a strange and overwhelming sense of déjà vu. Of familiarity.

It's a yellow station wagon. The same yellow station wagon that picked her up after she leapt from the car that night. It's George's car.

It doesn't make any sense, yet it doesn't matter. She's found exactly what she was looking for the whole time. And as the doors close behind her in the ambulance, and she sees the paramedic strapping a tiny little oxygen mask over her baby's face, she knows that everything is going to be okay.

Inside the warm, dry ambulance, she closes her eyes, and the silver clasp closes shut. She is safe.

Ruby and her mother climb into the back of the station wagon and Gloria gets in the driver's side.

"There are blankets in the way back," Gloria says into the rearview mirror.

Before she fastens her seat belt, Ruby gets on her knees and peers into the cluttered back of the station wagon. She finds two blankets and pulls them into the backseat. She hands one to her mother and then wraps one around herself. Her entire body is shaking with cold and something else.

"I'm taking you both to the hospital," Gloria says.

Ruby feels something stop in her chest, like a plug getting sucked back into a drain. She looks at her mother, afraid of what she will see. The last time her mother went to the hospital, they had swaddled her like a baby, made her arms useless. She had felt embarrassed for her mother, guilty with her own inability to help her. But now her mother just nods and looks out the window as they make their way through the high grass of the field and back onto the dirt road.

The wind is strong, but inside the car, they are safe.

Gloria follows the ambulance, which announces itself with high-pitched wails and glaring red lights. Everything inside the station wagon is imbued with red. She looks at her mother, and thinks she could just be blushing. The color of her cheeks that of shame.

"Who is she?" Gloria asks, finally, as they get onto the road and are driving fast down the main road toward town. "That girl?"

She looks in the rearview mirror again and catches Ruby's eye.

Ruby shakes her head. She doesn't know. Despite everything they've been through together over the last week, despite the fact that she has fed her and cared for her and tried to keep her safe, she has no idea who she is. And she thinks that perhaps she is the same mystery to her own mother. Her mother, who has been absent for nearly the last two years of her life, who has let her slip away like so much sand through careless fingers.

"She knows what happened to Jess," Ruby's mother says suddenly, and Ruby turns to her.

"What?" Ruby says, and Gloria turns her head as though whatever she is seeing in the rearview mirror is not enough.

"She was there," she says. "At the bridge."

There are haunted bridges all over the world. Ruby has studied them with the same sort of morbid curiosity she used to have for ghost stories. Her dad told the best ones. Ones he and his brothers used to tell around the campfire when they were kids.

The Golden Gate Bridge is the most famous one, haunted by suicides mostly but also by the *SS Tennessee,* which wrecked and sank near the bridge in the 1850s. People still claim that they can hear the screams, the voices of the dying through the thick San Francisco fog at night. In 1891, a train derailed in the middle of the night while crossing the Bostian Bridge in North Carolina. Thirty people were killed. Visitors to the bridge claim that at 3 A.M. on the anniversary of the accident each year, it is as though it is happening all over again. There is the sound of the cars crashing into the ravine below, the screams of the passengers inside. But the story that has always fascinated Ruby the most is that of Emily's Bridge, which is right here in Vermont. Ruby has never been there, but her father said that he has. Nobody can seem to get the story straight though. One version is that this woman, Emily, was supposed to meet her lover at the bridge to elope, but that when he never arrived, she hung herself from the rafters. The other version is that Emily was left at the altar by her lover and, in a rage, she took off in a horse-drawn wagon in which she plummeted to her death at the bridge. People go to the bridge to try to catch a glimpse of Emily's ghost. Some people claim they hear the sounds of a girl screaming, of horses, hear a loud banging sound, and feel a woman's gentle touch on their skin. It bothers Ruby that nobody knows what really happened to Emily.

Ruby doesn't know much about ghosts, but she knows that they're supposed to be the people who died with unfinished business. She wonders about Jess, about what sort of things might not be settled for him.

The night of the accident, when she and her mother returned to the house, there was a cup of cocoa sitting on the counter, a little bit of the cocoa powder spilled next to it. Jess used to hate the tiny marshmallows that came in those packets, so he'd pick them out before stirring the powder into the hot milk. She remembers her mother staring at the mug, holding it in her hands. She couldn't wash it or even move it from the counter top for weeks. Every single day it was a reminder that Jess had stood here, plucking marshmallows out of his cocoa, not knowing that in a few hours he would be gone.

Ghosts usually haunt the places where they died. They return looking for some sort of closure, some way to pass through to the afterlife. In every culture in the world there are ghosts. On every continent and in every country. She thinks about Nessa. And how she has haunted their lives as well. For months after the accident, her mother insisted that there was another car at the bridge that night. But her father couldn't remember anything about the accident except for the moment when the steering wheel crushed his legs. Her mother pleaded with her father, with Gloria, with *her* to believe that there was someone else there. Someone who saw what happened, who didn't stop. Bunk promised he would find the car, but how do you begin to search for the invisible? How do you find a ghost?

But Nessa is *not* a ghost. She is real, and

she is here.

"How are you feeling?" Gloria asks, peeking into the hospital room where Ruby and her mother lie in separate beds. Her mother has, somehow, fallen asleep. Gloria pulls the thin curtain between them across, separating them. "The doctor says you're going to be okay," Gloria says to Ruby. "You look like you've taken a mud bath."

Ruby remembers only then that her entire body was caked in mud, like she is one of those bog people she learned about at school, their bodies preserved in a cast made of peat. The bog people were ghosts in their own way, she thinks.

"Listen, I'm going to try to reach your dad again," Gloria says, squeezing her hand. "I'll also check on Nessa and the baby, and Grover too."

She had almost forgotten that Grover is also somewhere in this hospital.

"Can I pick you up something from the cafeteria on my way back?" Gloria asks. "Jell-O? Some chocolate pudding?"

Ruby nods. She is so hungry.

The nurse lets her shower and then dresses Ruby in clean hospital pajamas that have teddy bears all over them as though she is just a little girl. And while normally this would make her feel really awkward, it feels

496

nice to be taken care of.

"We're going to have you spend the night with us," the nurse says, as if this is a slumber party instead of the hospital. The nurse takes her temperature one more time and then says, "You've had quite an adventure. Try to get some rest."

Gloria comes back an hour later, clutching a chocolate pudding in one hand. Her eyes are red, swollen.

"Are you crying?" Ruby asks.

"Just sad about Grover," she says.

"Is he going to die?" Ruby asks.

"Someday," she says, smiling sadly. "But hopefully some *other* day."

She knows that Gloria does not believe in God, that Izzy's family is agnostic. *That means unsure,* is how Gloria explained it. *Because no matter what anybody says, nobody knows for sure.* She remembers that Gloria's uncertainty made her feel strange. When she was little, she thought that grown-ups knew almost everything. They knew the definitions of words (*barometer, gelatinous, persuasive*). Her father and Bunk could fix almost anything that broke. They always knew what to do when there was an emergency. And they knew the answers to most of her questions: *Why does the sun go down at night? Where does rain come from? Where is the tallest building in the world? The longest bridge?* And if they didn't know the answers, they knew where to find them. But God was a different story. And when she asked, it wasn't like the questions she had about where babies came from. She knew there were some questions that made her mother blush and her father change the subject. But this was not one of those questions. This question made her mother's face go white. It made the color slip away from her face, disappearing like an Etch A Sketch drawing after you shake it.

"Where is Jess now?" she had asked that night, Jess's cup of cocoa still sitting there on the counter, and her mother had shaken her head. She didn't know. She couldn't find the answer to this in the big dusty World Book on the shelf; she couldn't Google it. Her father also had no answers. He mumbled something about heaven, but you could tell he was unconvinced and it was just something to say so that she would stop asking questions.

It was then that Ruby realized that grown-ups *don't* know everything. They can't answer every question, and they can't fix everything that's broken. That there are some questions that don't have answers. And there are some broken things that can never be fixed.

Before the accident, she'd never felt afraid. Not really. She'd never felt anything but safe. She'd been stupid, but she'd trusted the world to stay the same. But then, in an instant, Jess was gone and nobody in the world could tell her where he went. Her parents couldn't bear to look at each other anymore, and her mother was afraid of everything. It was as though Ruby had been walking on a high wire all this time, and never looked down. But now here she was, suspended on the most dangerous of bridges, with nothing below her to catch her if she fell.

"You try to get some sleep, sweetie," Gloria says. "I'll check back in on you in a little bit."

Ruby can hear her mother murmuring softly to the doctor on the other side of the curtain. It makes her think of the nights after Jess had fallen asleep, and she would listen to her parents talking on the other side of the wall. It always made her feel peaceful, to listen to the soft sound of their conversation as she fell asleep at night. But now she needs more than her mother's voice. She needs to see her, to touch her.

"Mama?" she says softly.

"Yeah, baby?"

"I'm scared about Daddy," she says.

"Here, let me," the nurse says and parts the curtain between them.

Ruby slips off her bed and stands up, goes to her mother's bed and lies her head down on her mother's pale lap. "He's going to be okay," her mother says, and Ruby lets herself believe, if only for now, that her mother has this answer.

It is nearly impossible to differentiate this night from those other nights. While the world spins on and on, reckless and unpredictable and ever-changing, the hospital is like a strange and untouched island. An antiseptic bubble of both time and space. This night could be any night. It could be the night of the accident when the nurses had to restrain her to keep her from tearing out her own hair. From running down the long bright corridors. It could also be the night last spring when she came back. When she realized that everything she thought was true was a lie. That the earth is not round at all, but rather that it has edges, and that she was standing on one, peering into the darkness below. That night, they'd restrained her too, though they didn't need to. She had given up then, her mind failing her, her body failing her as well.

The *tick tick* of machines, the *hush hush*

of slippered feet across the linoleum. The antiseptic stink; the smell of sickness disguised. Like cologne slapped onto a sweaty man. Like air freshener in a house where an animal has died.

The other nights she had wanted to be left alone. She had wanted to simply close her eyes and slip inside herself, into the safe dark pit at the center of her chest. She'd wanted only to not speak, to not hear, to not smell or see or feel. But now, with Ruby curled next to her in this bed, their bodies pressed together and balancing delicately on the narrow expanse of mattress, she wants only to go home.

But home is gone. Home is a splintered fractured building carried away by the river. Home is nothing but a cement hole in the ground. Home is a memory.

This thought is stunning. Like trying to ponder infinity. To grasp ahold of the insides of a black hole. To imagine the depths of the ocean or how long ago a star died.

Gloria comes into the room again, and she has a sad smile on her face.

"Did you reach him?" Sylvie asks, afraid of Gloria's answer.

She shakes her head. "Not yet."

*Robert.* Robert is somewhere out there in the storm. And she knows now that there are no safe places: roads collapse, bridges crumble, even houses get swept away.

"I'm sure he just isn't getting reception in this weather, or maybe his battery died," Gloria says unconvincingly, sitting down in a plastic molded chair next to the bed. She absently picks up the blue plastic pitcher the nurse left with ice water earlier.

Sylvie nods and strokes Ruby's hair. Ruby is curled up in the bed next to Sylvie, half-asleep.

"How is the baby?" Sylvie asks.

"They've taken her to the NICU, but she's a tough little one."

"And the girl?"

"She's okay too. Sleeping, I think."

It is so hard to think past this moment. Normally, her mind would be reeling, like gears *click, click, clicking,* anticipating the next moment and the next, creating a chain of endless possibilities. What will she tell Robert about the girl? How will they find the man who was driving the car? What will happen to the baby? But suddenly, the gears grind to a halt.

She smells something familiar. Something so lovely and impossible, she is completely overwhelmed by it.

She leans down and breathes the scent of Ruby's hair. Closes her eyes and is completely transported. It's only shampoo. But in that scent is an entire world she has forgotten. For a brisk and beautiful moment, she is nothing, *not a thing,* only this child's mother. She is kneeling on the cold tile floor next to the bathtub, rubbing the soap into her hair in quiet lazy circles. She is sitting on the couch, the blue glow of the TV in front of her as she combs out the tangles. (She is careful to hold her hair at the scalp as she tugs through the knots so as not to hurt her.) Here she is running one tine of the comb down the center of her scalp to make a part, twisting the hairbands Ruby loves with the colored plastic balls at the end to make two ponytails. Here she is crying as she cuts those first dark curls, catching them on a towel spread across Ruby's lap. Here she is when Ruby has fallen asleep at night, pressing her face into her hair to smell the sweet child smell of her, the innocent scent of her. It smells like neither winter nor summer; this soapy smell is seasonless. Timeless.

Her throat feels thick with this simple remembrance.

There is the muffled sound of a phone. It is ringing inside Gloria's giant purse. She fishes around inside, her face lost in concentration.

Finally, she pulls it from her purse and clicks it on. "Hello?" she says.

"Robert?"

Silence.

"Oh, Bunk, thank God. Where are you?"

■ ■ ■ ■

# AFTER THE STORM

■ ■ ■ ■

It is Nessa's eighteenth birthday today. This is what she thinks when she wakes up to the bright and unfamiliar light of the sun, to the growingly familiar sound of her baby fussing. *Wren,* her little songbird. She sits up, rubbing the sleep from her eyes, and looks around the room. Gloria had asked her what her favorite color was, and she'd said purple. And so now, the walls are a soft silvery shade of purple, and the curtains and bed are white. It is like the room she dreamed when she was little. The room she imagined even as they moved from one apartment to the next to the next.

The man who helped her, George Downs, who lived here before, is in a nursing home now. Gloria took her to see him, to meet him a week ago. Nessa worried he would have no memory of her, of that night. But when they came into the room, his eyes lit up, and she could see recognition flicker in his face. As if he were recalling a dream. He wasn't able to speak, the stroke he'd suffered after he went to the hospital had stolen his words. And this shared loss made her feel even closer to him. She sat next to him for nearly an hour, not speaking, simply holding his hand. Before she left, she whispered softly, "Thank you," something she had been waiting nearly a year to say to him.

She can smell breakfast cooking in the other room. Gloria's husband, Neil, makes these pancakes that look like something from a Dr. Seuss book. He has promised her Dutch babies and bacon and the vanilla coffee she has grown to depend upon.

They found an old crib out in the garage, but the baby sleeps with her in this big bed (it is the biggest bed she has ever had). Wren lies flat on her back with her arms and legs splayed out, like a teenage boy instead of a newborn. She is nothing like babies are supposed to be. She is happy, easy, wanting nothing more than to eat and sleep.

Nessa rolls over and peers closely at Wren's sleeping face. She touches the soft swirls of her dark hair with the tips of her fingers. Her skin is untouched, so soft that when she strokes her cheek, it feels as though she is only touching air. She tries to imagine her own mother lying next to her eighteen years ago, wonders if she felt this same strange bliss, this delirious happiness. This overwhelming sense of peace.

Wren stirs, and she is glad. She gets nervous when she sleeps for too long. Sometimes she wants to wake her, just to watch her eyes struggle to focus. To see the faint recollection that follows this confusion. She knows that soon she will begin to understand that Nessa is her mother, that she is the one who loves her, the one who will take care of her. The one who will keep her safe. And she *will* keep her safe. She will protect her. This is where the legacy from her mother disappears.

This week will be a busy one. Wren has a doctor's appointment. Nessa has to go to the social services office and sign up for WIC, for Medicaid, for all those things that will help them until she gets on her feet. She has also promised Sylvie that she will make a statement to the police, to tell them the true story of what happened that night. Gloria says that she also needs to tell them what Declan did to her for all those months leading up to the accident, reminding her again and again that this is not her fault. That she was only a child. It won't be that simple, of course. The barn where he lived is empty now, abandoned. They will have to find him, and when they do, there will be charges, an arraignment, an arrest, a trial. She knows she will be asked to testify, to sit across from him, even as she speaks out against him. She only hopes that her words are powerful enough to bring Sylvie and Robert the justice they so badly need.

She knows she also needs to find her mother, though the urgency of this has lessened now. Gloria has offered to help her, when she's ready. It could be as simple as searching Facebook. As Google. As calling Information. Or it could be more difficult. She does worry that if she waits too long, it will be too late, that like her grandfather, her mother may have slipped away when she wasn't looking. She doesn't know what she will say when she finds her; she just needs to trust her voice this time. To ask the questions that remain. To say what needs to be said.

Gloria has a friend who owns a coffee shop who has offered Nessa a part-time job, and she will finish up high school online. Neil says she can enroll in some classes at the college as soon as she is done. She is overwhelmed by their generosity. She wishes there were words for the enormous gratitude she feels. *Thank you* is too small. Too ordinary a phrase for this tremendous kindness. And so she offers all that she has. Hands to help wash and dry dishes, to chop vegetables, to help Gloria unload the kiln with her fragile treasures inside.

School has started for Ruby, and so Nessa sees her most days. She comes home with Izzy and they sit at the big wooden table in the kitchen to do their homework before disappearing upstairs to do whatever it is that eleven-year-old girls do. She watches them with a strange fascination and longing. It is hard to remember herself at eleven. It seems she has always been this age, seventeen now eighteen. It seems that she never had that wild gorgeous innocence that these girls have. She has no memory of being this young. This beautifully young.

But now, it feels as though she's grown into the older woman she has always been. It's as though her body has finally caught up with her mind. She loves the soft pouch of her stomach, the swell and pull of her breasts. She loves her fat thighs, her tired back, the dark moons under her eyes. She loves this body, this woman's body that instead of being stolen from, *gives*.

It is her eighteenth birthday, and she is a woman. A mother. And, she thinks, as she looks around this sun-filled room, colored leaves pressing against the window like bits of colored glass inside a kaleidoscope, that maybe finding *home* is as simple, and as difficult, as finding *hope*.

It is hard to remember each other. It is hard to recollect the ease and familiarity with which they used to interact. It is nearly impossible to capture the way they used to take each other for granted. The way they used to make each other feel safe.

Robert is damaged. His body ravaged by the accident. He has lost so much, and must be reminded of the absence each time he looks at the place where his legs used to be. At the things he can no longer do. At the cruelties of a world that rarely compensates or complies with his new needs.

"What do you want?" she asks him, wondering when the last time was that anyone asked him this. "Do you want to move to North Carolina?"

He studies her as though he is leery of her sincerity. This distrust is something she will never get used to, but she is the one who has brought it about. She is the one to blame for his inability to believe in her.

"No," he says. "I thought I did."

And so she nods.

Robert has always run away. This is what he does. He flees. He seeks. And she hunkers down. She stays; she closes herself up. What they need is a compromise. What they need is to meet somewhere in between. They need to find this bridge, the one that will traverse the chasm that has grown between them.

For now, what this means is that she lives in a rented house in town while he stays three streets over at Bunk's. Ruby passes between them, spending every other night with her. Robert comes over those nights for dinner. And they sit together around the small wooden table, big enough only for three. And after Ruby goes to bed, they talk. Sometimes, they talk about the future. About where to go from here. But most of the time, they talk about the past. The waters between, the *now,* are treacherous, they both know this and they are still looking for the materials to use to build this bridge. It is not something to be thrown together haphazardly. Bridges built in haste are never safe. This is something that Ruby has taught them both.

One night in October when the moon

outside is as bright as the sun, they sit together on the porch, looking out at the leaves that rush across the street like a river. Sylvie turns to Robert. And she wonders at how he can be both so familiar and so unknowable at the same time. How have they grown so far apart?

"I need you," Sylvie says, feeling her heart pulsing in her throat.

He turns to look at her. She thinks it is the first time he has looked at her, really looked at her since Jess died. And she wonders what he sees. For a moment, she is afraid. Terrified that she has made a terrible mistake. That exposing her vulnerability like this will ruin her. That he could destroy her now.

But his eyes are bright, reflecting the harvest moon that looms in the sky. And he takes her hand, rubs his thumb along the veins that run like rivers on her flesh. And he nods. "I'm here, Sylvie. I'm not going anywhere."

The night of the contest, Sylvie and Robert go together to the middle school. They park in the brightly lit parking lot and she helps him out of the car and into his chair. He doesn't need her to push his chair, and so she walks beside him, noting the ease with

which he navigates the sidewalks and walkways and ramps. They nod and smile at the
other parents who have come to watch their
children compete, and Sylvie focuses on
each moment. On each breath. She is learning to listen to her body's responses and to
use both her breath and her logic to calm
herself. It is not easy, but it helps. She has a
long, long way to go. But each outing like
this, each trip to the grocery store that ends
well, each visit with Gloria, feels like an accomplishment.

Ruby is here already. She's been here all
afternoon with the other competitors. She
and Izzy have repaired what was broken in
their friendship, but Ruby has insisted on
doing this alone. Gloria and Neil and Izzy
are sitting in the front row. They have saved
the aisle seat for her, and there is room for
Robert's chair next to it.

"Hi," Gloria says, standing up and reaching out for Sylvie. And Sylvie lets her in,
lets her hold her. She imagines Gloria's
arms as something designed to support her,
to hold her up. The architecture of elbows
and shoulders as something built for support. All of these tricks help.

When it is Ruby's turn to present her
bridge, Sylvie feels something strange in the
pit of her stomach. It is not fear exactly, not

the crippling anxiety to which she has grown accustomed, but rather a happy sort of tension. Anticipation? It is difficult to locate this emotion on a map that has been dominated by fear. Identify and let go, her therapist says. *I am nervous for her,* Sylvie thinks. *I am excited for her.*

As she watches Ruby explain about load, about suspension, about the importance of the design, Sylvie marvels at Ruby's patience, at her attention to detail. It makes her think of the birds, and she wonders if maybe this is one other gift she has given her.

Ruby stands in front of her model bridge, this impossibly gorgeous and delicate construction, and Sylvie holds her breath as the judge places first one brick on its slight deck and then another and another. And *this* feeling, the one swelling inside the place where the chasm used to be, like a flood, like a rushing river, is not fear but rather *wonder* and *pride.* Because their daughter, despite everything, has built something both beautiful and indestructible.

There are a million stories and poems about bridges. Mrs. Jenkins, her sixth-grade English teacher, says that writers and poets have always been drawn to bridges to help them explain the distance between people and places and how those gaps can be traversed. There is a mystery about bridges. A good bridge evokes both respect and wonder.

Ruby reads about the people who built the bridges. She studies their lives, reads about their dreams. Santiago Calatrava, Thomas Telford, Christian Menn, Gustave Eiffel. She studies not only their architecture, their designs, but their lives. She thinks that everything that has happened to them influences the way they solve the problem of how to traverse a chasm. How their lives are the beams and trusses, the cantilevers and arches.

She imagines herself one day building a

bridge that floats across a large body of water. A bridge that is both beautiful and indestructible, that relies on nothing but the water beneath it. She thinks about the people that will walk across its deck, who will drive over its incredible expanse. She imagines how it will connect one place to another, make the journey one that people will talk about long after they have crossed the bridge.

She reads the poems about bridges as well. Nessa gave her a Longfellow poem she found, and she told her to read it aloud. To feel the way the words trip across your tongue. Sitting on the edge of Nessa's bed as she feeds the baby, Ruby reads aloud to her. Wren is quiet, suckling and cooing, and the air is still around them:

Yet whenever I cross the river
On its bridge with wooden piers,
Like the odor of brine from the ocean
Comes the thought of other years.

And I think how many thousands
Of care-encumbered men,
Each bearing his burden of sorrow,
Have crossed the bridge since then.

She thinks about a procession of men,

521

each with their own sorrow, what sort of design might help bear that impossible load. She dreams the architecture of forgiveness, of understanding required to endure those burdens. This is the kind of bridge she'll make one day, she thinks, as both Nessa and the baby drift off to sleep. This one, right here.

# A READING GROUP GUIDE:
# THE FOREVER BRIDGE

## T. GREENWOOD

The following discussion questions are included to enhance your group's reading of *The Forever Bridge.*

# DISCUSSION QUESTIONS

1. Discuss Ruby's obsession with bridges. How does the theme of bridge building manifest throughout the novel? What is meant by the title, *The Forever Bridge*

2. How does the author depict the mothers in this story (Sylvie, Nessa, Nessa's mother, Gloria)? Compare Ruby's relationships with Sylvie and Gloria.

3. Sylvie suffers from crippling agoraphobia, but explains that her anxiety began long before the accident. Have you ever felt such debilitating fear?

4. Discuss how Sylvie and Ruby individually remember Jess throughout the novel. How did his death in particular affect them separately and as a family?

5. Nessa returns to Quimby for a number

of reasons. Discuss them and the resolution for each. Do you think she'll stay this time? If you were Nessa, would you seek out your missing mother?

6. This novel is about mothers and daughters, but it's about female friendships as well. Discuss the rift that grows between Ruby and Izzy. Between Gloria and Sylvie. Have you ever experienced the loss of a female friend?

7. Fate plays an important role in this story. How does it factor into the relationships between the three main characters? Do you believe in destiny?

8. Throughout the novel Sylvie practices taxidermy, specifically on birds. What is the significance of this hobby for her and as a metaphor in the novel? What do you think she gets out of it? After Hurricane Irene washes away her home and all of her careful work, do you think she takes it up again, or have its benefits been exhausted?

9. Nessa comes to redefine the idea of "home" throughout the course of the novel. What does "home" mean for each

of these characters? What does it mean to you?

10. Another theme of *The Forever Bridge* is loss: Nessa's voice and childhood, Jess, friendship, and, after the storm, shelter. What else has been lost? Have all of these things been found again? Do you think that everything that is lost can be recaptured?

11. Discuss silence in this novel, particularly Nessa's mutism. Is her silence a weakness or an assertion of her own will?

12. The men are largely absent from the story, but they have an impact on these characters nevertheless. Discuss the roles that Robert, George, Mica, and Declan play in these women's lives.

13. A few chapters (the "here is" chapters) are written in second-person point of view. Why are they written in that style? What effect does that point of view and the "here is" style have on those scenes? What effect does it have on you, the reader?

14. How does the storm both threaten these characters and force them into action?

# ABOUT THE AUTHOR

**T. Greenwood** is the author of nine critically acclaimed novels. She has received numerous grants for her writing, including a National Endowment for the Art Literature Fellowship and a grant from the Maryland State Arts Council. She lives with her family in San Diego, California, where she teaches creative writing, studies photography, and continues to write. Her website is www.tgreenwood.com.

The employees of Thorndike Press hope you have enjoyed this Large Print book. All our Thorndike, Wheeler, and Kennebec Large Print titles are designed for easy reading, and all our books are made to last. Other Thorndike Press Large Print books are available at your library, through selected bookstores, or directly from us.

For information about titles, please call:
(800) 223-1244

or visit our Web site at:
http://gale.cengage.com/thorndike

To share your comments, please write:
Publisher
Thorndike Press
10 Water St., Suite 310
Waterville, ME 04901